P8-CQF-814

D0020502

Camping with Unicorns

Another Phoebe and Her Unicorn Adventure

Complete Your Phoebe and Her Unicorn Collection

Phoebe and Her Unicorn
Dana Simpson

Unicorn on a Roll
Another Phoebe and Her Unicorn Adventure
Dana Simpson

Unicorn vs. Goblins
Another Phoebe and Her Unicorn Adventure
Dana Simpson

Razzle Dazzle Unicorn
Another Phoebe and Her Unicorn Adventure
Dana Simpson

Unicorn Crossing
Another Phoebe and Her Unicorn Adventure
Dana Simpson

Phoebe and Her Unicorn in
The Magic Storm
Dana Simpson

Unicorn of Many Hats
Another Phoebe and Her Unicorn Adventure
Dana Simpson

Phoebe and Her Unicorn in
Unicorn Theater
Dana Simpson

Unicorn Bowling
Another Phoebe and Her Unicorn Adventure
Dana Simpson

The Unicorn Whisperer
Another Phoebe and Her Unicorn Adventure
Dana Simpson

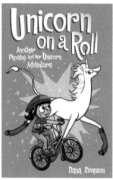

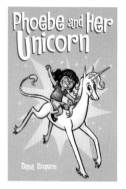

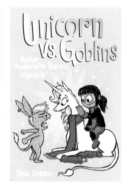

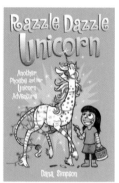

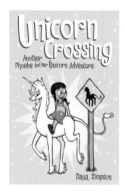

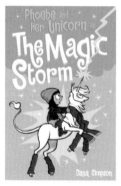

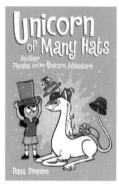

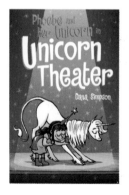

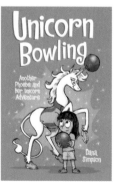

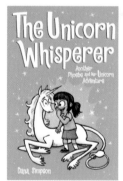

Camping with Unicorns

Another
Phoebe and Her Unicorn Adventure

Dana Simpson

Andrews McMeel
PUBLISHING®

Hey, kids!

Check out the glossary starting on page 173
if you come across words you don't know.

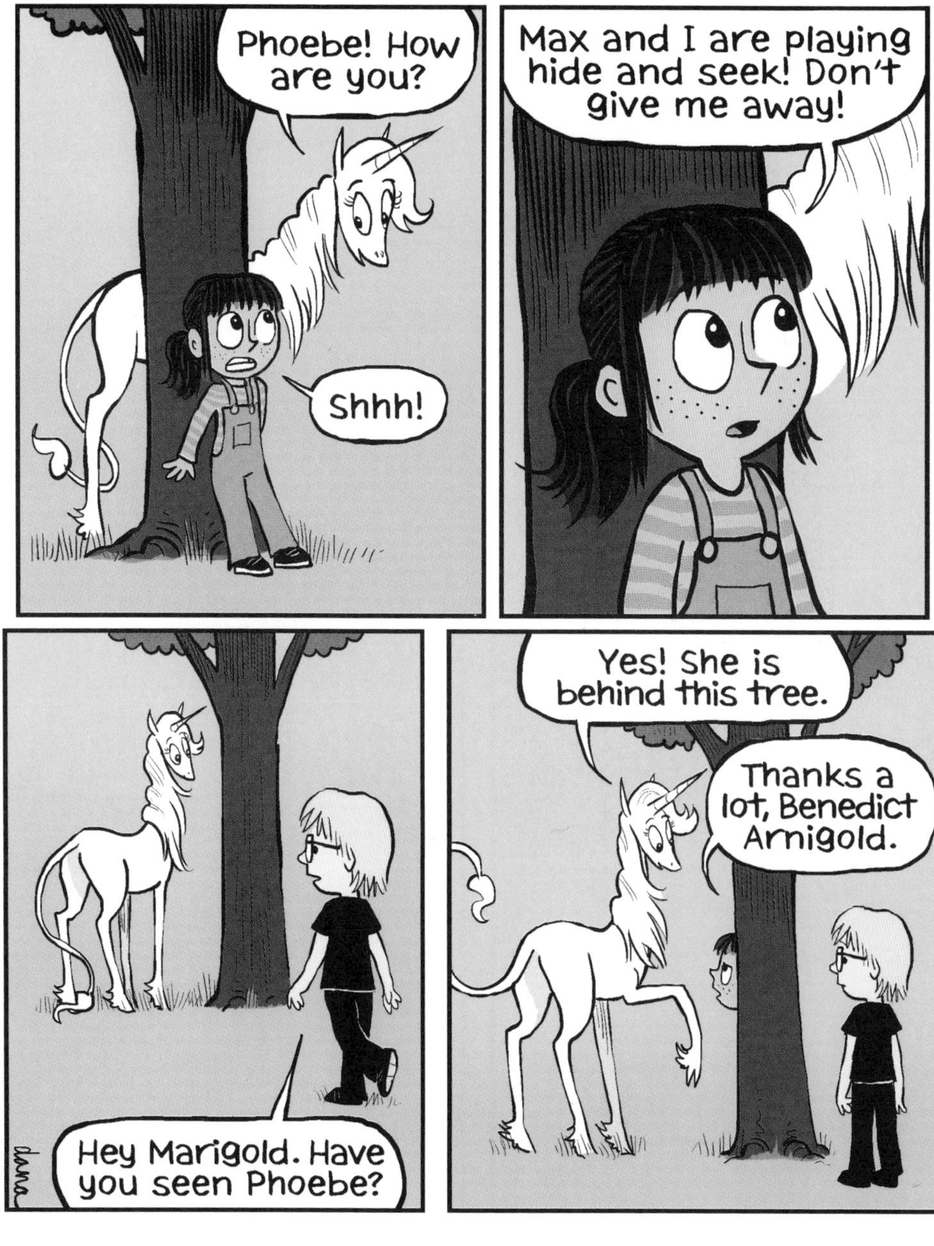
Phoebe! How are you?
Shhh!
Max and I are playing hide and seek! Don't give me away!
Hey Marigold. Have you seen Phoebe?
Yes! She is behind this tree.
Thanks a lot, Benedict Arnigold.

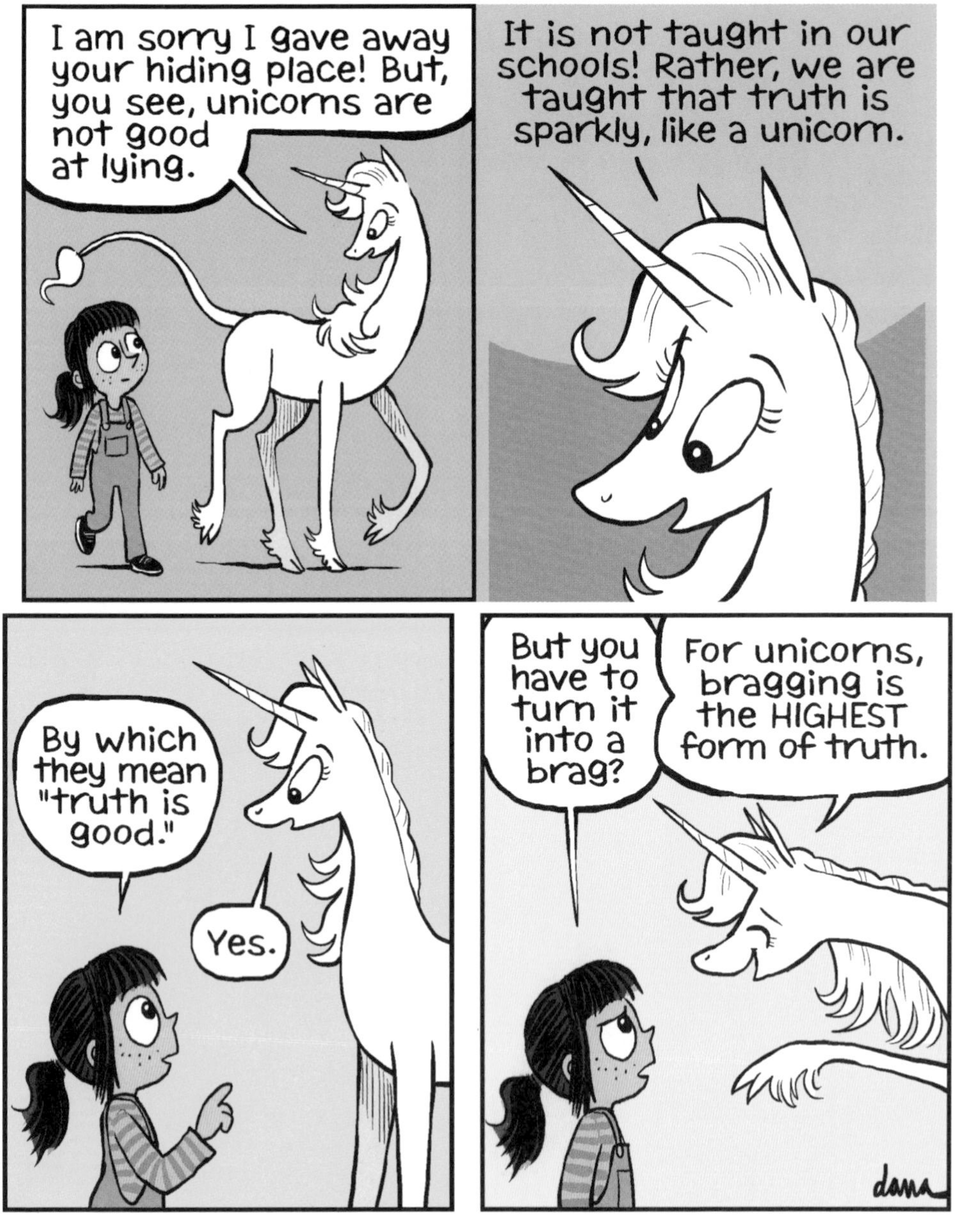
I am sorry I gave away your hiding place! But, you see, unicorns are not good at lying.
It is not taught in our schools! Rather, we are taught that truth is sparkly, like a unicorn.
By which they mean "truth is good."
Yes.
But you have to turn it into a brag?
For unicorns, bragging is the HIGHEST form of truth.
dana

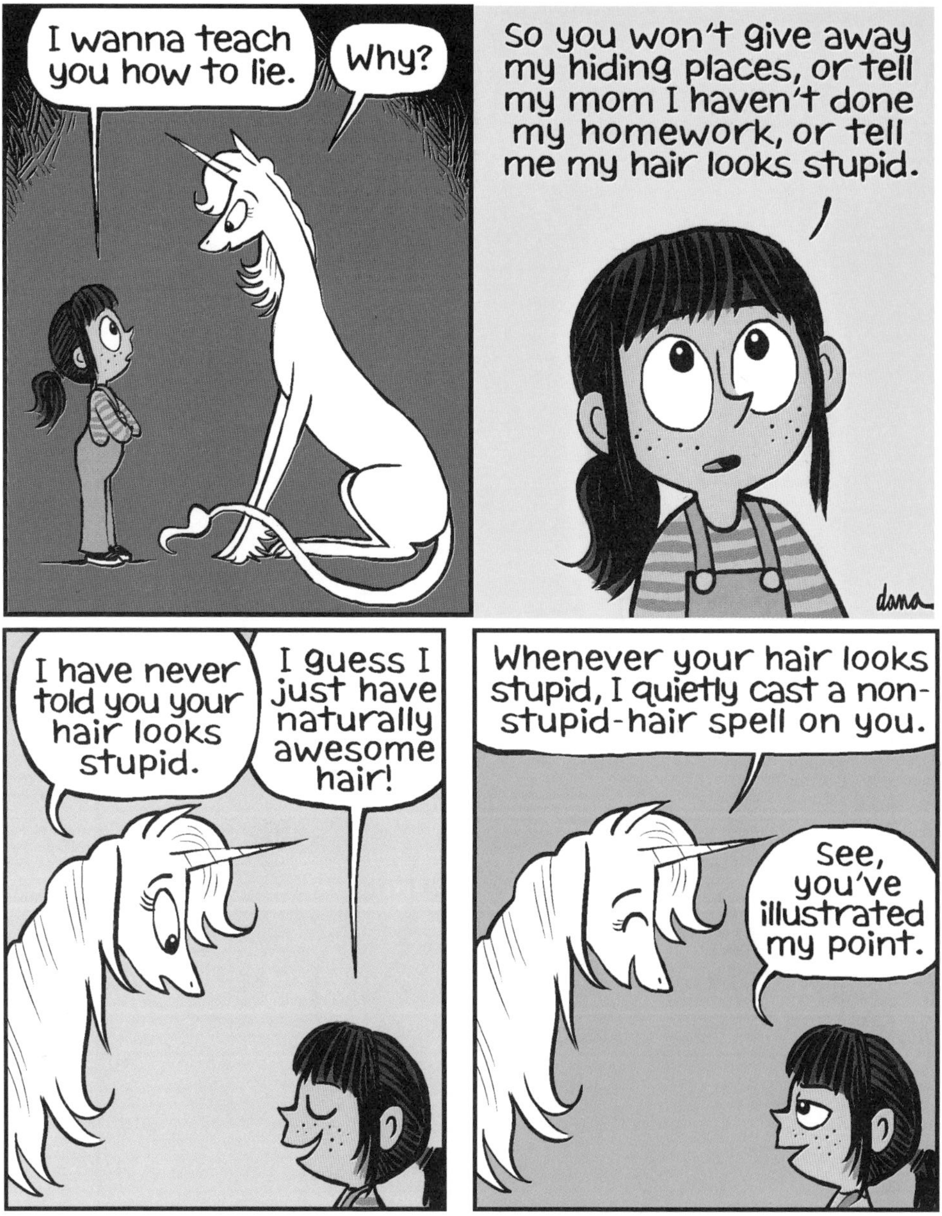
I wanna teach you how to lie.
Why?
So you won't give away my hiding places, or tell my mom I haven't done my homework, or tell me my hair looks stupid.
dana
I have never told you your hair looks stupid.
I guess I just have naturally awesome hair!
Whenever your hair looks stupid, I quietly cast a non-stupid-hair spell on you.
See, you've illustrated my point.

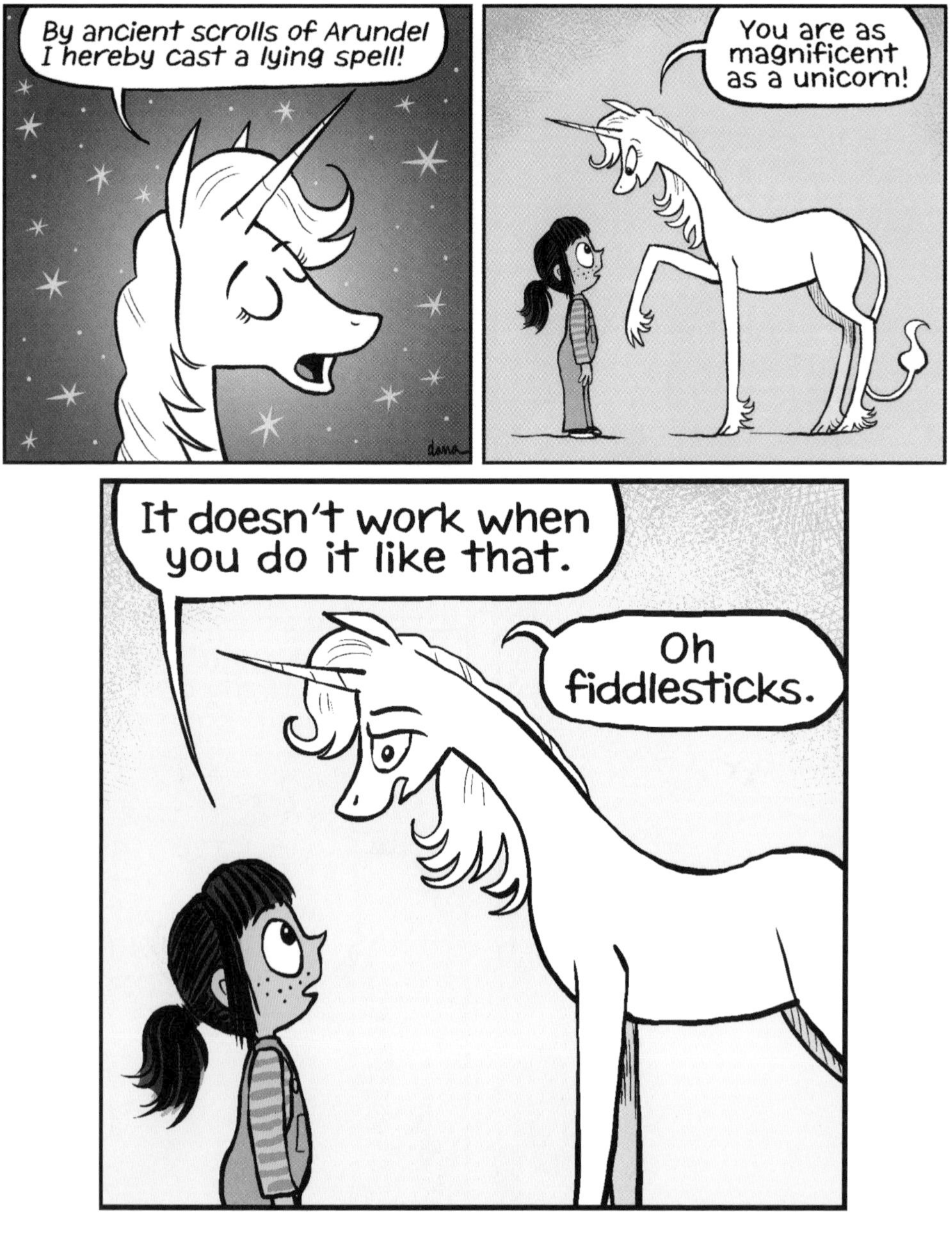
By ancient scrolls of Arundel I hereby cast a lying spell!
You are as magnificent as a unicorn!
It doesn't work when you do it like that.
Oh fiddlesticks.

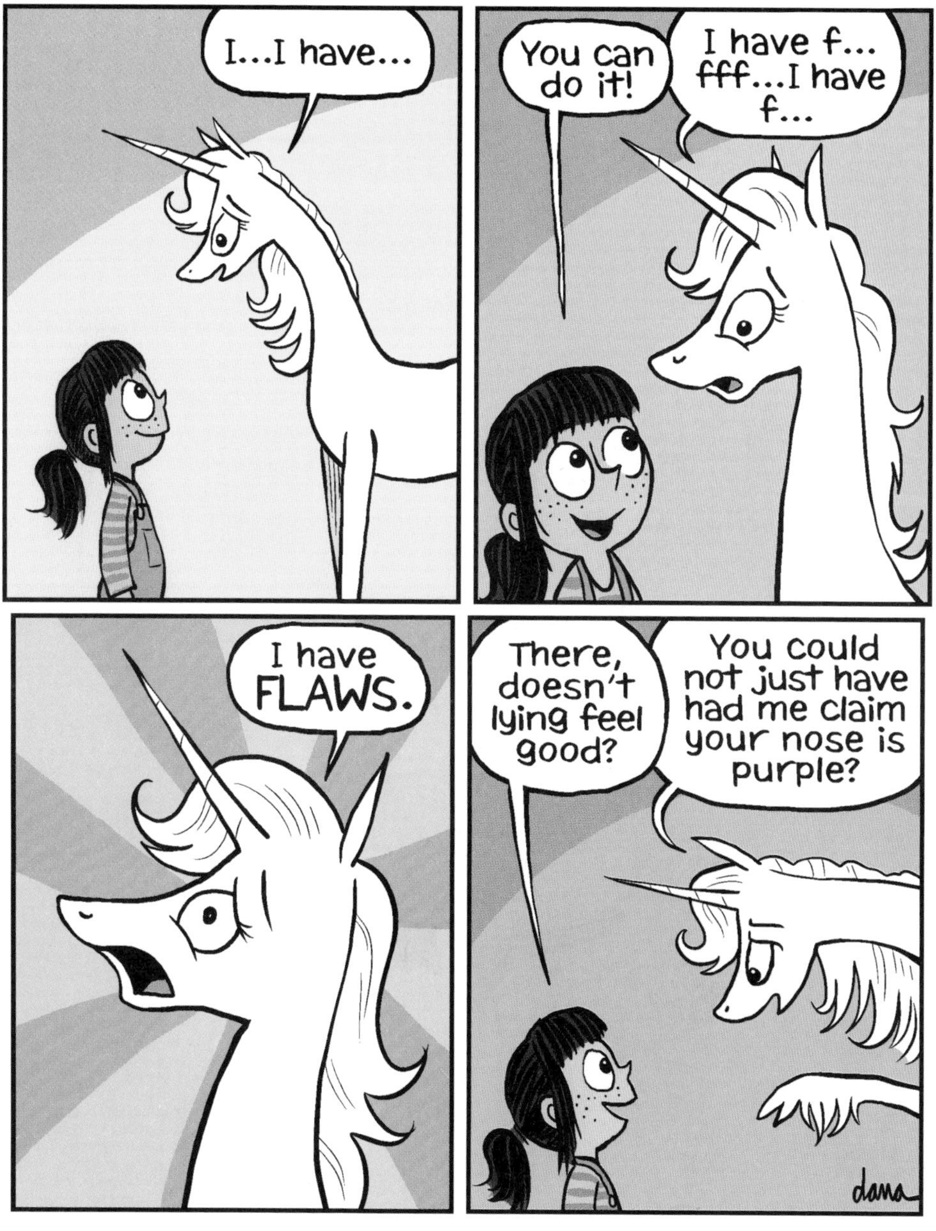
I...I have...
You can do it!
I have f... fff...I have f...
I have FLAWS.
There, doesn't lying feel good?
You could not just have had me claim your nose is purple?
dana

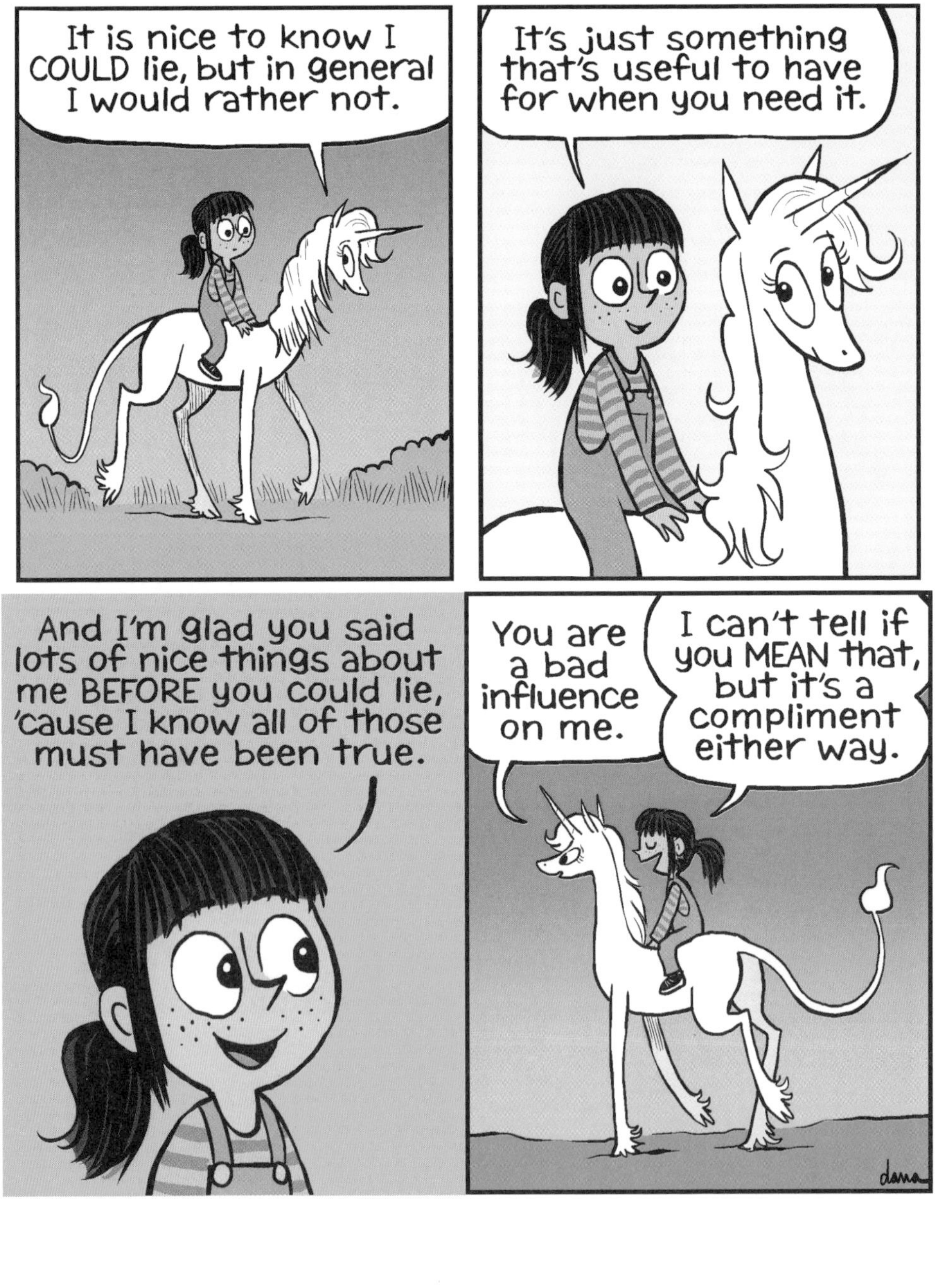
It is nice to know I COULD lie, but in general I would rather not.
It's just something that's useful to have for when you need it.
And I'm glad you said lots of nice things about me BEFORE you could lie, 'cause I know all of those must have been true.
You are a bad influence on me.
I can't tell if you MEAN that, but it's a compliment either way.
dana

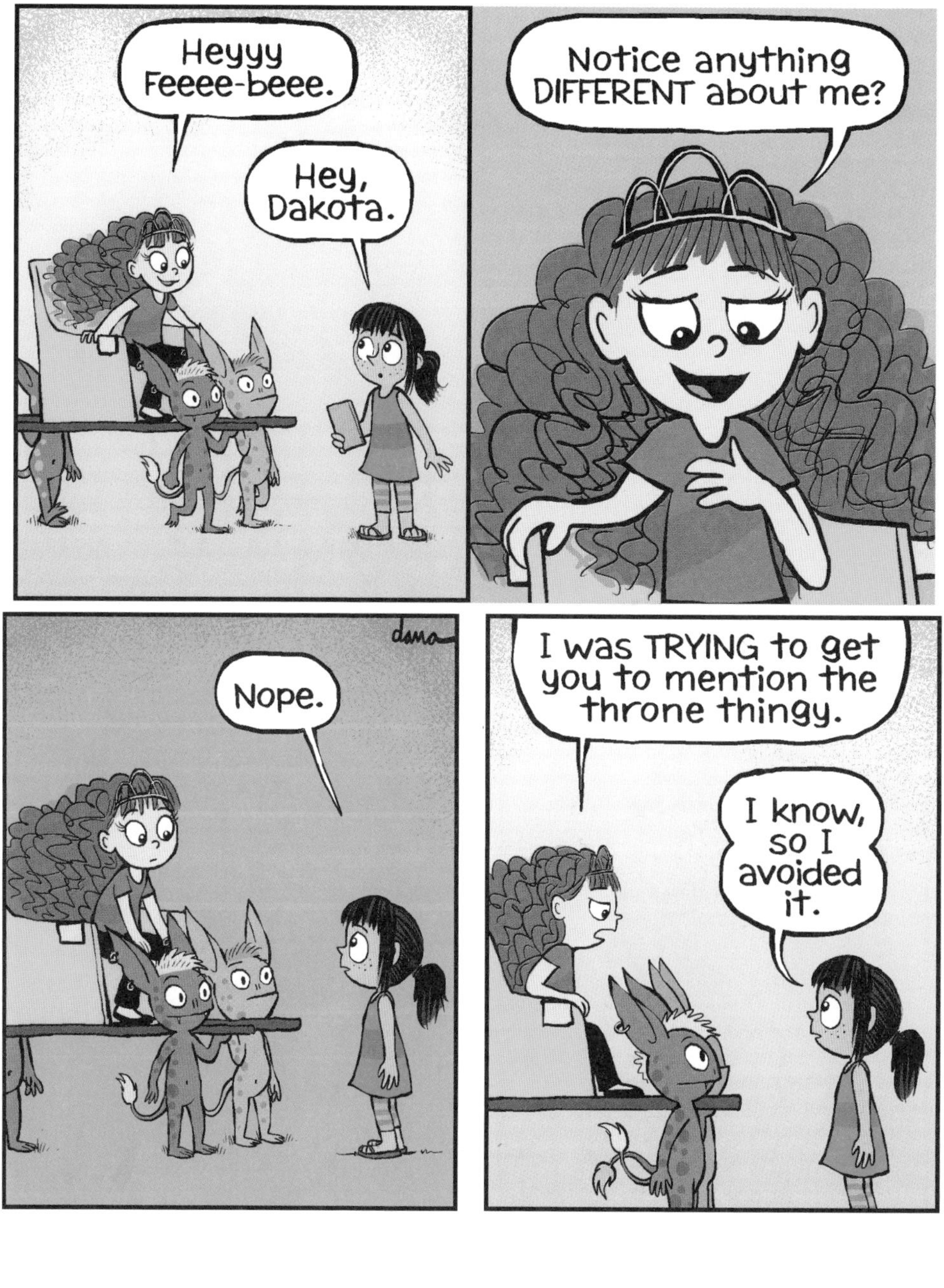
Heyyy Feeee-beee.
Hey, Dakota.
Notice anything DIFFERENT about me?
Nope.
I was TRYING to get you to mention the throne thingy.
I know, so I avoided it.

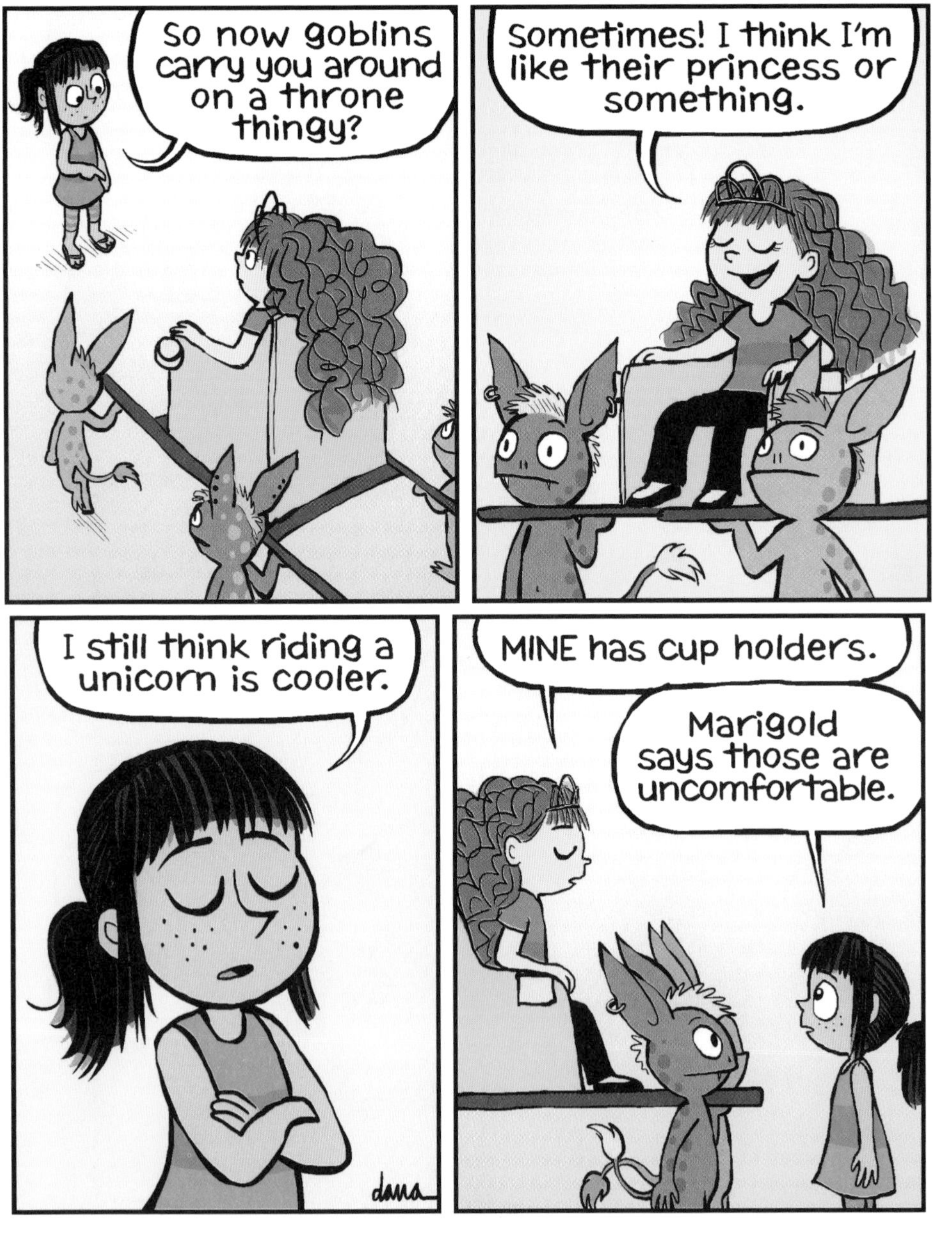
So now goblins carry you around on a throne thingy?
Sometimes! I think I'm like their princess or something.
I still think riding a unicorn is cooler.
dana
MINE has cup holders.
Marigold says those are uncomfortable.

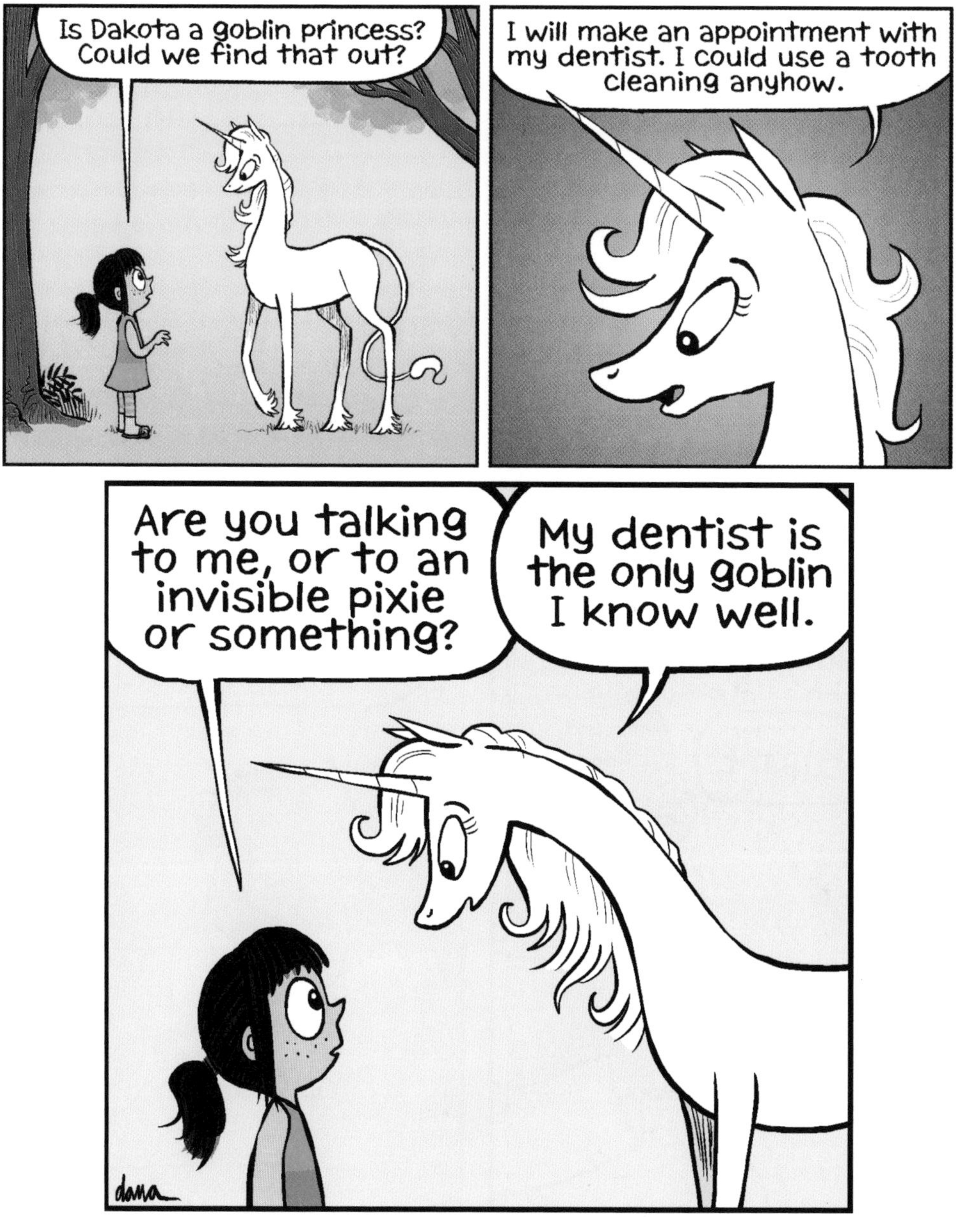
Is Dakota a goblin princess? Could we find that out?
I will make an appointment with my dentist. I could use a tooth cleaning anyhow.
Are you talking to me, or to an invisible pixie or something?
My dentist is the only goblin I know well.
dana

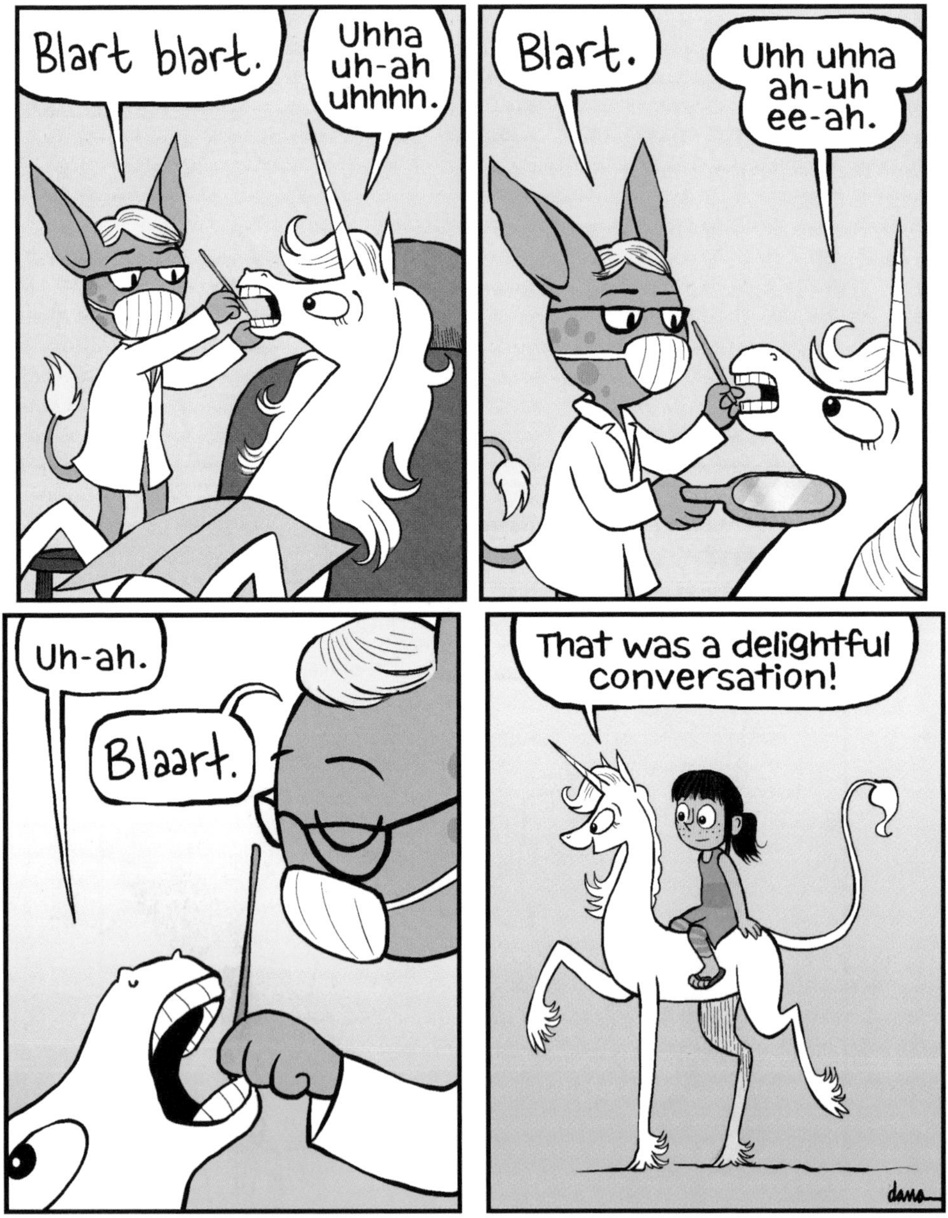

Blart blart.
Uhha uh-ah uhhhh.
Blart.
Uhh uhha ah-uh ee-ah.
Uh-ah.
Blaart.
That was a delightful conversation!
dana

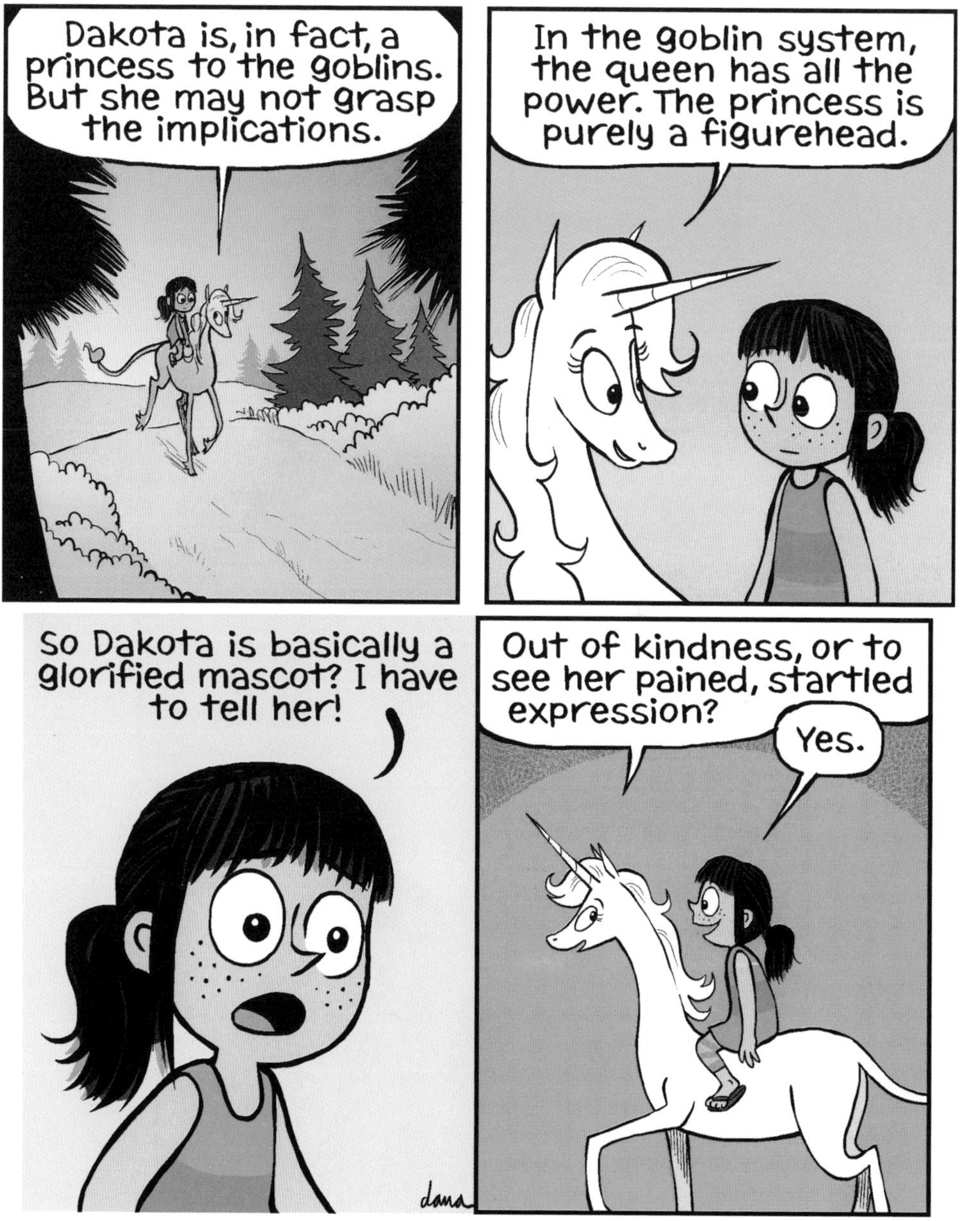
Dakota is, in fact, a princess to the goblins. But she may not grasp the implications.
In the goblin system, the queen has all the power. The princess is purely a figurehead.
So Dakota is basically a glorified mascot? I have to tell her!
Out of kindness, or to see her pained, startled expression?
Yes.
dana

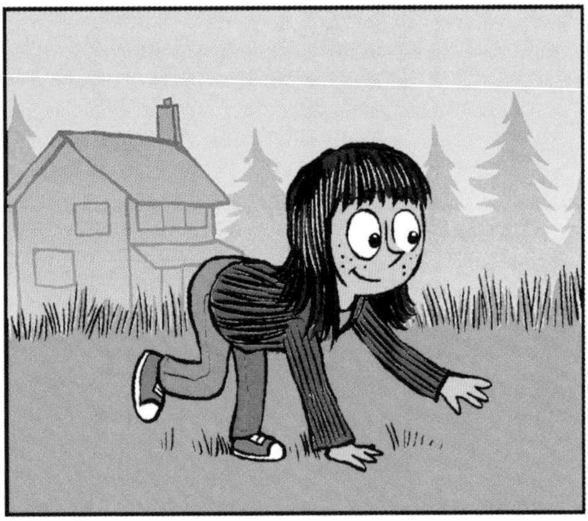

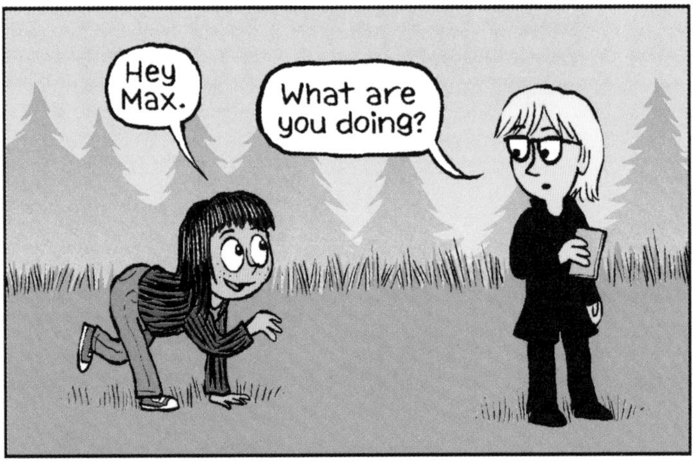
Hey Max.
What are you doing?

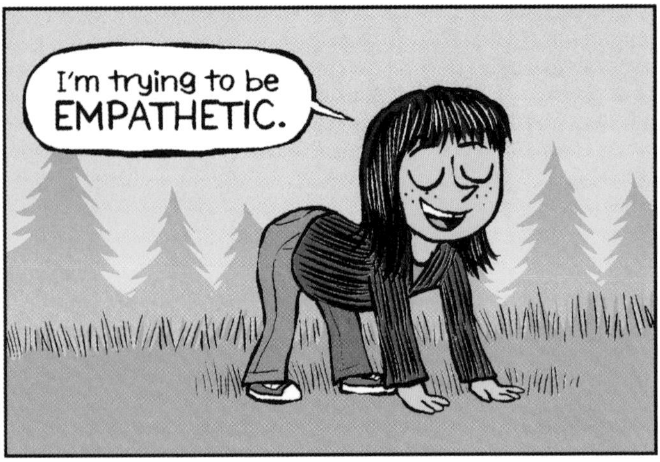
I'm trying to be EMPATHETIC.

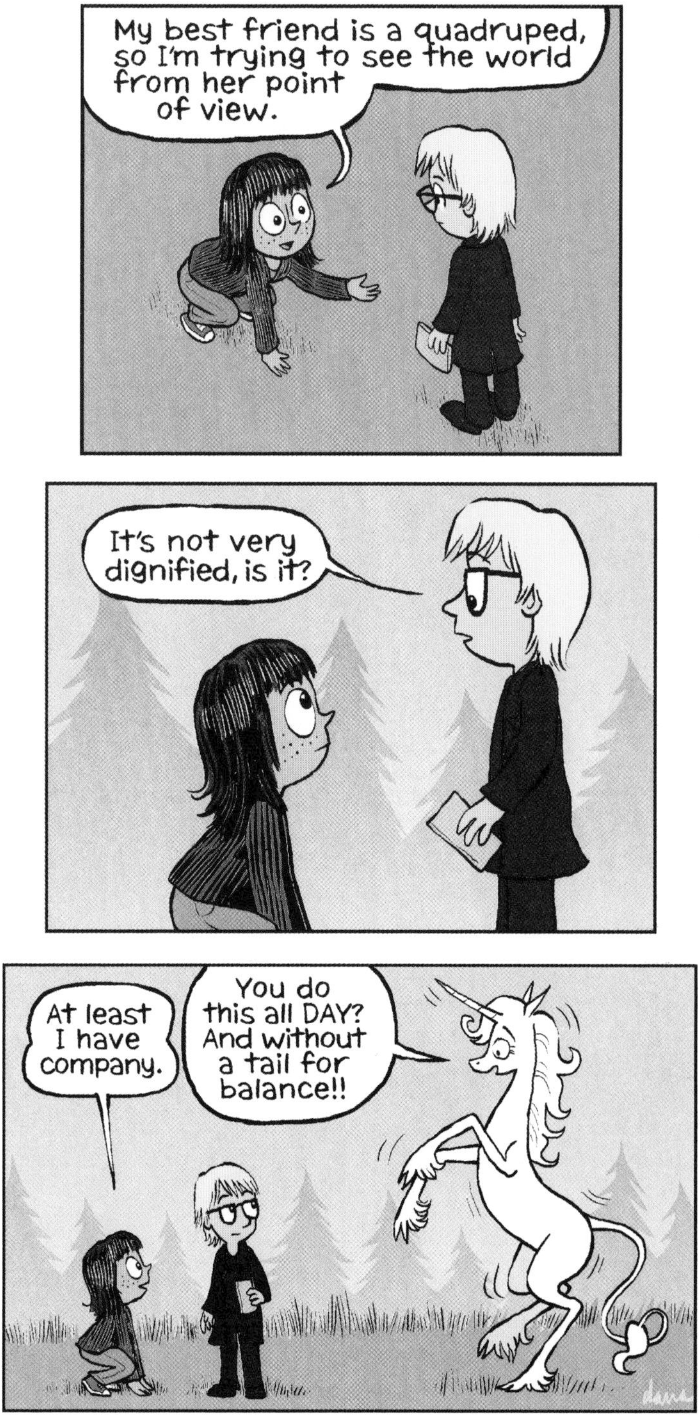
My best friend is a quadruped, so I'm trying to see the world from her point of view.
It's not very dignified, is it?
At least I have company.
You do this all DAY? And without a tail for balance!!
dana

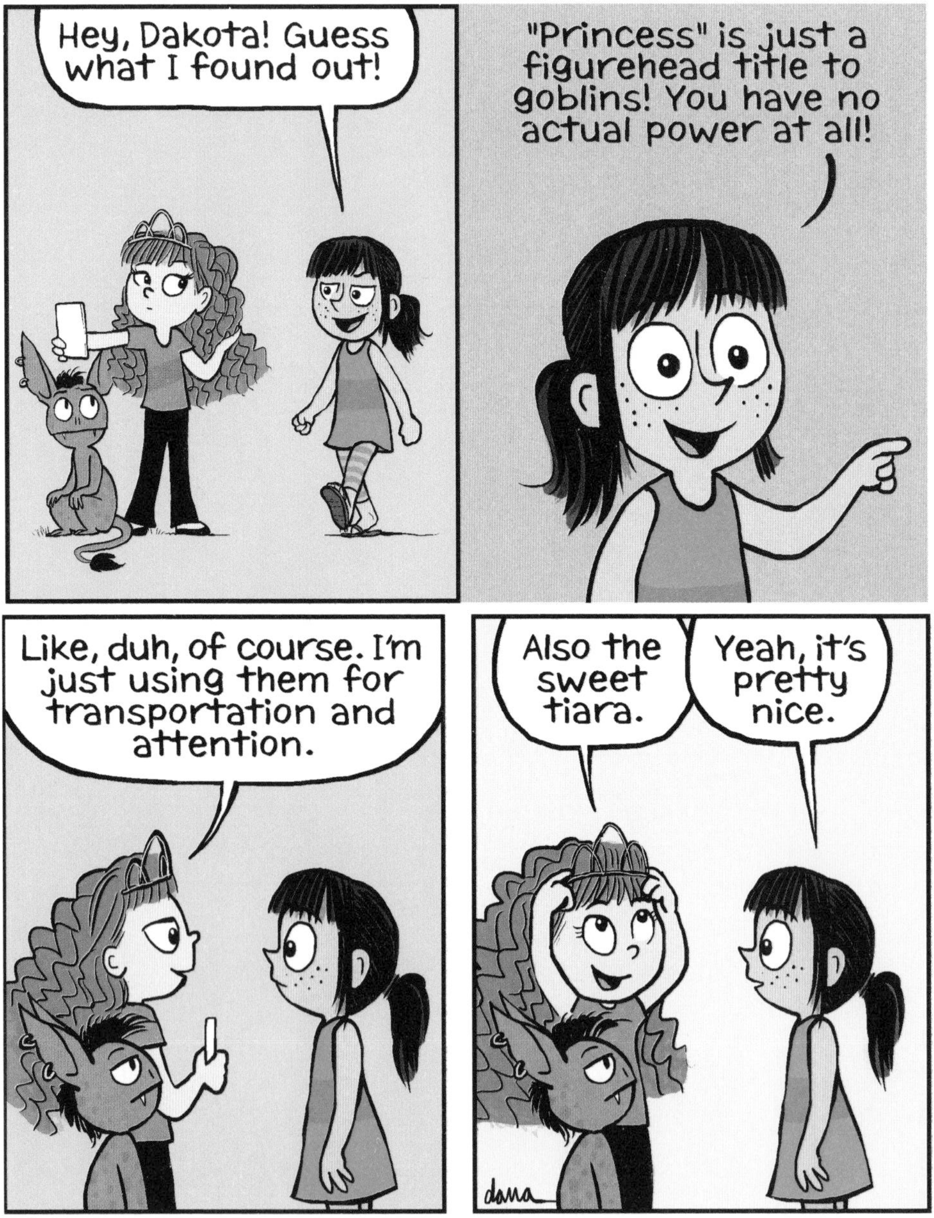
Hey, Dakota! Guess what I found out!
"Princess" is just a figurehead title to goblins! You have no actual power at all!
Like, duh, of course. I'm just using them for transportation and attention.
Also the sweet tiara.
Yeah, it's pretty nice.
dana

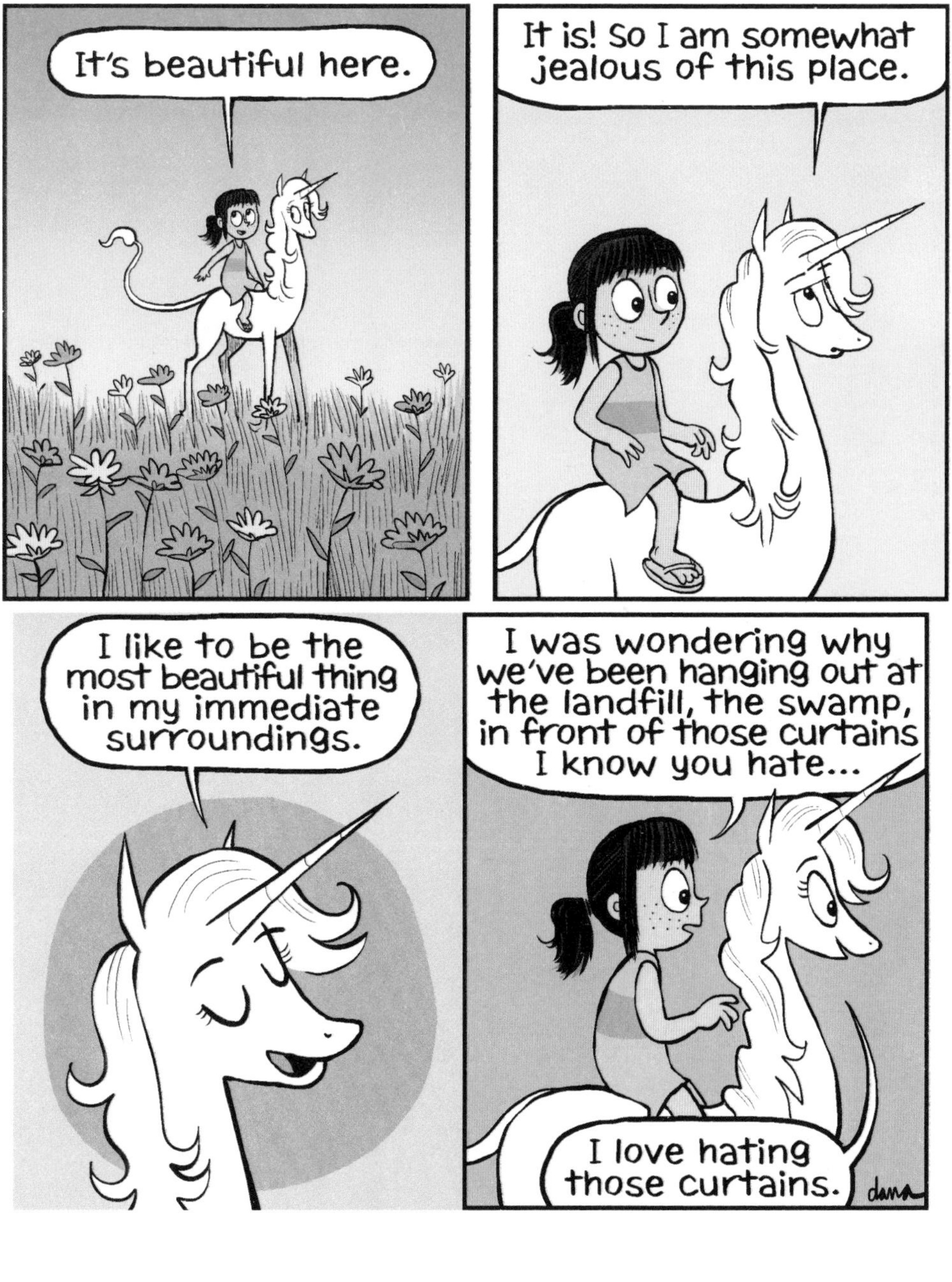
It's beautiful here.
It is! So I am somewhat jealous of this place.
I like to be the most beautiful thing in my immediate surroundings.
I was wondering why we've been hanging out at the landfill, the swamp, in front of those curtains I know you hate...
I love hating those curtains.
dana

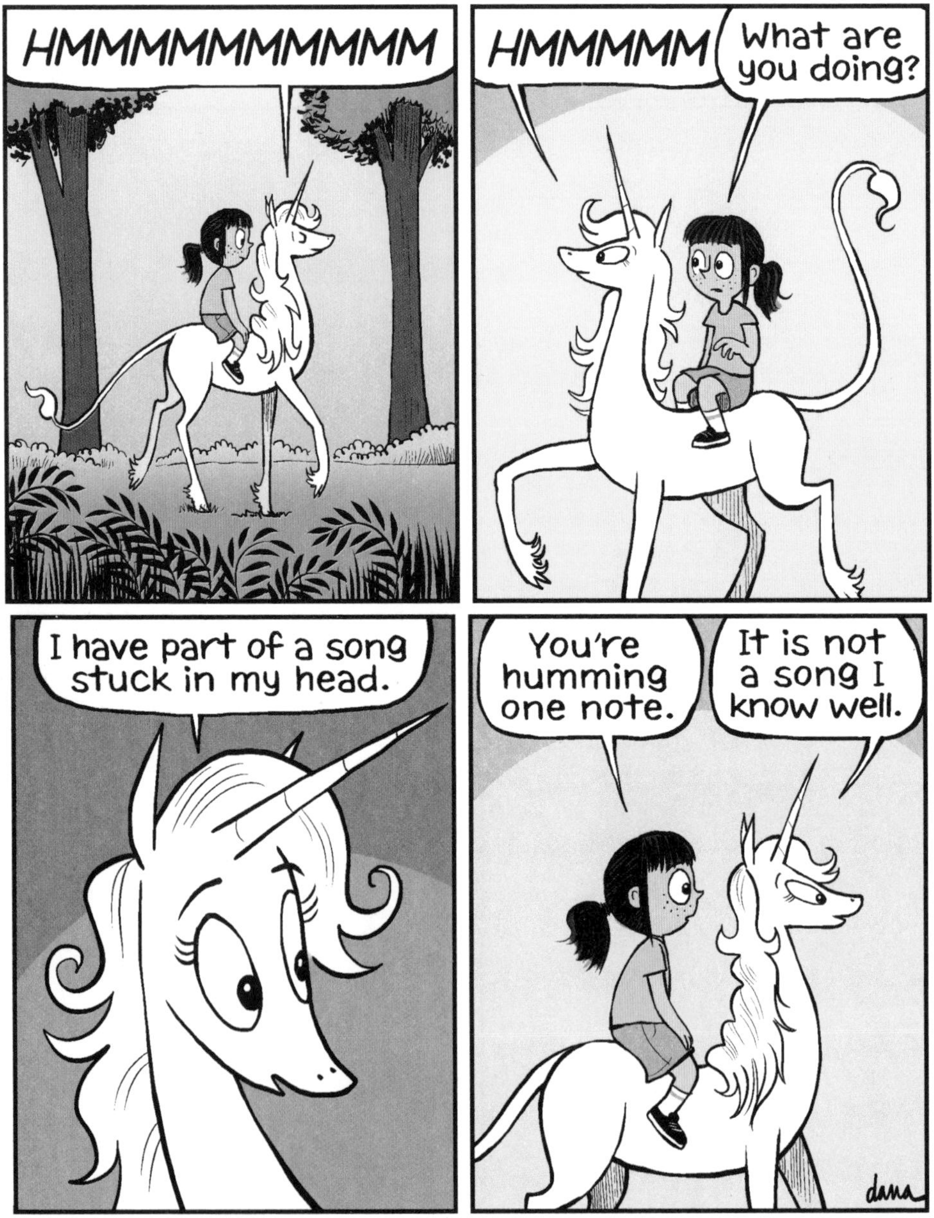
HMMMMMMMMMM
HMMMMM
What are you doing?
I have part of a song stuck in my head.
You're humming one note.
It is not a song I know well.
dana

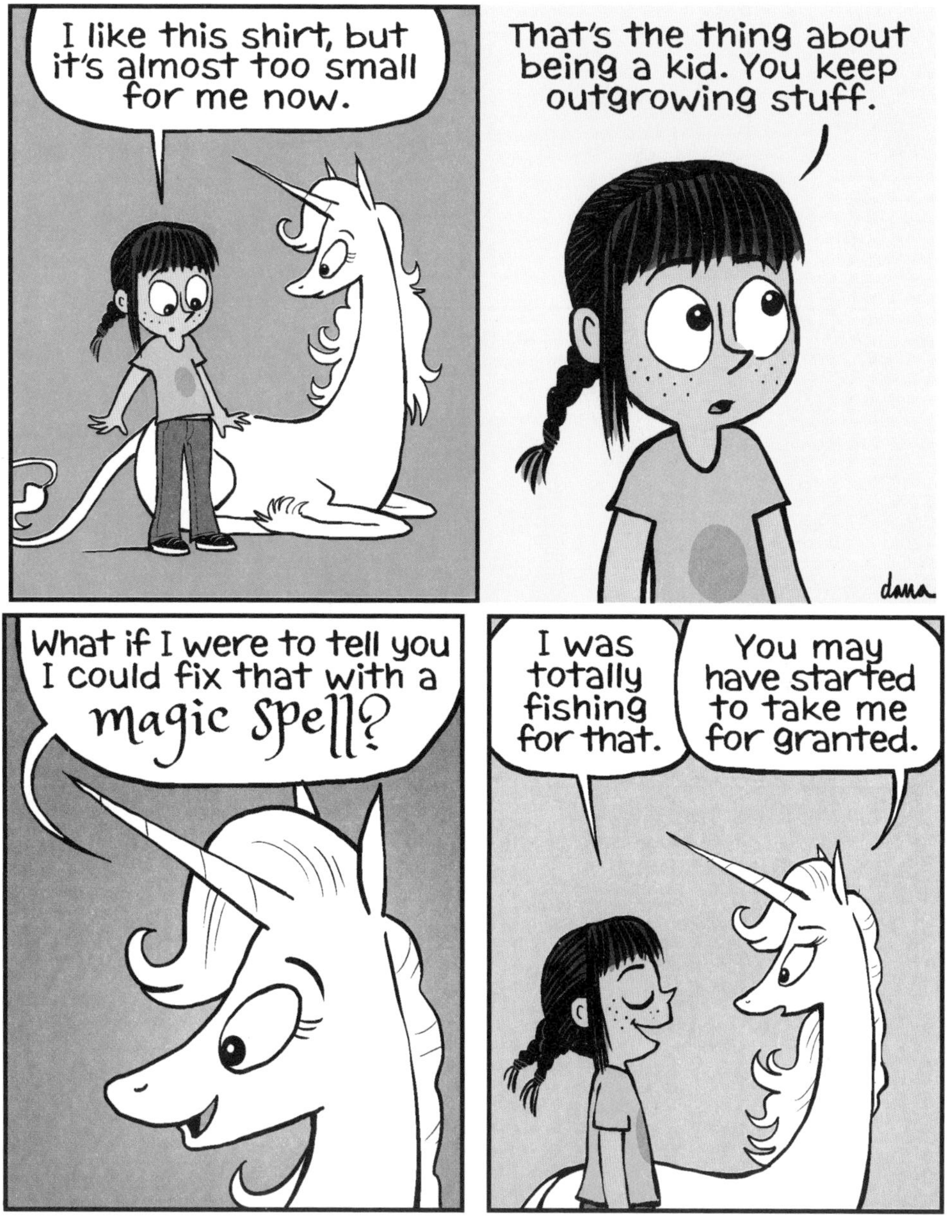
I like this shirt, but it's almost too small for me now.
That's the thing about being a kid. You keep outgrowing stuff.
dana
What if I were to tell you I could fix that with a magic spell?
I was totally fishing for that.
You may have started to take me for granted.

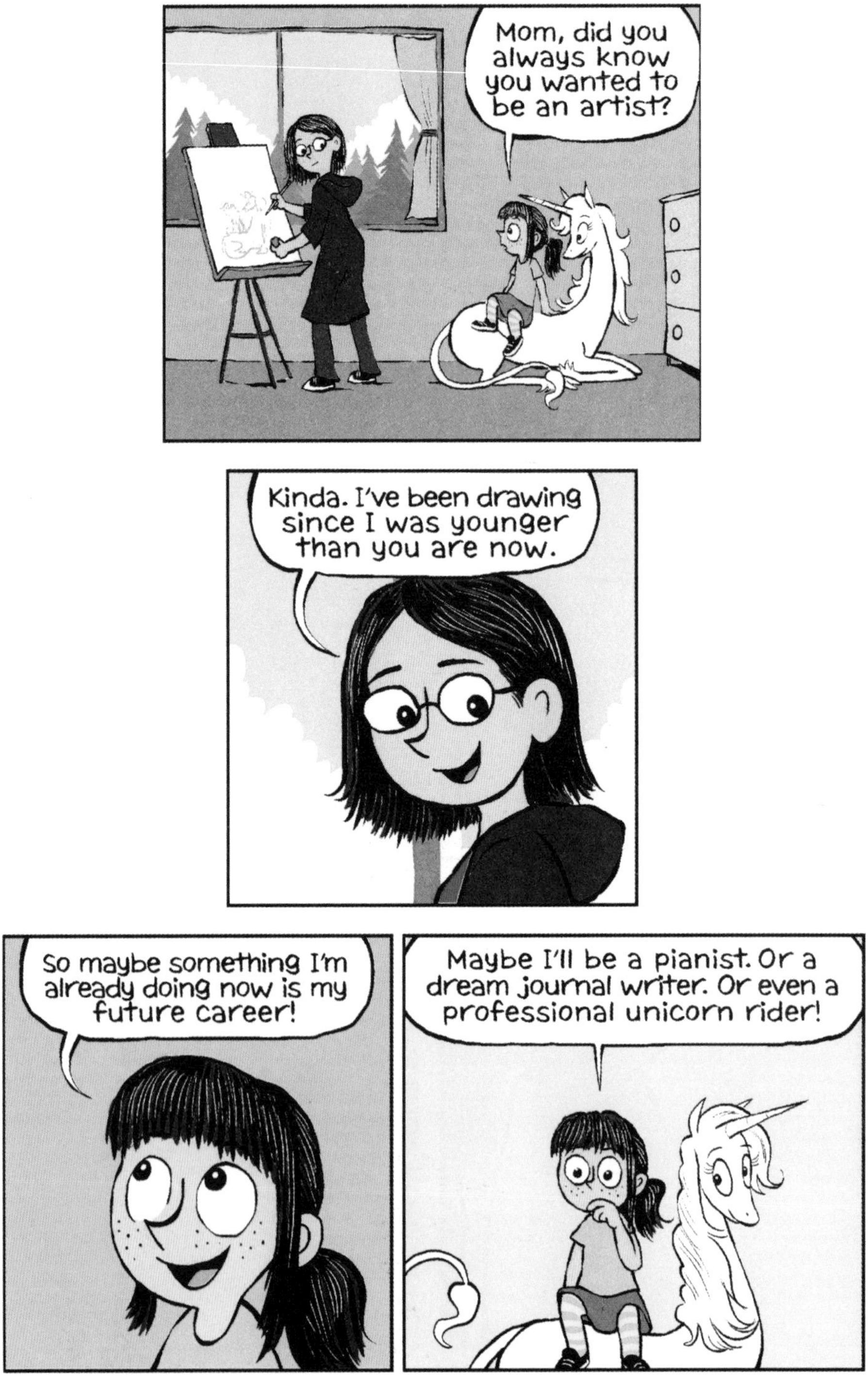

Mom, did you always know you wanted to be an artist?
Kinda. I've been drawing since I was younger than you are now.
So maybe something I'm already doing now is my future career!
Maybe I'll be a pianist. Or a dream journal writer. Or even a professional unicorn rider!

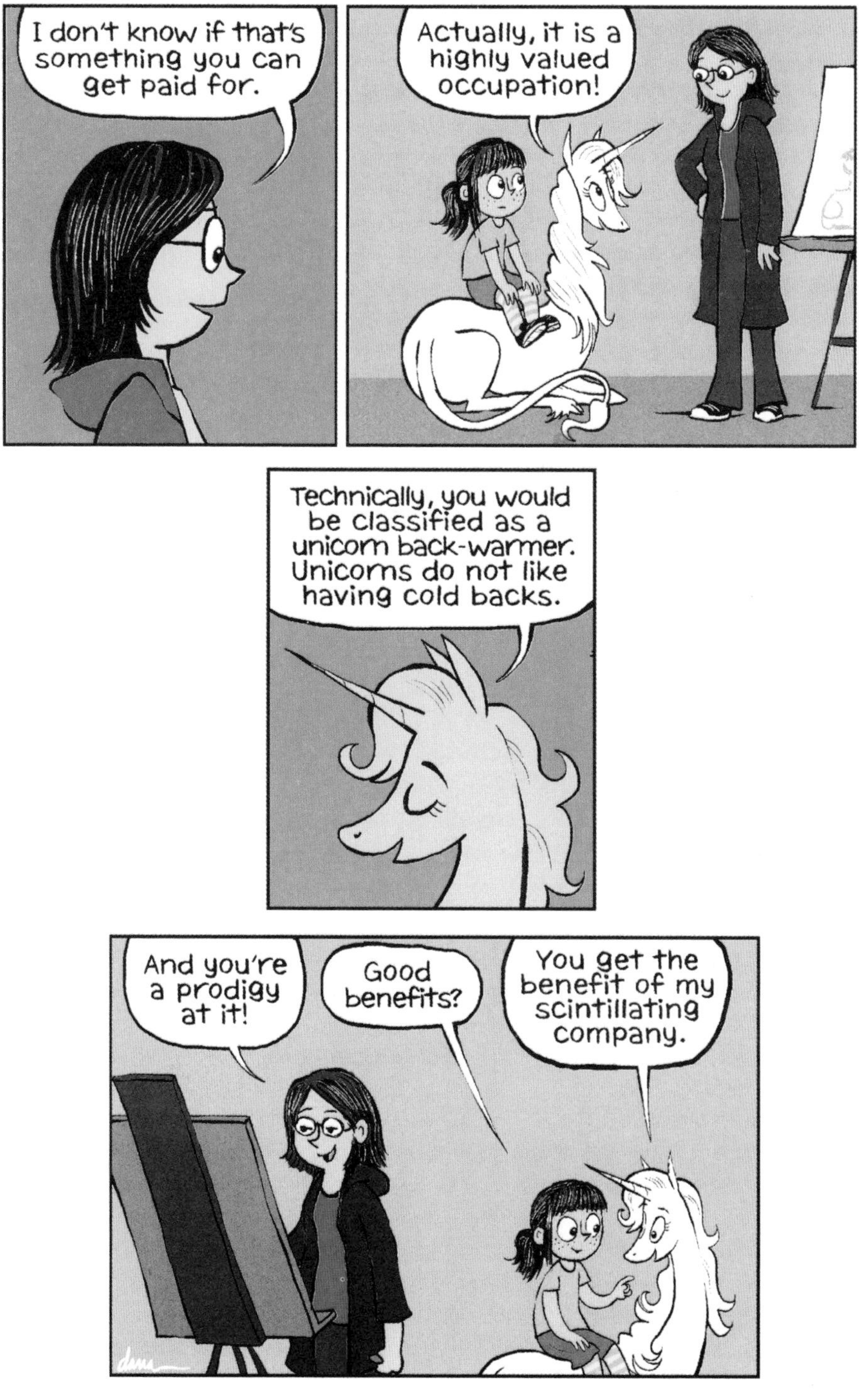
I don't know if that's something you can get paid for.
Actually, it is a highly valued occupation!
Technically, you would be classified as a unicorn back-warmer. Unicorns do not like having cold backs.
And you're a prodigy at it!
Good benefits?
You get the benefit of my scintillating company.

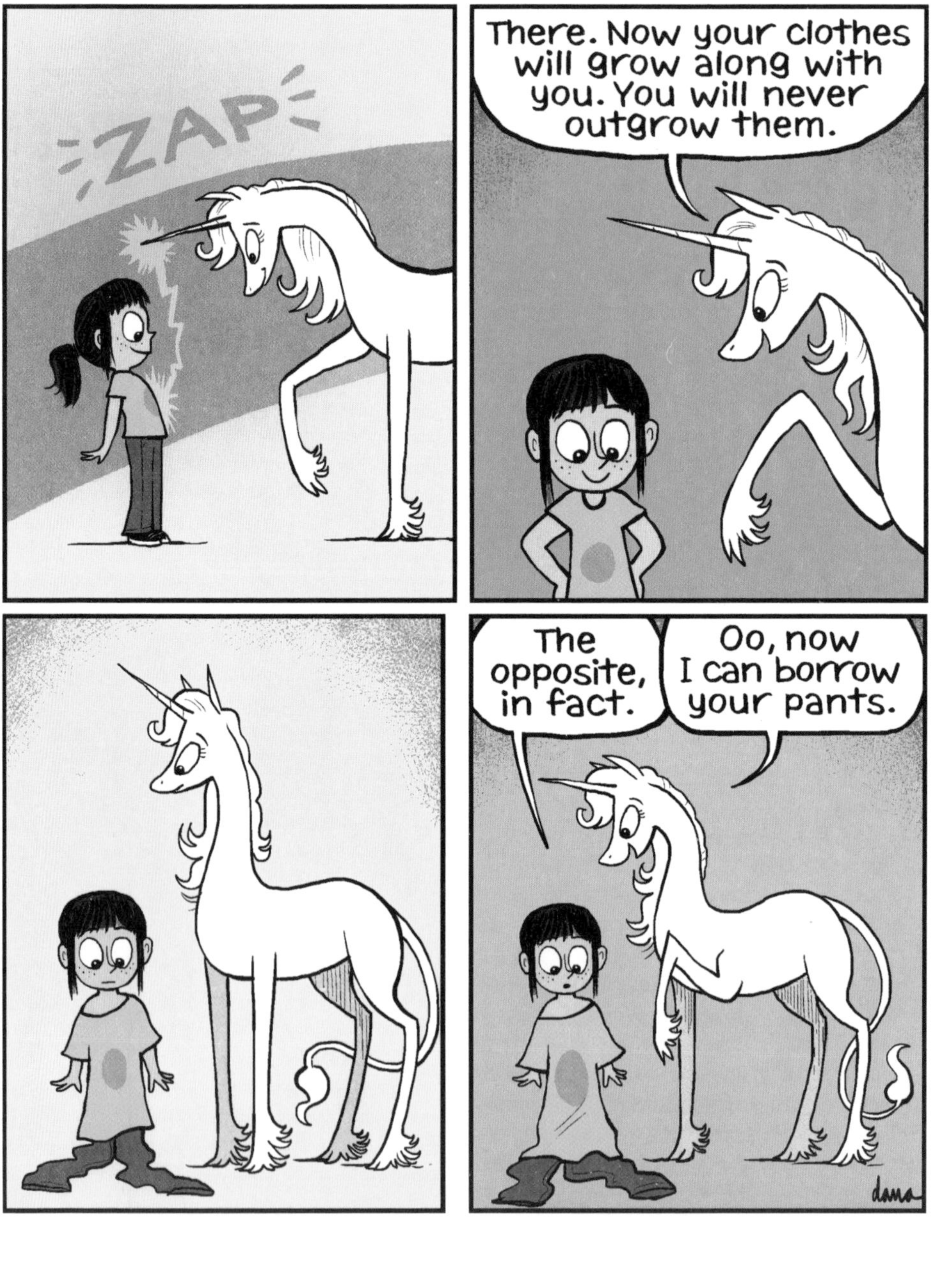
ZAP
There. Now your clothes will grow along with you. You will never outgrow them.
The opposite, in fact.
Oo, now I can borrow your pants.
dana

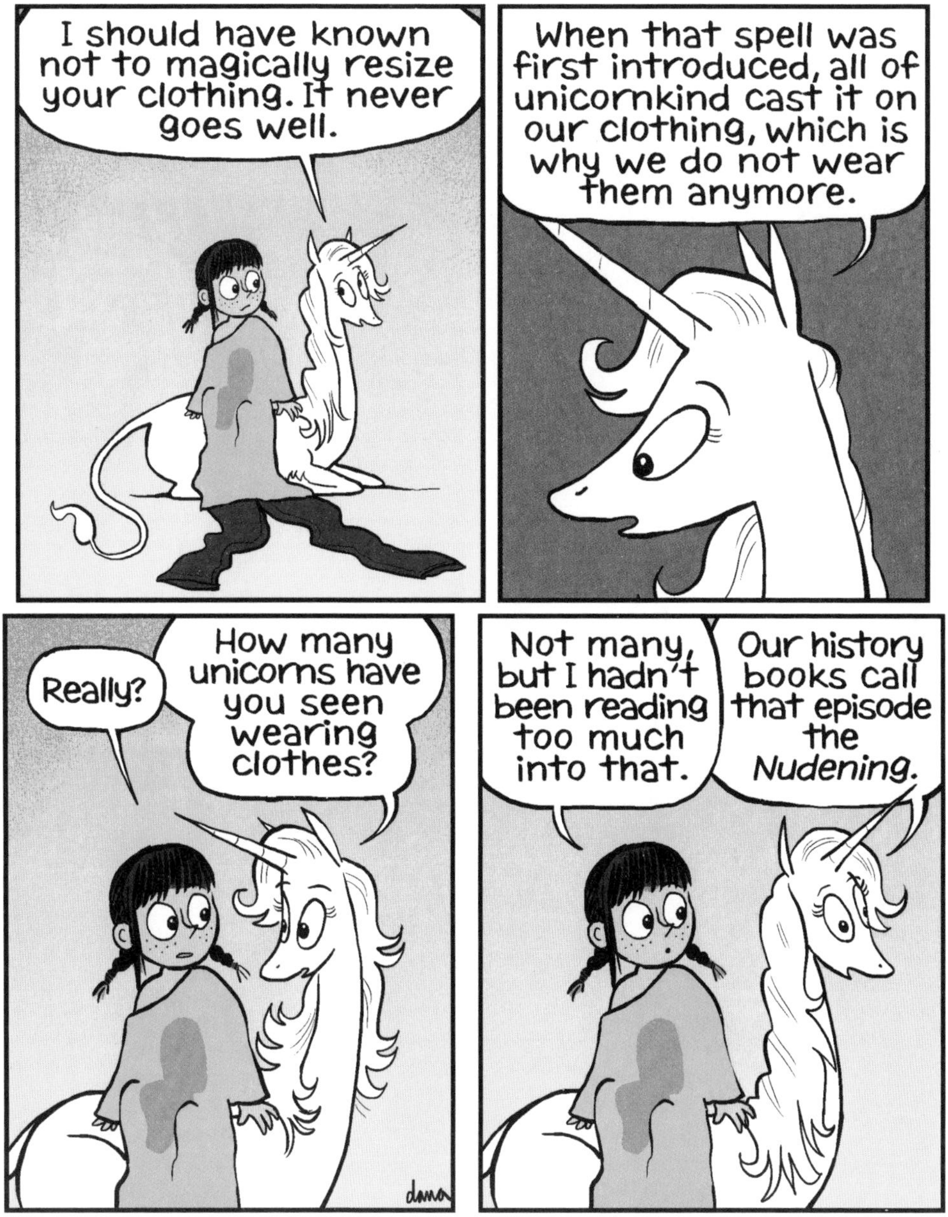

I should have known not to magically resize your clothing. It never goes well.
When that spell was first introduced, all of unicornkind cast it on our clothing, which is why we do not wear them anymore.
Really?
How many unicorns have you seen wearing clothes?
Not many, but I hadn't been reading too much into that.
Our history books call that episode the *Nudening*.
dana

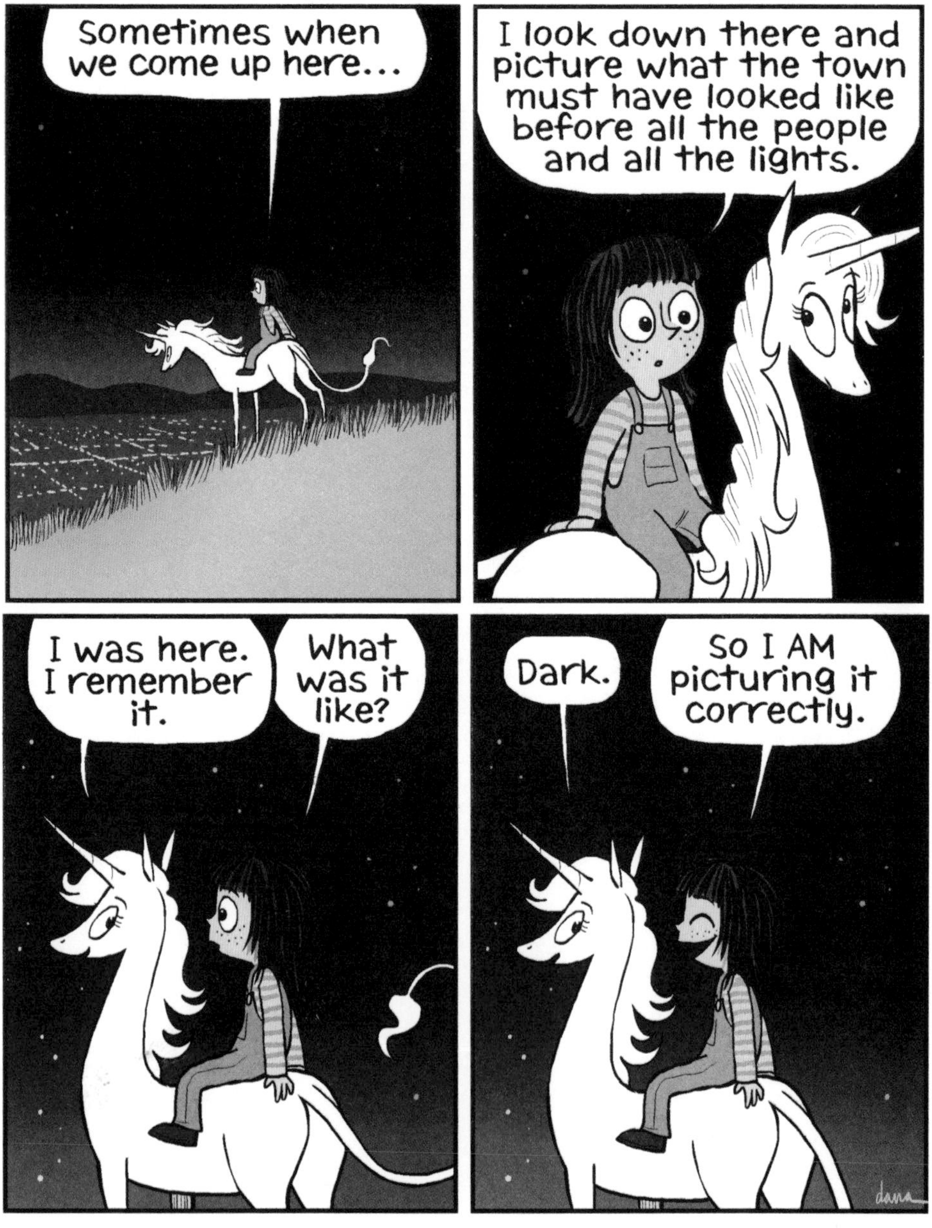
Sometimes when we come up here...
I look down there and picture what the town must have looked like before all the people and all the lights.
I was here. I remember it.
What was it like?
Dark.
So I AM picturing it correctly.
dana

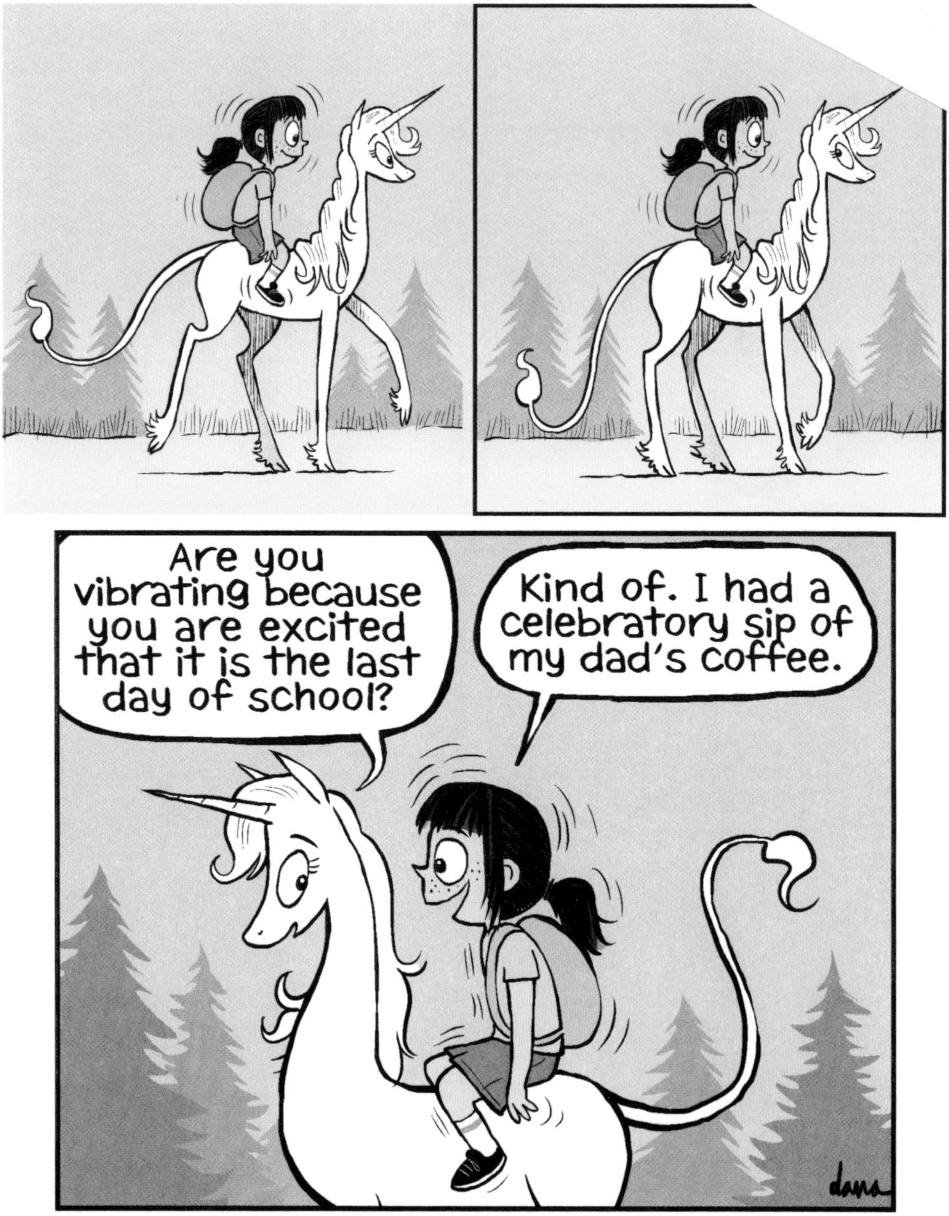
Are you vibrating because you are excited that it is the last day of school?
Kind of. I had a celebratory sip of my dad's coffee.
dana

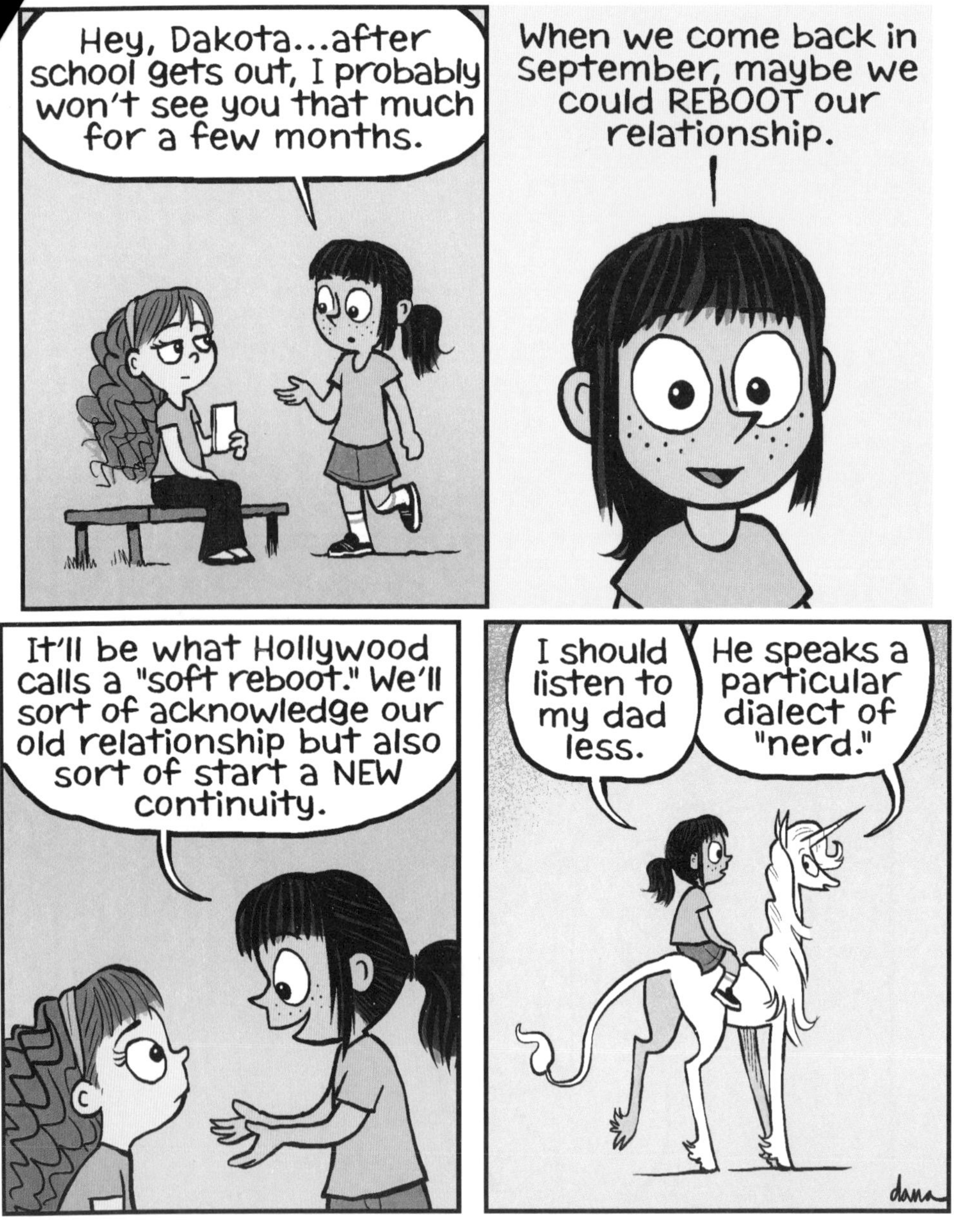
Hey, Dakota...after school gets out, I probably won't see you that much for a few months.
When we come back in September, maybe we could REBOOT our relationship.
It'll be what Hollywood calls a "soft reboot." We'll sort of acknowledge our old relationship but also sort of start a NEW continuity.
I should listen to my dad less.
He speaks a particular dialect of "nerd."
dana

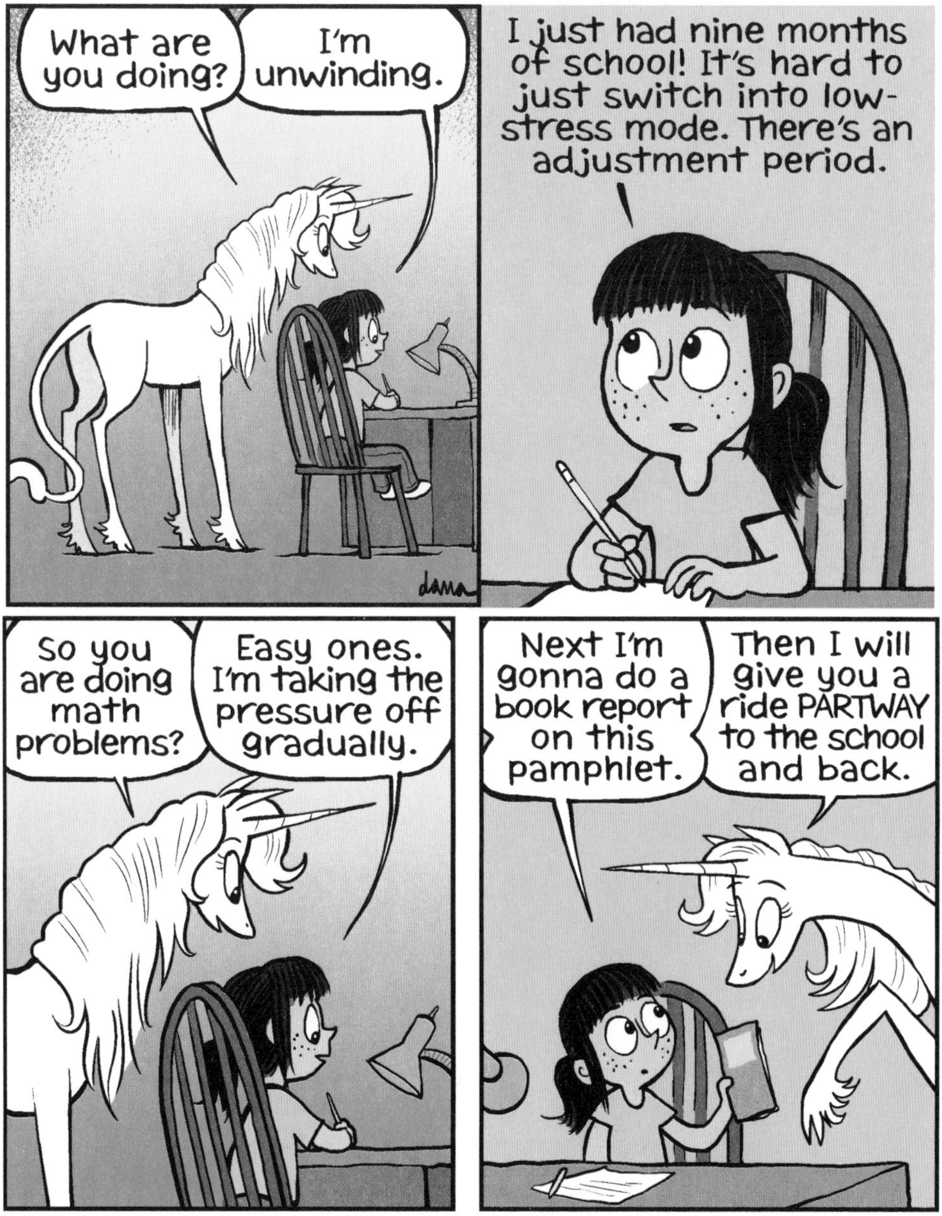
What are you doing?
I'm unwinding.
I just had nine months of school! It's hard to just switch into low-stress mode. There's an adjustment period.
dana
So you are doing math problems?
Easy ones. I'm taking the pressure off gradually.
Next I'm gonna do a book report on this pamphlet.
Then I will give you a ride PARTWAY to the school and back.

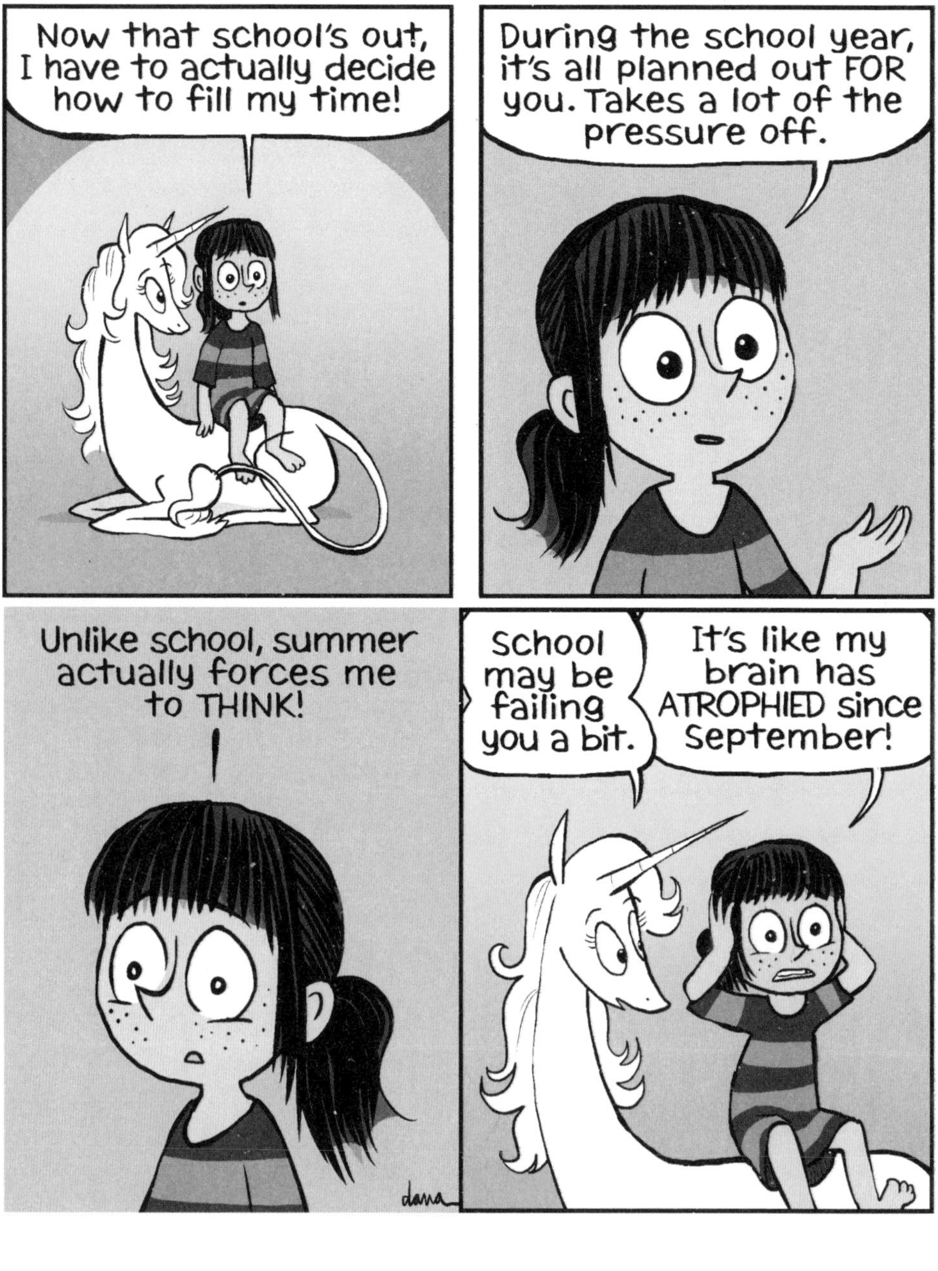
Now that school's out, I have to actually decide how to fill my time!
During the school year, it's all planned out FOR you. Takes a lot of the pressure off.
Unlike school, summer actually forces me to THINK!
It's like my brain has ATROPHIED since September!
School may be failing you a bit.
dana

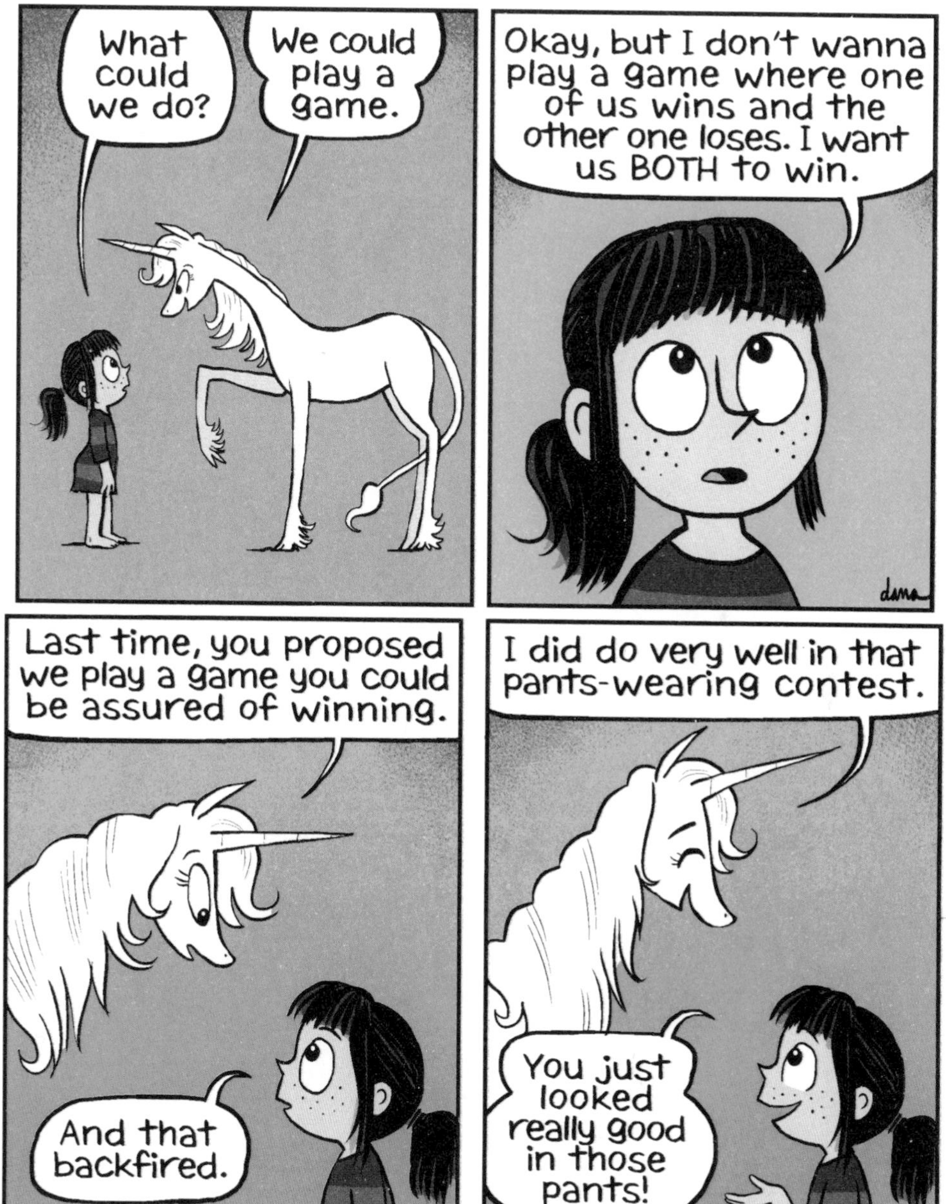
What could we do?
We could play a game.
Okay, but I don't wanna play a game where one of us wins and the other one loses. I want us BOTH to win.
dana
Last time, you proposed we play a game you could be assured of winning.
And that backfired.
I did do very well in that pants-wearing contest.
You just looked really good in those pants!

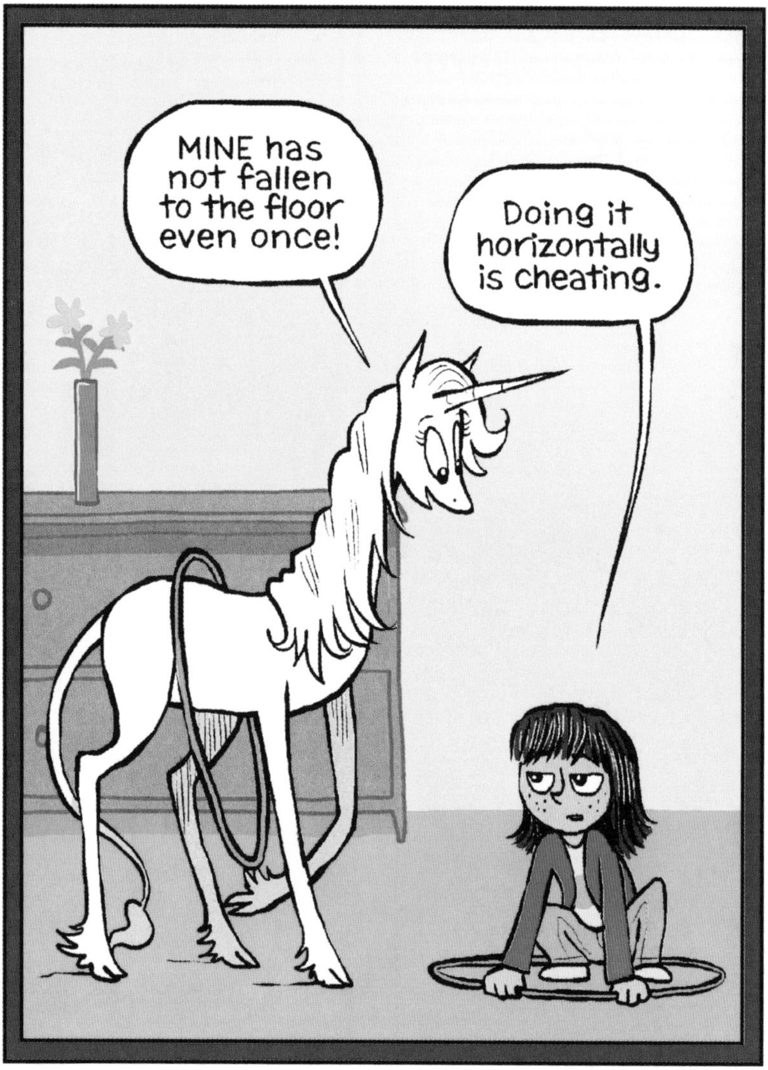
MINE has not fallen to the floor even once!
Doing it horizontally is cheating.

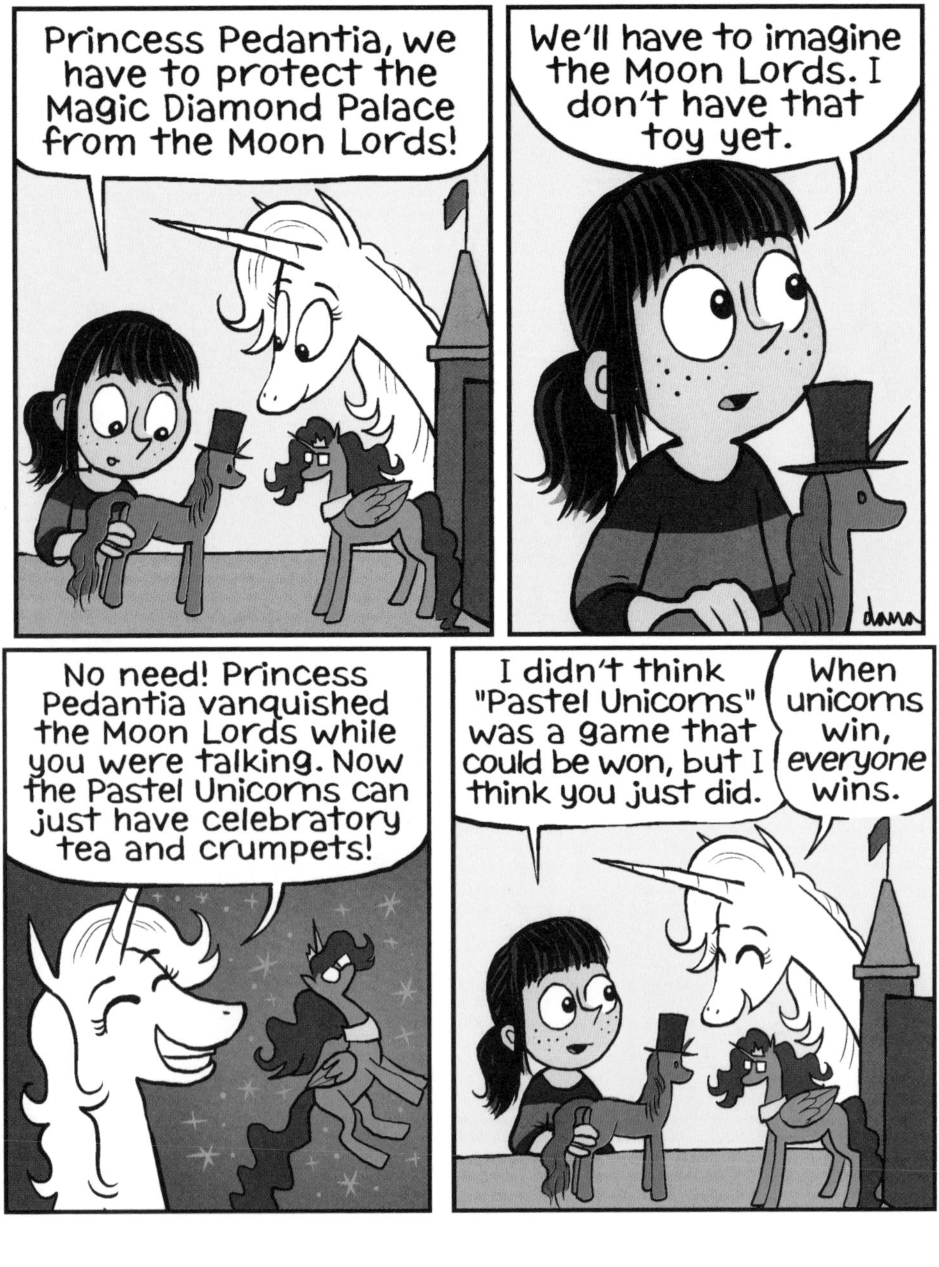
Princess Pedantia, we have to protect the Magic Diamond Palace from the Moon Lords!
We'll have to imagine the Moon Lords. I don't have that toy yet.
dana
No need! Princess Pedantia vanquished the Moon Lords while you were talking. Now the Pastel Unicorns can just have celebratory tea and crumpets!
I didn't think "Pastel Unicorns" was a game that could be won, but I think you just did.
When unicorns win, *everyone* wins.

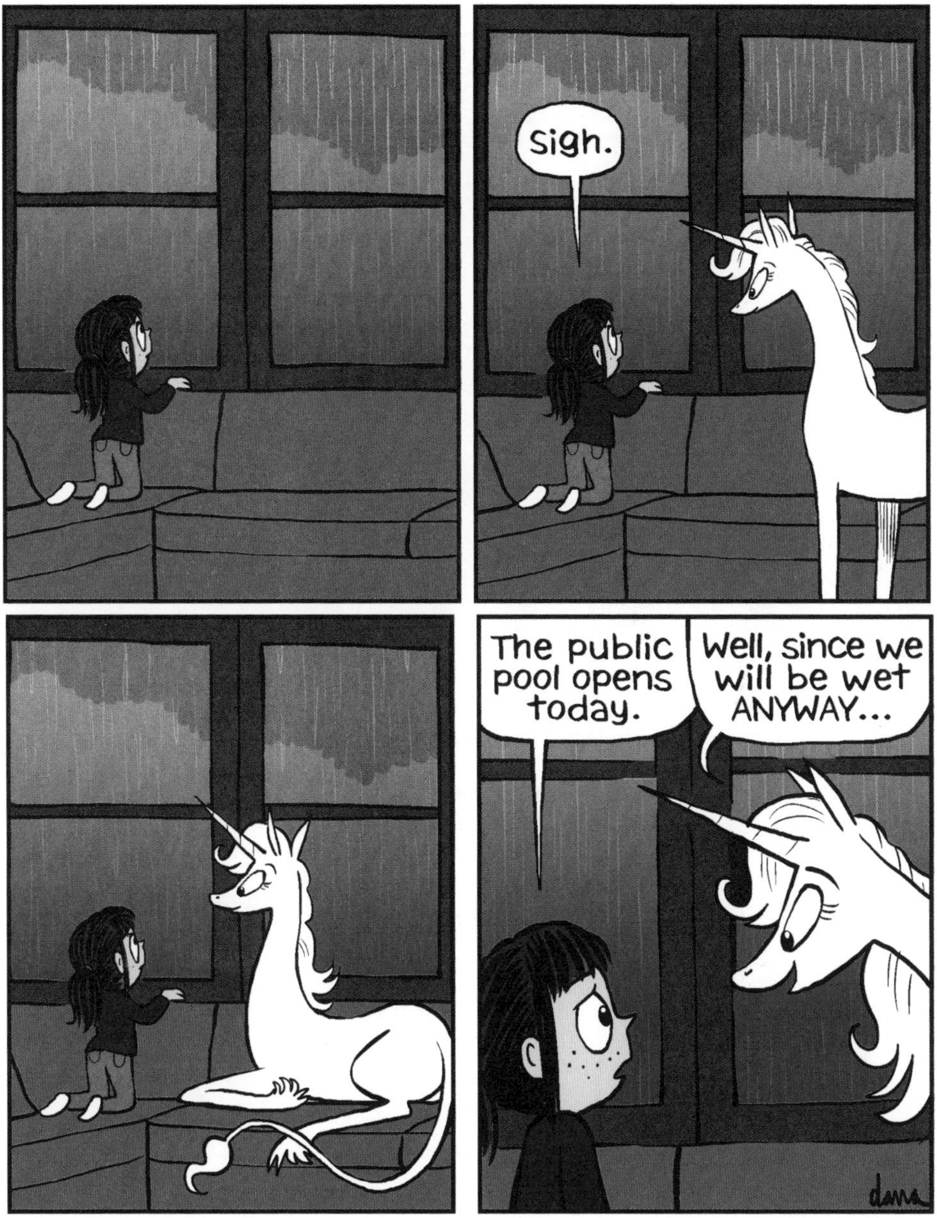

Sigh.
The public pool opens today.
Well, since we will be wet ANYWAY...
dana

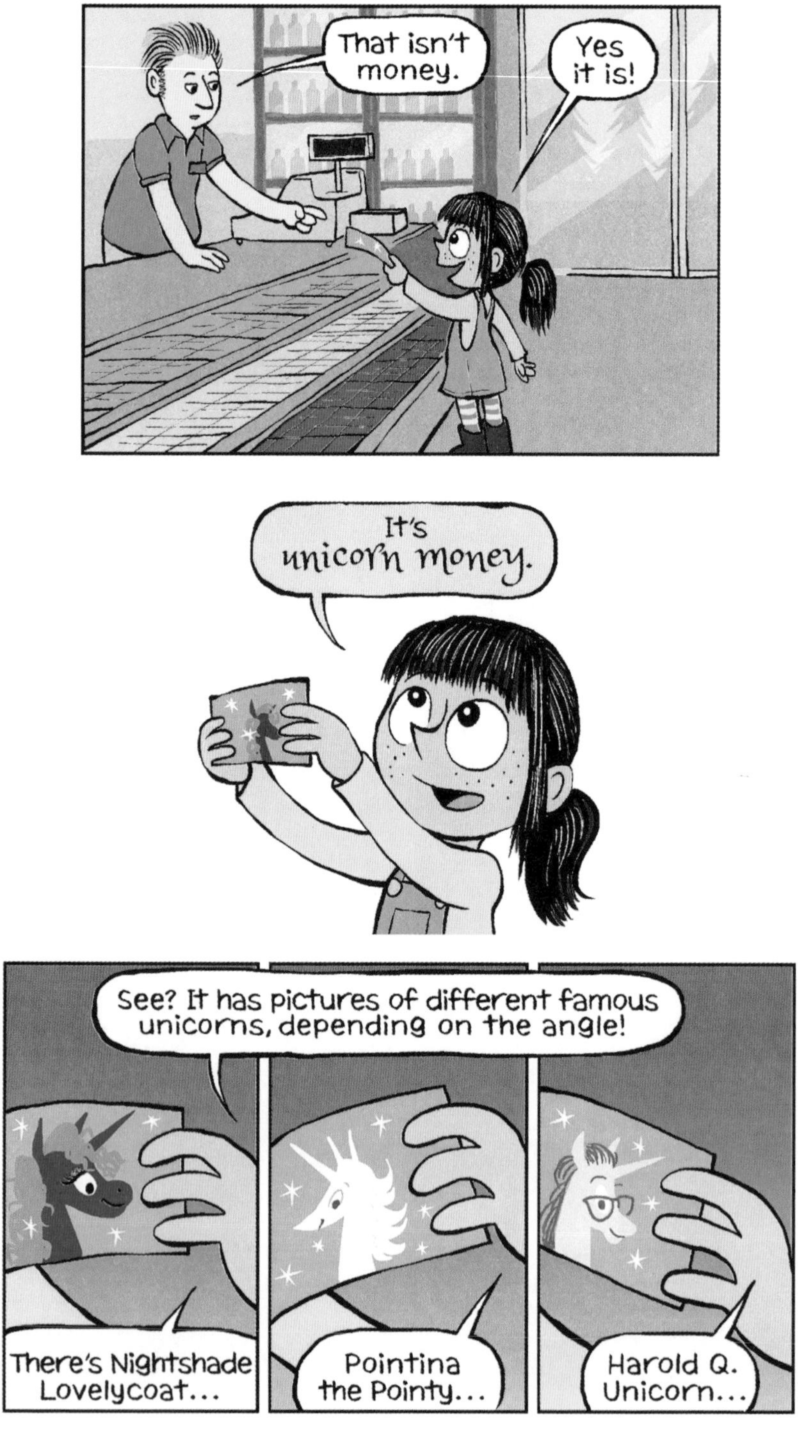
That isn't money.
Yes it is!
It's unicorn money.
See? It has pictures of different famous unicorns, depending on the angle!
There's Nightshade Lovelycoat...
Pointina the Pointy...
Harold Q. Unicorn...

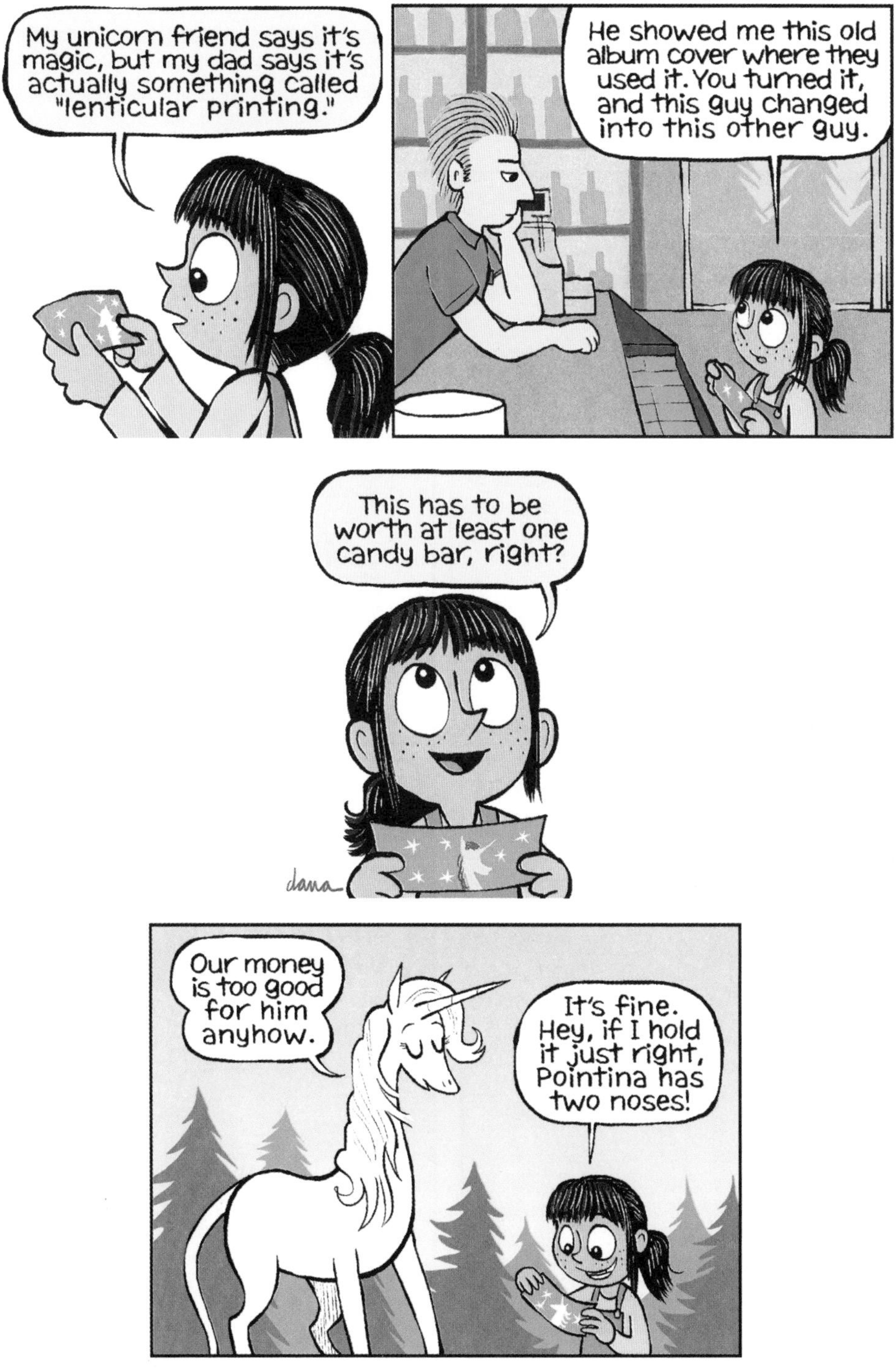
My unicorn friend says it's magic, but my dad says it's actually something called "lenticular printing."
He showed me this old album cover where they used it. You turned it, and this guy changed into this other guy.
This has to be worth at least one candy bar, right?
Our money is too good for him anyhow.
It's fine. Hey, if I hold it just right, Pointina has two noses!

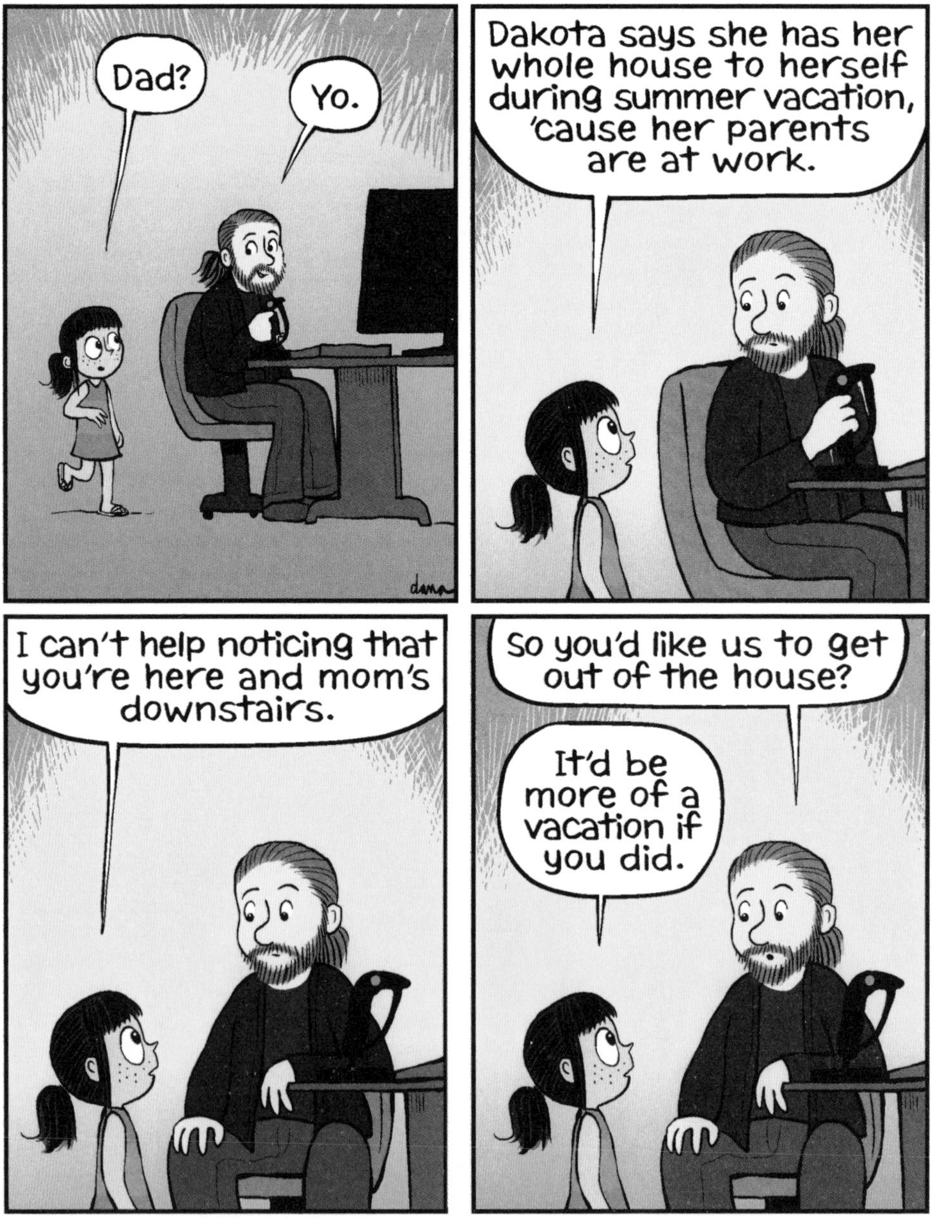
Dad?
Yo.
Dakota says she has her whole house to herself during summer vacation, 'cause her parents are at work.
I can't help noticing that you're here and mom's downstairs.
So you'd like us to get out of the house?
It'd be more of a vacation if you did.

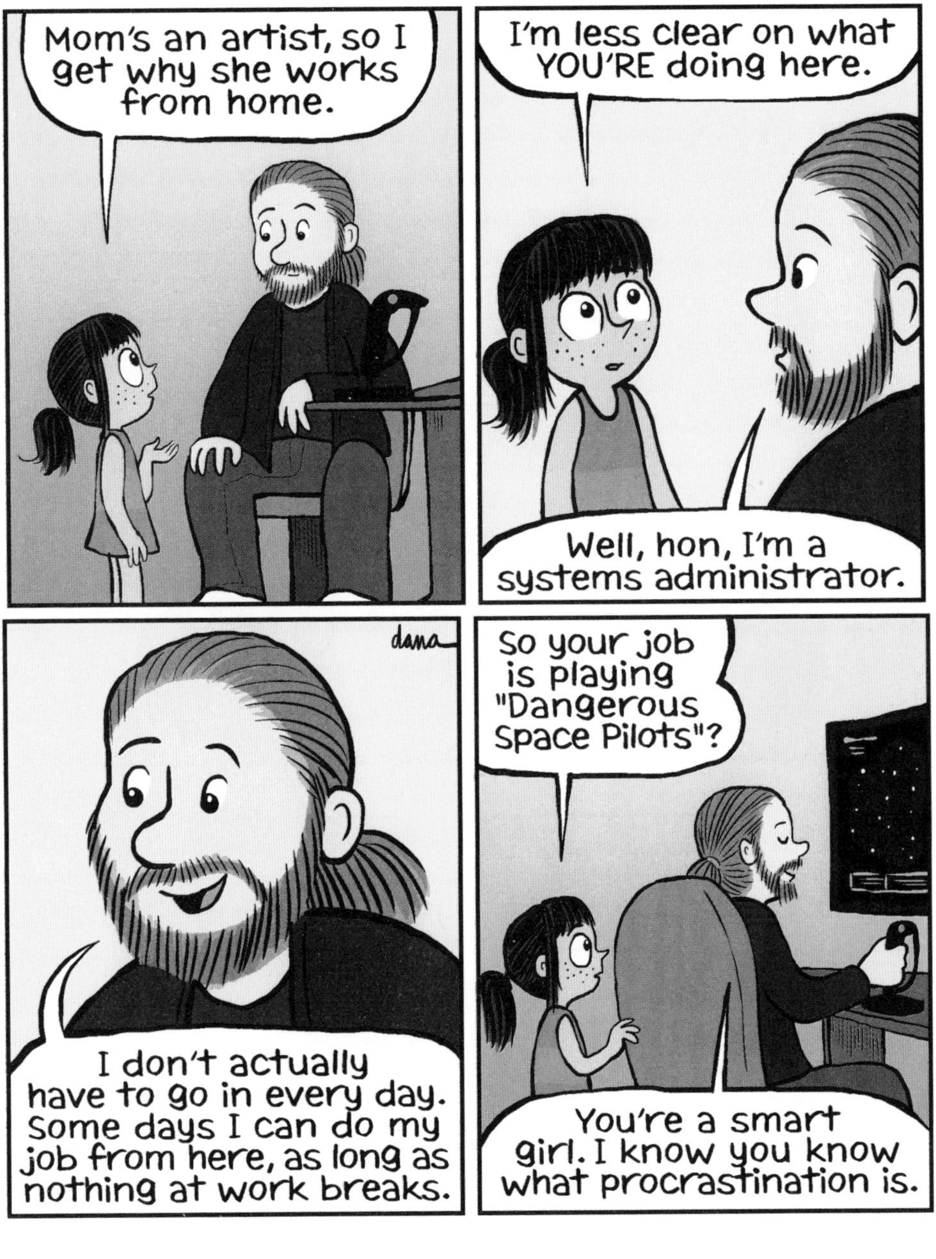
Mom's an artist, so I get why she works from home.
I'm less clear on what YOU'RE doing here.
Well, hon, I'm a systems administrator.
dana
I don't actually have to go in every day. Some days I can do my job from here, as long as nothing at work breaks.
So your job is playing "Dangerous Space Pilots"?
You're a smart girl. I know you know what procrastination is.

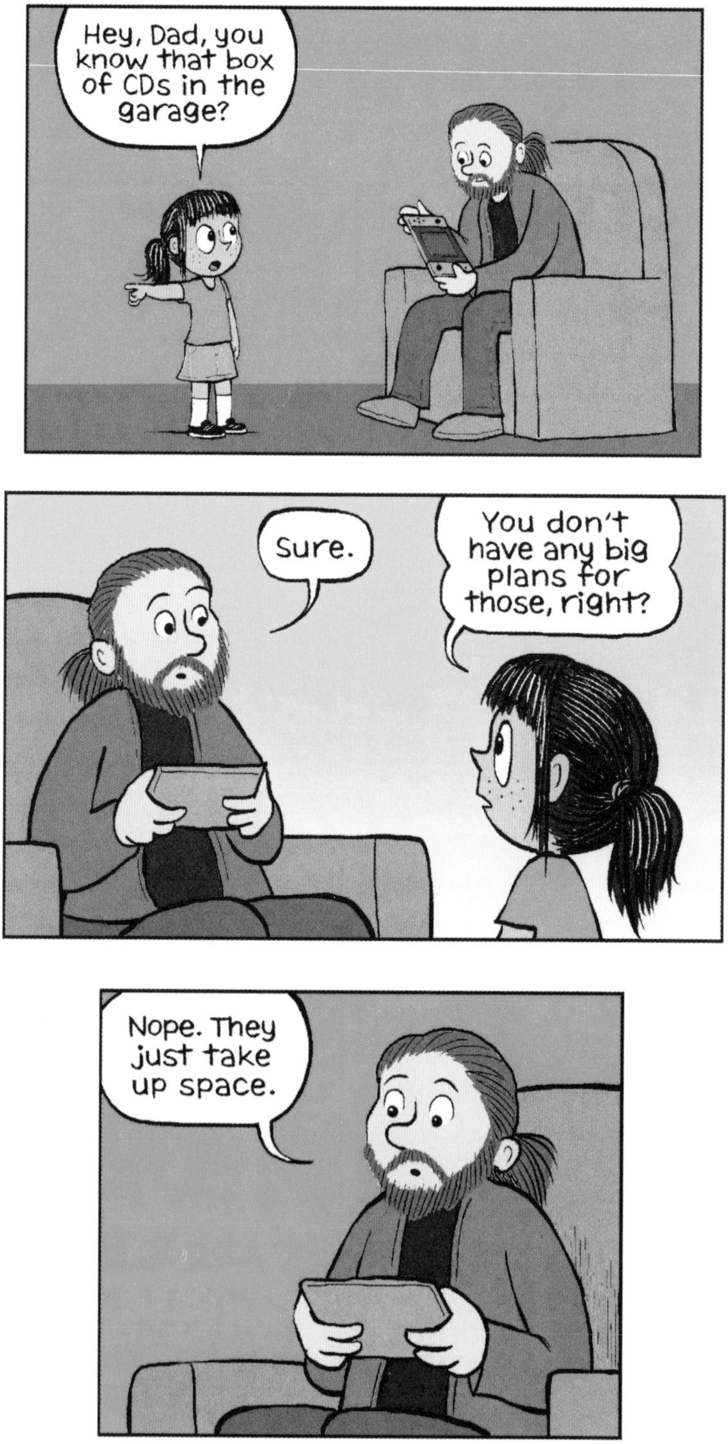
Hey, Dad, you know that box of CDs in the garage?
Sure.
You don't have any big plans for those, right?
Nope. They just take up space.

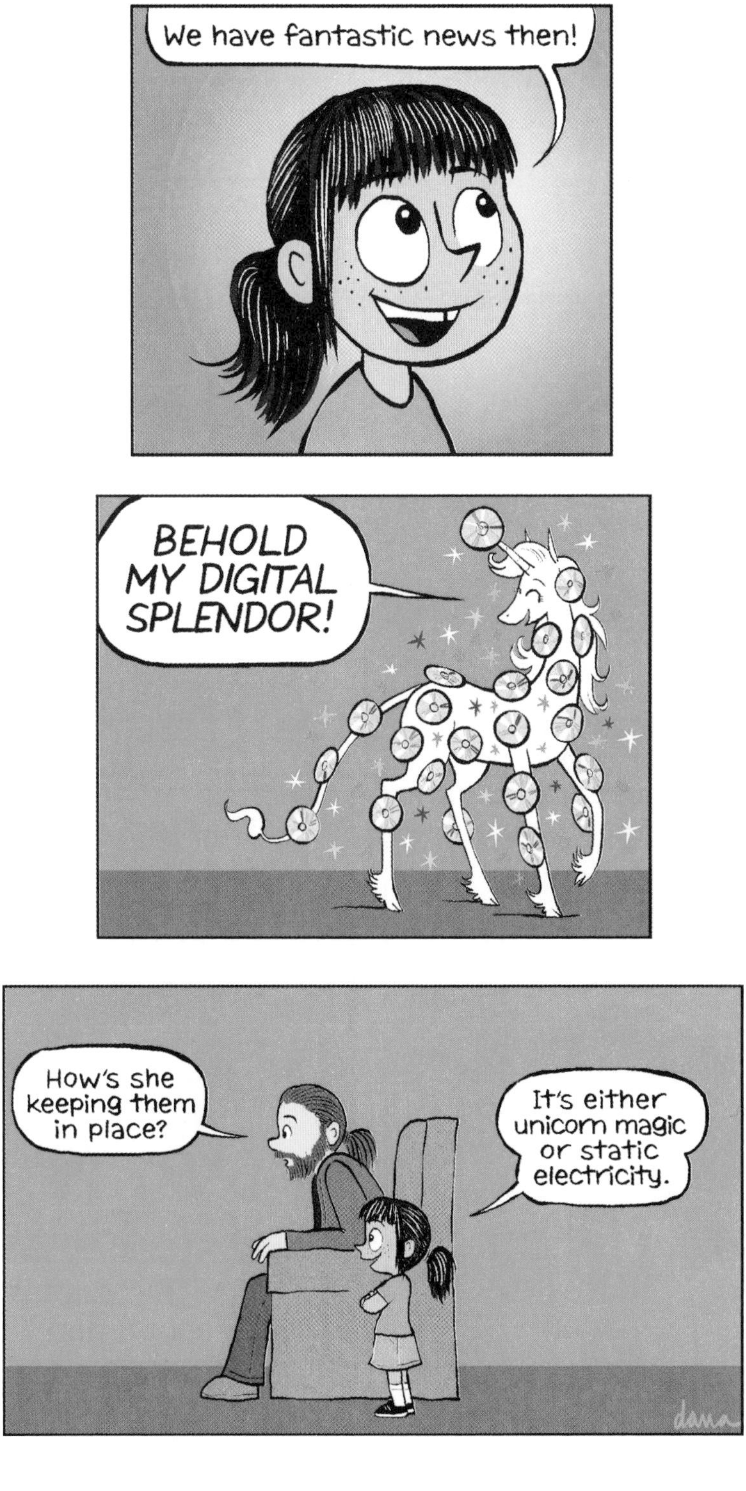
We have fantastic news then!
BEHOLD MY DIGITAL SPLENDOR!
How's she keeping them in place?
It's either unicorn magic or static electricity.

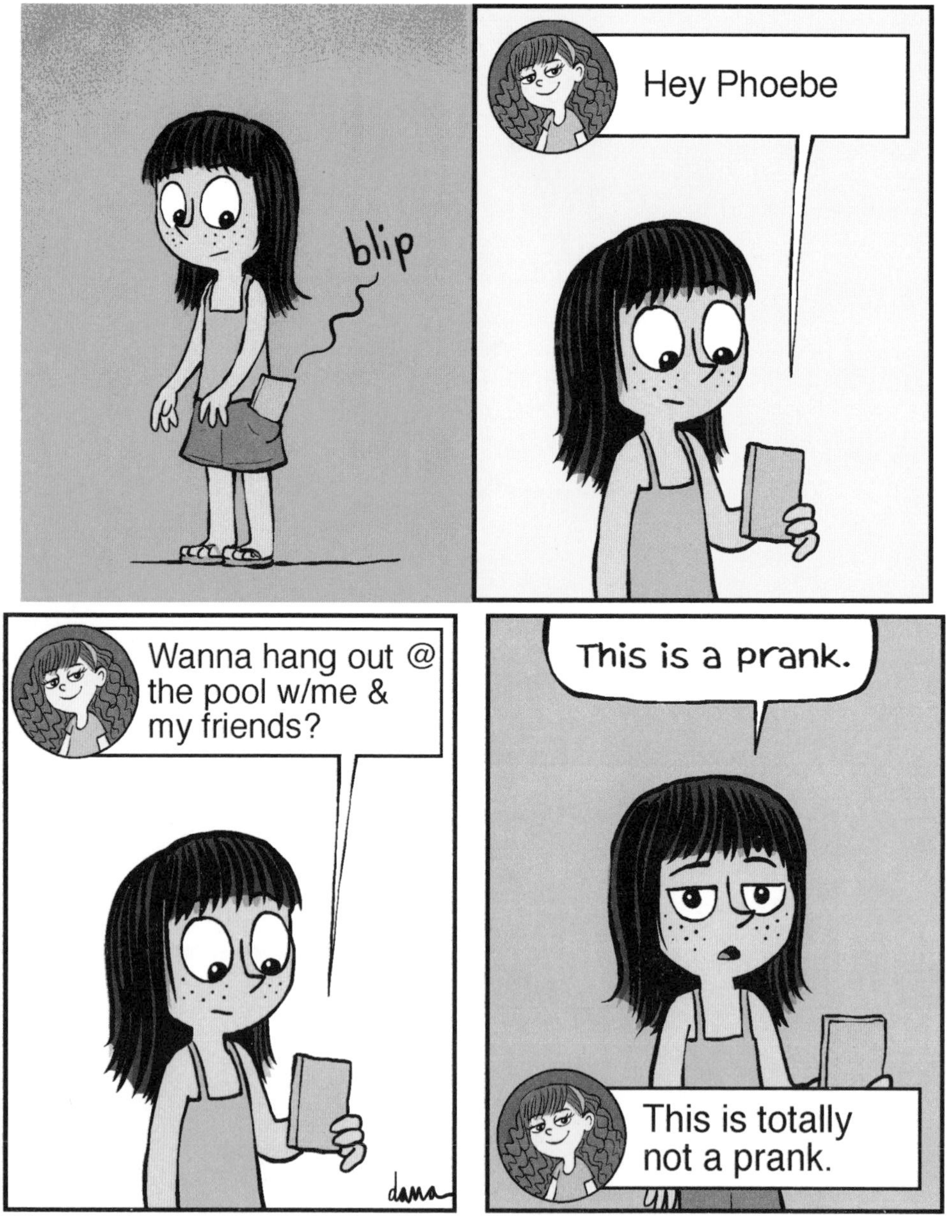
blip
Hey Phoebe
Wanna hang out @ the pool w/me & my friends?
dana
This is a prank.
This is totally not a prank.

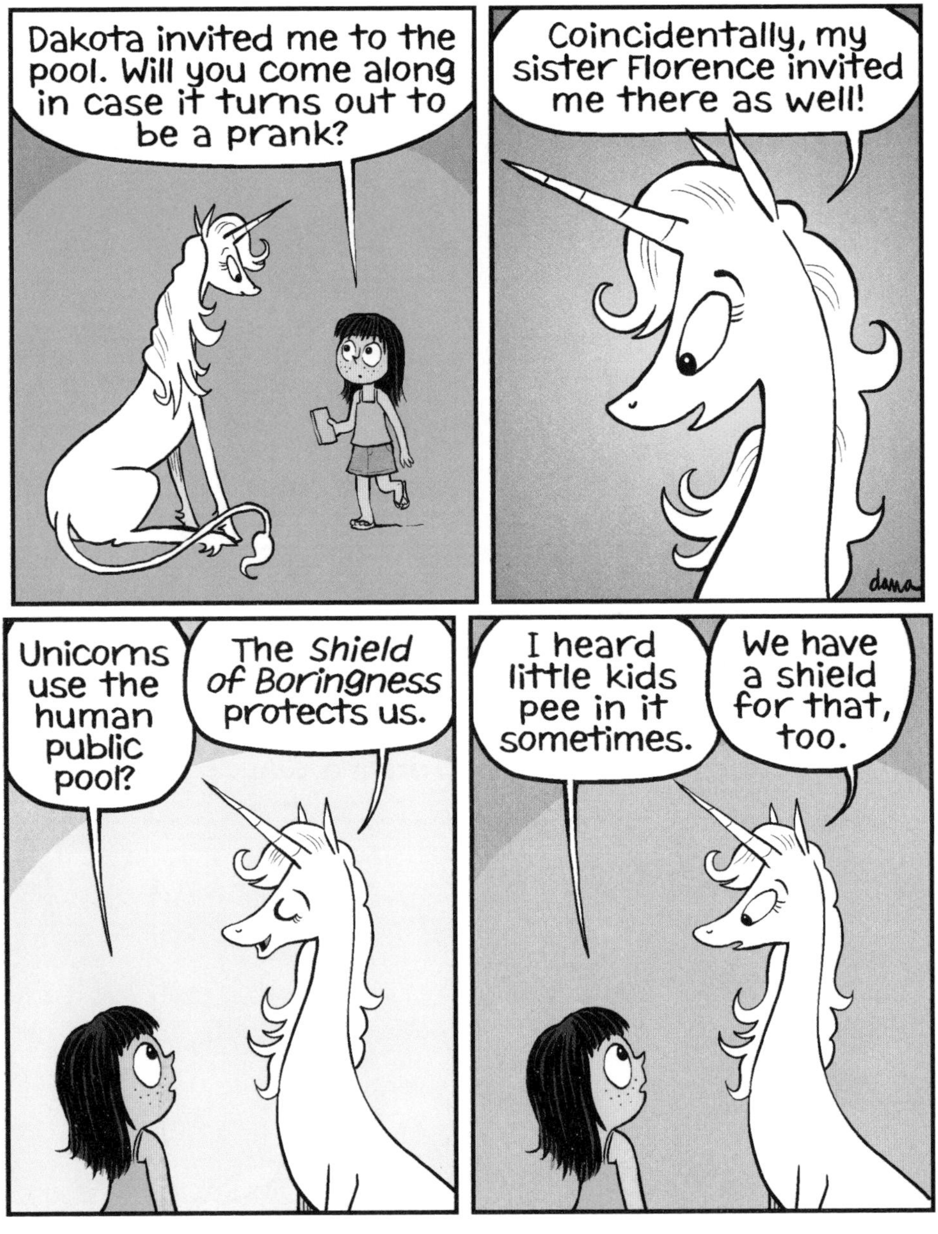
Dakota invited me to the pool. Will you come along in case it turns out to be a prank?
Coincidentally, my sister Florence invited me there as well!
dana
Unicorns use the human public pool?
The *Shield of Boringness* protects us.
I heard little kids pee in it sometimes.
We have a shield for that, too.

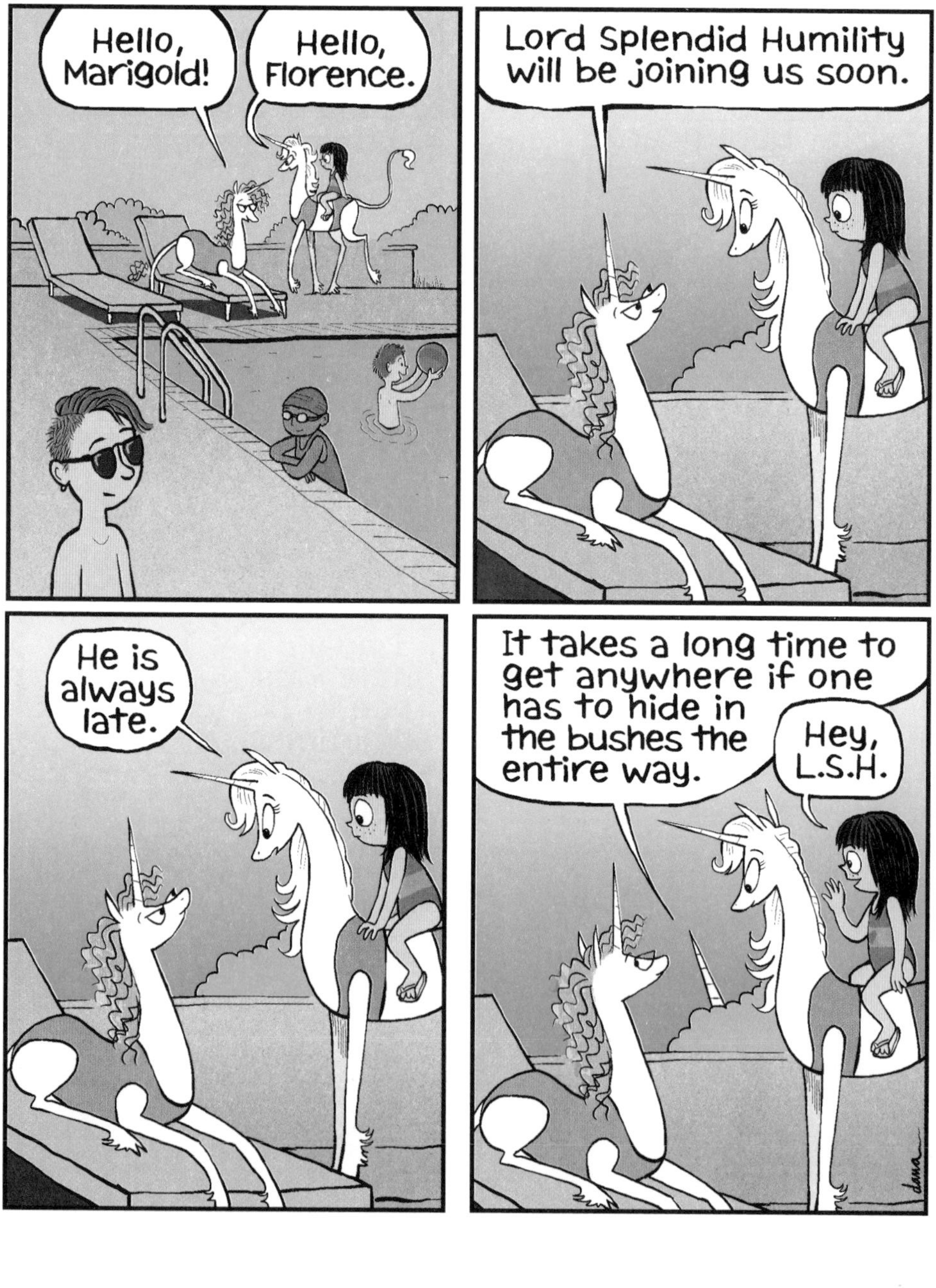
Hello, Marigold!
Hello, Florence.
Lord Splendid Humility will be joining us soon.
He is always late.
It takes a long time to get anywhere if one has to hide in the bushes the entire way.
Hey, L.S.H.

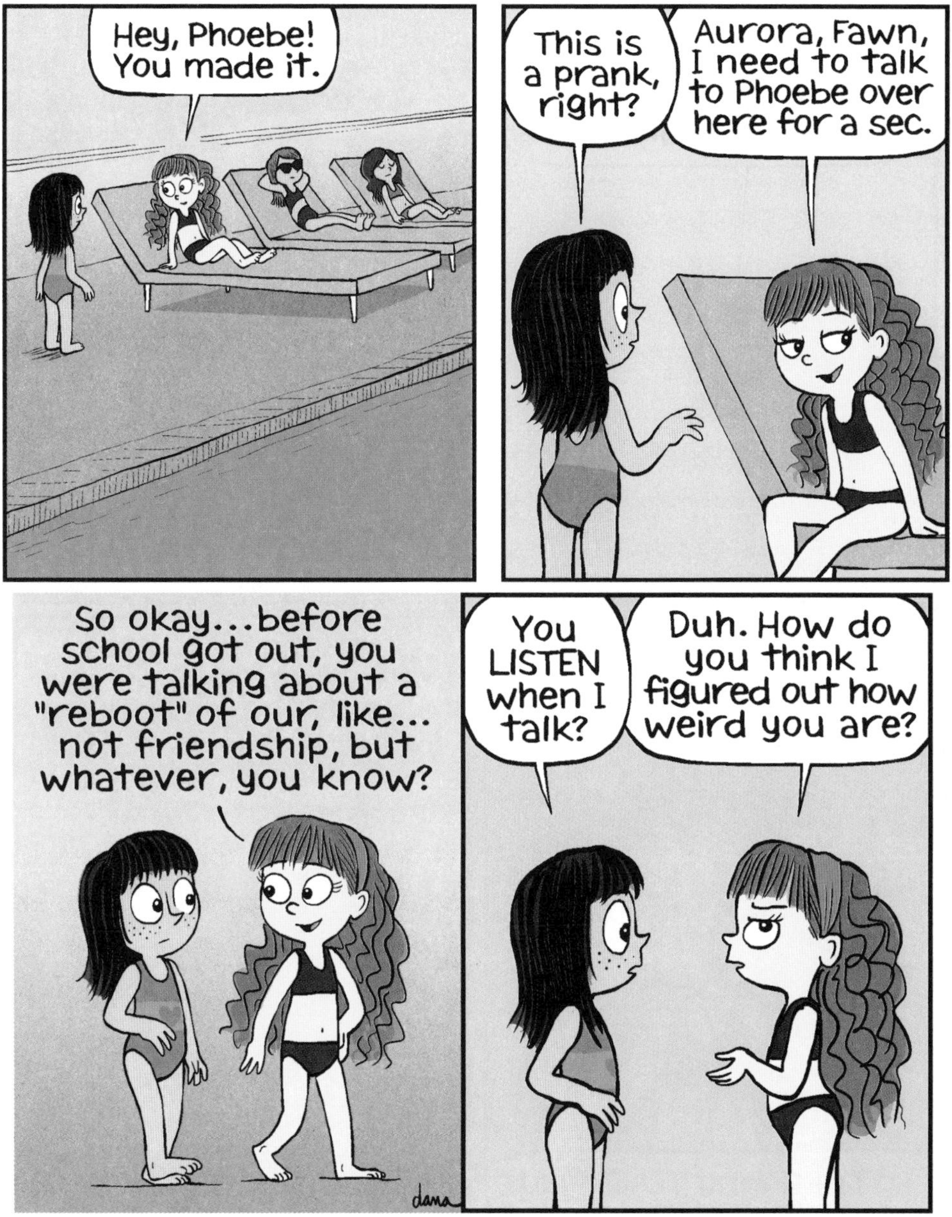
Hey, Phoebe! You made it.
This is a prank, right?
Aurora, Fawn, I need to talk to Phoebe over here for a sec.
So okay...before school got out, you were talking about a "reboot" of our, like... not friendship, but whatever, you know?
You LISTEN when I talk?
Duh. How do you think I figured out how weird you are?
dana

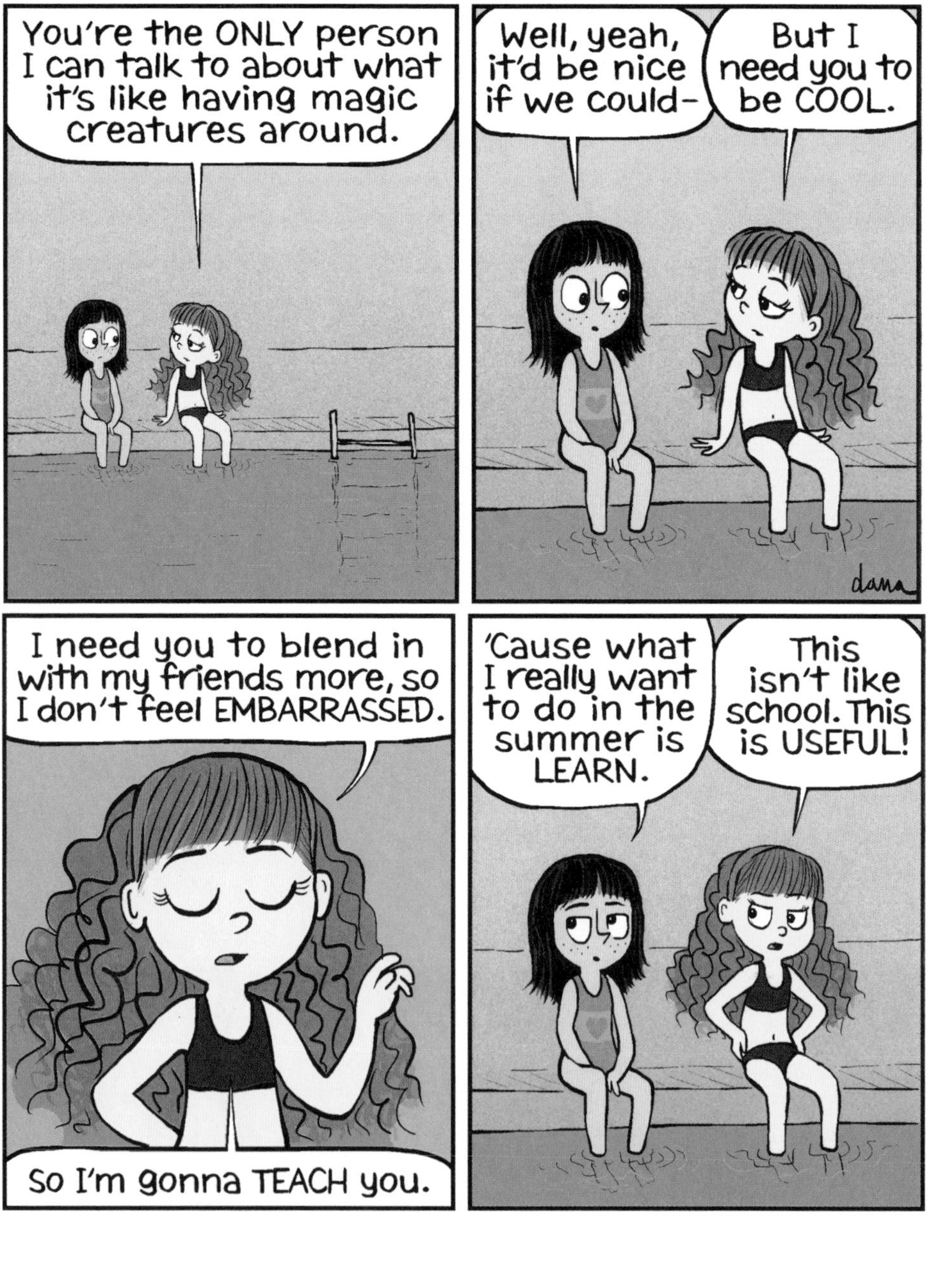
You're the ONLY person I can talk to about what it's like having magic creatures around.
Well, yeah, it'd be nice if we could-
But I need you to be COOL.
dana
I need you to blend in with my friends more, so I don't feel EMBARRASSED.
So I'm gonna TEACH you.
'Cause what I really want to do in the summer is LEARN.
This isn't like school. This is USEFUL!

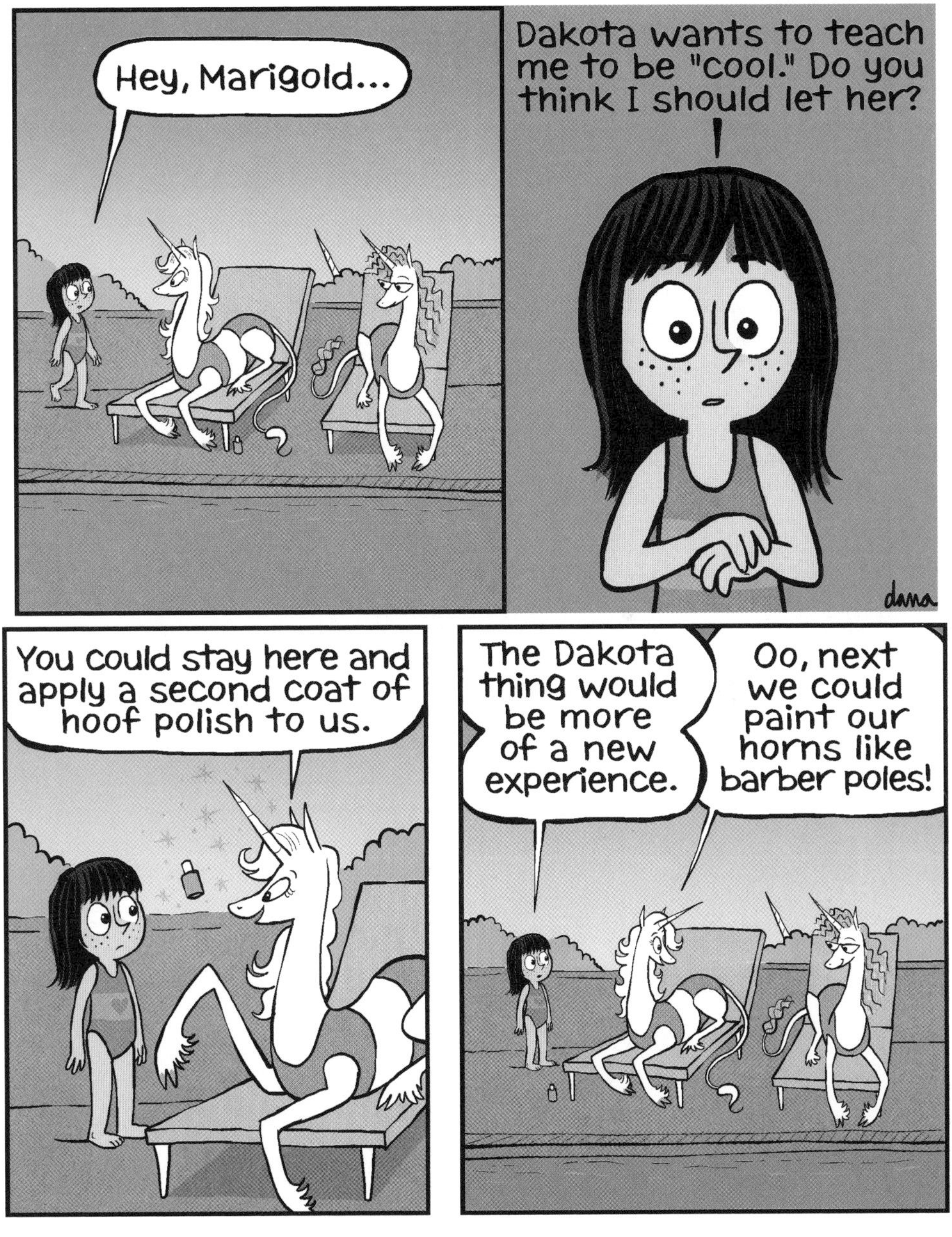

Hey, Marigold...
Dakota wants to teach me to be "cool." Do you think I should let her?
dana
You could stay here and apply a second coat of hoof polish to us.
The Dakota thing would be more of a new experience.
Oo, next we could paint our horns like barber poles!

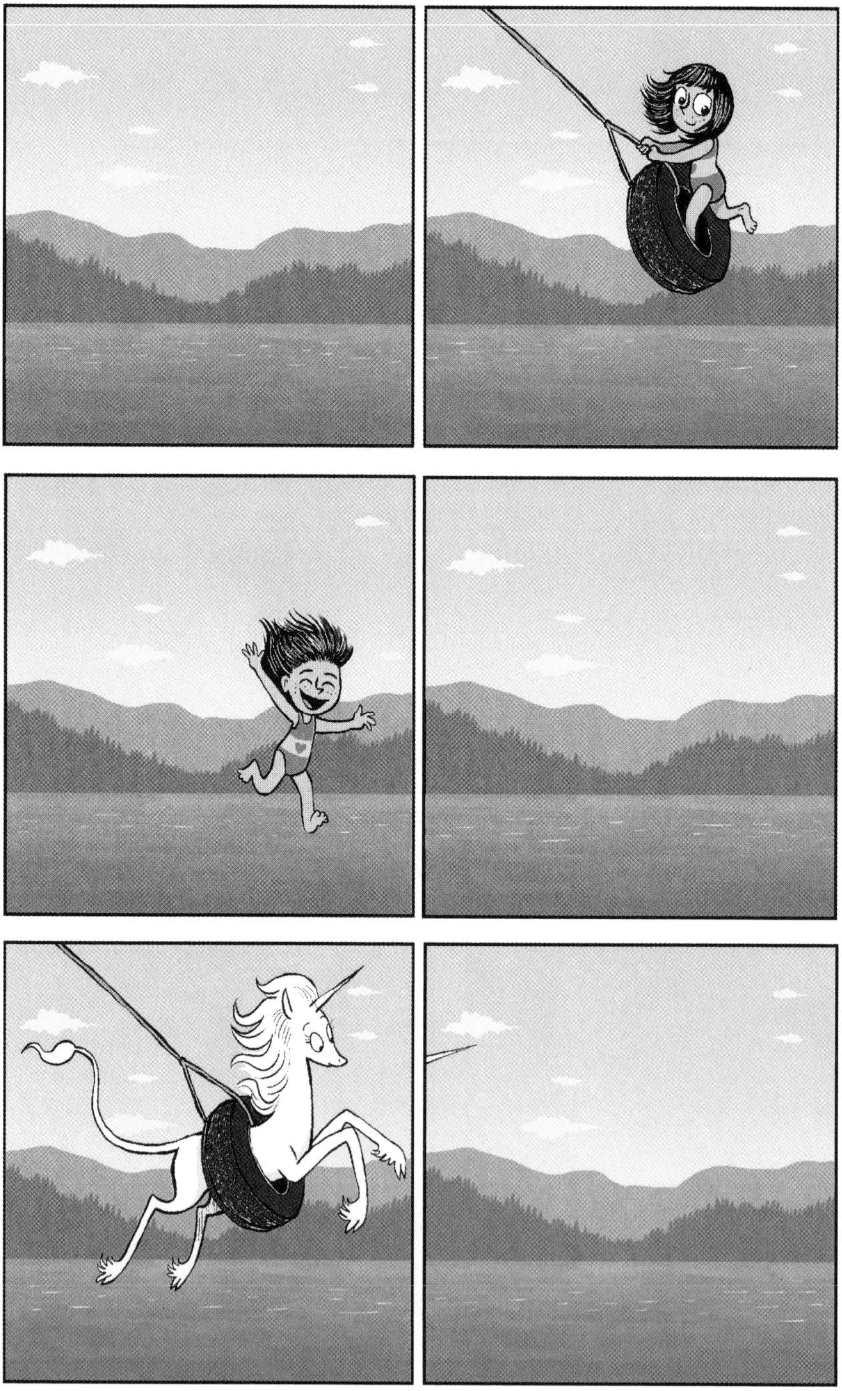

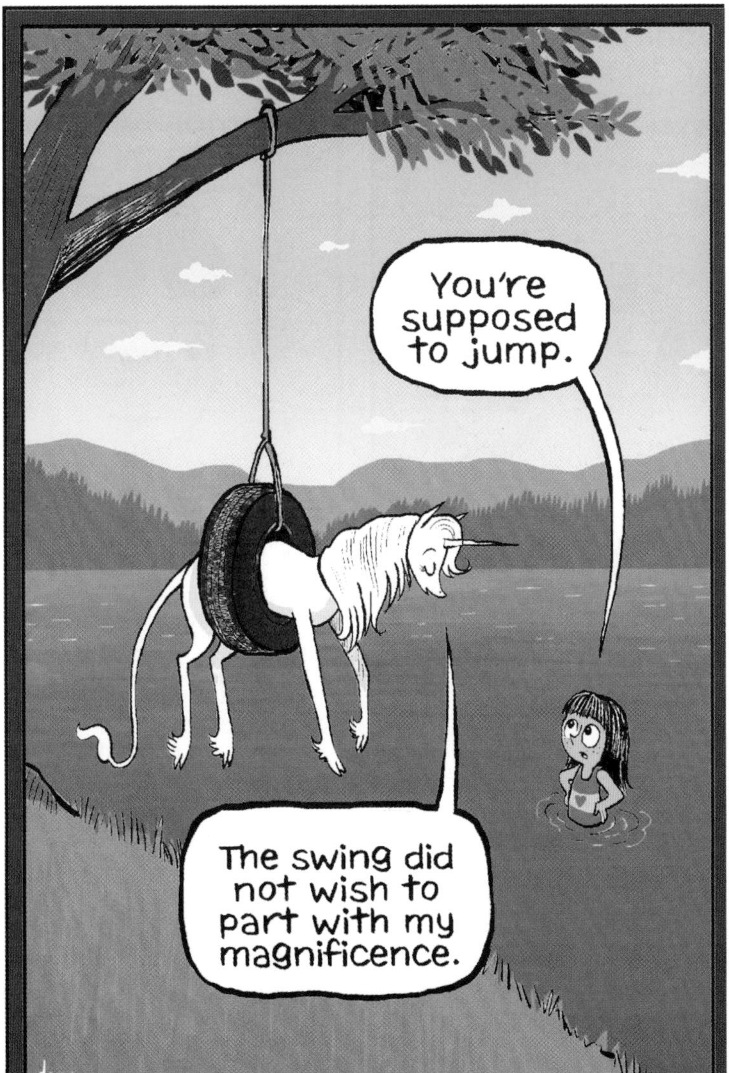
You're supposed to jump.
The swing did not wish to part with my magnificence.
dana

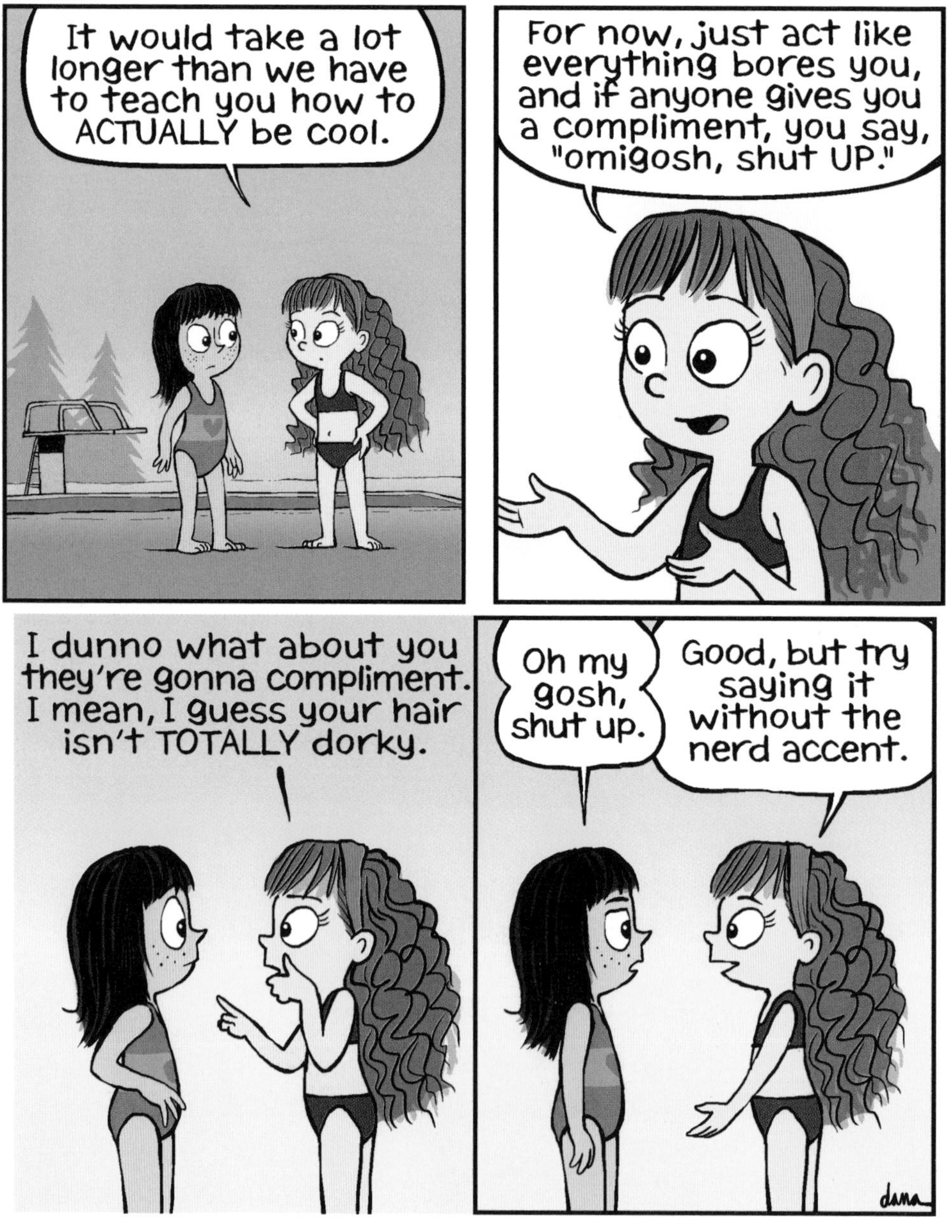
It would take a lot longer than we have to teach you how to ACTUALLY be cool.
For now, just act like everything bores you, and if anyone gives you a compliment, you say, "omigosh, shut UP."
I dunno what about you they're gonna compliment. I mean, I guess your hair isn't TOTALLY dorky.
Oh my gosh, shut up.
Good, but try saying it without the nerd accent.
dana

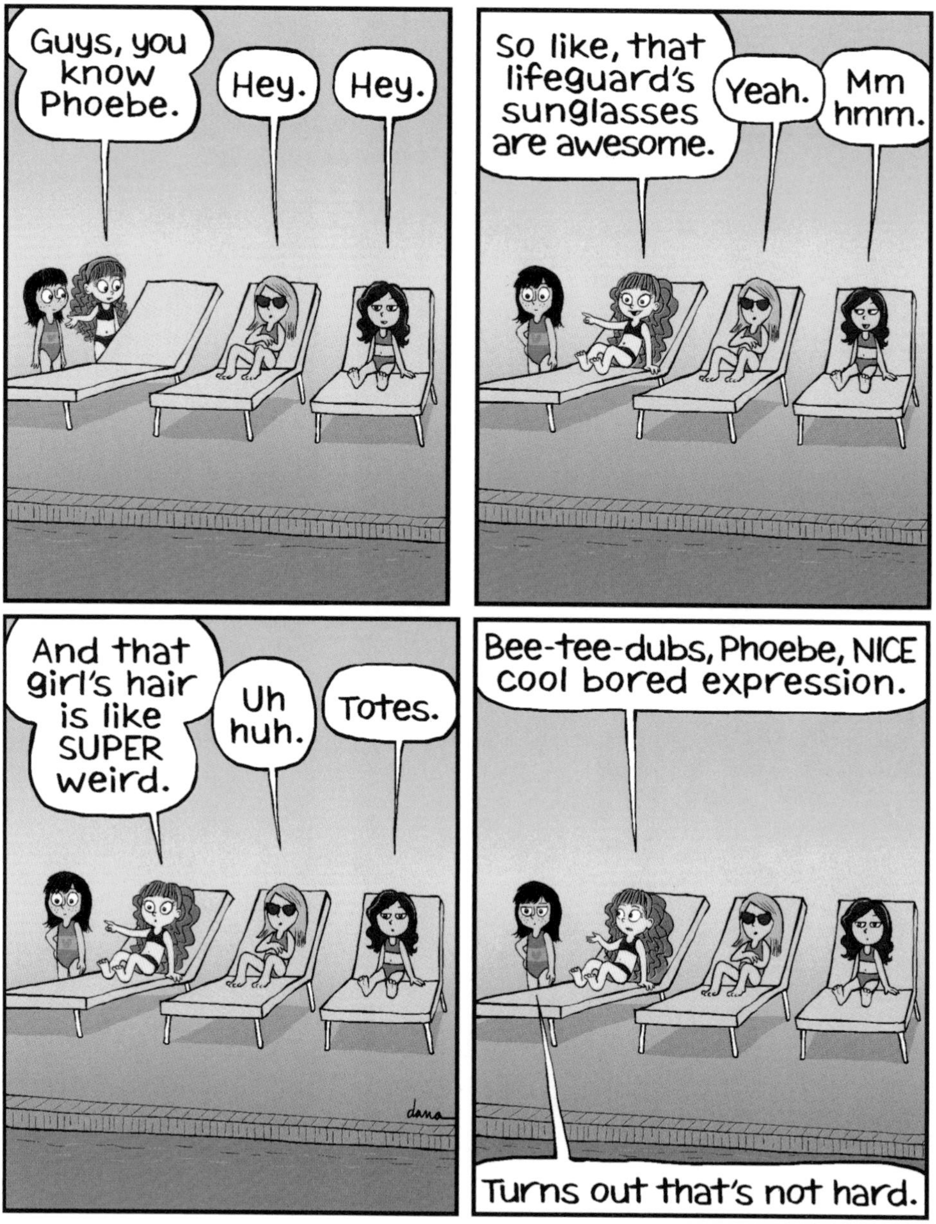
Guys, you know Phoebe.
Hey.
Hey.
So like, that lifeguard's sunglasses are awesome.
Yeah.
Mm hmm.
And that girl's hair is like SUPER weird.
Uh huh.
Totes.
dana
Bee-tee-dubs, Phoebe, NICE cool bored expression.
Turns out that's not hard.

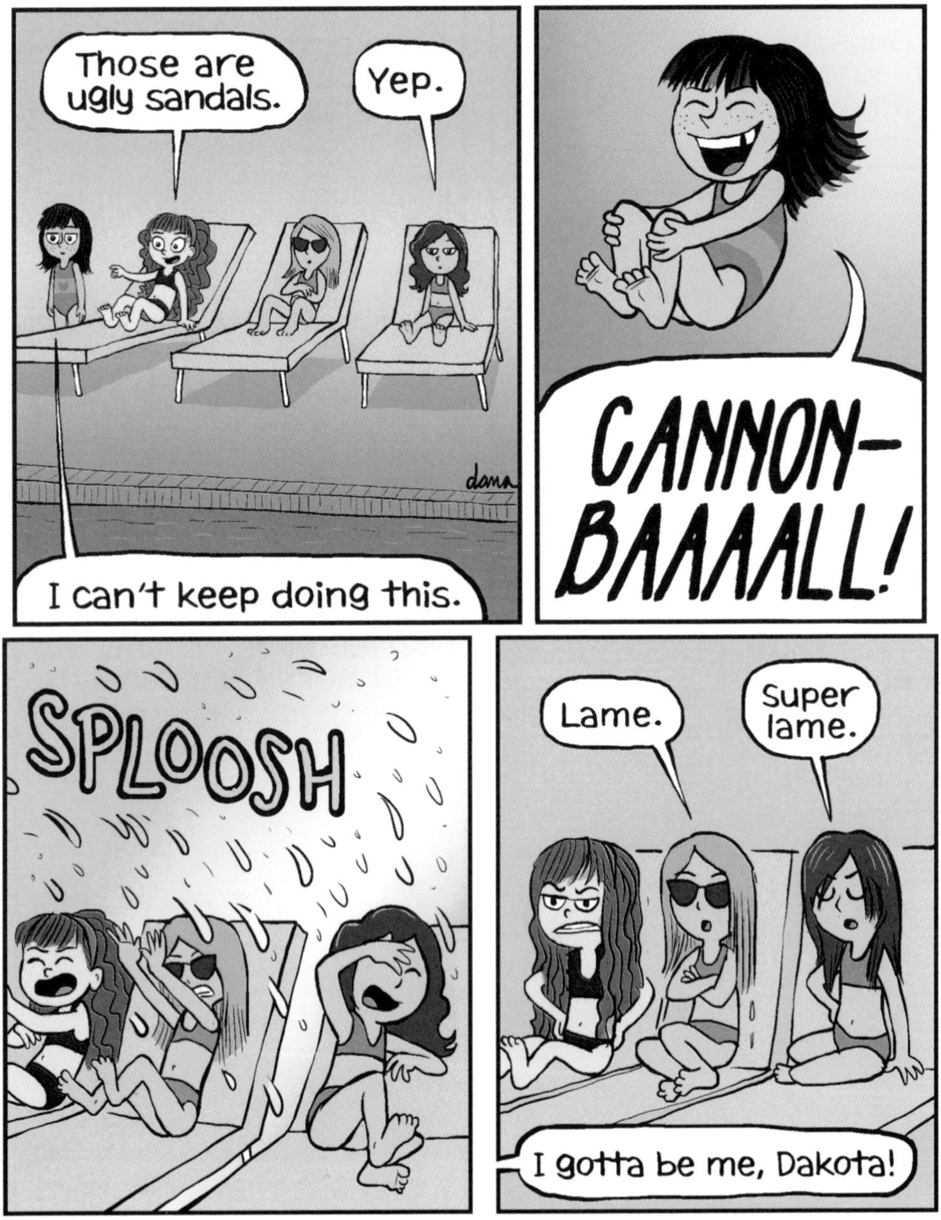
Those are ugly sandals.
Yep.
I can't keep doing this.
CANNON-BAAAALL!
SPLOOSH
Lame.
Super lame.
I gotta be me, Dakota!

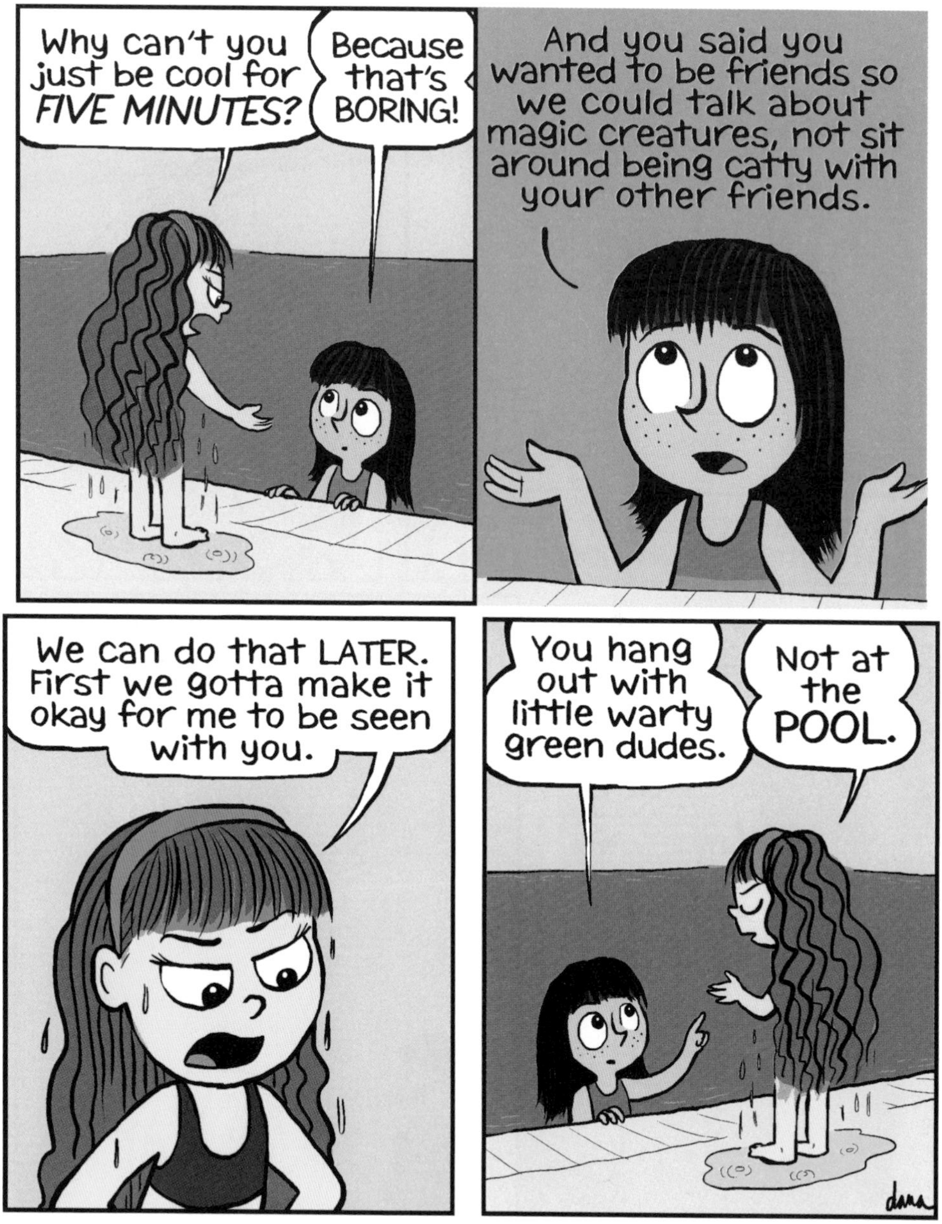
Why can't you just be cool for *FIVE MINUTES?*
Because that's BORING!
And you said you wanted to be friends so we could talk about magic creatures, not sit around being catty with your other friends.
We can do that LATER. First we gotta make it okay for me to be seen with you.
You hang out with little warty green dudes.
Not at the POOL.
dana

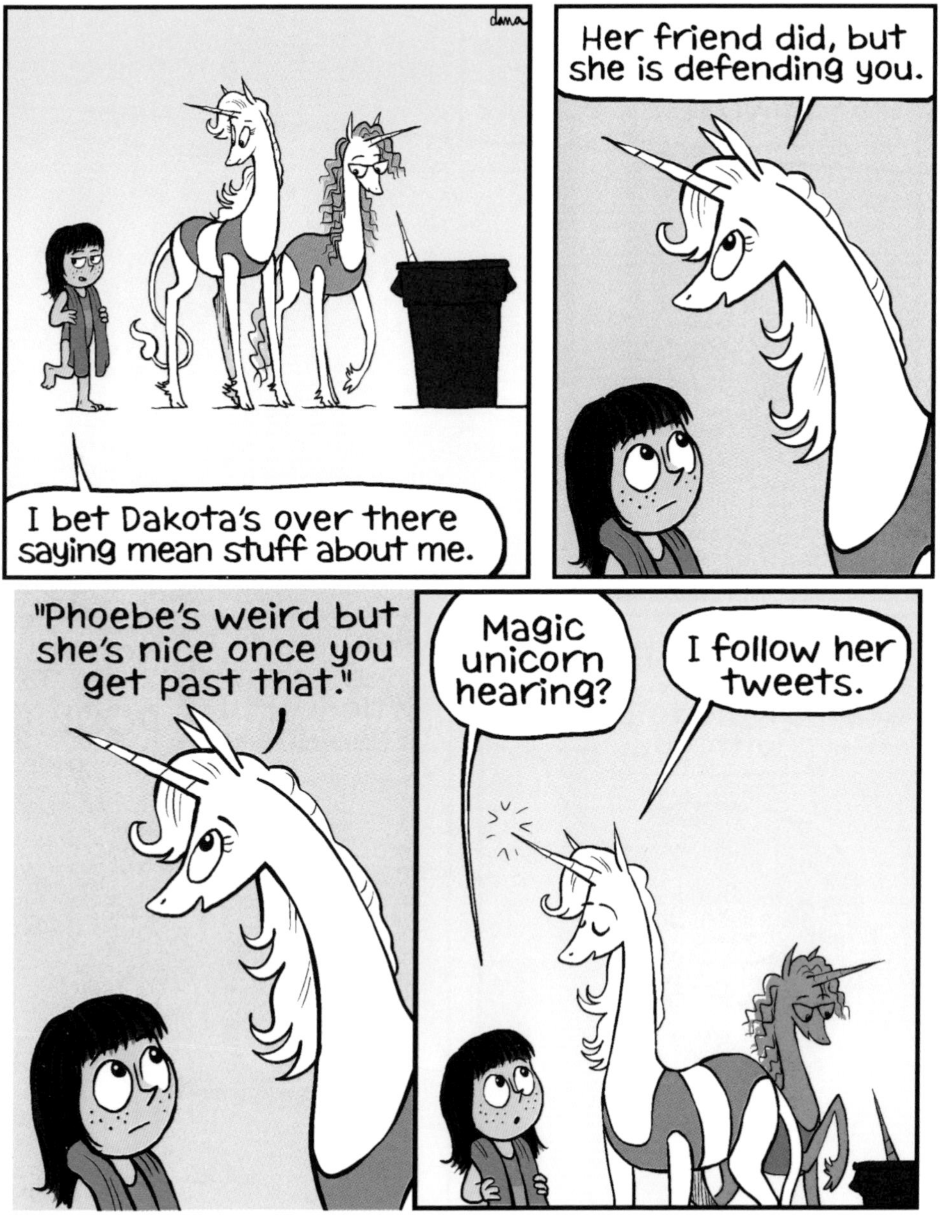
dana
I bet Dakota's over there saying mean stuff about me.
Her friend did, but she is defending you.
"Phoebe's weird but she's nice once you get past that."
Magic unicorn hearing?
I follow her tweets.

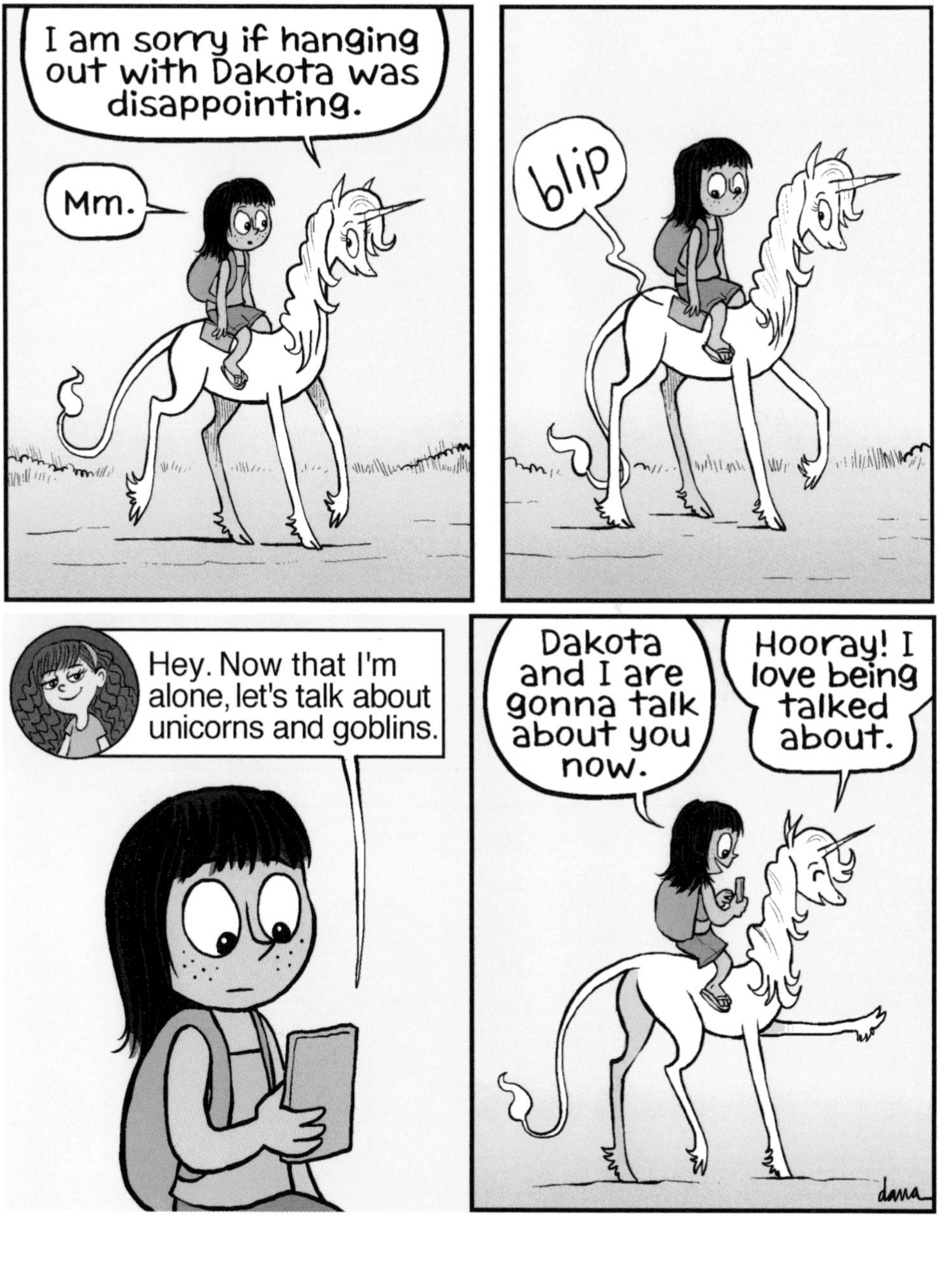
I am sorry if hanging out with Dakota was disappointing.
Mm.
blip
Hey. Now that I'm alone, let's talk about unicorns and goblins.
Dakota and I are gonna talk about you now.
Hooray! I love being talked about.
dana

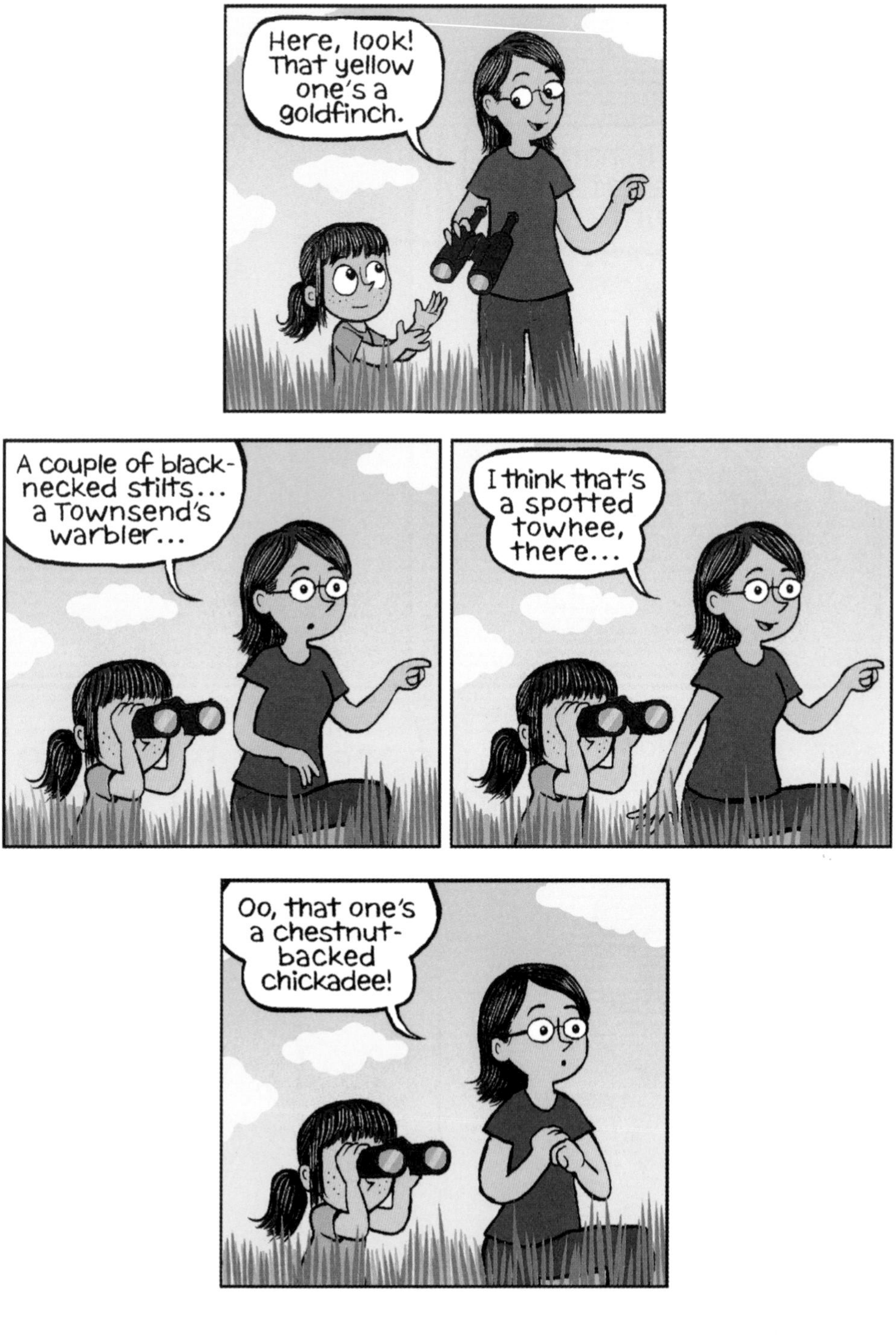
Here, look! That yellow one's a goldfinch.
A couple of black-necked stilts... a Townsend's warbler...
I think that's a spotted towhee, there...
Oo, that one's a chestnut-backed chickadee!

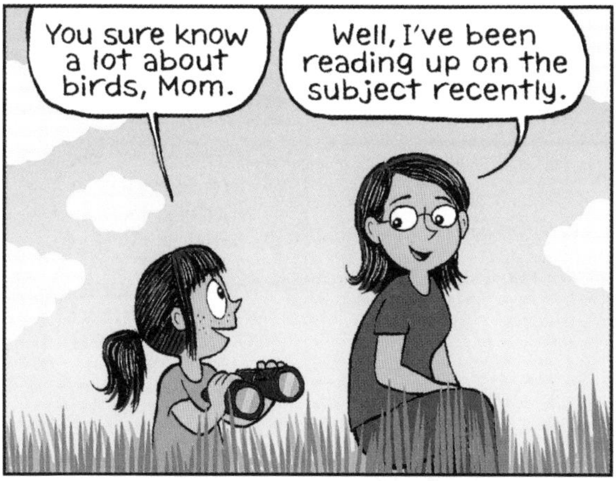
You sure know a lot about birds, Mom.
Well, I've been reading up on the subject recently.

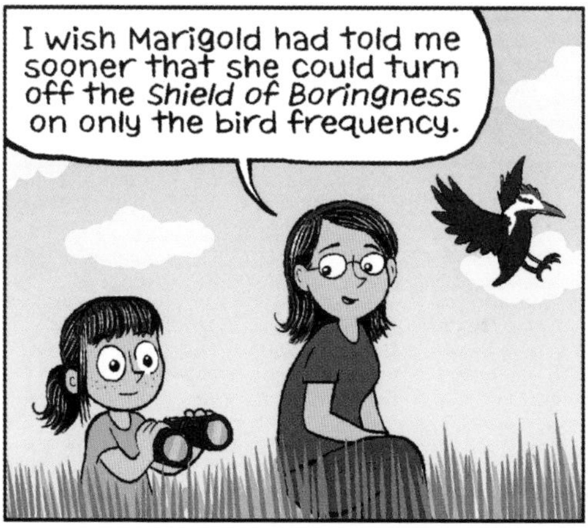
I wish Marigold had told me sooner that she could turn off the *Shield of Boringness* on only the bird frequency.

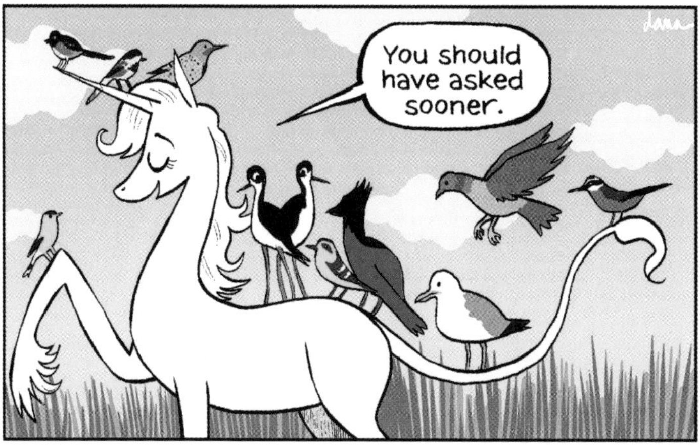
You should have asked sooner.

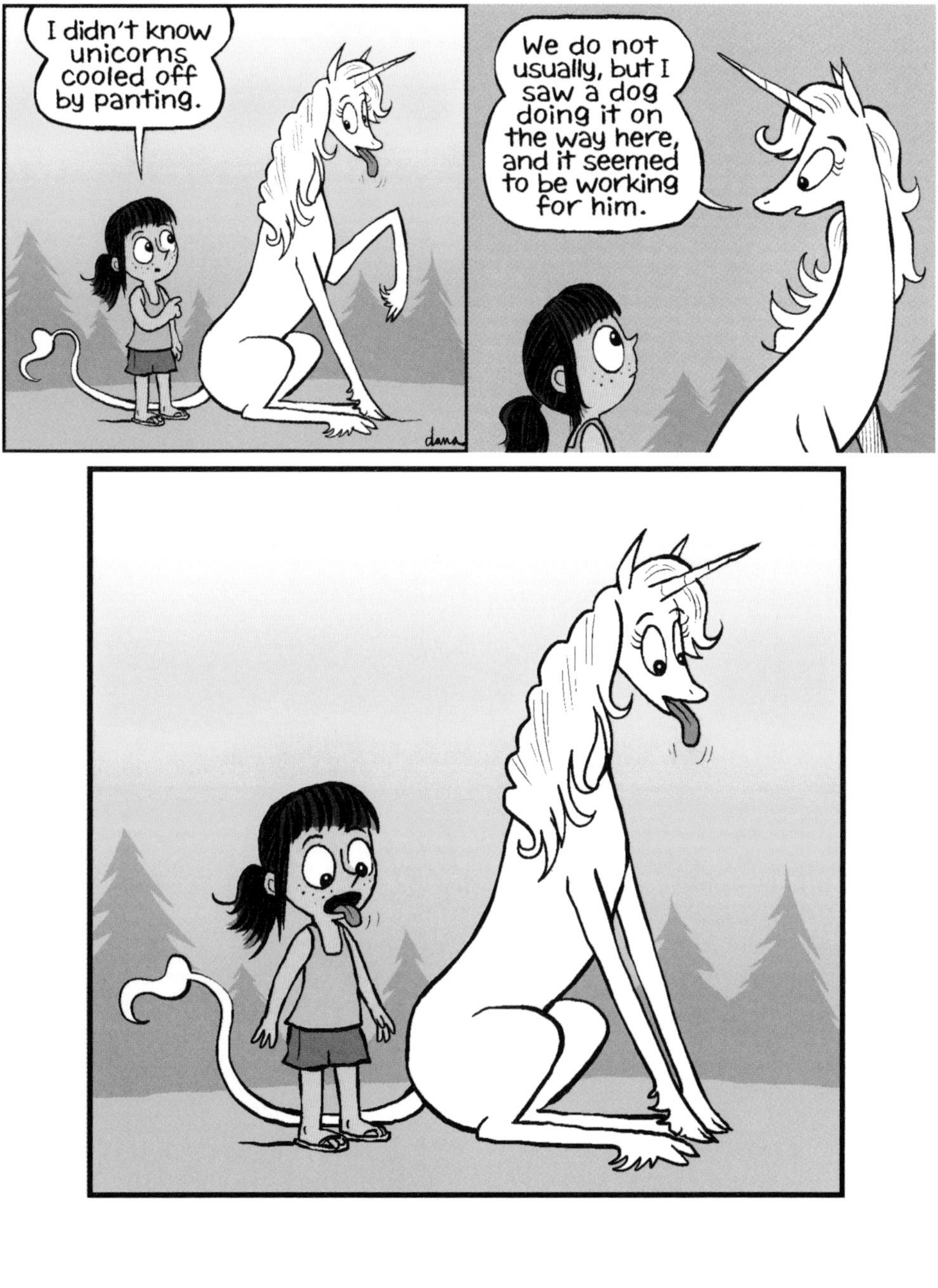
I didn't know unicorns cooled off by panting.
We do not usually, but I saw a dog doing it on the way here, and it seemed to be working for him.
dana

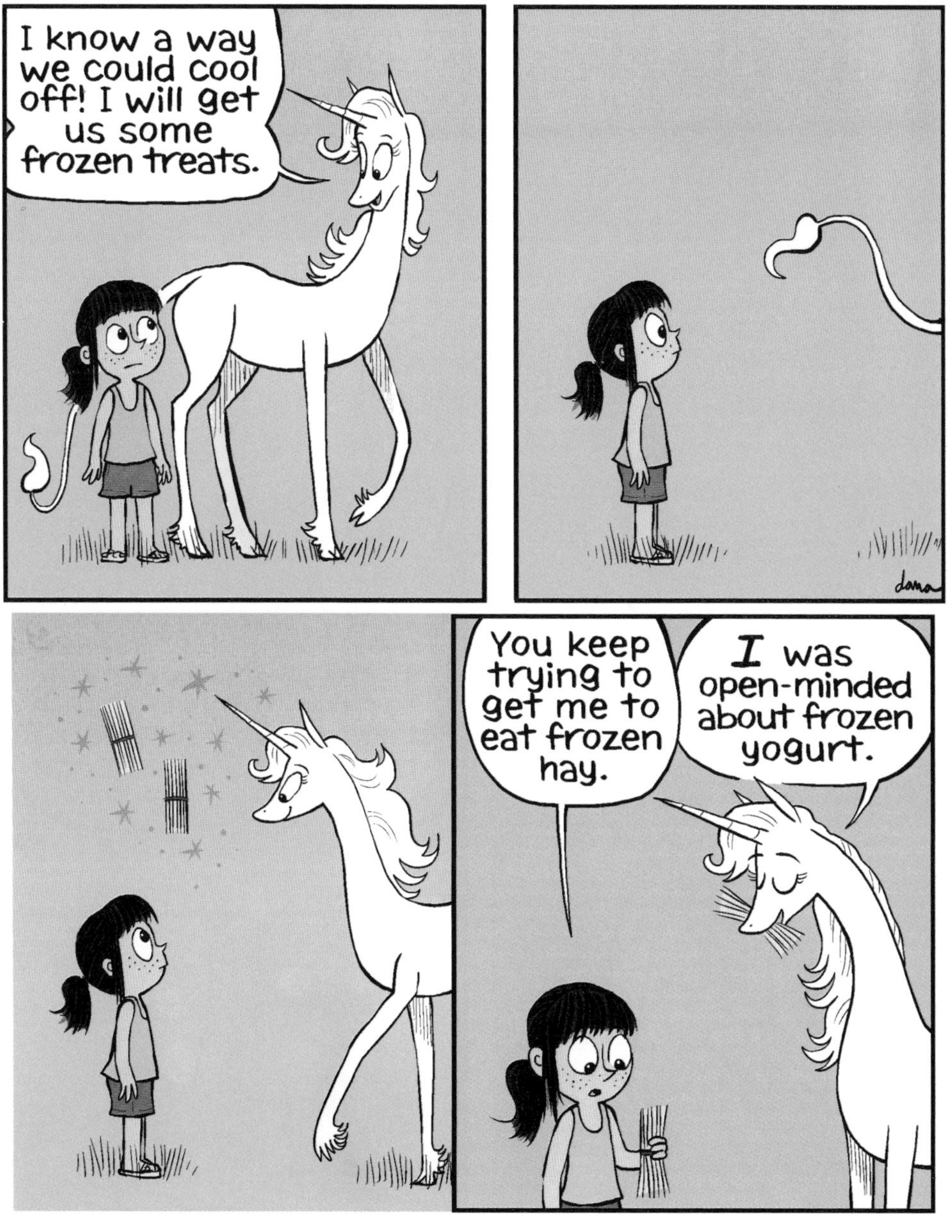
I know a way we could cool off! I will get us some frozen treats.
You keep trying to get me to eat frozen hay.
I was open-minded about frozen yogurt.

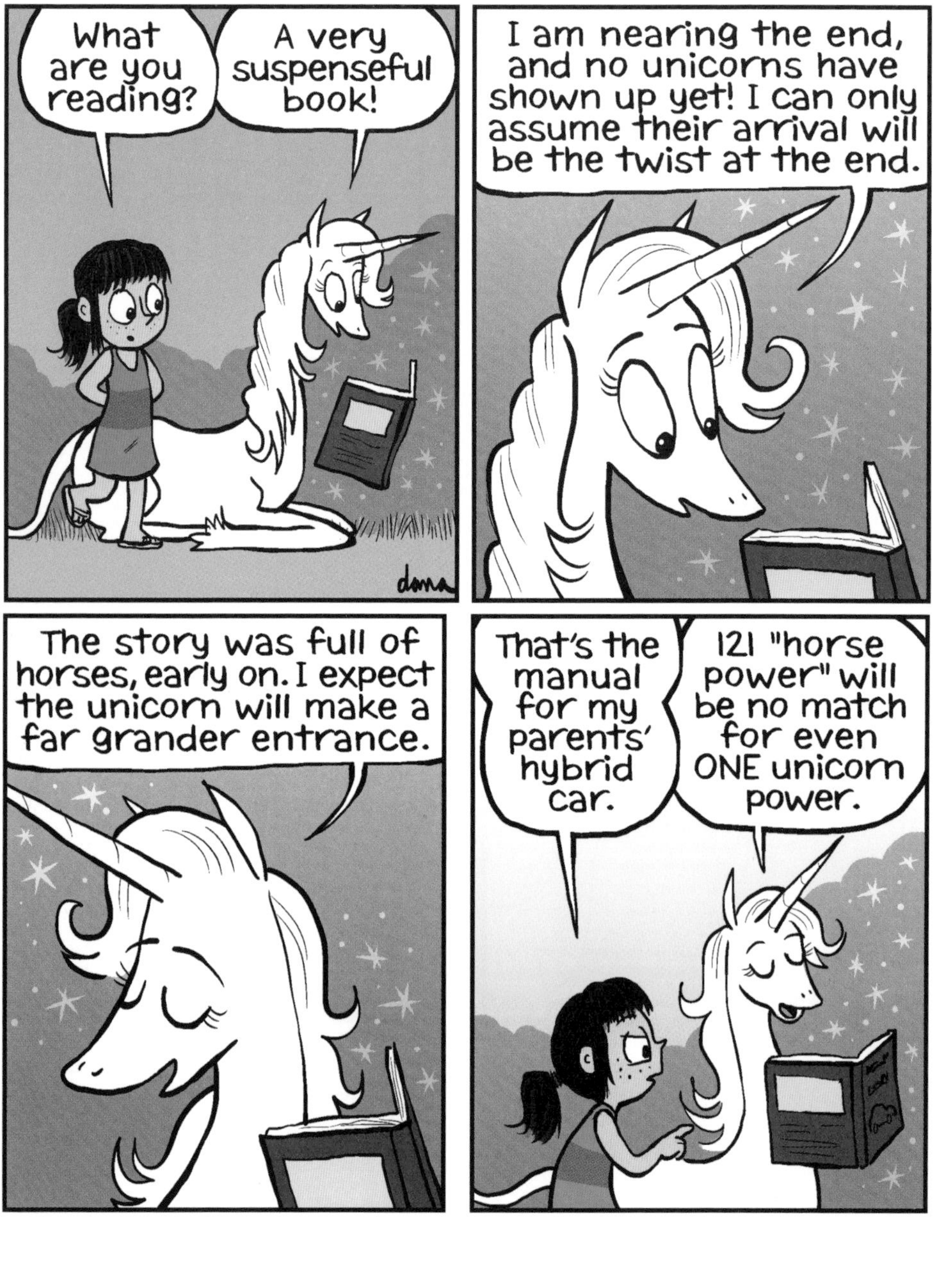
What are you reading?
A very suspenseful book!
I am nearing the end, and no unicorns have shown up yet! I can only assume their arrival will be the twist at the end.
The story was full of horses, early on. I expect the unicorn will make a far grander entrance.
That's the manual for my parents' hybrid car.
121 "horse power" will be no match for even ONE unicorn power.

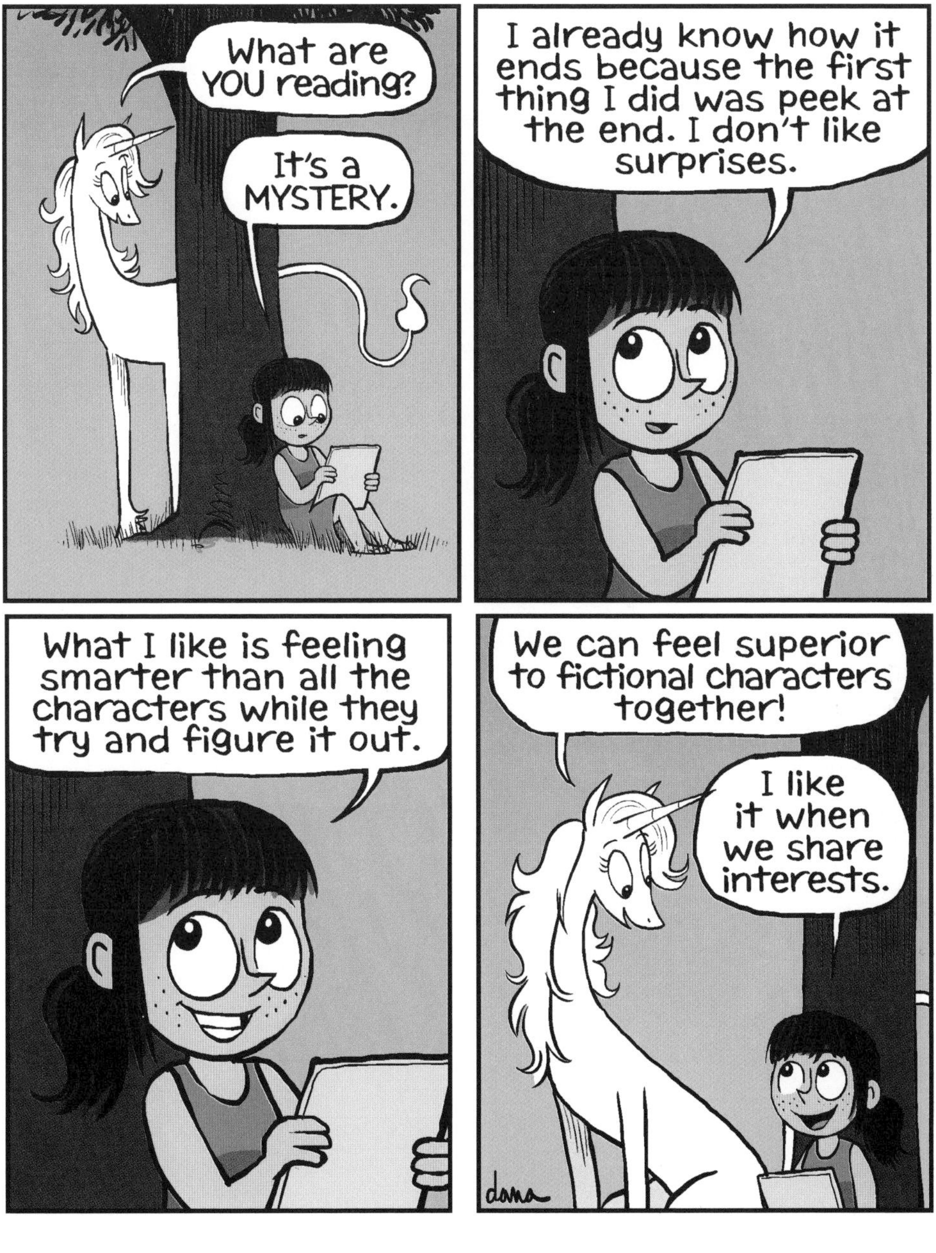

What are YOU reading?
It's a MYSTERY.
I already know how it ends because the first thing I did was peek at the end. I don't like surprises.
What I like is feeling smarter than all the characters while they try and figure it out.
We can feel superior to fictional characters together!
I like it when we share interests.
dana

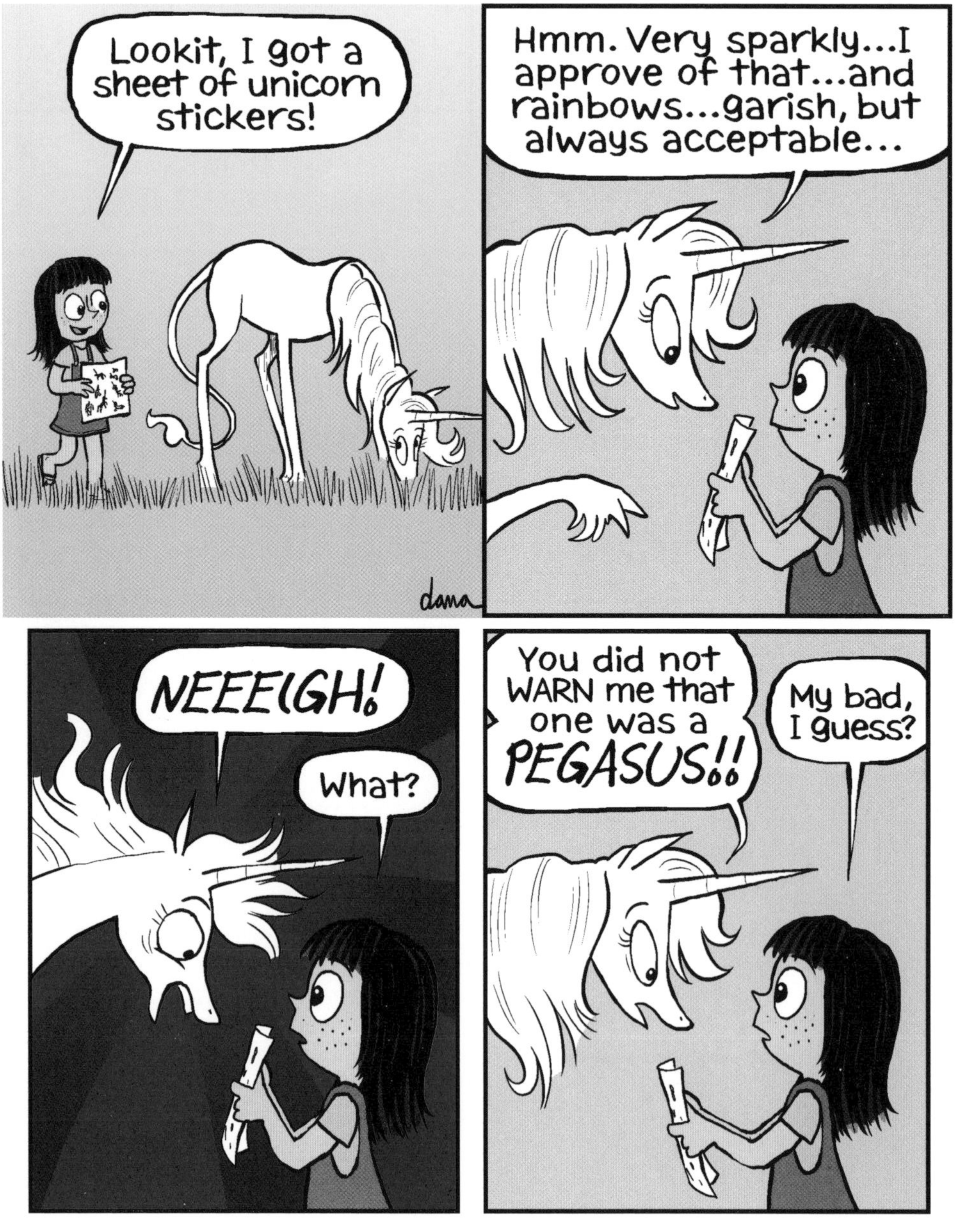
Lookit, I got a sheet of unicorn stickers!
Hmm. Very sparkly...I approve of that...and rainbows...garish, but always acceptable...
NEEEIGH!
What?
You did not WARN me that one was a PEGASUS!!
My bad, I guess?

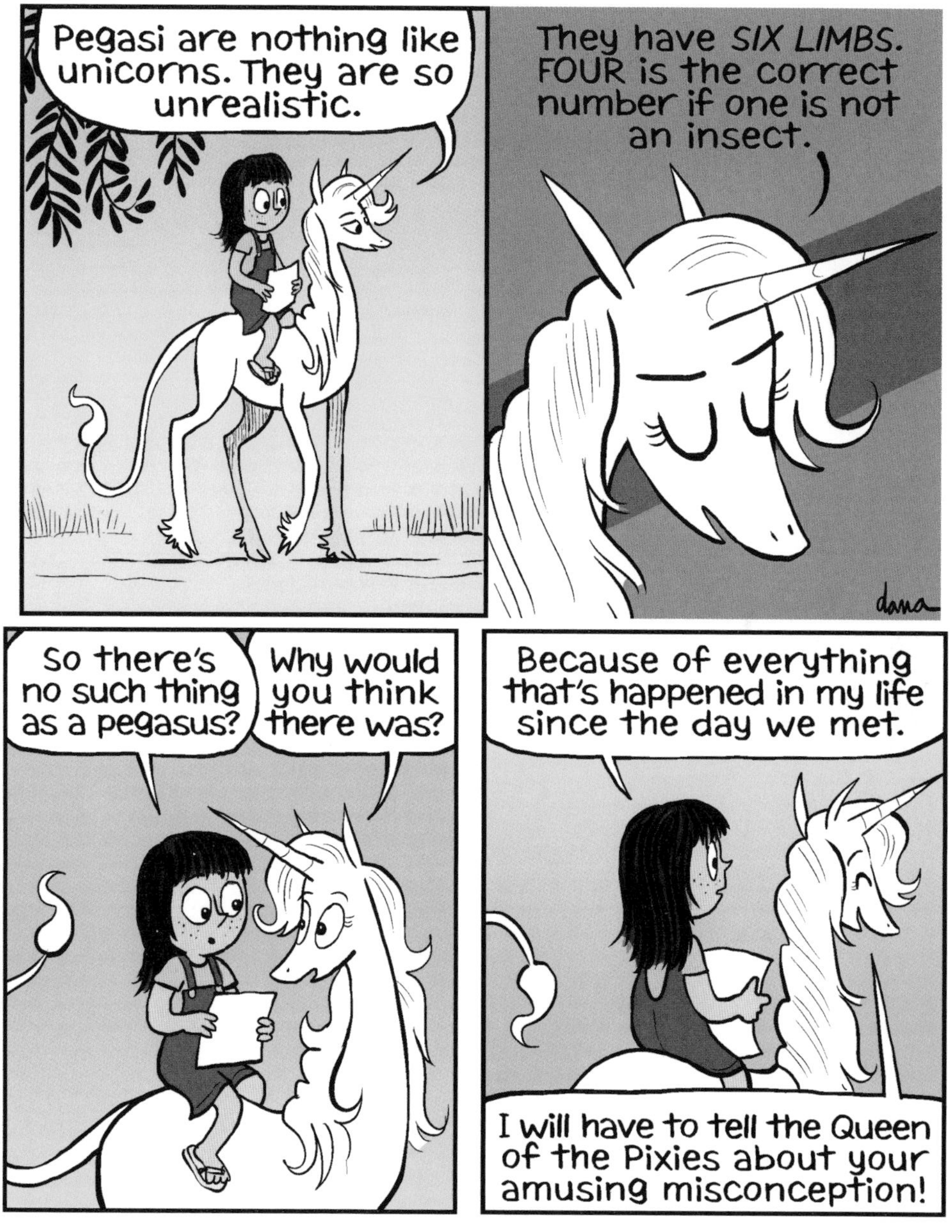
Pegasi are nothing like unicorns. They are so unrealistic.
They have SIX LIMBS. FOUR is the correct number if one is not an insect.
dana
So there's no such thing as a pegasus?
Why would you think there was?
Because of everything that's happened in my life since the day we met.
I will have to tell the Queen of the Pixies about your amusing misconception!

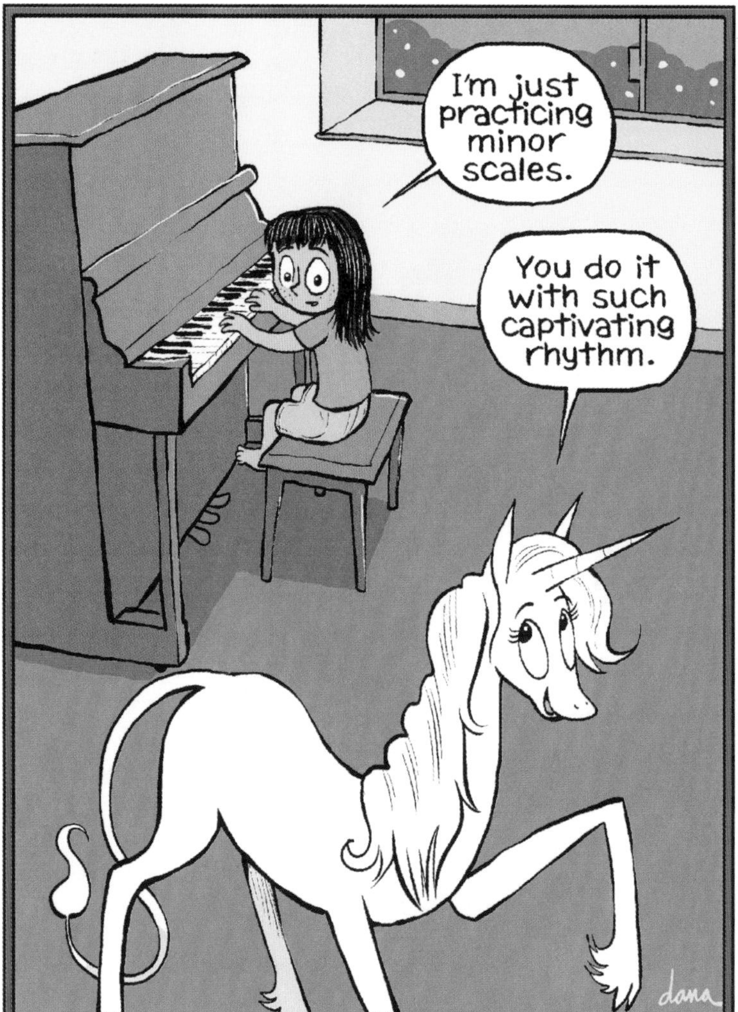
I'm just practicing minor scales.
You do it with such captivating rhythm.
dana

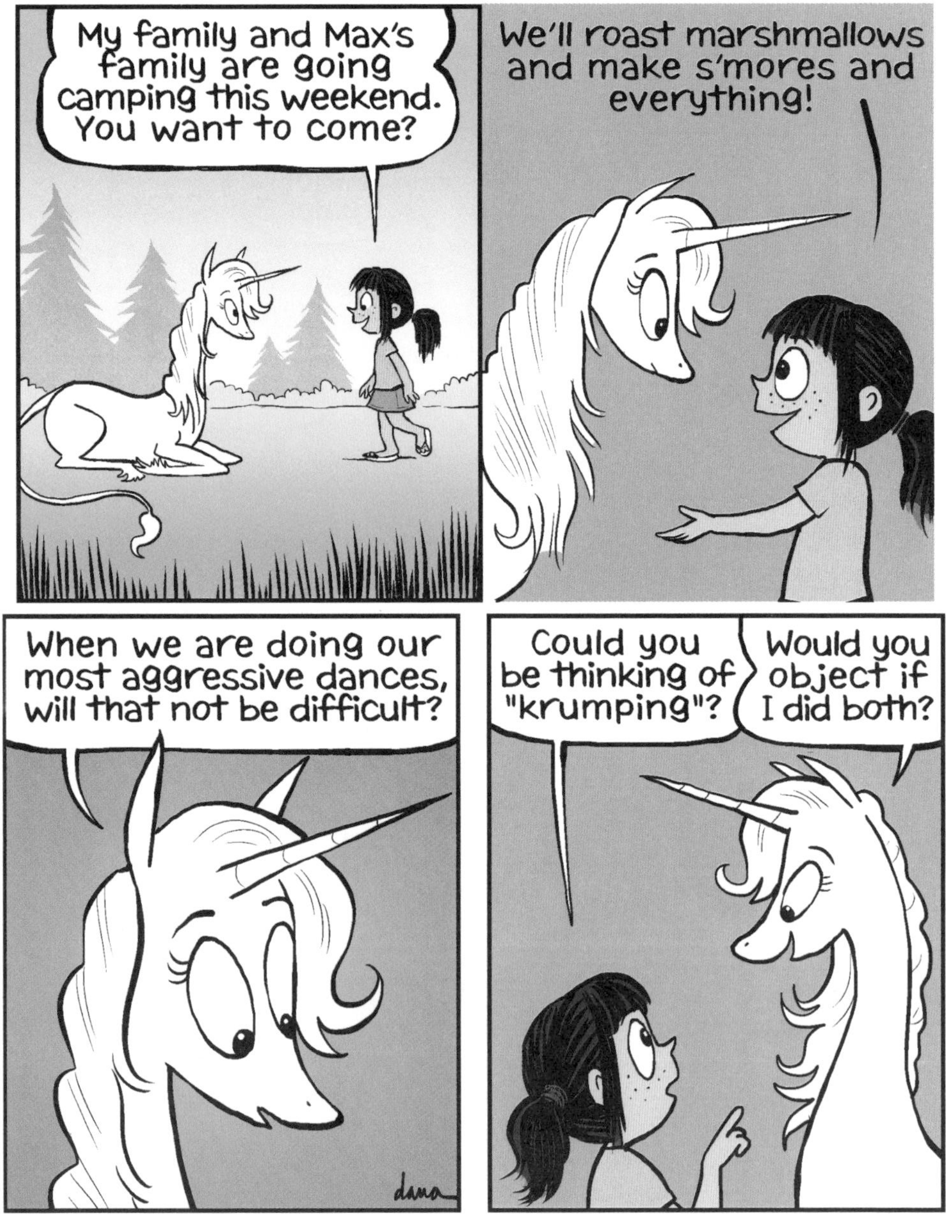
My family and Max's family are going camping this weekend. You want to come?
We'll roast marshmallows and make s'mores and everything!
When we are doing our most aggressive dances, will that not be difficult?
Could you be thinking of "krumping"?
Would you object if I did both?
dana

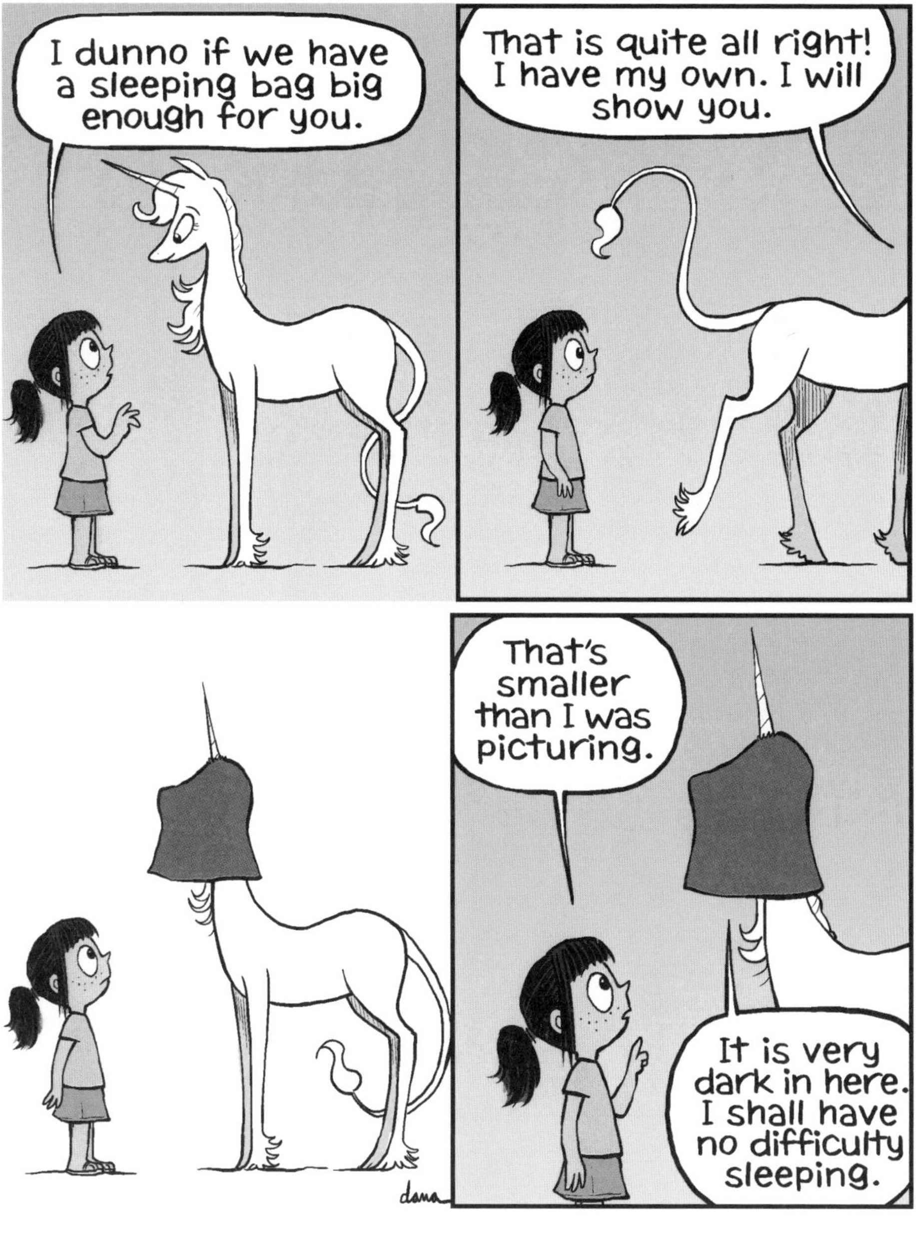
I dunno if we have a sleeping bag big enough for you.
That is quite all right! I have my own. I will show you.
That's smaller than I was picturing.
It is very dark in here. I shall have no difficulty sleeping.
dana

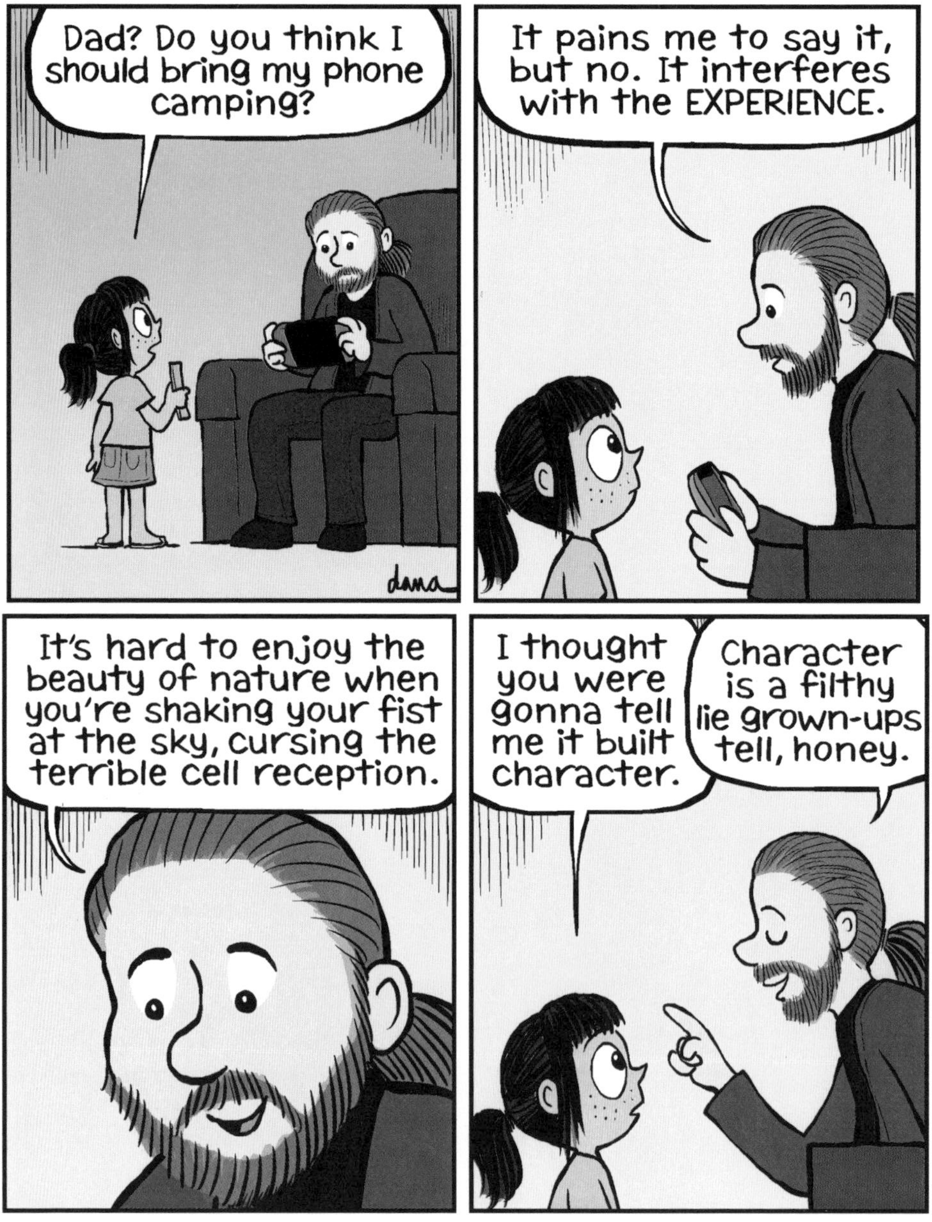
Dad? Do you think I should bring my phone camping?
It pains me to say it, but no. It interferes with the EXPERIENCE.
It's hard to enjoy the beauty of nature when you're shaking your fist at the sky, cursing the terrible cell reception.
I thought you were gonna tell me it built character.
Character is a filthy lie grown-ups tell, honey.

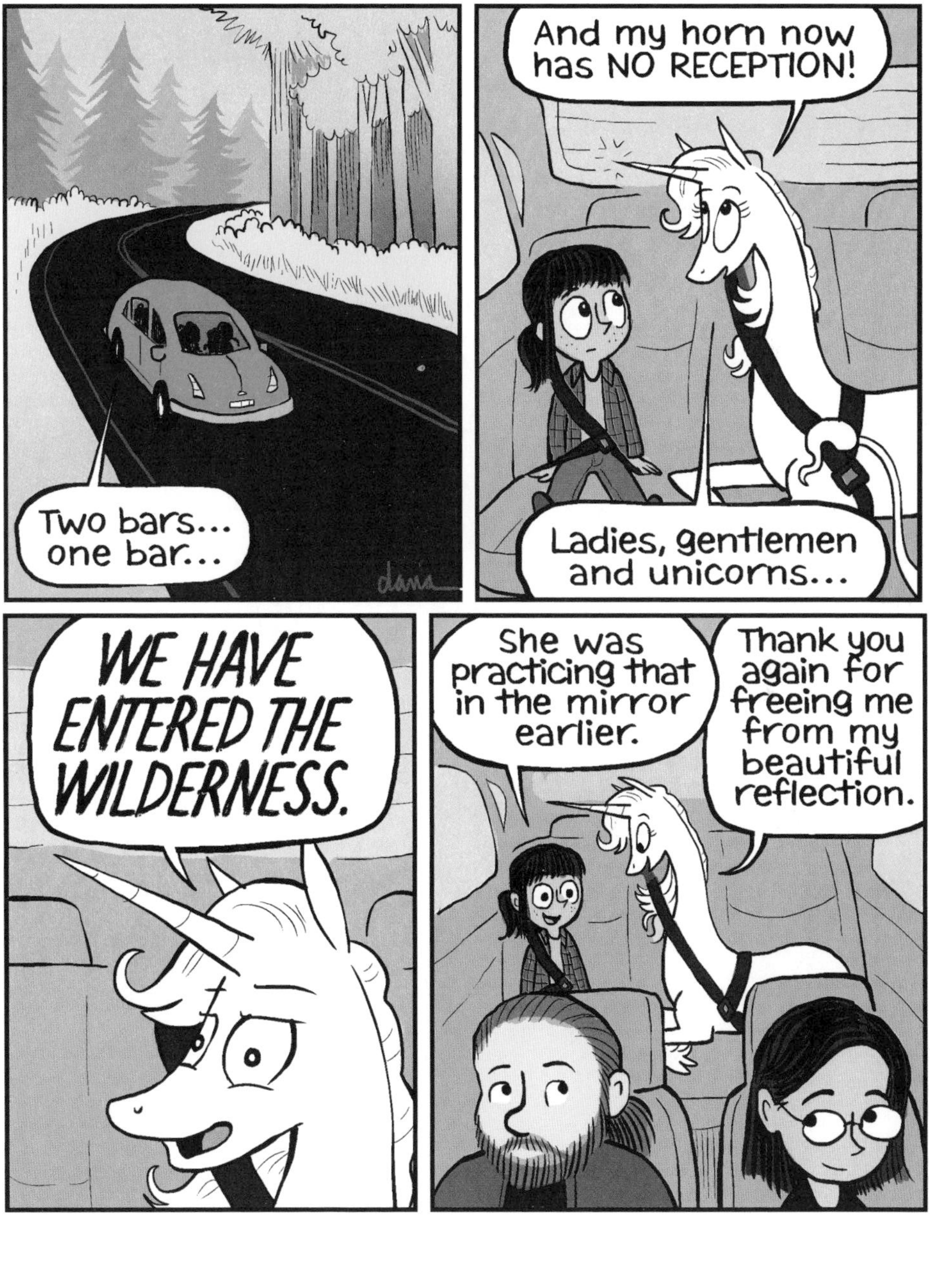

Two bars...
one bar...
And my horn now has NO RECEPTION!
Ladies, gentlemen and unicorns...
WE HAVE ENTERED THE WILDERNESS.
She was practicing that in the mirror earlier.
Thank you again for freeing me from my beautiful reflection.

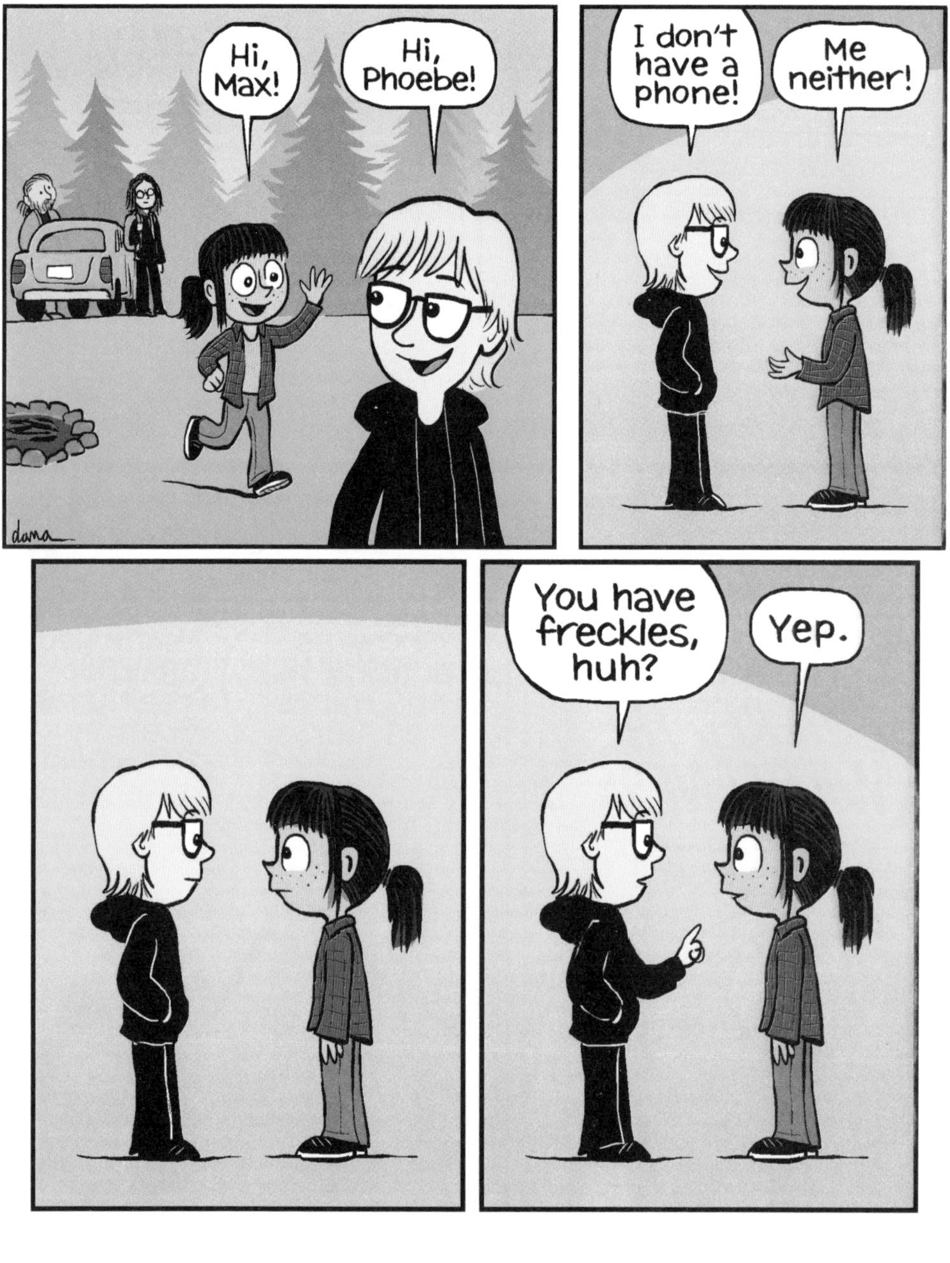
Hi, Max!
Hi, Phoebe!
dana
I don't have a phone!
Me neither!
You have freckles, huh?
Yep.

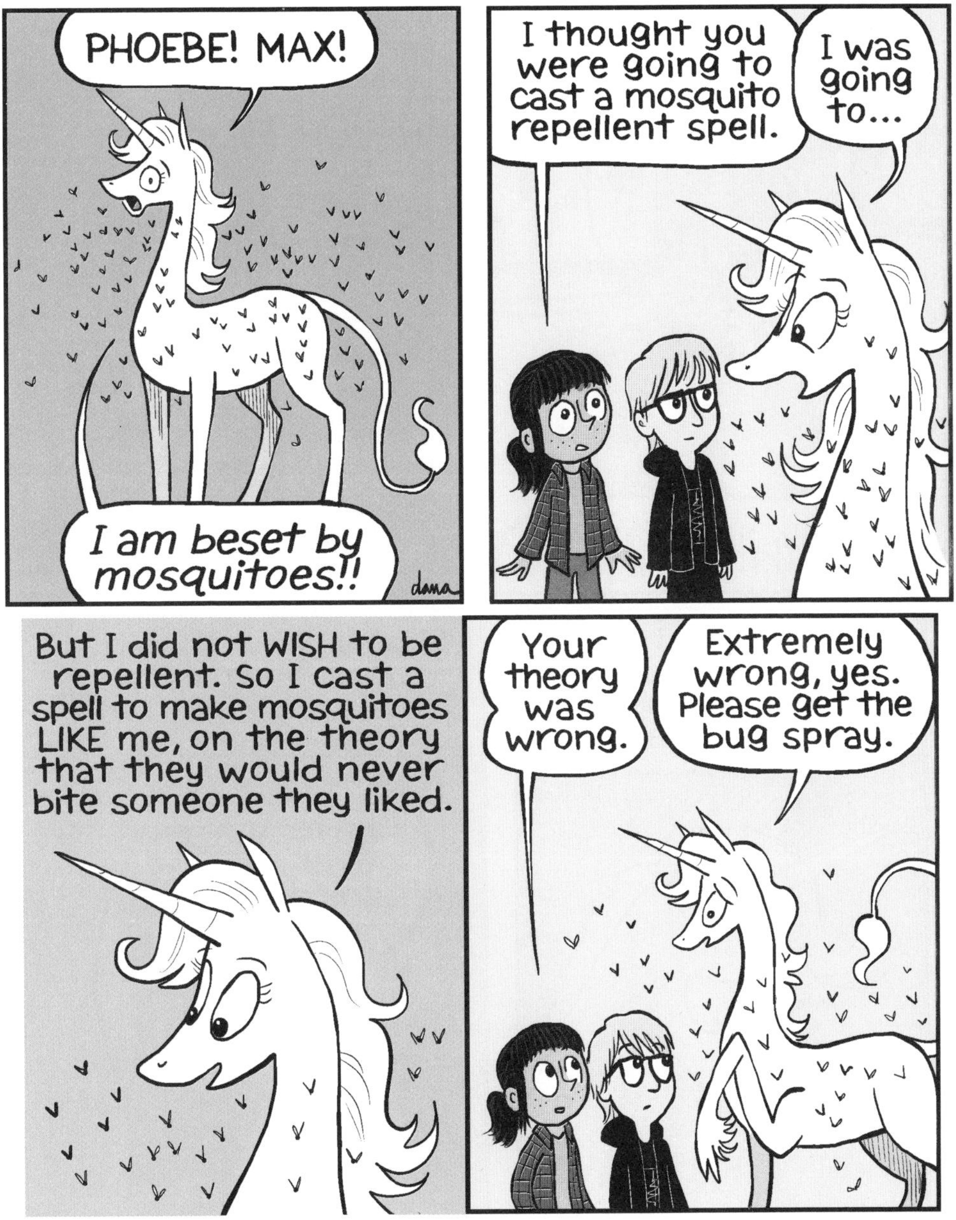
PHOEBE! MAX!
I am beset by mosquitoes!!
dana
I thought you were going to cast a mosquito repellent spell.
I was going to...
But I did not WISH to be repellent. So I cast a spell to make mosquitoes LIKE me, on the theory that they would never bite someone they liked.
Your theory was wrong.
Extremely wrong, yes. Please get the bug spray.

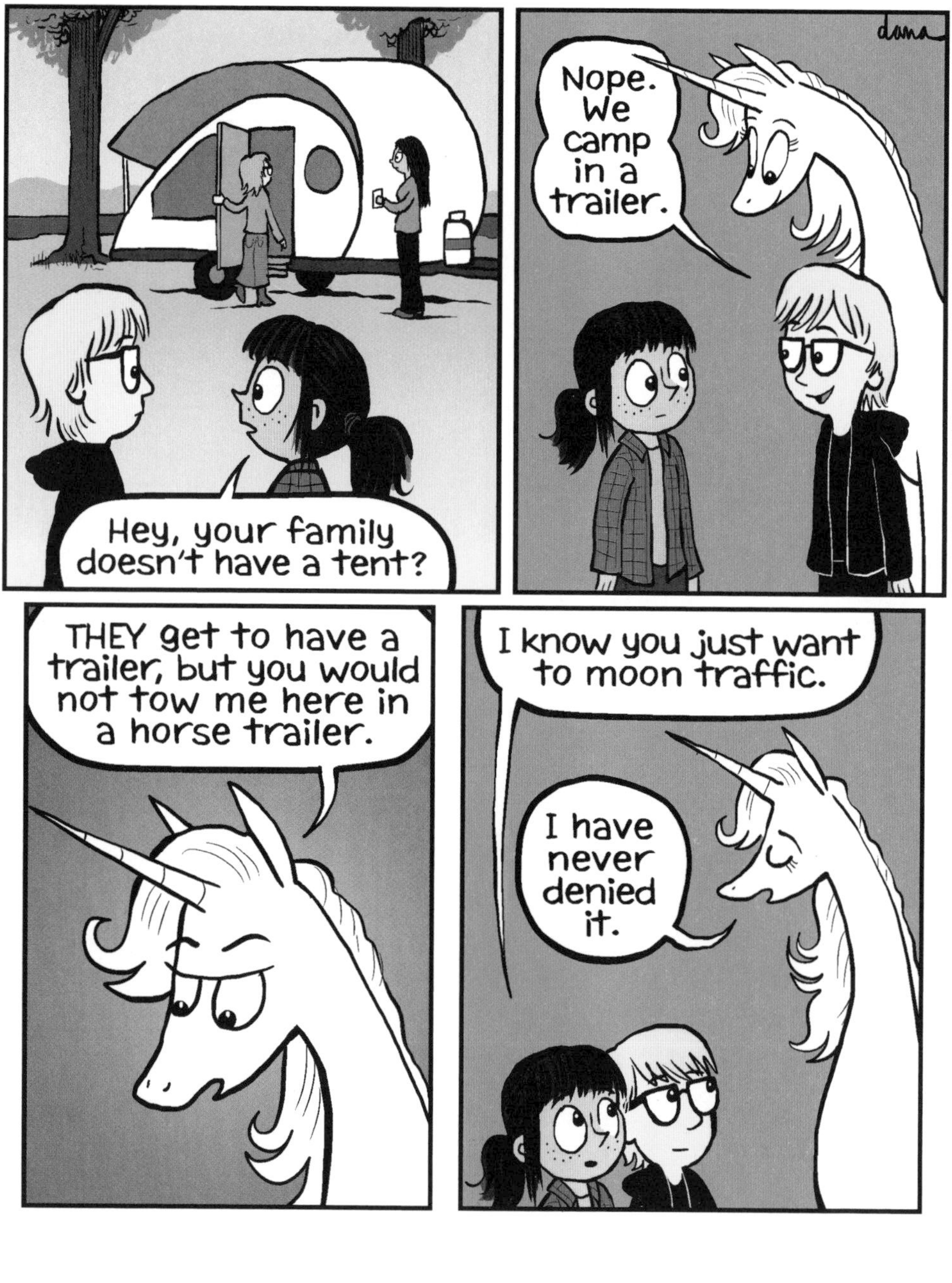
Hey, your family doesn't have a tent?
dana
Nope. We camp in a trailer.
THEY get to have a trailer, but you would not tow me here in a horse trailer.
I know you just want to moon traffic.
I have never denied it.

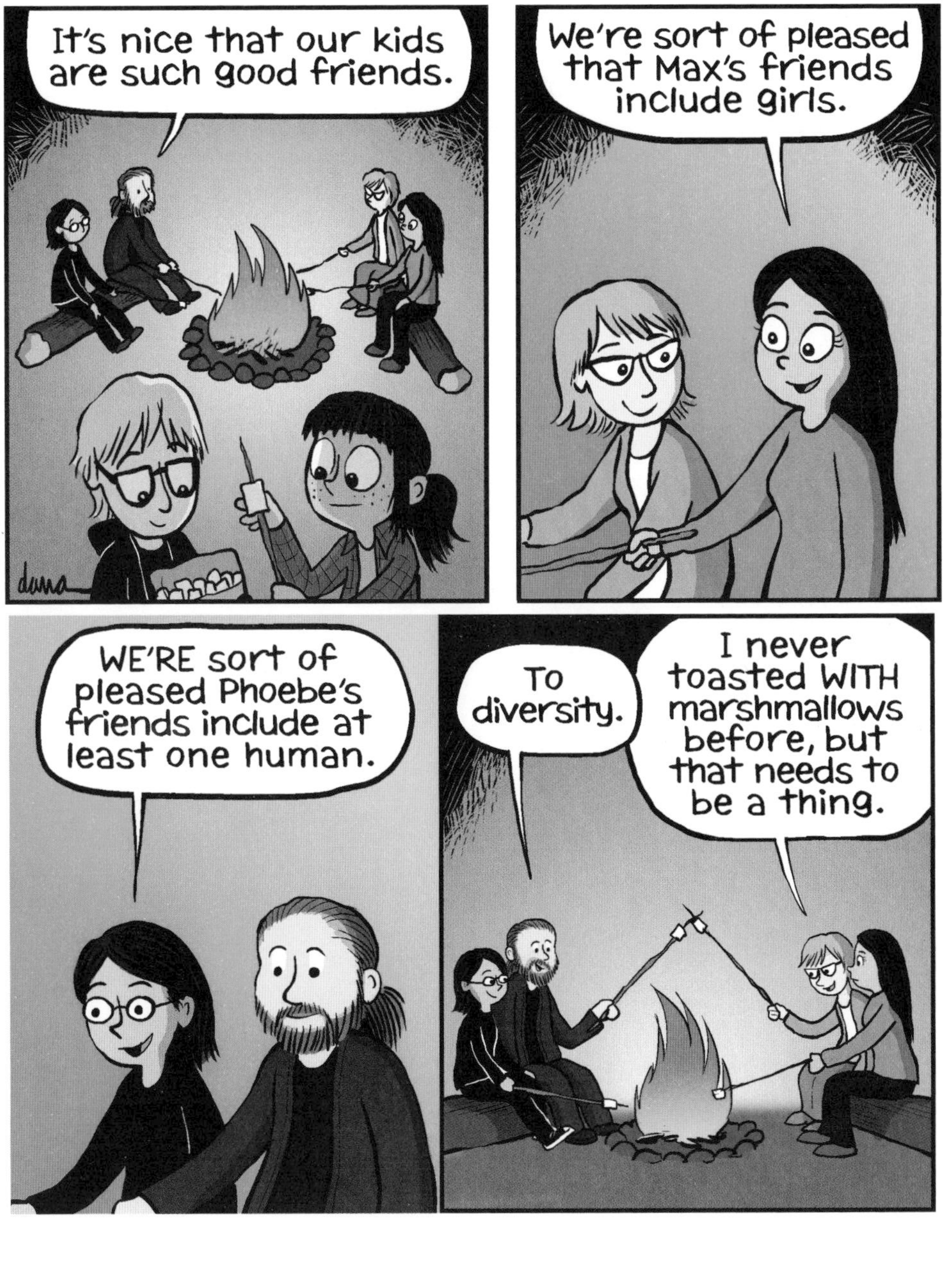
It's nice that our kids are such good friends.
We're sort of pleased that Max's friends include girls.
WE'RE sort of pleased Phoebe's friends include at least one human.
To diversity.
I never toasted WITH marshmallows before, but that needs to be a thing.
dana

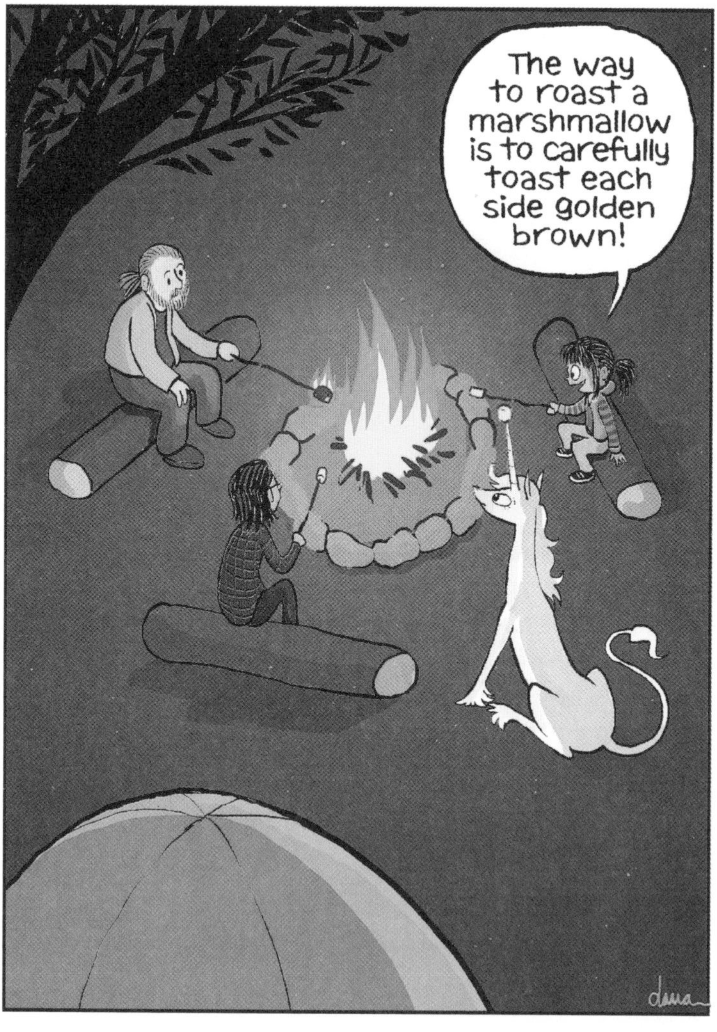
The way to roast a marshmallow is to carefully toast each side golden brown!
dana

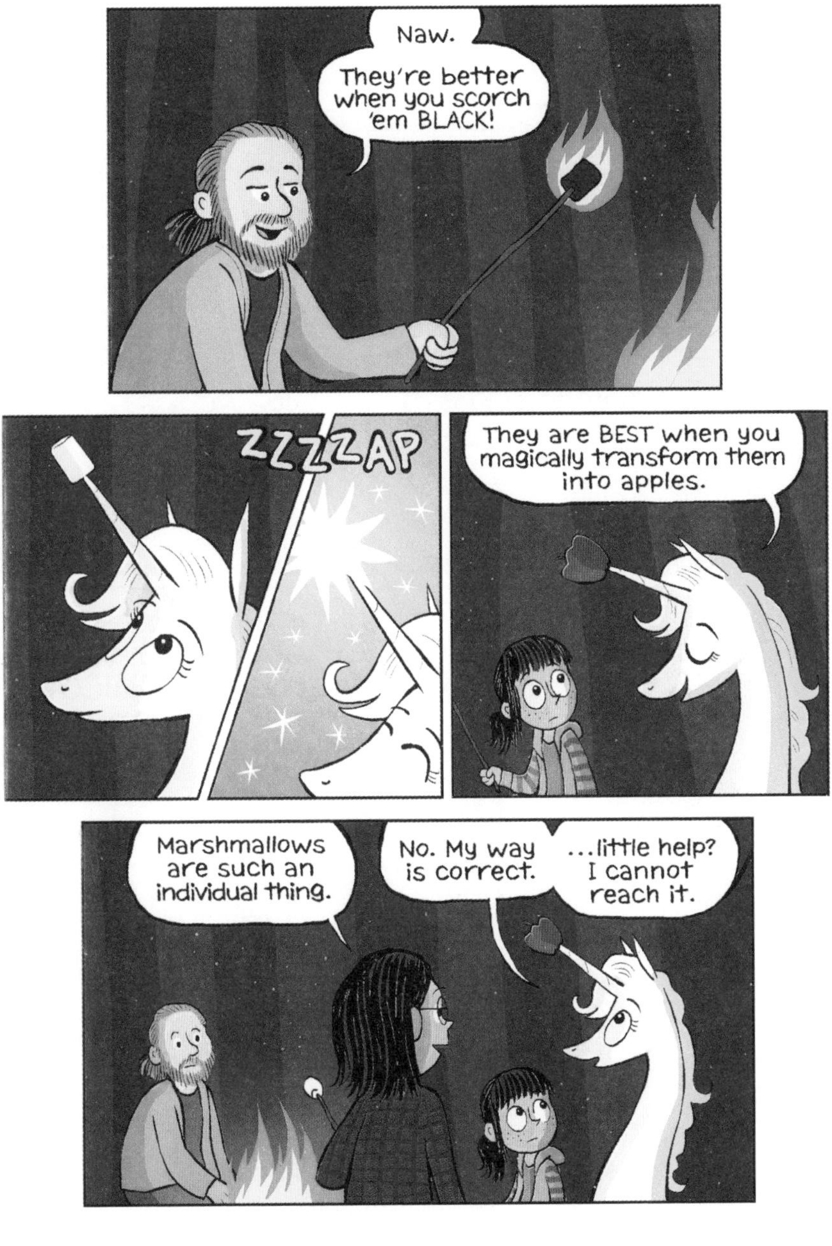
Naw.
They're better when you scorch 'em BLACK!
ZZZZAP
They are BEST when you magically transform them into apples.
Marshmallows are such an individual thing.
No. My way is correct.
...little help? I cannot reach it.

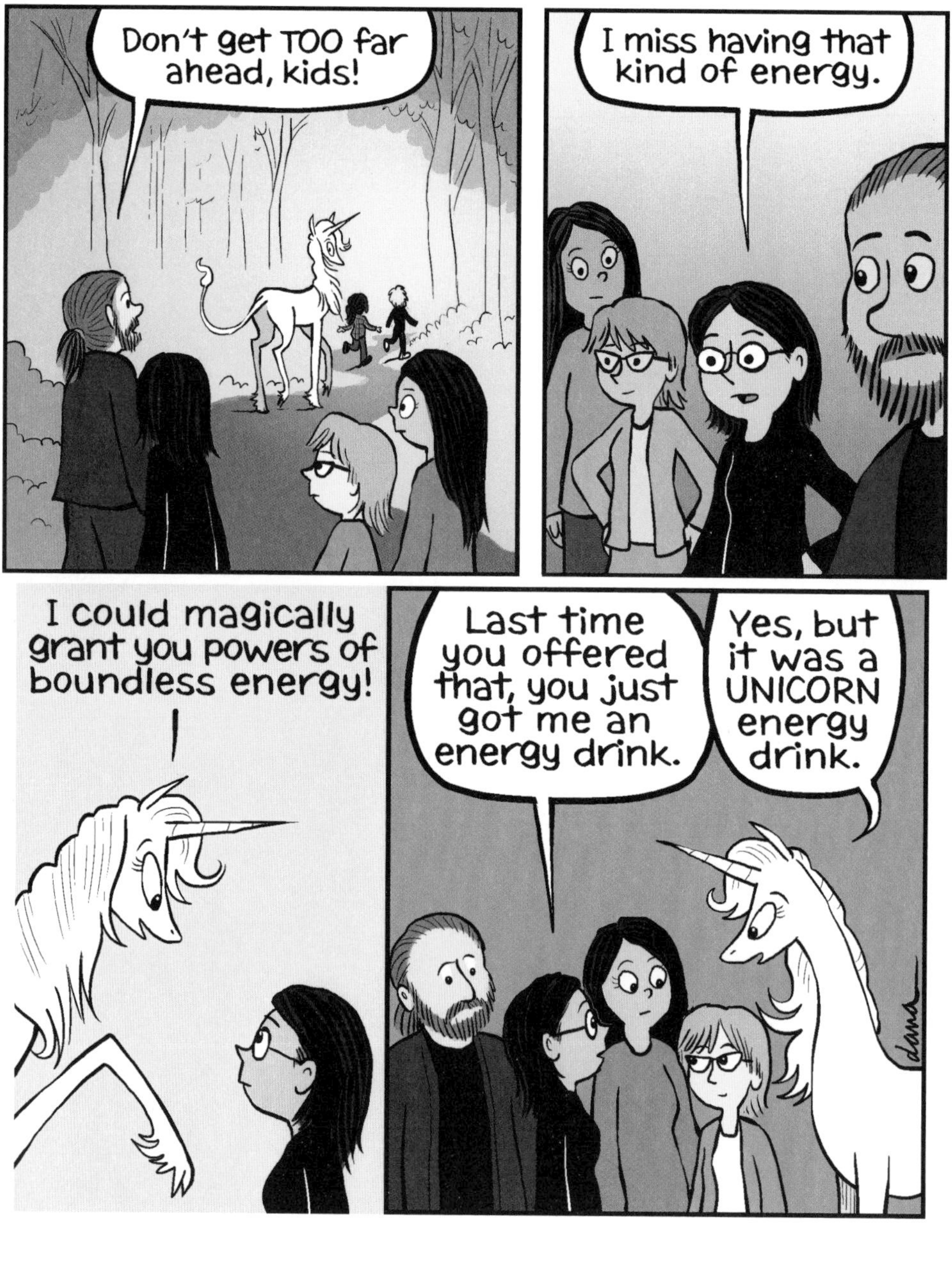
Don't get TOO far ahead, kids!
I miss having that kind of energy.
I could magically grant you powers of boundless energy!
Last time you offered that, you just got me an energy drink.
Yes, but it was a UNICORN energy drink.
dana

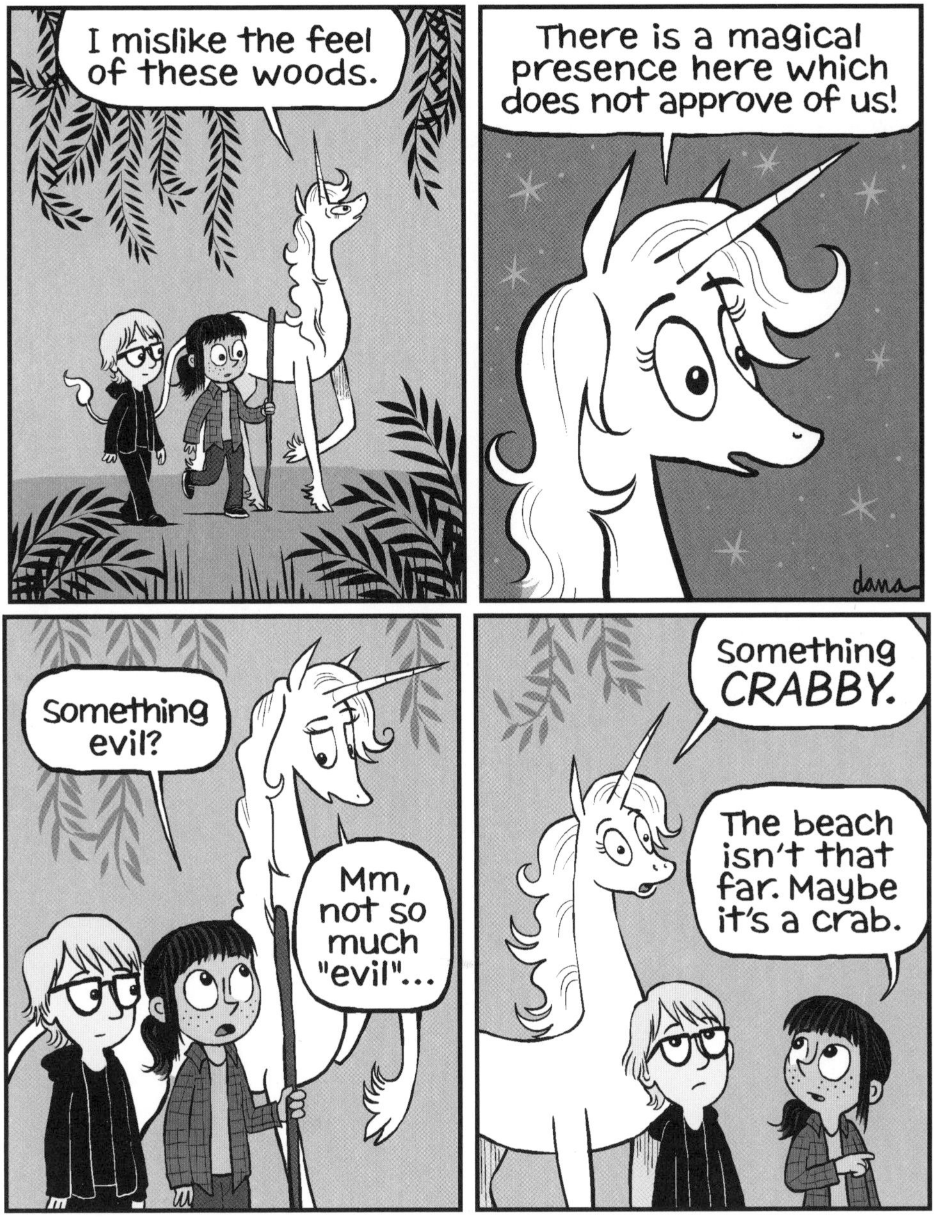
I mislike the feel of these woods.
There is a magical presence here which does not approve of us!
dana
Something evil?
Mm, not so much "evil"...
Something CRABBY.
The beach isn't that far. Maybe it's a crab.

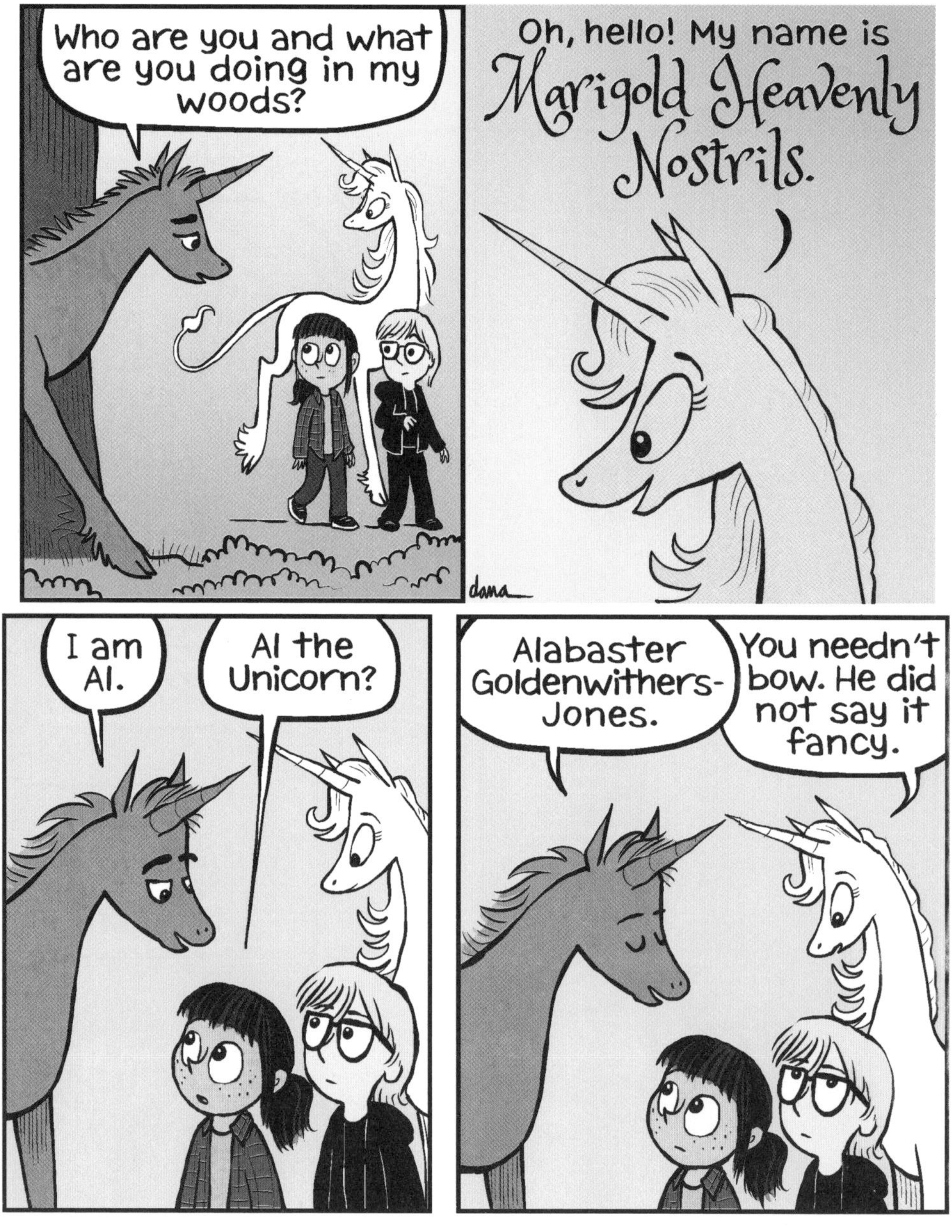
Who are you and what are you doing in my woods?
Oh, hello! My name is Marigold Heavenly Nostrils.
dana
I am Al.
Al the Unicorn?
Alabaster Goldenwithers-Jones.
You needn't bow. He did not say it fancy.

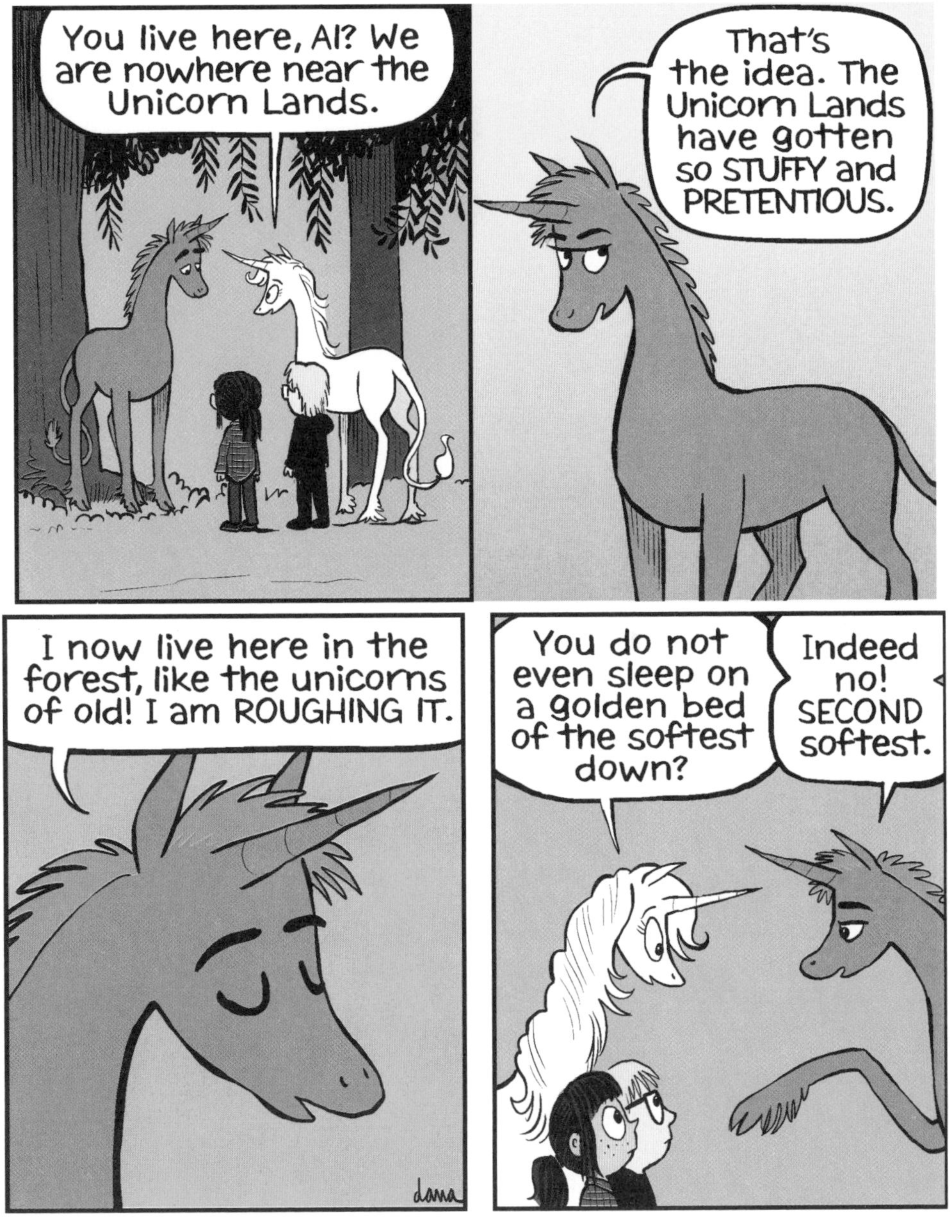
You live here, Al? We are nowhere near the Unicorn Lands.
That's the idea. The Unicorn Lands have gotten so STUFFY and PRETENTIOUS.
I now live here in the forest, like the unicorns of old! I am ROUGHING IT.
You do not even sleep on a golden bed of the softest down?
Indeed no! SECOND softest.
dana

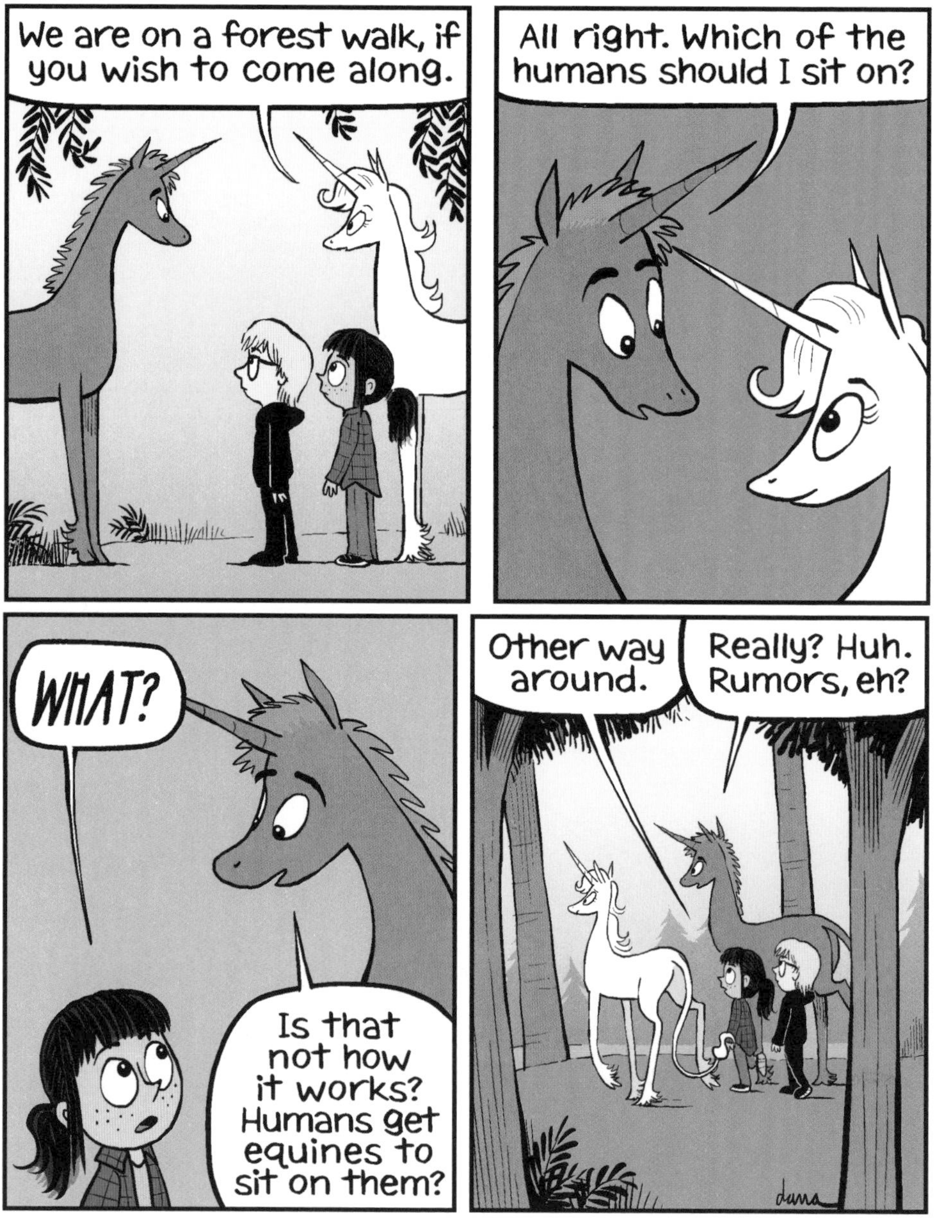
We are on a forest walk, if you wish to come along.
All right. Which of the humans should I sit on?
WHAT?
Is that not how it works? Humans get equines to sit on them?
Other way around.
Really? Huh. Rumors, eh?
dana

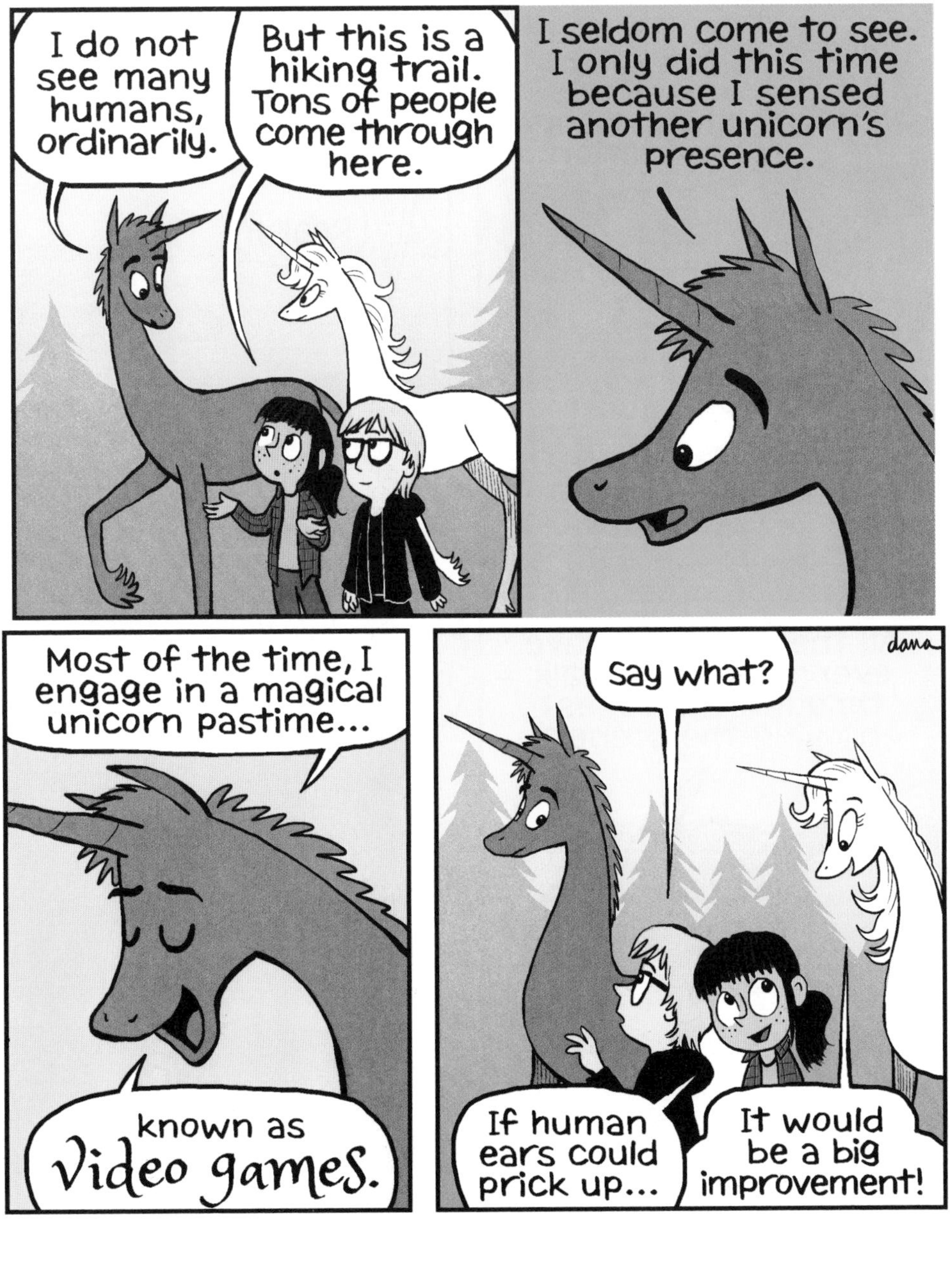
I do not see many humans, ordinarily.
But this is a hiking trail. Tons of people come through here.
I seldom come to see. I only did this time because I sensed another unicorn's presence.
Most of the time, I engage in a magical unicorn pastime...
known as Video games.
dana
Say what?
If human ears could prick up...
It would be a big improvement!

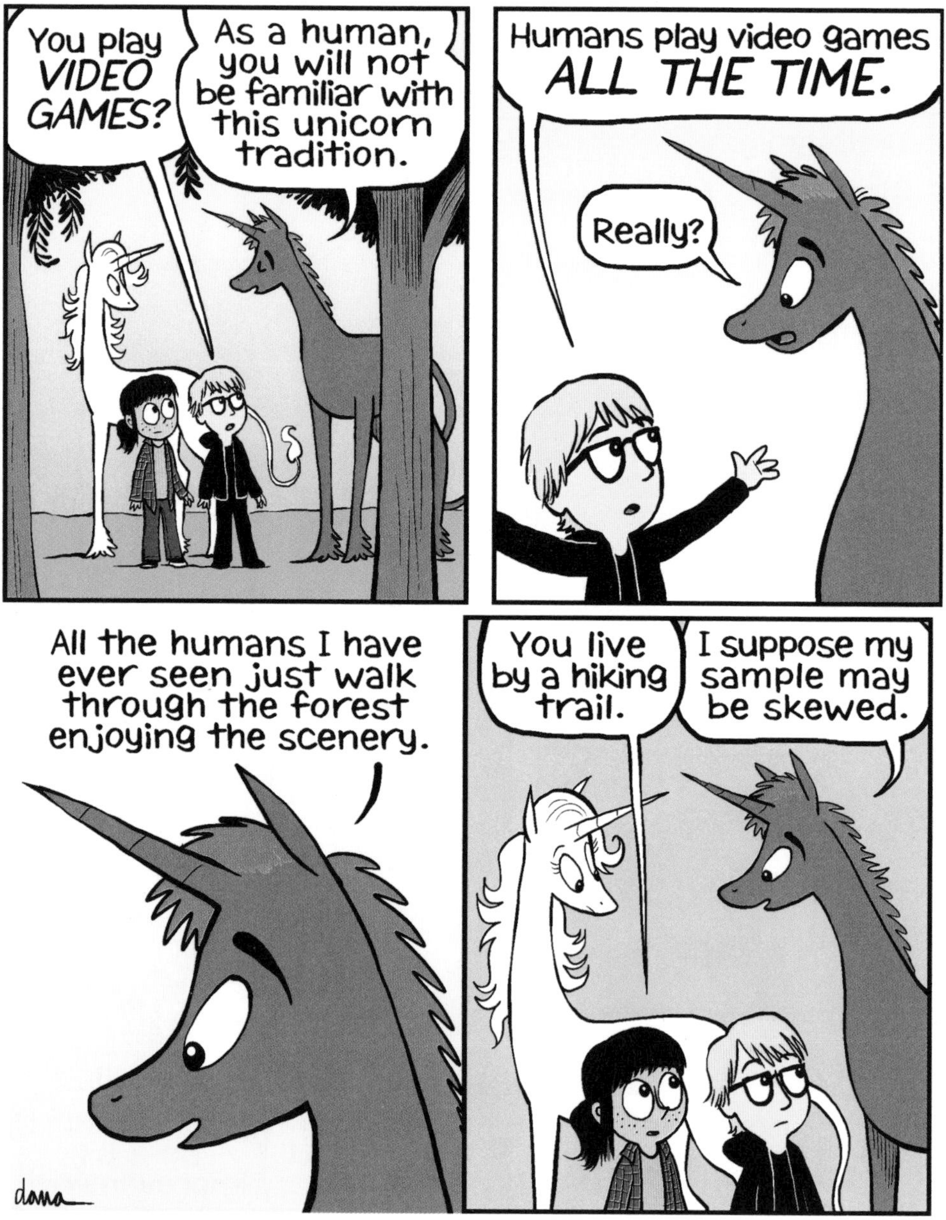
You play VIDEO GAMES?
As a human, you will not be familiar with this unicorn tradition.
Humans play video games ALL THE TIME.
Really?
All the humans I have ever seen just walk through the forest enjoying the scenery.
You live by a hiking trail.
I suppose my sample may be skewed.
dana

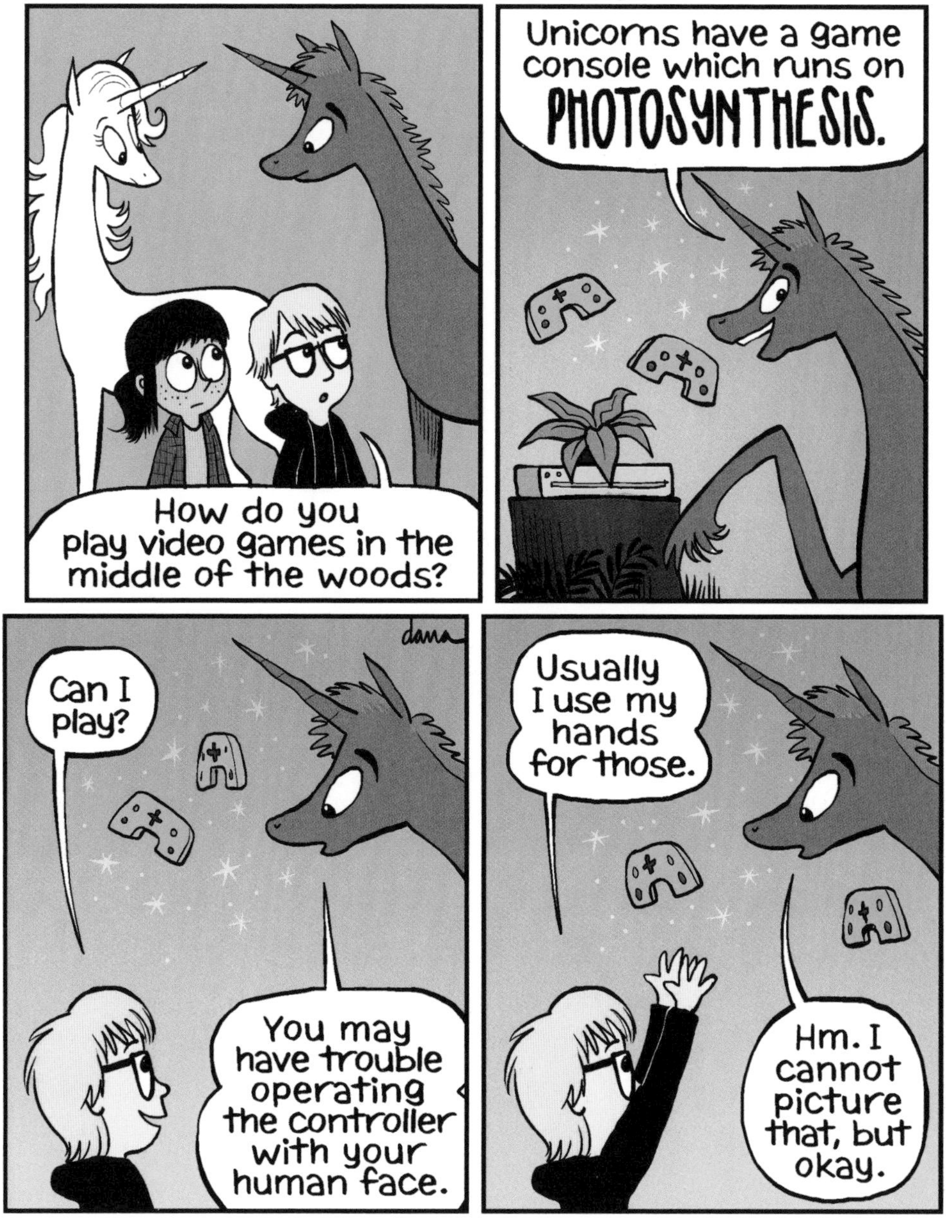
How do you play video games in the middle of the woods?
Unicorns have a game console which runs on PHOTOSYNTHESIS.
dana
Can I play?
You may have trouble operating the controller with your human face.
Usually I use my hands for those.
Hm. I cannot picture that, but okay.

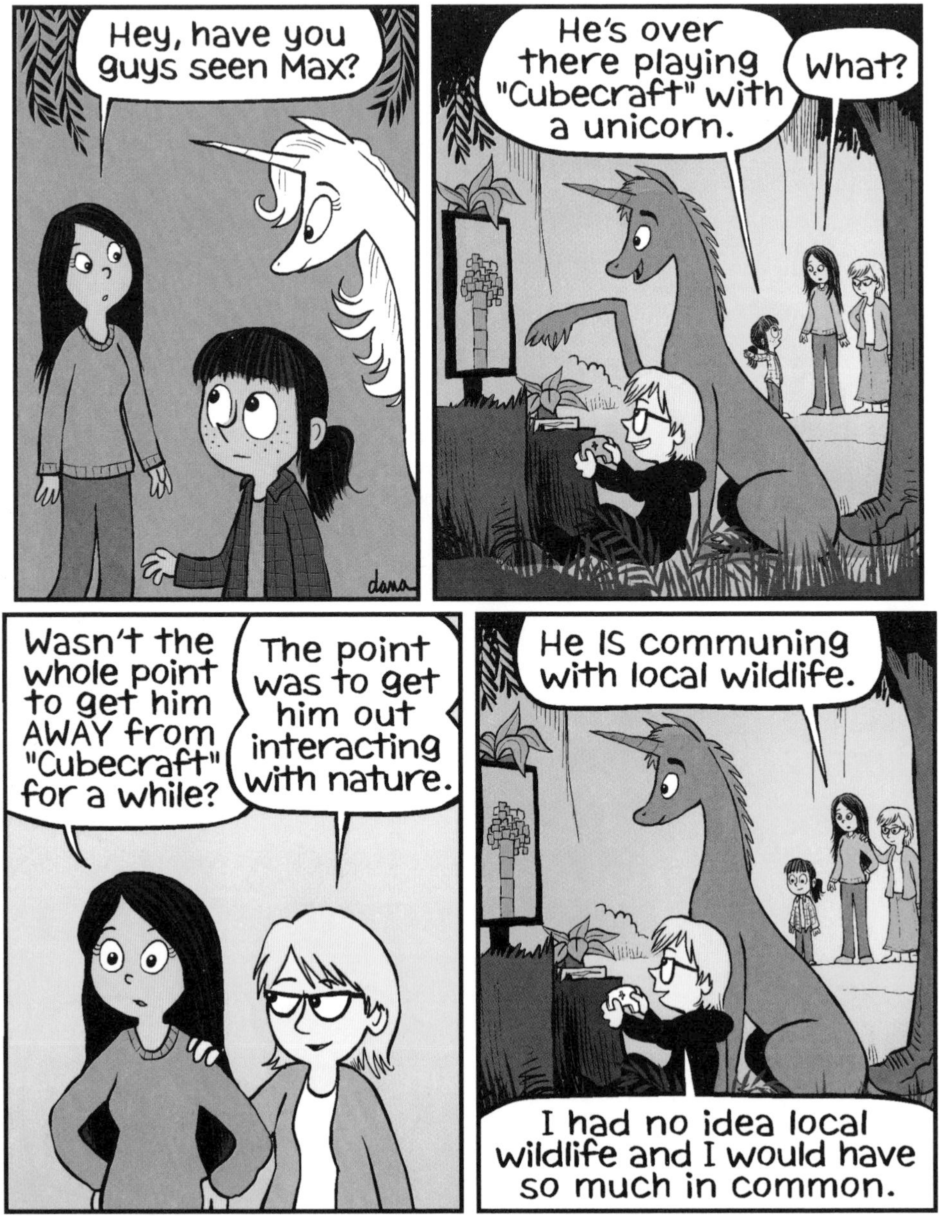
Hey, have you guys seen Max?
He's over there playing "Cubecraft" with a unicorn.
What?
Wasn't the whole point to get him AWAY from "Cubecraft" for a while?
The point was to get him out interacting with nature.
He IS communing with local wildlife.
I had no idea local wildlife and I would have so much in common.

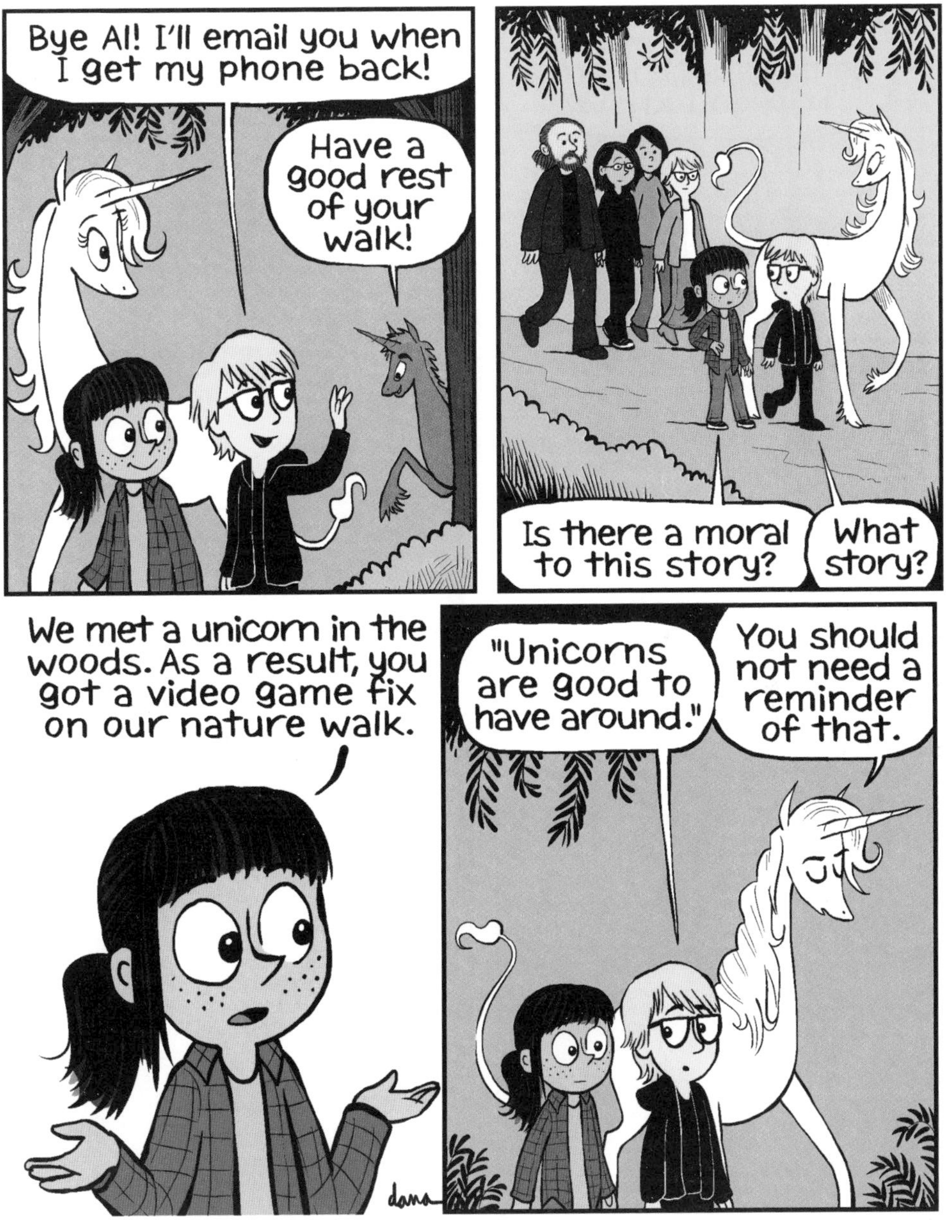
Bye Al! I'll email you when I get my phone back!
Have a good rest of your walk!
Is there a moral to this story?
What story?
We met a unicorn in the woods. As a result, you got a video game fix on our nature walk.
"Unicorns are good to have around."
You should not need a reminder of that.
dana

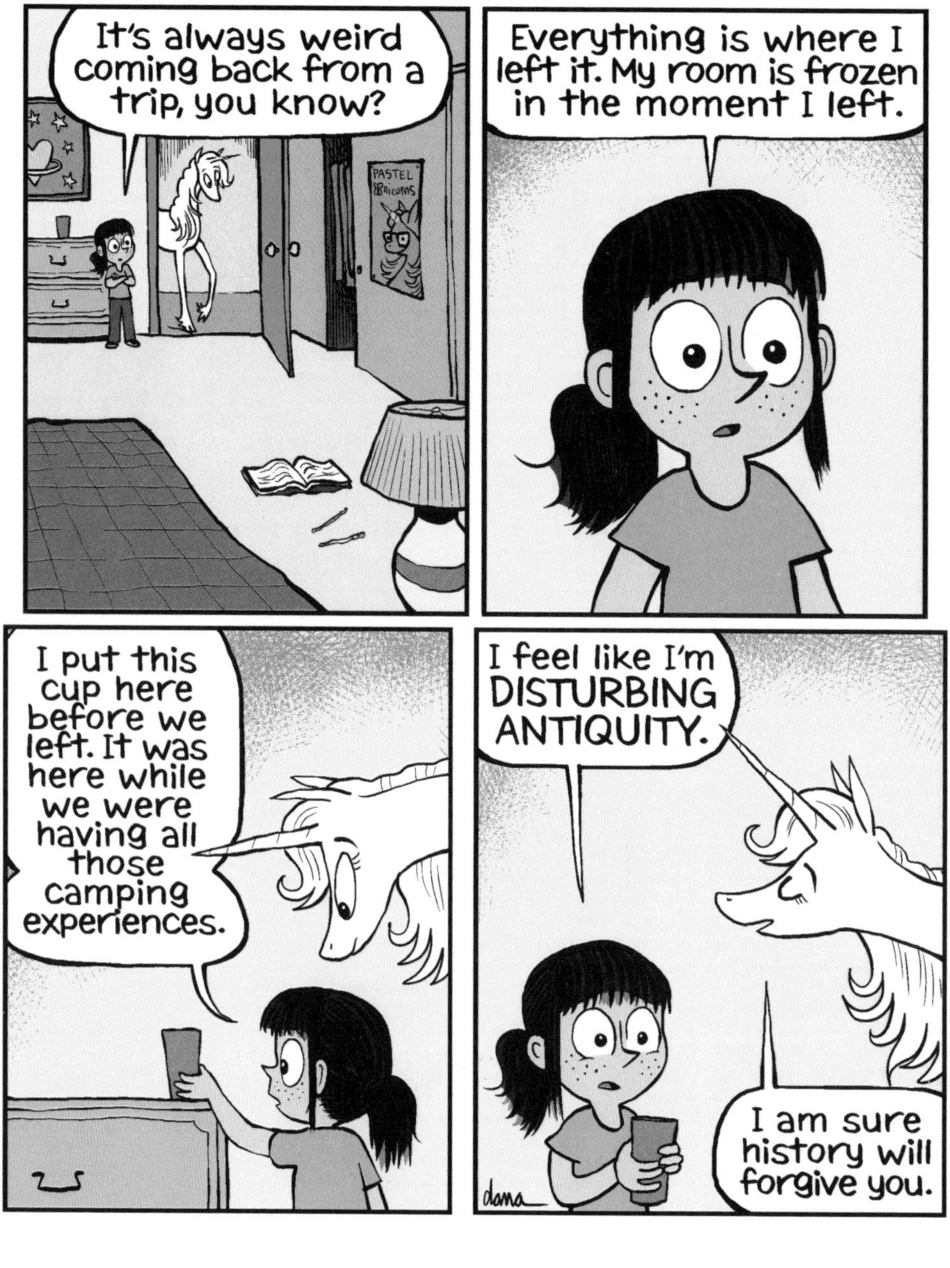
It's always weird coming back from a trip, you know?
PASTEL
Everything is where I left it. My room is frozen in the moment I left.
I put this cup here before we left. It was here while we were having all those camping experiences.
I feel like I'm DISTURBING ANTIQUITY.
I am sure history will forgive you.
dana

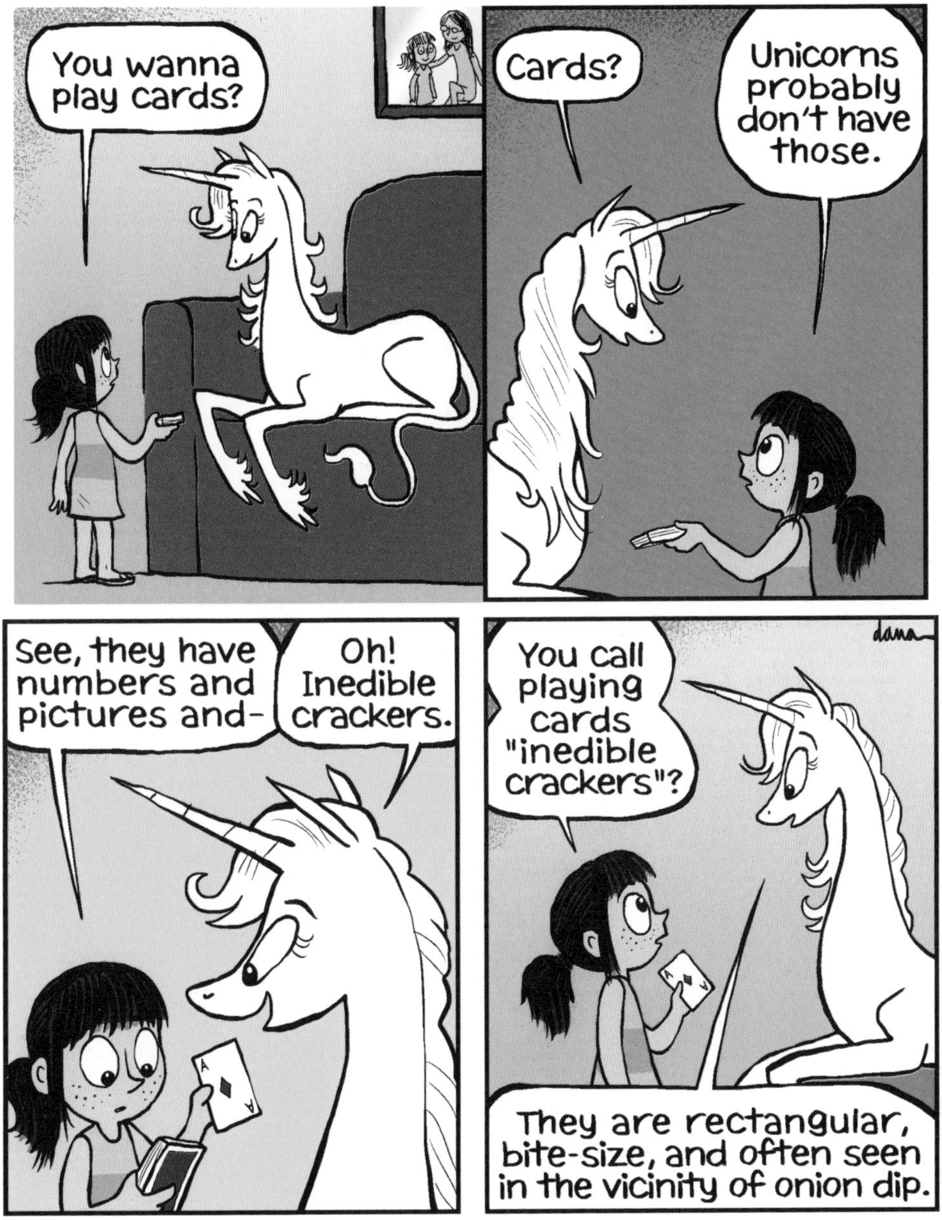
You wanna play cards?
Cards?
Unicorns probably don't have those.
See, they have numbers and pictures and-
Oh! Inedible crackers.
dana
You call playing cards "inedible crackers"?
They are rectangular, bite-size, and often seen in the vicinity of onion dip.

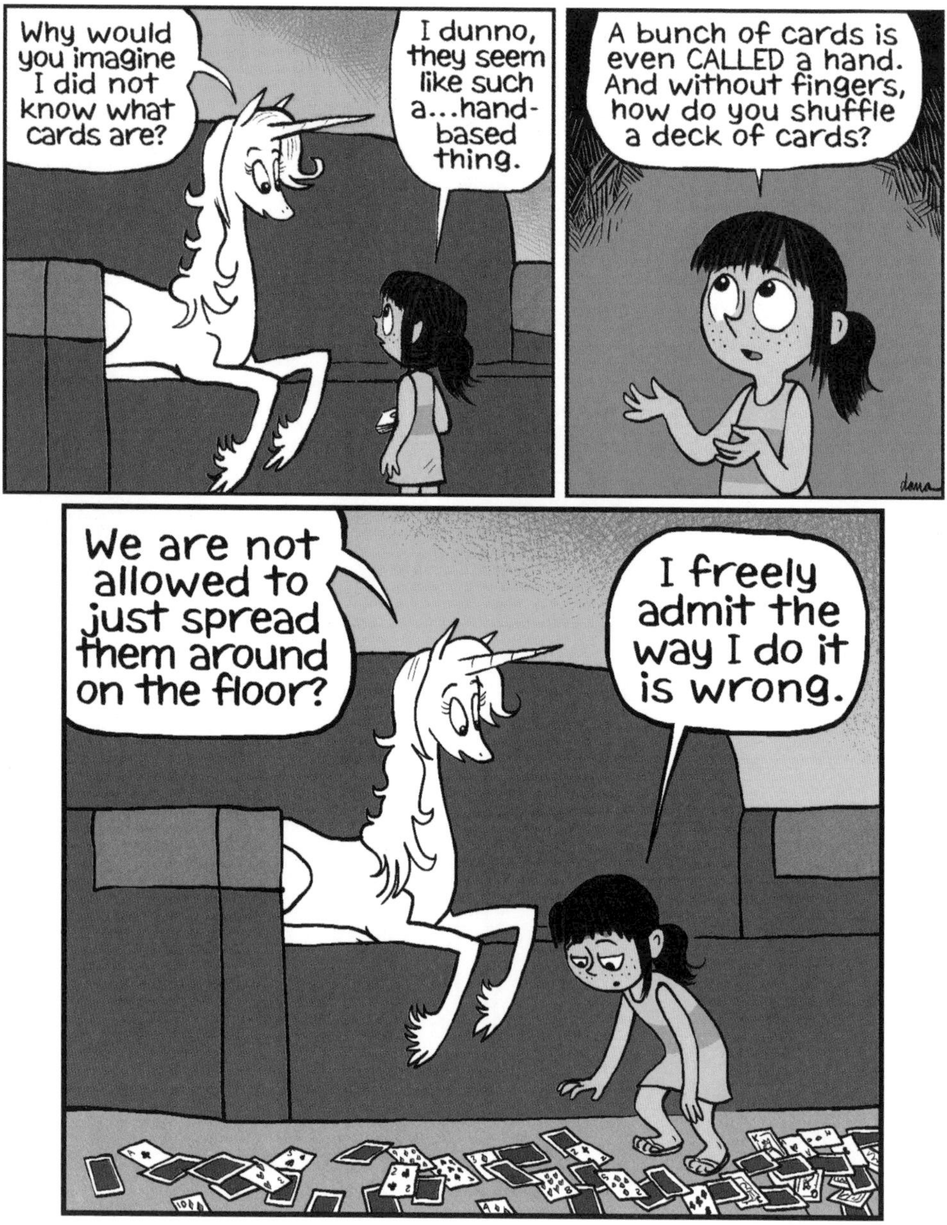
Why would you imagine I did not know what cards are?
I dunno, they seem like such a...hand-based thing.
A bunch of cards is even CALLED a hand. And without fingers, how do you shuffle a deck of cards?
We are not allowed to just spread them around on the floor?
I freely admit the way I do it is wrong.

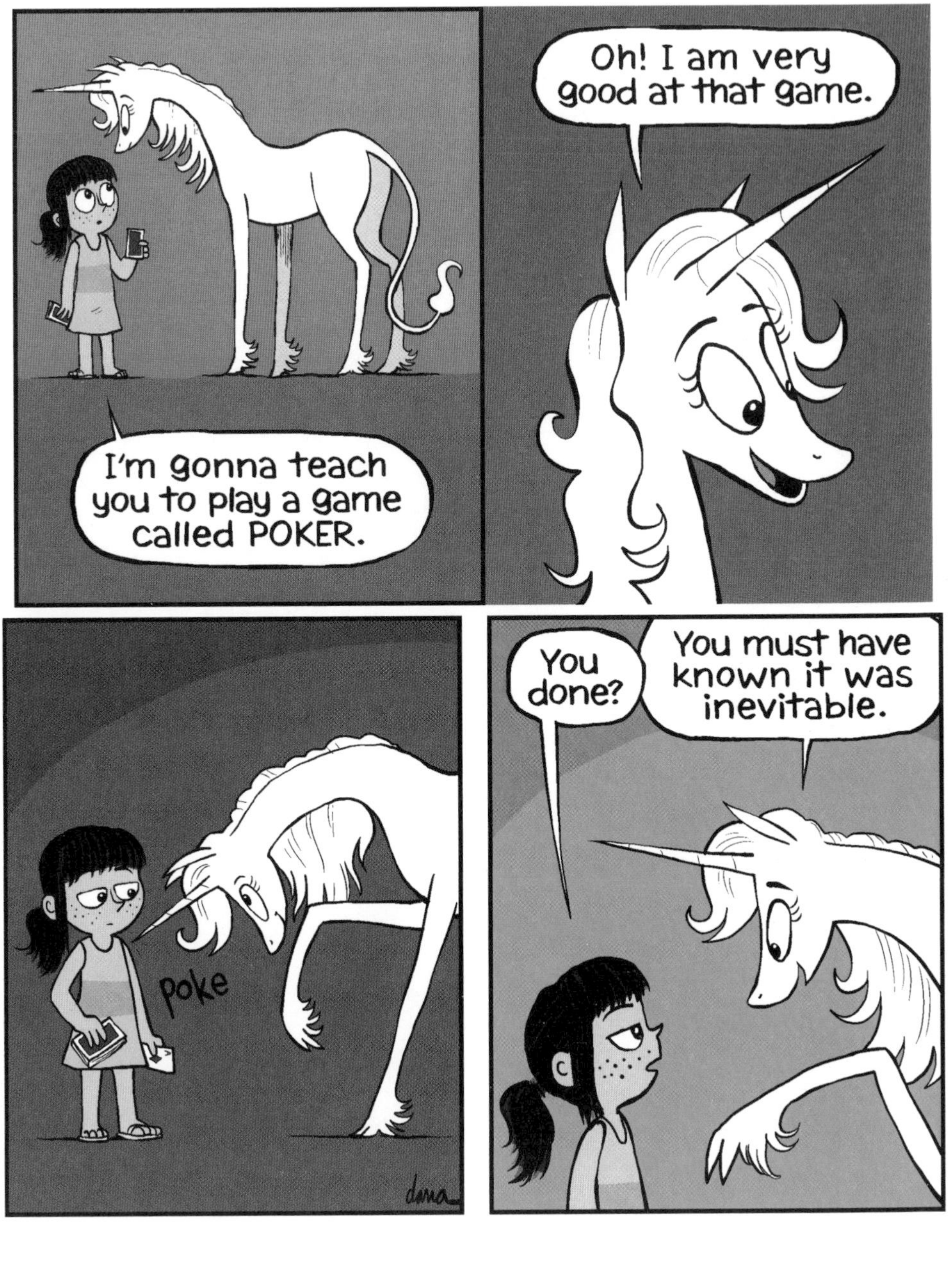
I'm gonna teach you to play a game called POKER.
Oh! I am very good at that game.
poke
You done?
You must have known it was inevitable.
dana

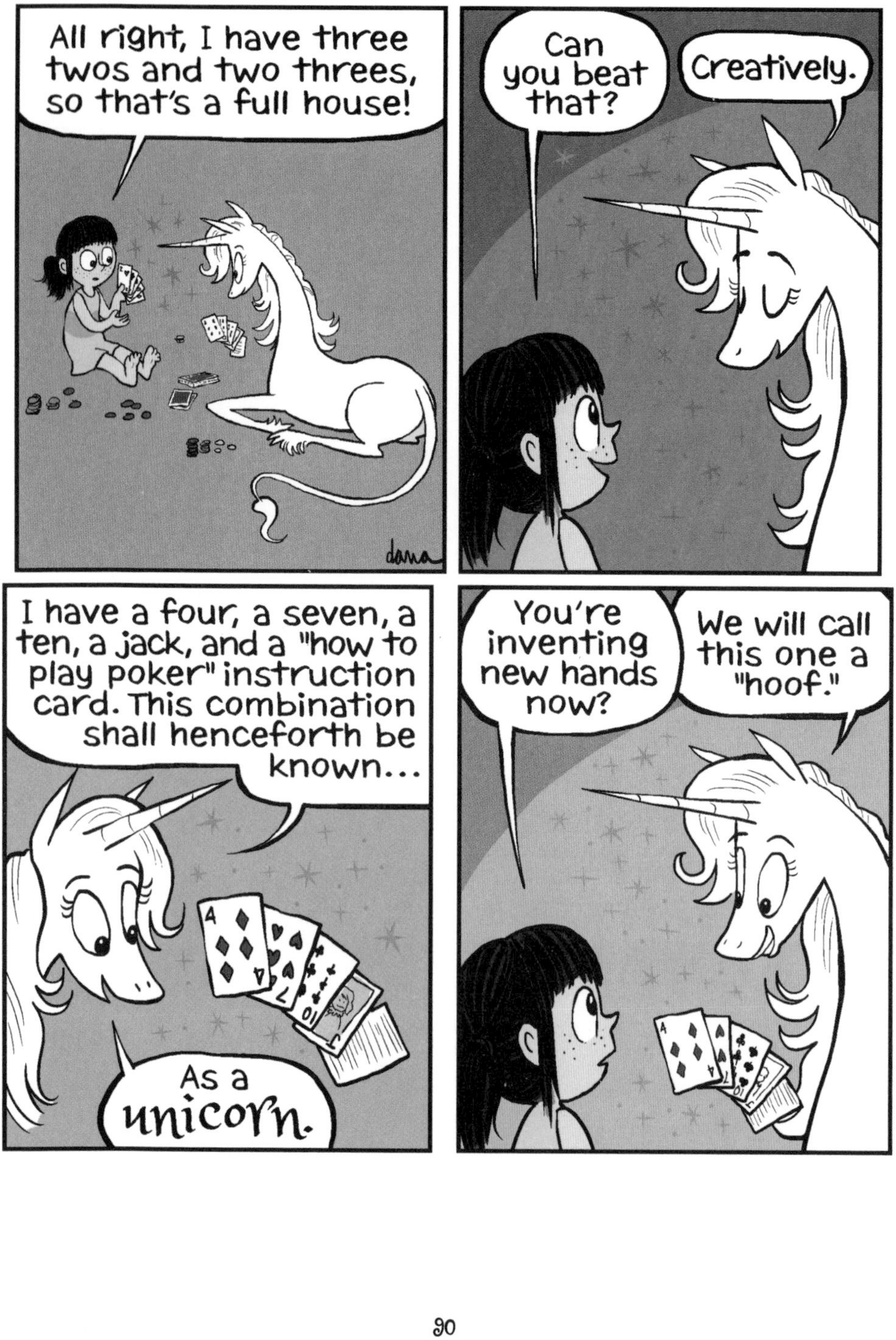
All right, I have three twos and two threes, so that's a full house!
Can you beat that?
Creatively.
I have a four, a seven, a ten, a jack, and a "how to play poker" instruction card. This combination shall henceforth be known...
As a unicorn.
You're inventing new hands now?
We will call this one a "hoof."

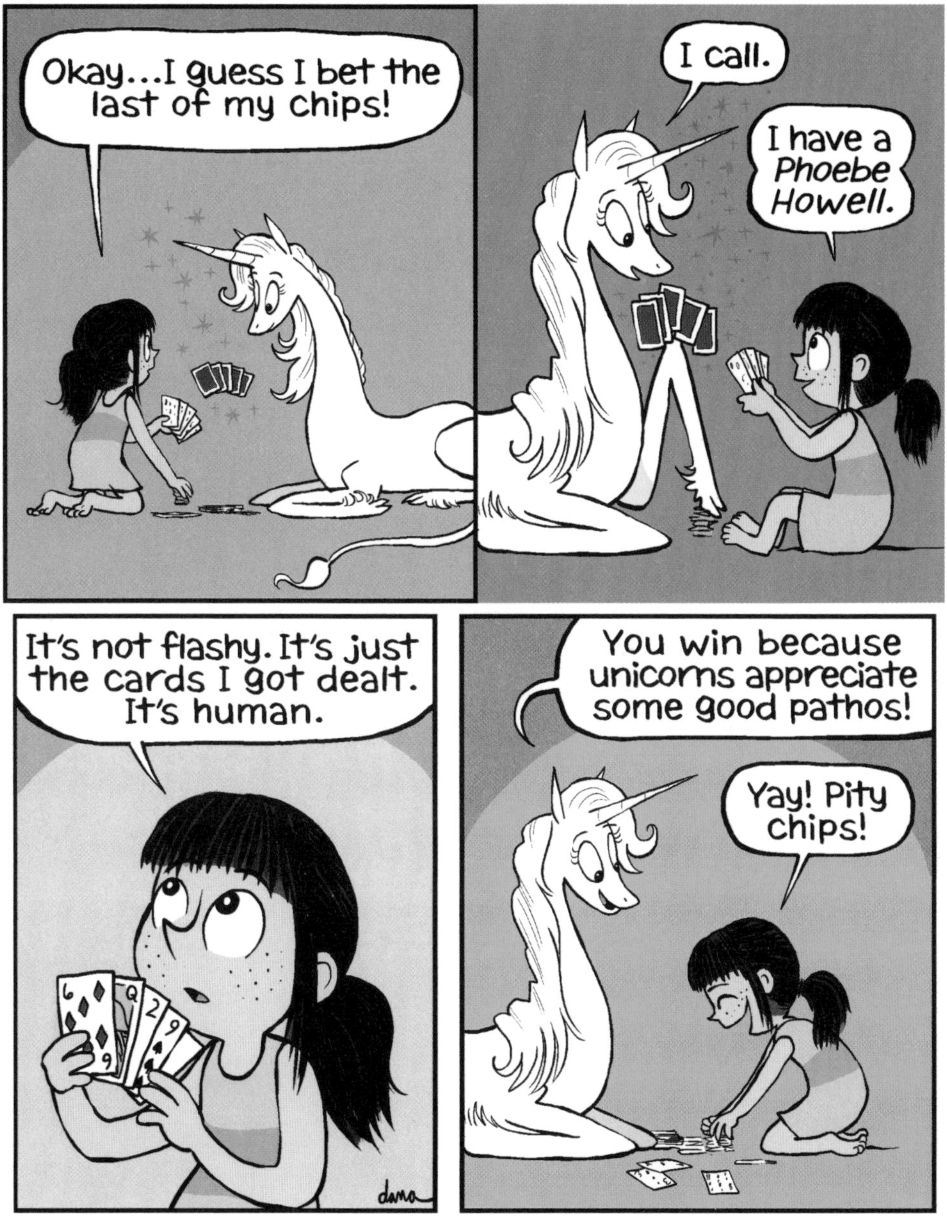
Okay...I guess I bet the last of my chips!
I call.
I have a *Phoebe Howell.*
It's not flashy. It's just the cards I got dealt. It's human.
You win because unicorns appreciate some good pathos!
Yay! Pity chips!

Look. There's the school.
It's weird seeing the school in summer. It's so...quiet and dark.
That is deceptive. In fact, school in summer is a HUB of magical activity.

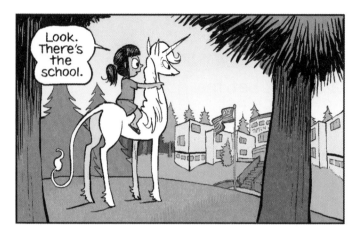

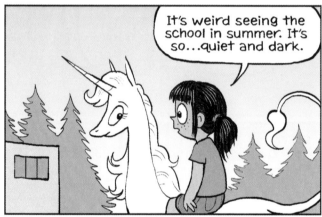

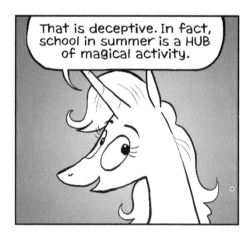

The local Pixie Guild holds their budget meeting, there are several wood nymph book clubs, and centaurs use it as a polling place.

I am sorry if I have robbed you of the mystery.

Figures that I only get to go there when it's BORING.

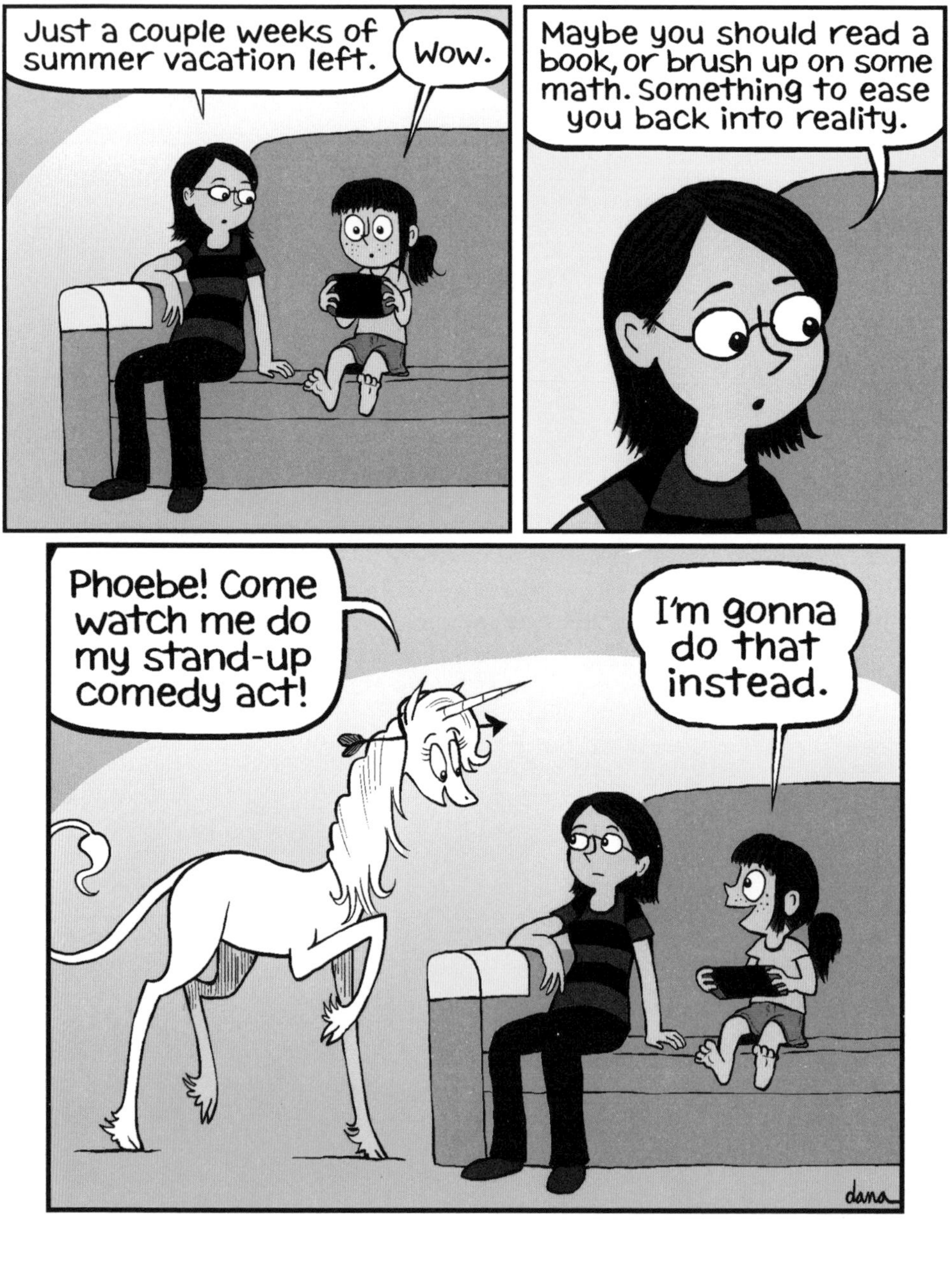
Just a couple weeks of summer vacation left.
Wow.
Maybe you should read a book, or brush up on some math. Something to ease you back into reality.
Phoebe! Come watch me do my stand-up comedy act!
I'm gonna do that instead.
dana

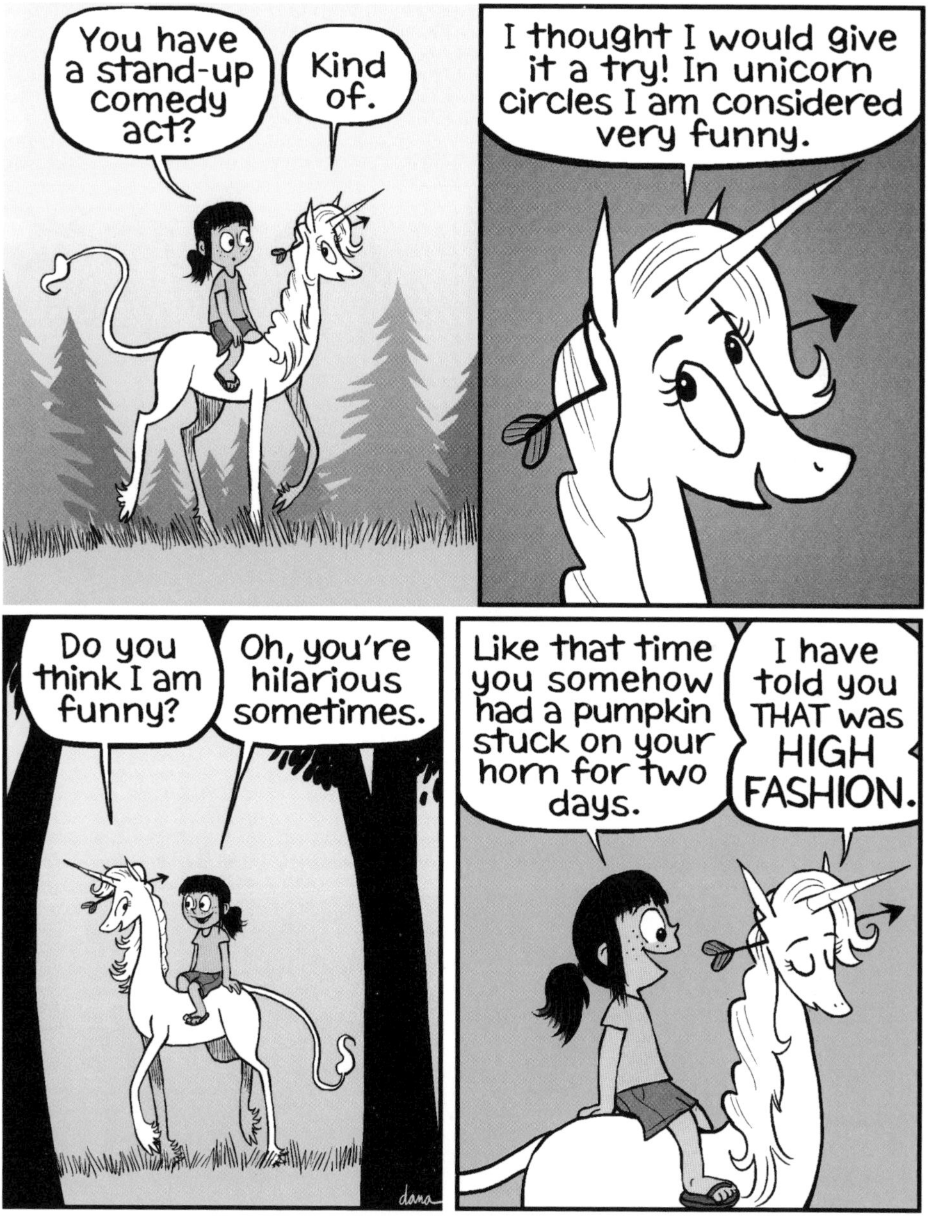
You have a stand-up comedy act?
Kind of.
I thought I would give it a try! In unicorn circles I am considered very funny.
Do you think I am funny?
Oh, you're hilarious sometimes.
Like that time you somehow had a pumpkin stuck on your horn for two days.
I have told you THAT was HIGH FASHION.
dana

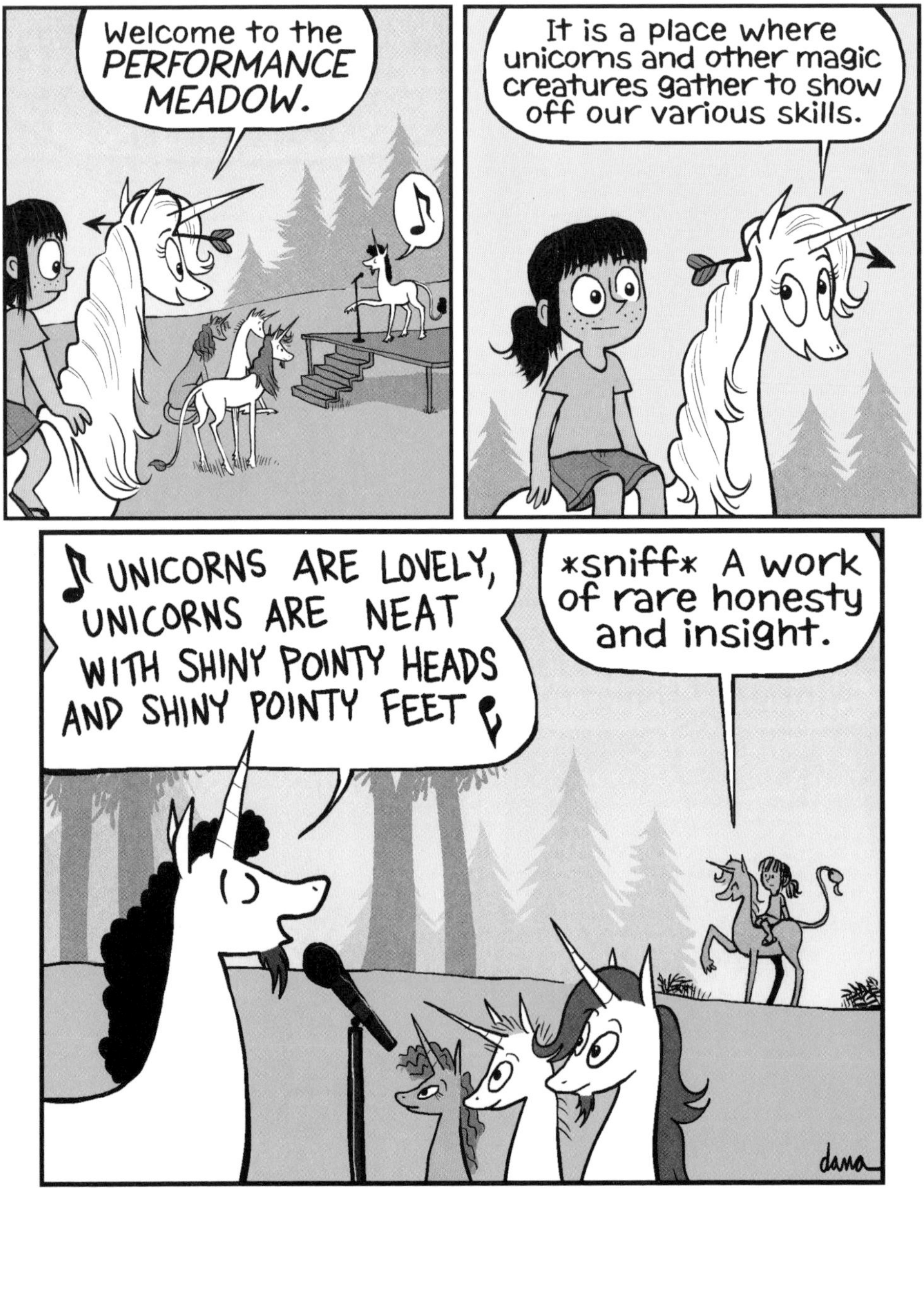
Welcome to the PERFORMANCE MEADOW.
It is a place where unicorns and other magic creatures gather to show off our various skills.
UNICORNS ARE LOVELY, UNICORNS ARE NEAT WITH SHINY POINTY HEADS AND SHINY POINTY FEET
sniff A work of rare honesty and insight.
dana

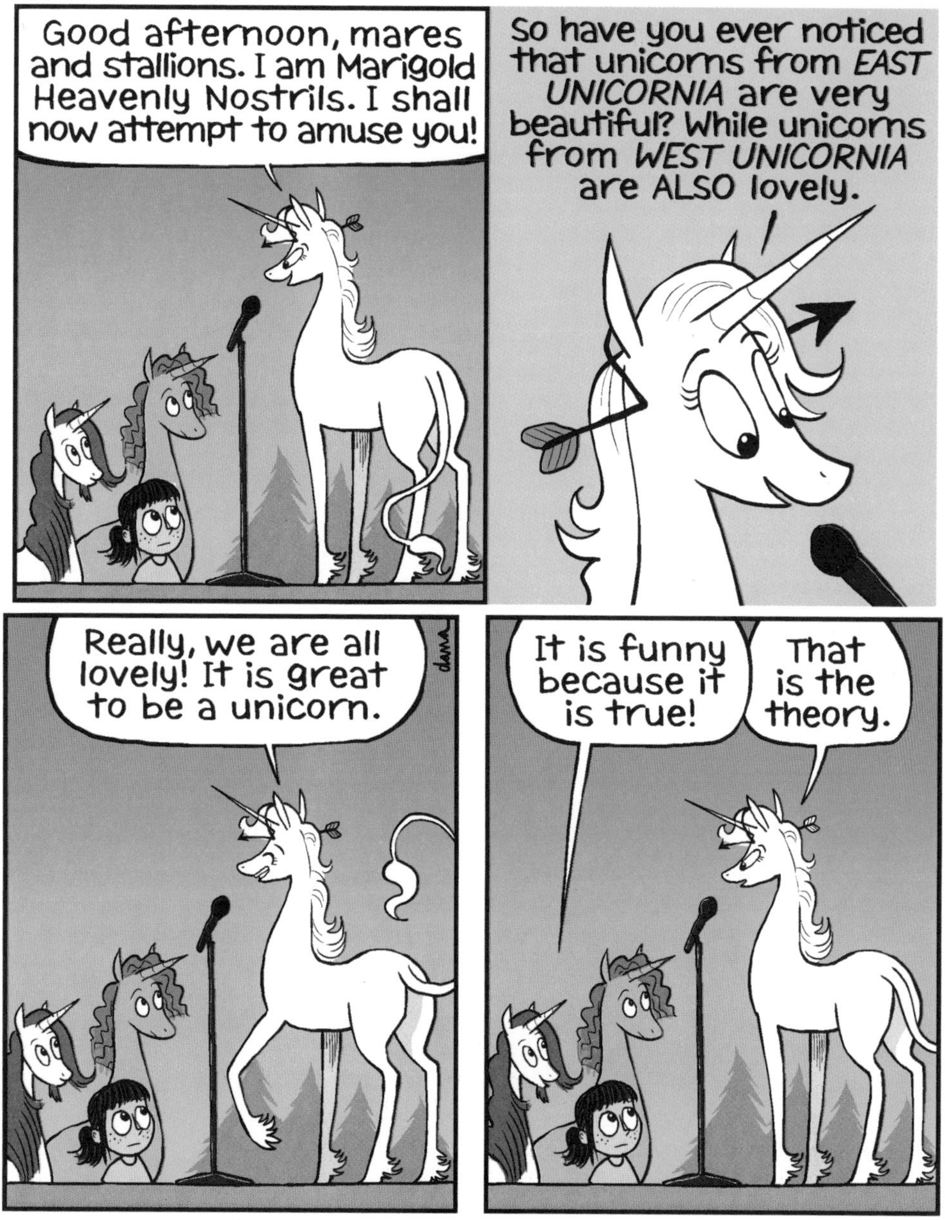
Good afternoon, mares and stallions. I am Marigold Heavenly Nostrils. I shall now attempt to amuse you!
So have you ever noticed that unicorns from EAST UNICORNIA are very beautiful? While unicorns from WEST UNICORNIA are ALSO lovely.
Really, we are all lovely! It is great to be a unicorn.
dana
It is funny because it is true!
That is the theory.

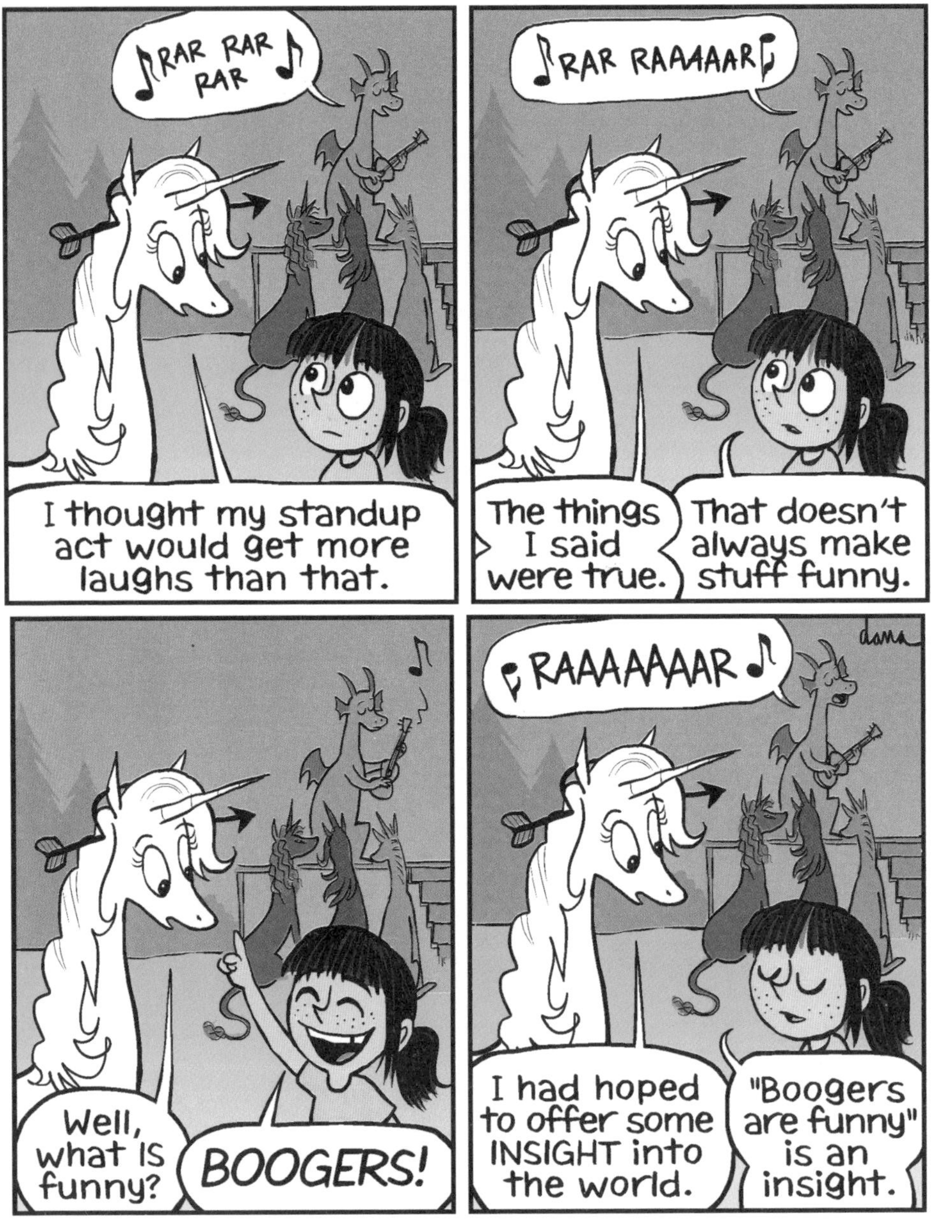
♪ RAR RAR RAR ♪
I thought my standup act would get more laughs than that.
♪ RAR RAAAAAR ♫
The things I said were true.
That doesn't always make stuff funny.
♪
Well, what IS funny?
BOOGERS!
♫ RAAAAAAAR ♪
I had hoped to offer some INSIGHT into the world.
"Boogers are funny" is an insight.

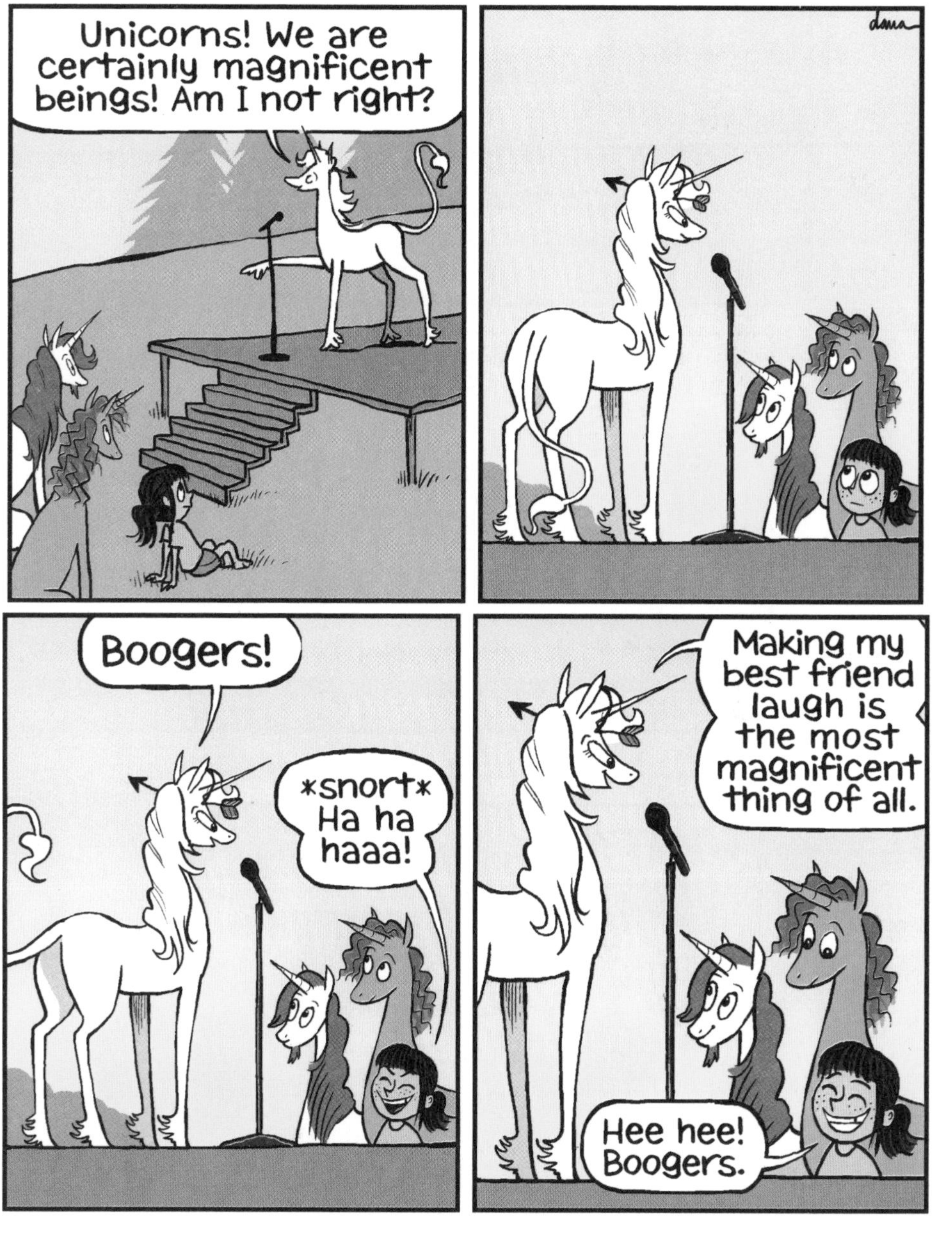

Unicorns! We are certainly magnificent beings! Am I not right?
dana
Boogers!
snort Ha ha haaa!
Making my best friend laugh is the most magnificent thing of all.
Hee hee! Boogers.

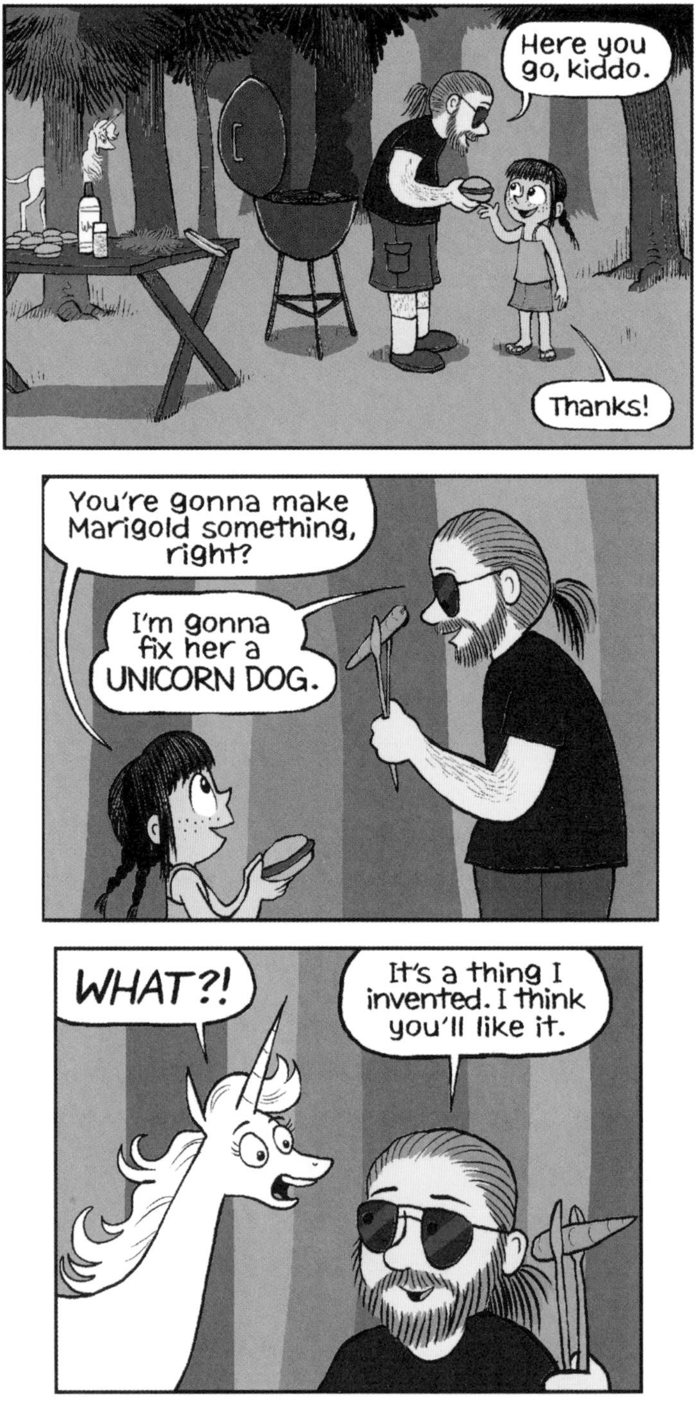
Here you go, kiddo.
Thanks!
You're gonna make Marigold something, right?
I'm gonna fix her a UNICORN DOG.
WHAT?!
It's a thing I invented. I think you'll like it.

It's a grilled carrot on a bun, on a bed of grass topped with whipped cream and cake sprinkles.

Oh! That is a relief.

I thought you were threatening my friend Chienne here!

Who just happens to be here right now?

Unicorn dogs are never far.

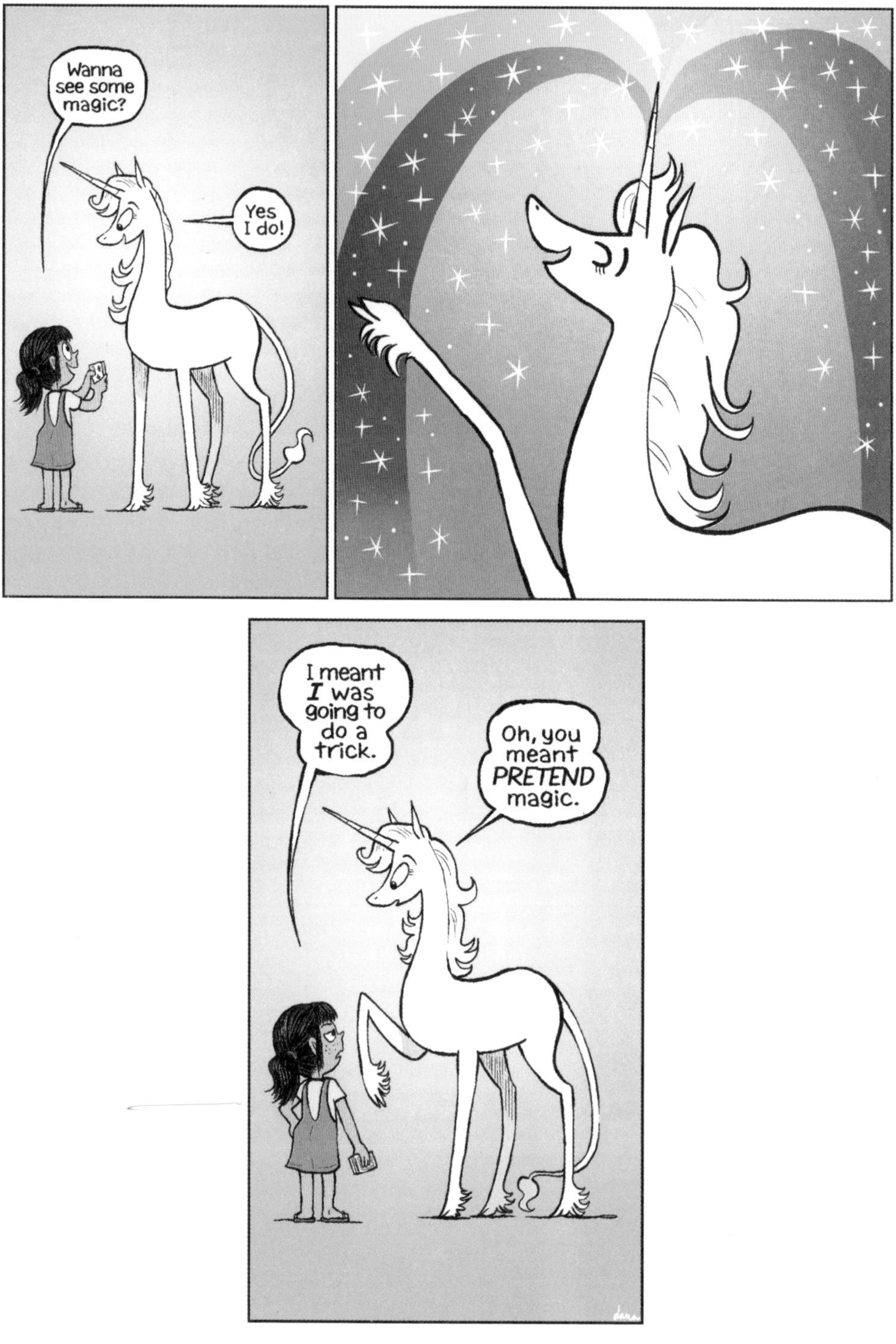
Wanna see some magic?
Yes I do!
I meant *I* was going to do a trick.
Oh, you meant PRETEND magic.

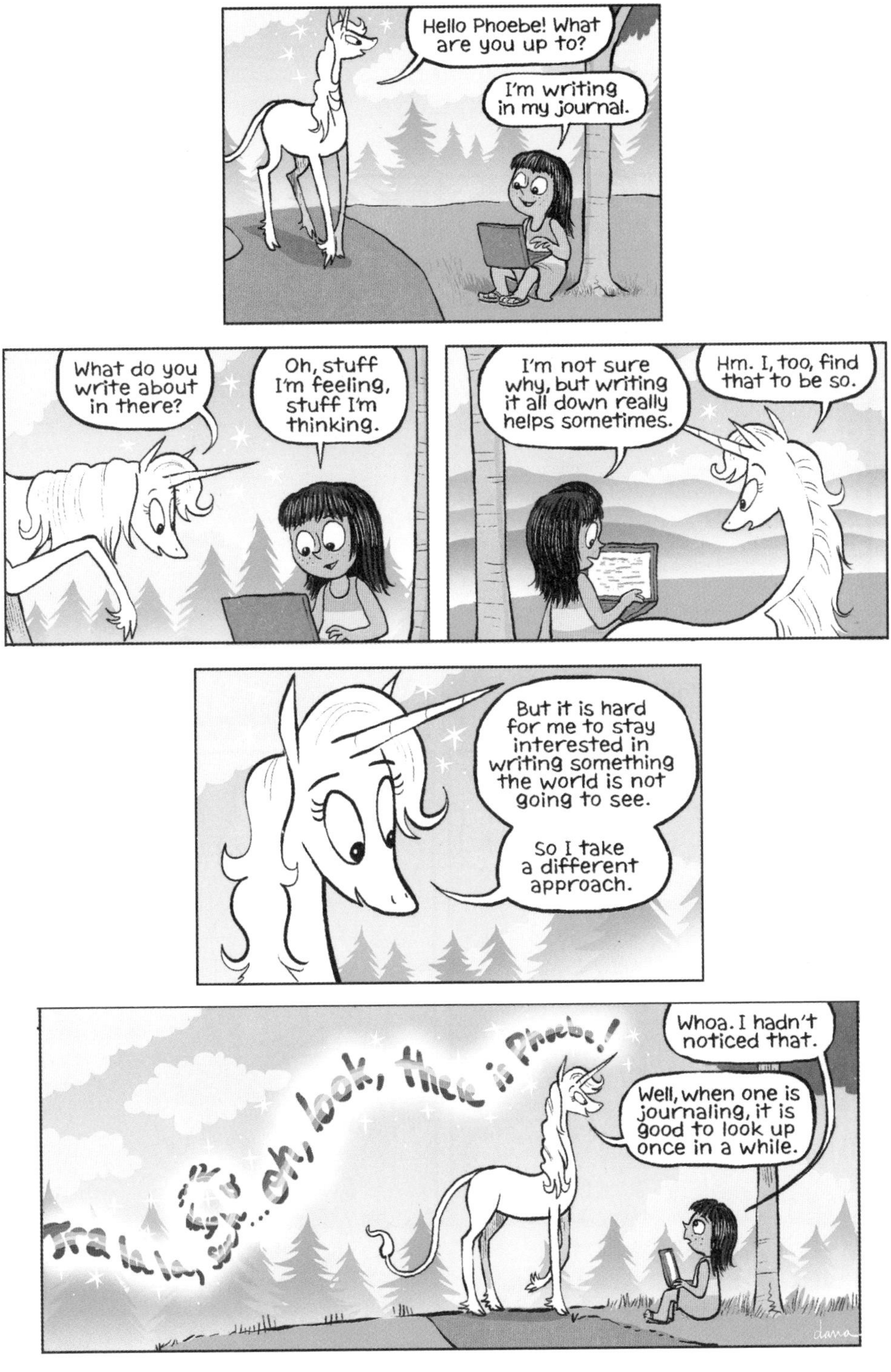

Hello Phoebe! What are you up to?
I'm writing in my journal.
What do you write about in there?
Oh, stuff I'm feeling, stuff I'm thinking.
I'm not sure why, but writing it all down really helps sometimes.
Hm. I, too, find that to be so.
But it is hard for me to stay interested in writing something the world is not going to see.
So I take a different approach.
Tra la la,
oh, look, there is Phoebe!
Whoa. I hadn't noticed that.
Well, when one is journaling, it is good to look up once in a while.

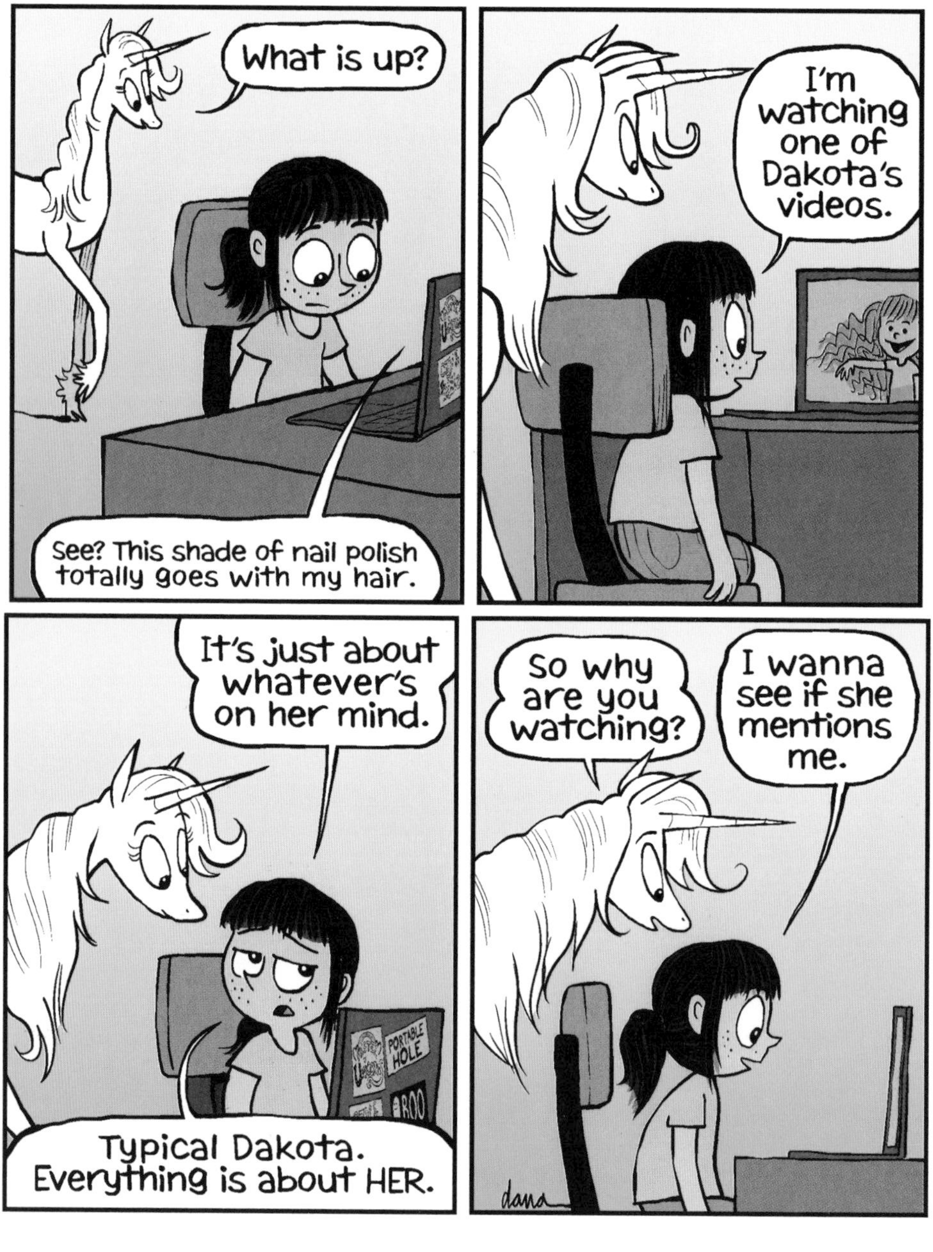
What is up?
See? This shade of nail polish totally goes with my hair.
I'm watching one of Dakota's videos.
It's just about whatever's on her mind.
PORTABLE HOLE
Typical Dakota. Everything is about HER.
So why are you watching?
I wanna see if she mentions me.
dana

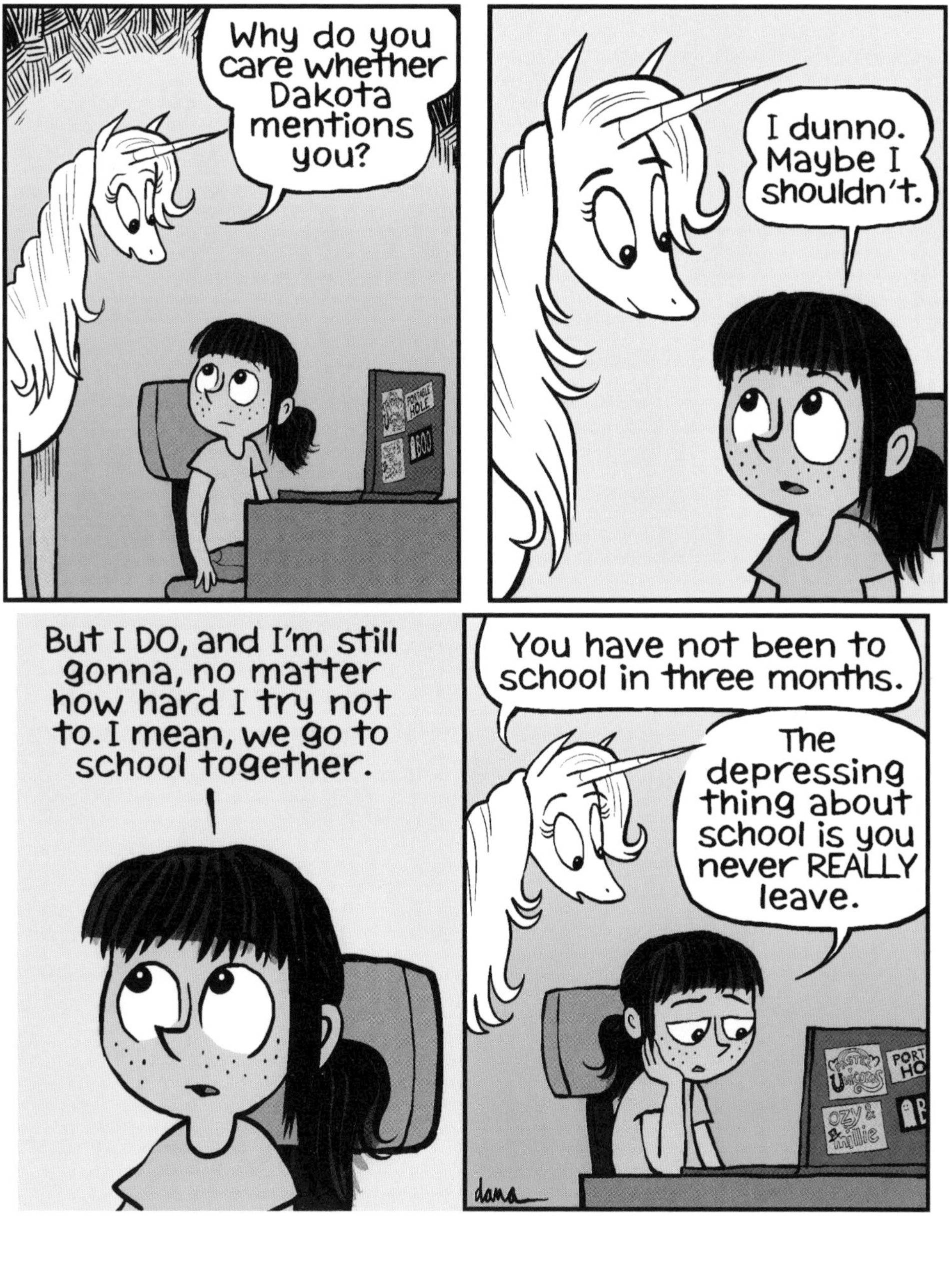

Why do you care whether Dakota mentions you?
I dunno. Maybe I shouldn't.
But I DO, and I'm still gonna, no matter how hard I try not to. I mean, we go to school together.
You have not been to school in three months.
The depressing thing about school is you never REALLY leave.

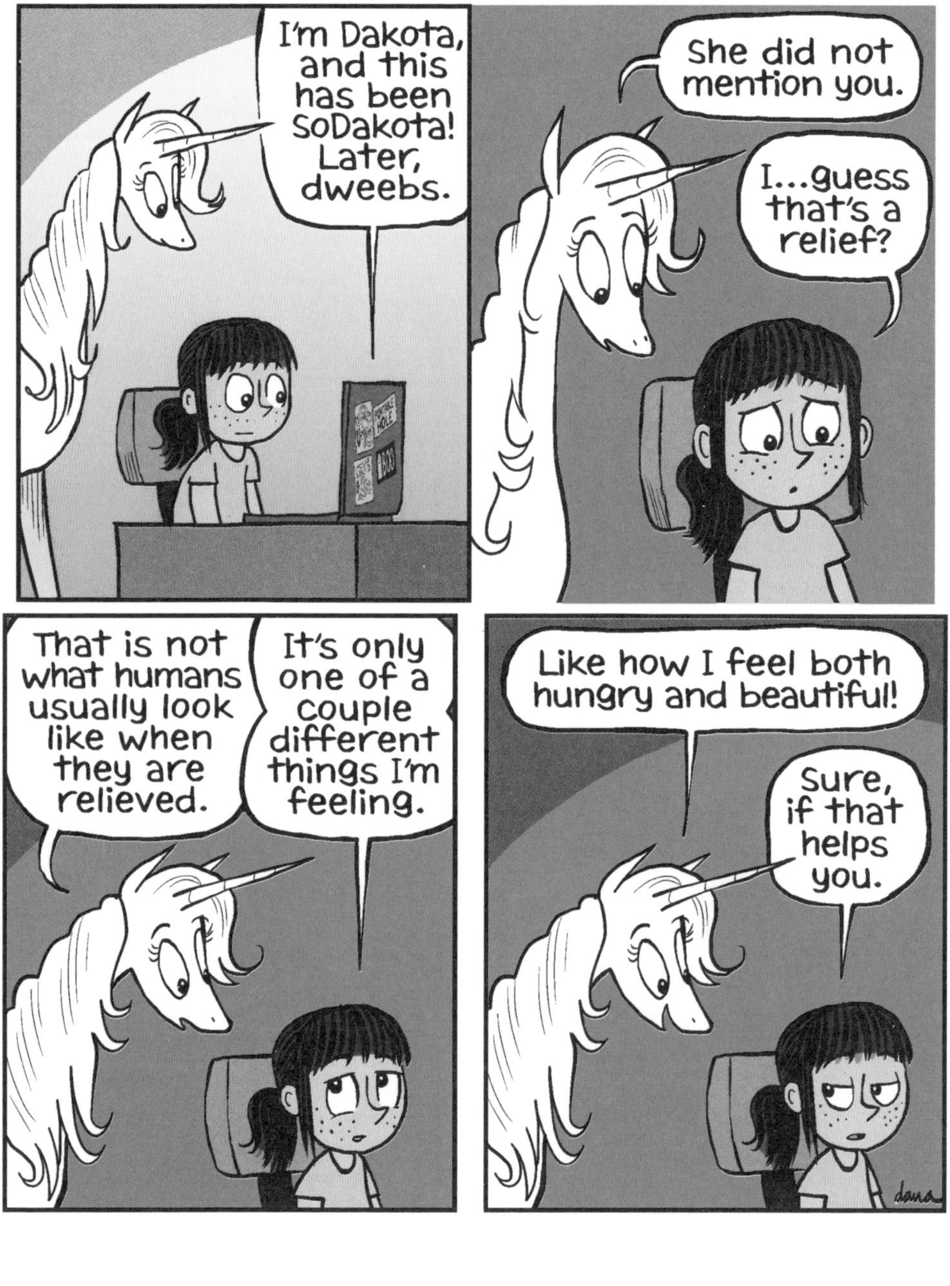
I'm Dakota, and this has been SoDakota! Later, dweebs.
She did not mention you.
I...guess that's a relief?
That is not what humans usually look like when they are relieved.
It's only one of a couple different things I'm feeling.
Like how I feel both hungry and beautiful!
Sure, if that helps you.

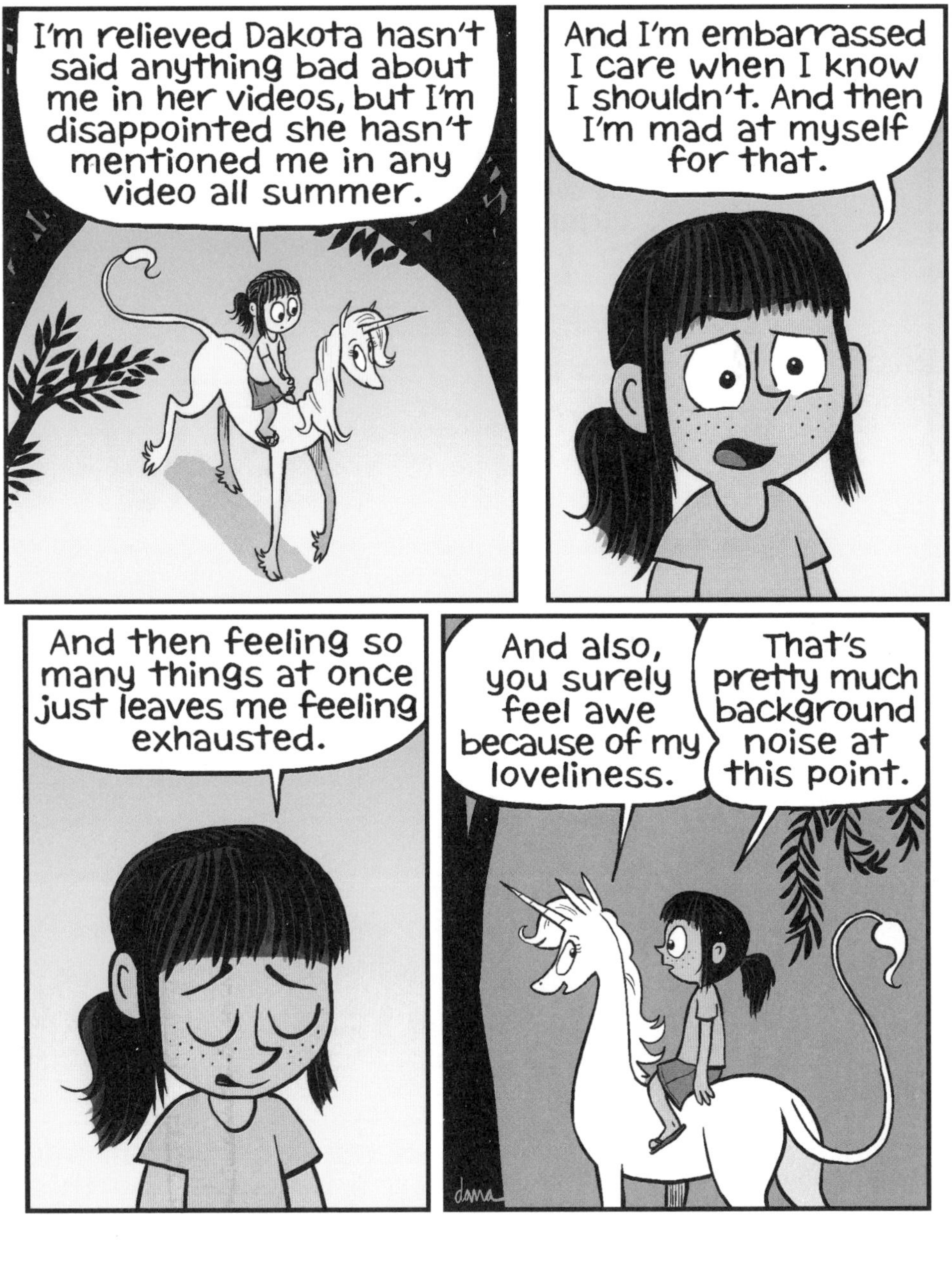
I'm relieved Dakota hasn't said anything bad about me in her videos, but I'm disappointed she hasn't mentioned me in any video all summer.
And I'm embarrassed I care when I know I shouldn't. And then I'm mad at myself for that.
And then feeling so many things at once just leaves me feeling exhausted.
And also, you surely feel awe because of my loveliness.
That's pretty much background noise at this point.
dana

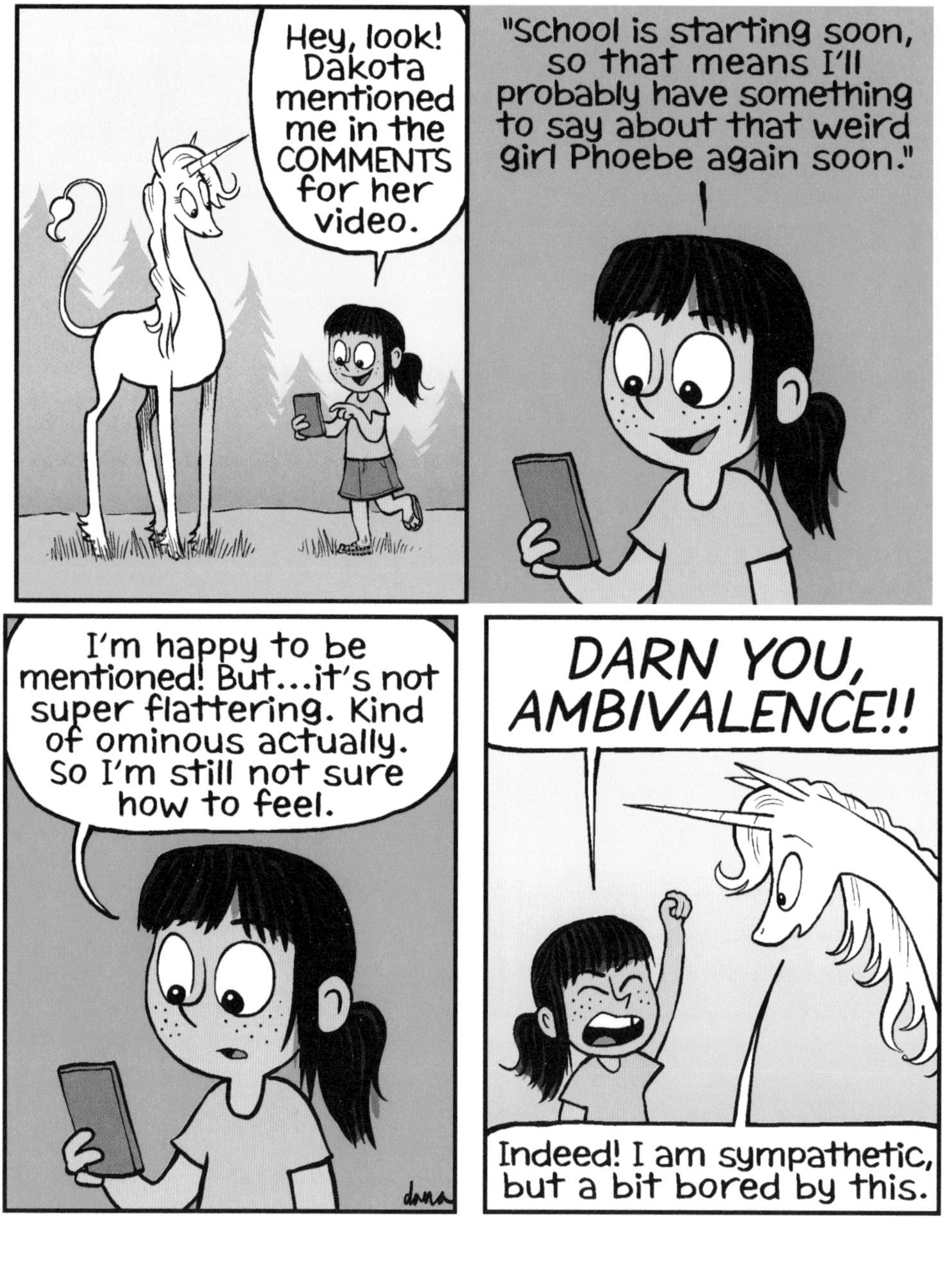
Hey, look! Dakota mentioned me in the COMMENTS for her video.
"School is starting soon, so that means I'll probably have something to say about that weird girl Phoebe again soon."
I'm happy to be mentioned! But...it's not super flattering. Kind of ominous actually. So I'm still not sure how to feel.
DARN YOU, AMBIVALENCE!!
Indeed! I am sympathetic, but a bit bored by this.
dana

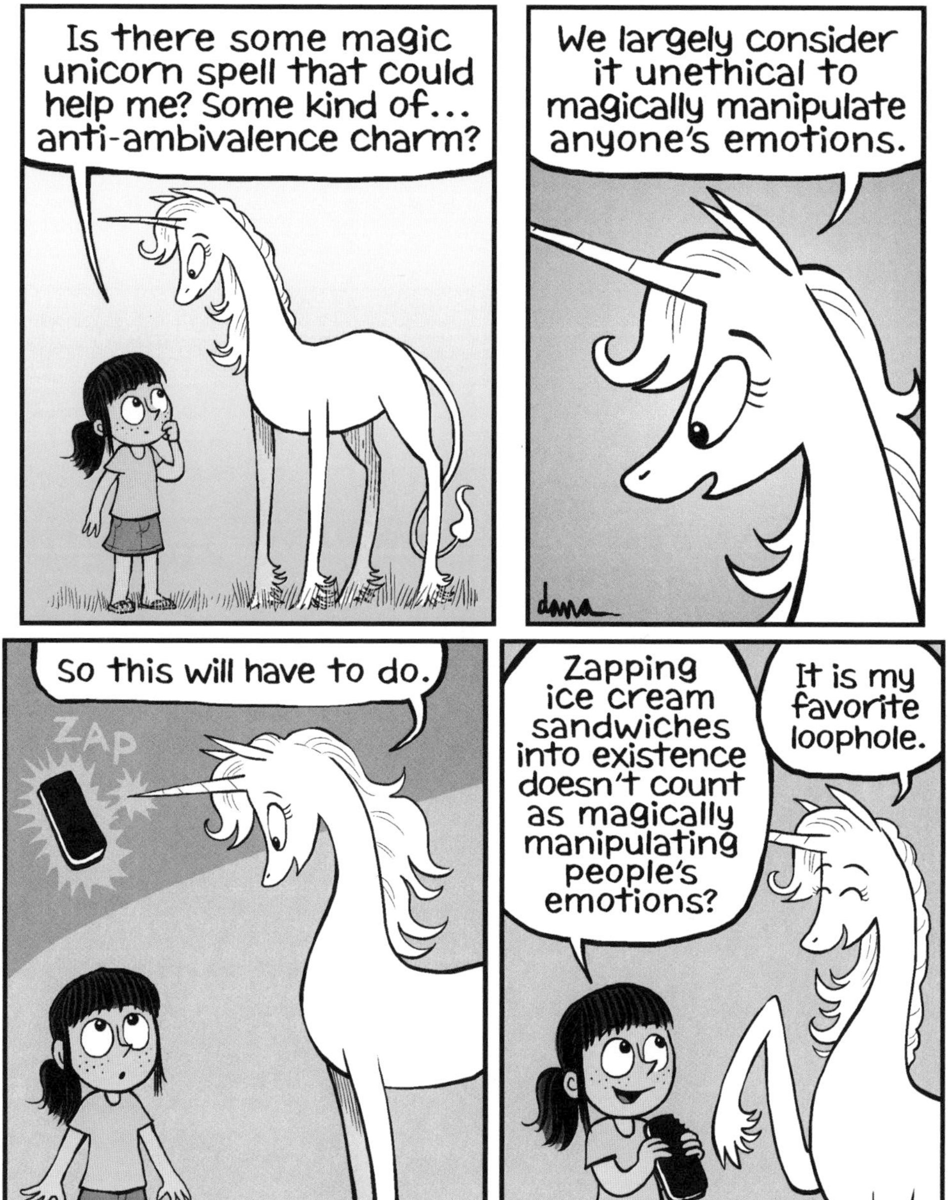
Is there some magic unicorn spell that could help me? Some kind of... anti-ambivalence charm?
We largely consider it unethical to magically manipulate anyone's emotions.
So this will have to do.
ZAP
Zapping ice cream sandwiches into existence doesn't count as magically manipulating people's emotions?
It is my favorite loophole.
dana

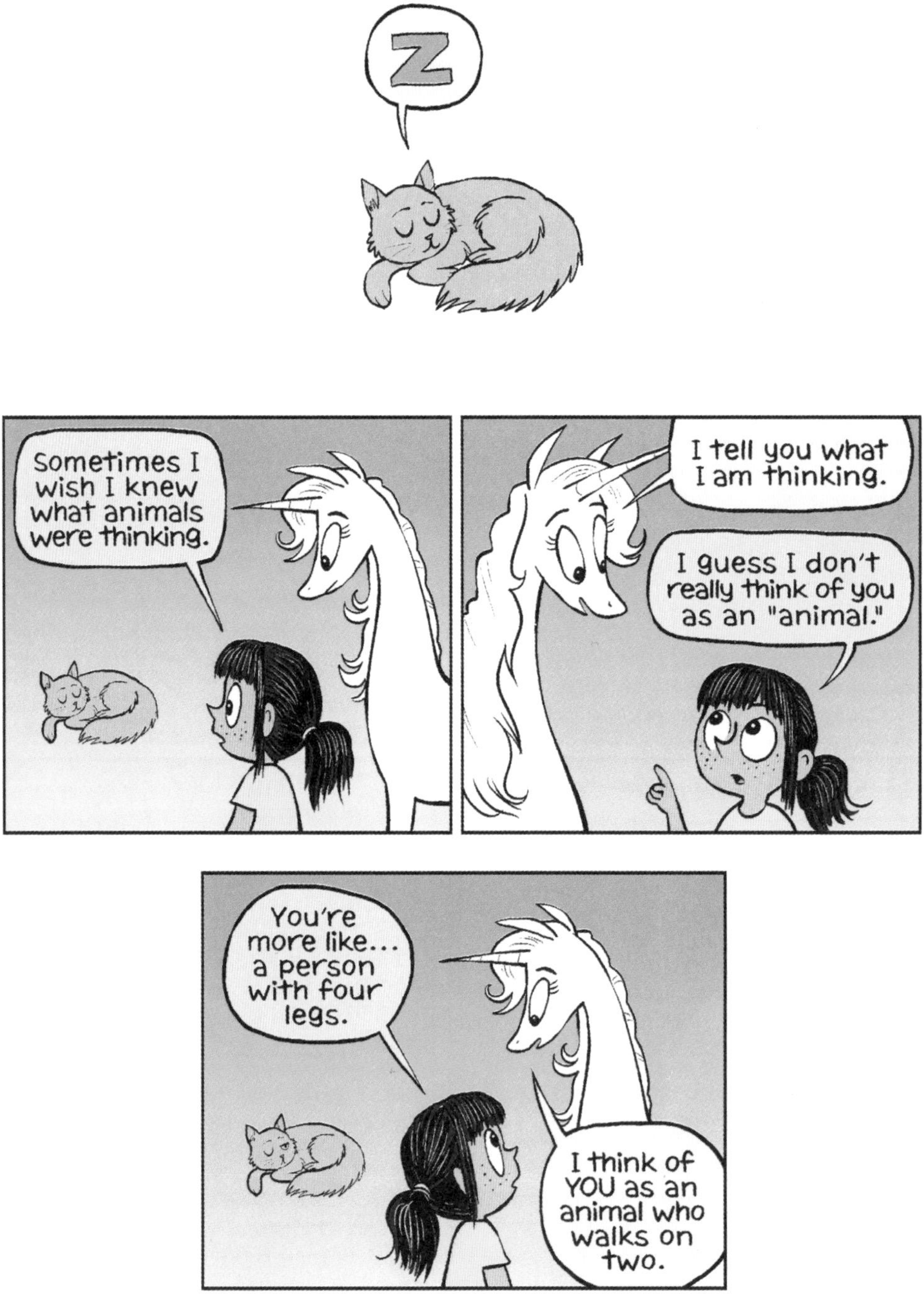
Z
Sometimes I wish I knew what animals were thinking.
I tell you what I am thinking.
I guess I don't really think of you as an "animal."
You're more like... a person with four legs.
I think of YOU as an animal who walks on two.

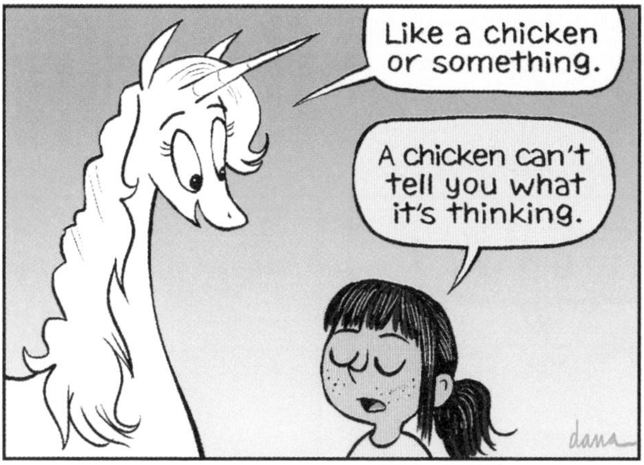
Like a chicken or something.
A chicken can't tell you what it's thinking.
dana

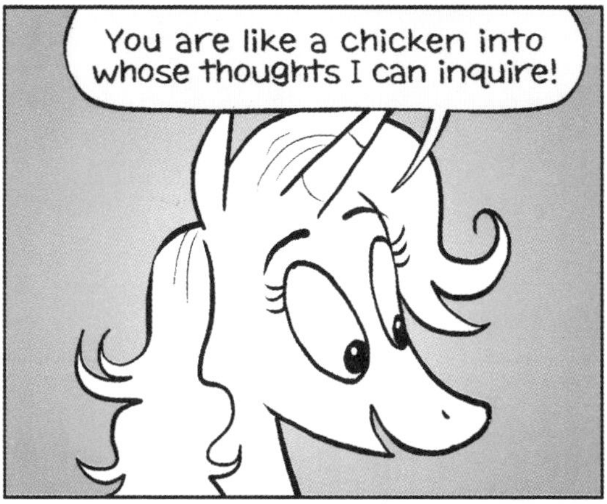
You are like a chicken into whose thoughts I can inquire!

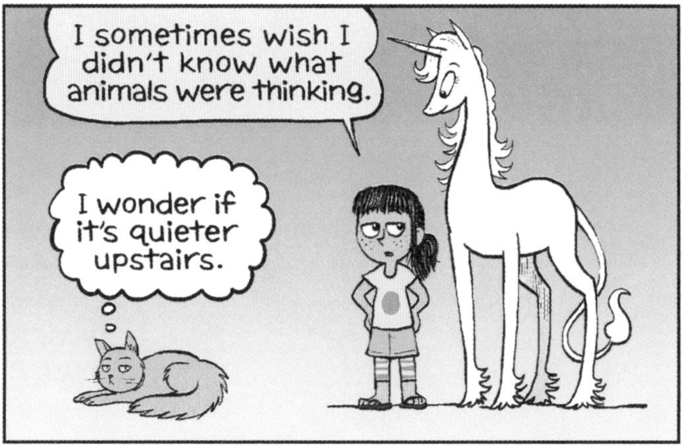
I sometimes wish I didn't know what animals were thinking.
I wonder if it's quieter upstairs.

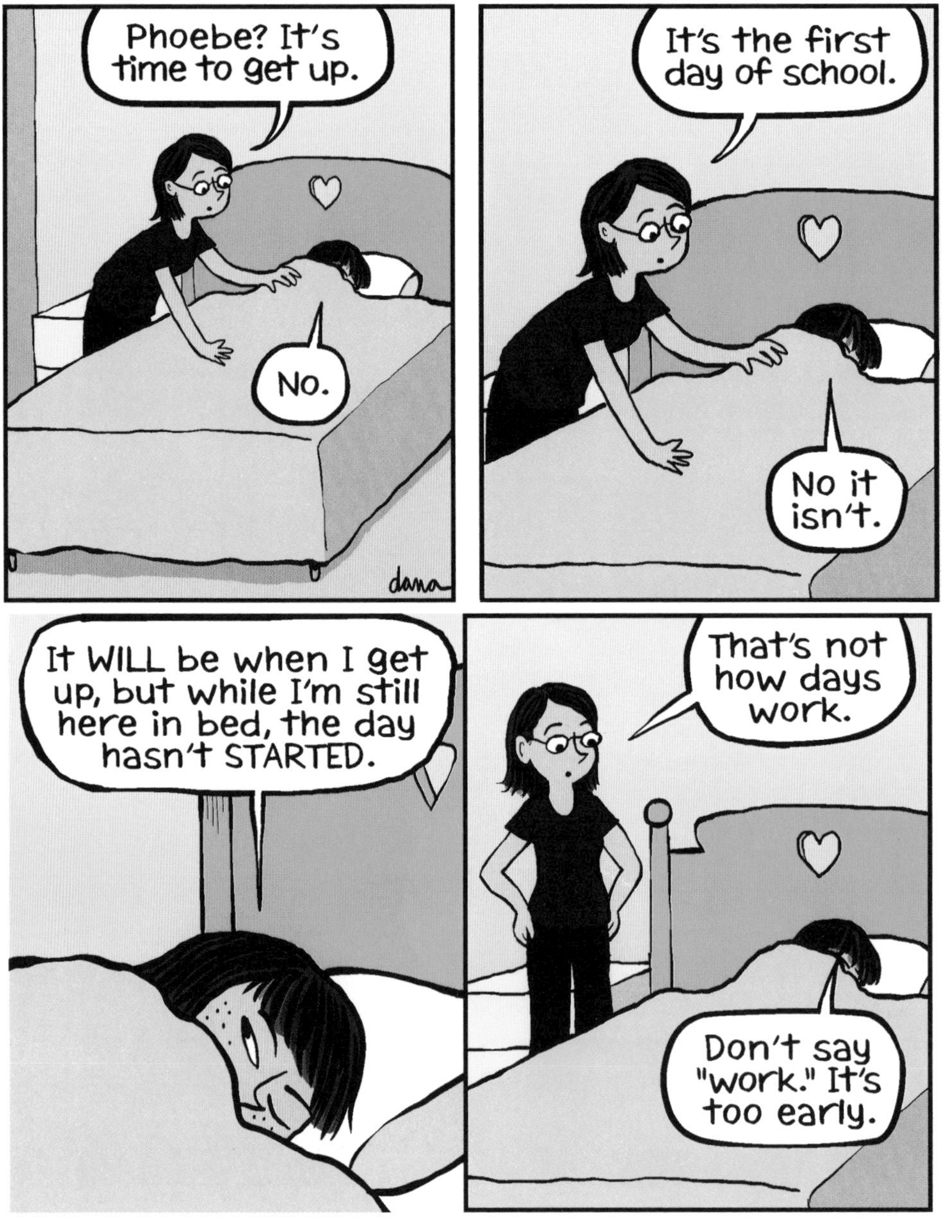

Phoebe? It's time to get up.
No.
dana
It's the first day of school.
No it isn't.
It WILL be when I get up, but while I'm still here in bed, the day hasn't STARTED.
That's not how days work.
Don't say "work." It's too early.

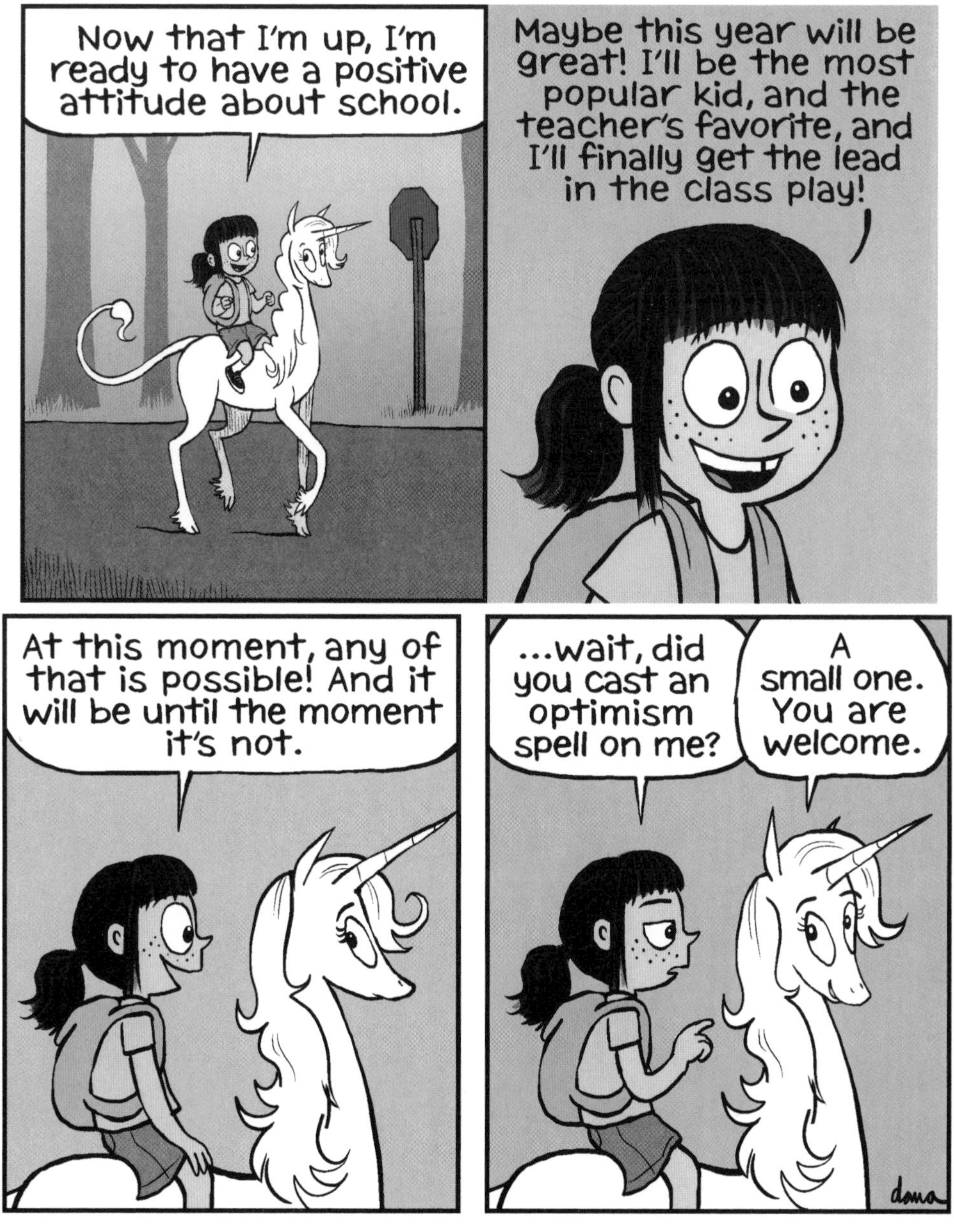
Now that I'm up, I'm ready to have a positive attitude about school.
Maybe this year will be great! I'll be the most popular kid, and the teacher's favorite, and I'll finally get the lead in the class play!
At this moment, any of that is possible! And it will be until the moment it's not.
...wait, did you cast an optimism spell on me?
A small one. You are welcome.
dana

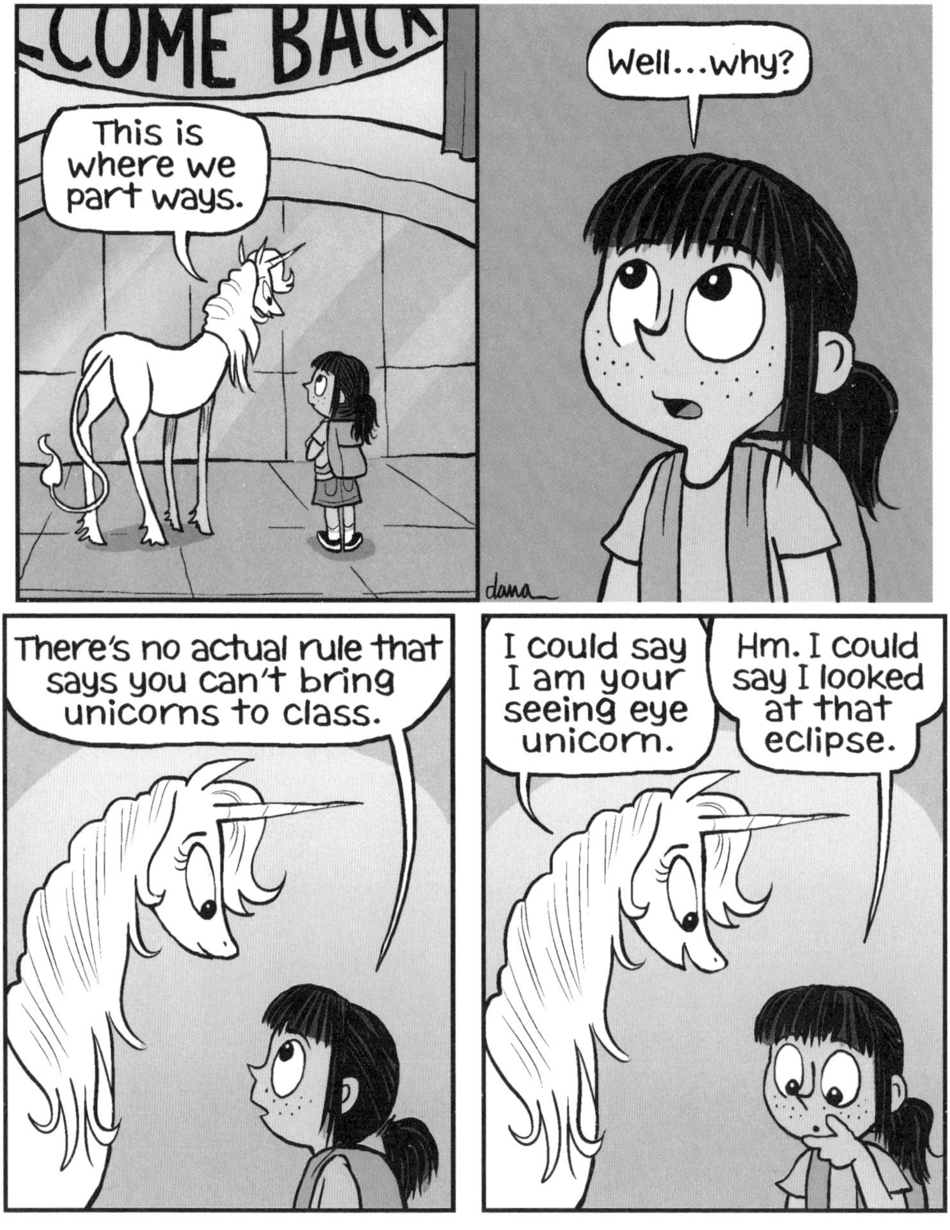
COME BACK
This is where we part ways.
Well...why?
There's no actual rule that says you can't bring unicorns to class.
I could say I am your seeing eye unicorn.
Hm. I could say I looked at that eclipse.

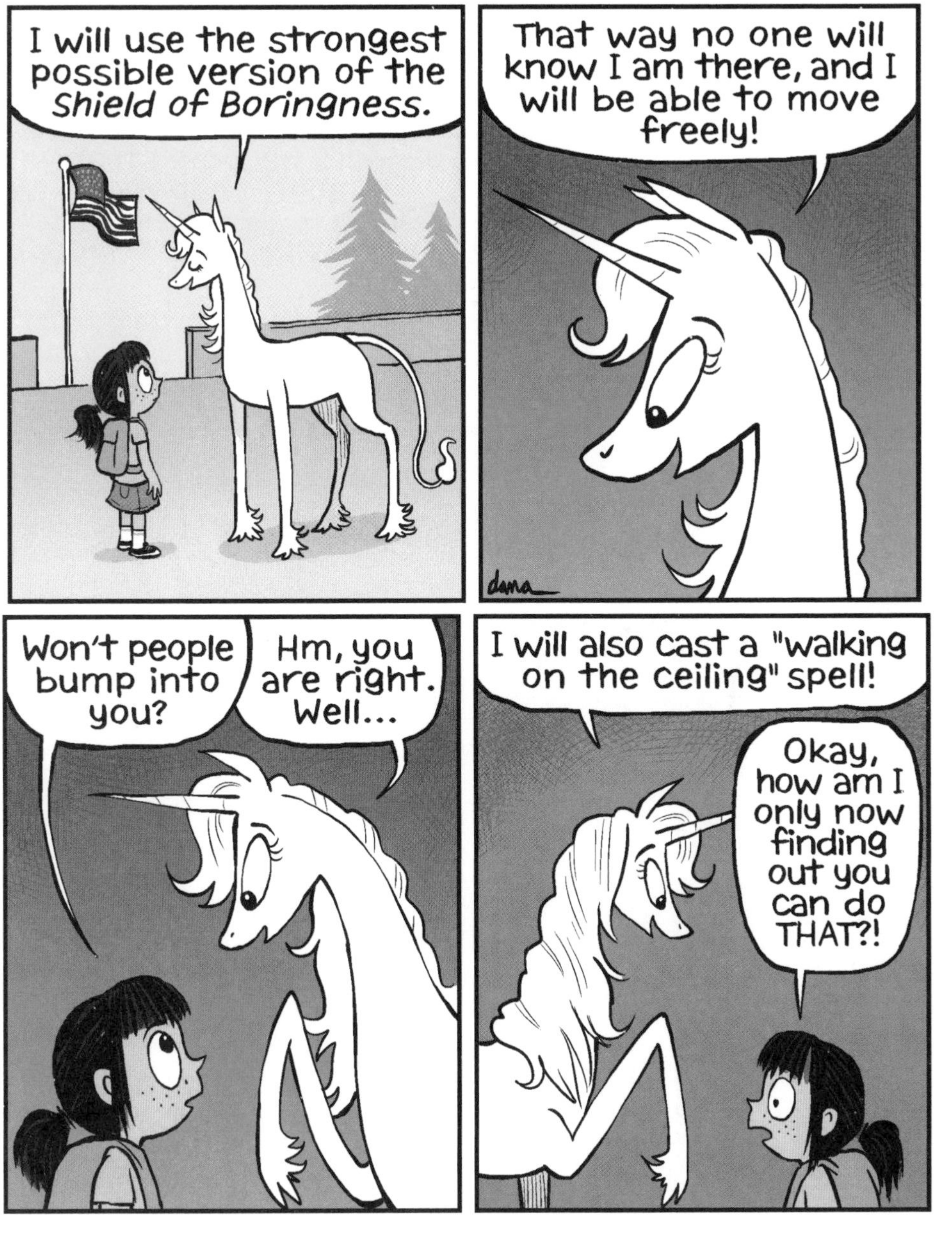
I will use the strongest possible version of the *Shield of Boringness.*
That way no one will know I am there, and I will be able to move freely!
dana
Won't people bump into you?
Hm, you are right. Well...
I will also cast a "walking on the ceiling" spell!
Okay, how am I only now finding out you can do THAT?!

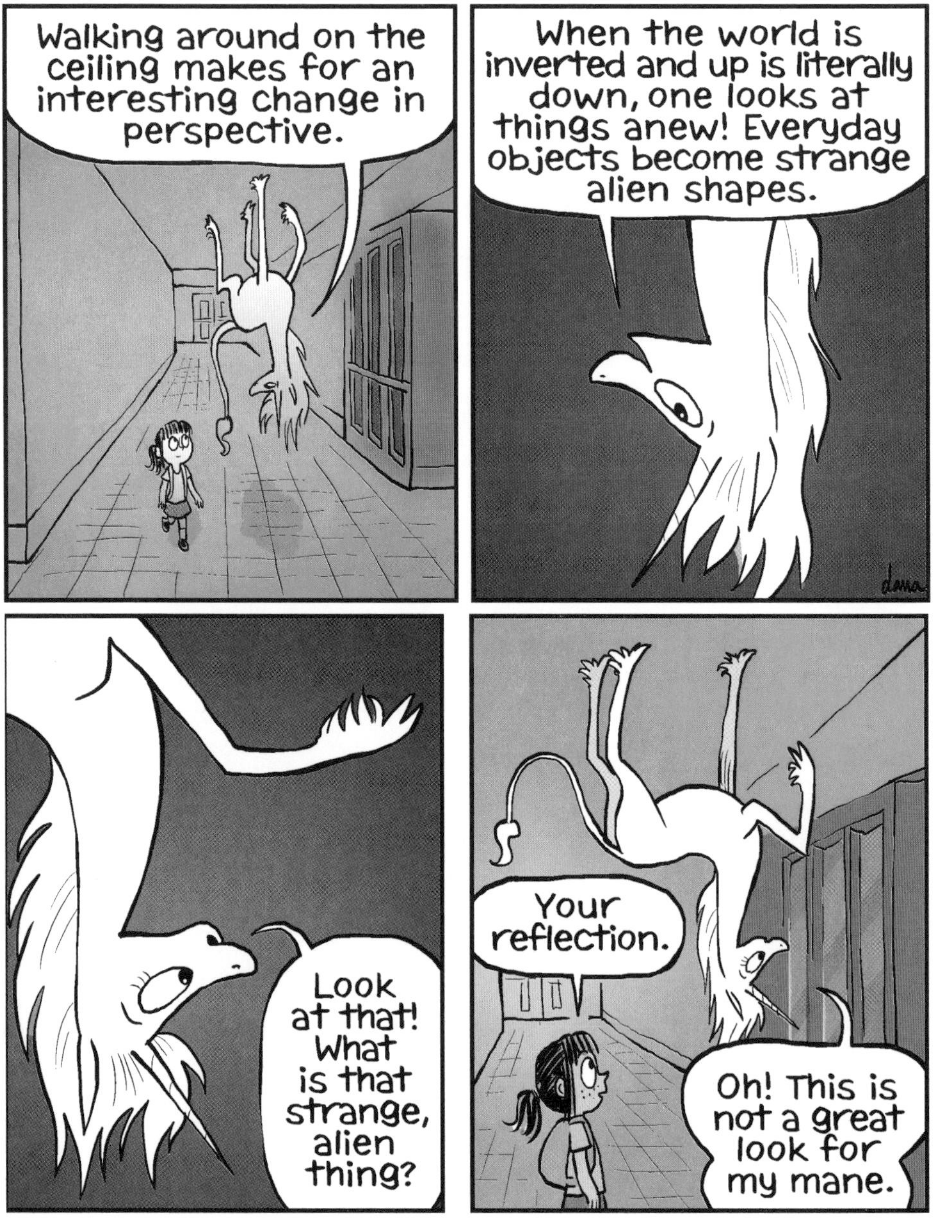
Walking around on the ceiling makes for an interesting change in perspective.
When the world is inverted and up is literally down, one looks at things anew! Everyday objects become strange alien shapes.
Look at that! What is that strange, alien thing?
Your reflection.
Oh! This is not a great look for my mane.

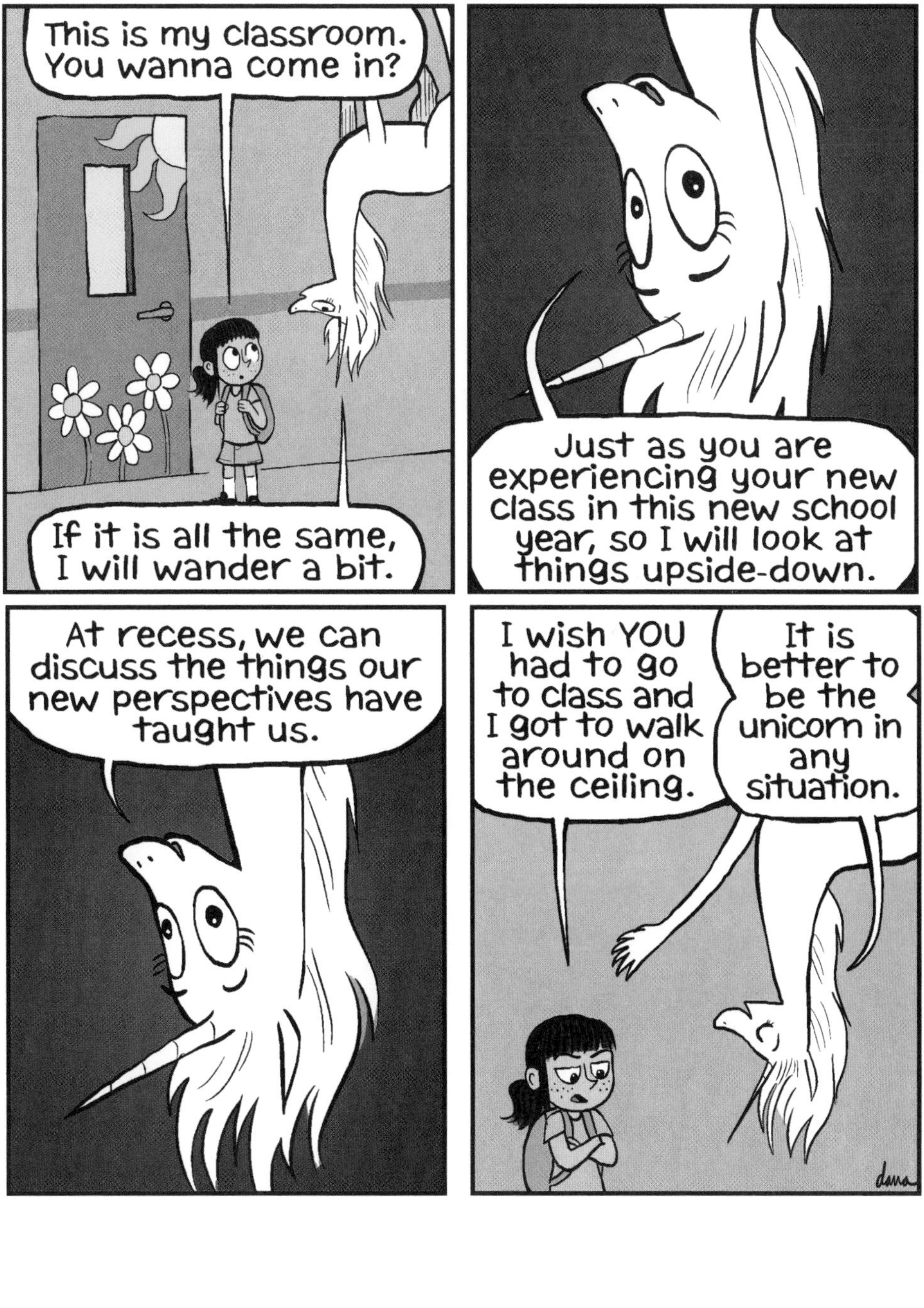
This is my classroom. You wanna come in?
If it is all the same, I will wander a bit.
Just as you are experiencing your new class in this new school year, so I will look at things upside-down.
At recess, we can discuss the things our new perspectives have taught us.
I wish YOU had to go to class and I got to walk around on the ceiling.
It is better to be the unicorn in any situation.
dana

It's subtle at first
The leaves get more red
And school is required
So I can't stay in bed
It is a lovely morning!
Good to know. Right now it's a green and orange blur.
But it's pretty much summer
In terms of the weather
I don't wear a coat when
We're riding together
Was that a raindrop?
Don't even JOKE about that.
dana

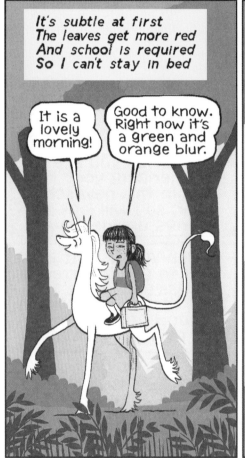

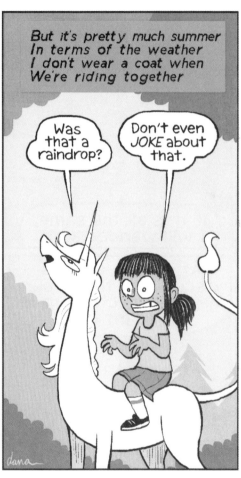

But then it gets colder
The skies get so dark
I need an umbrella
For rides in the park
If you can magically repel mud, what's with the boots?
Fashion!
When fall falls, it's farewell
To long sunny days
But shimmering unicorns
Make that okay.
You're sorta like a car with heated seats.
SEAT. So I am really more like a motorcycle.

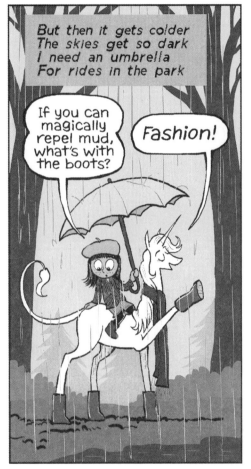

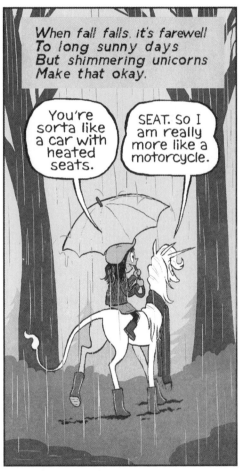

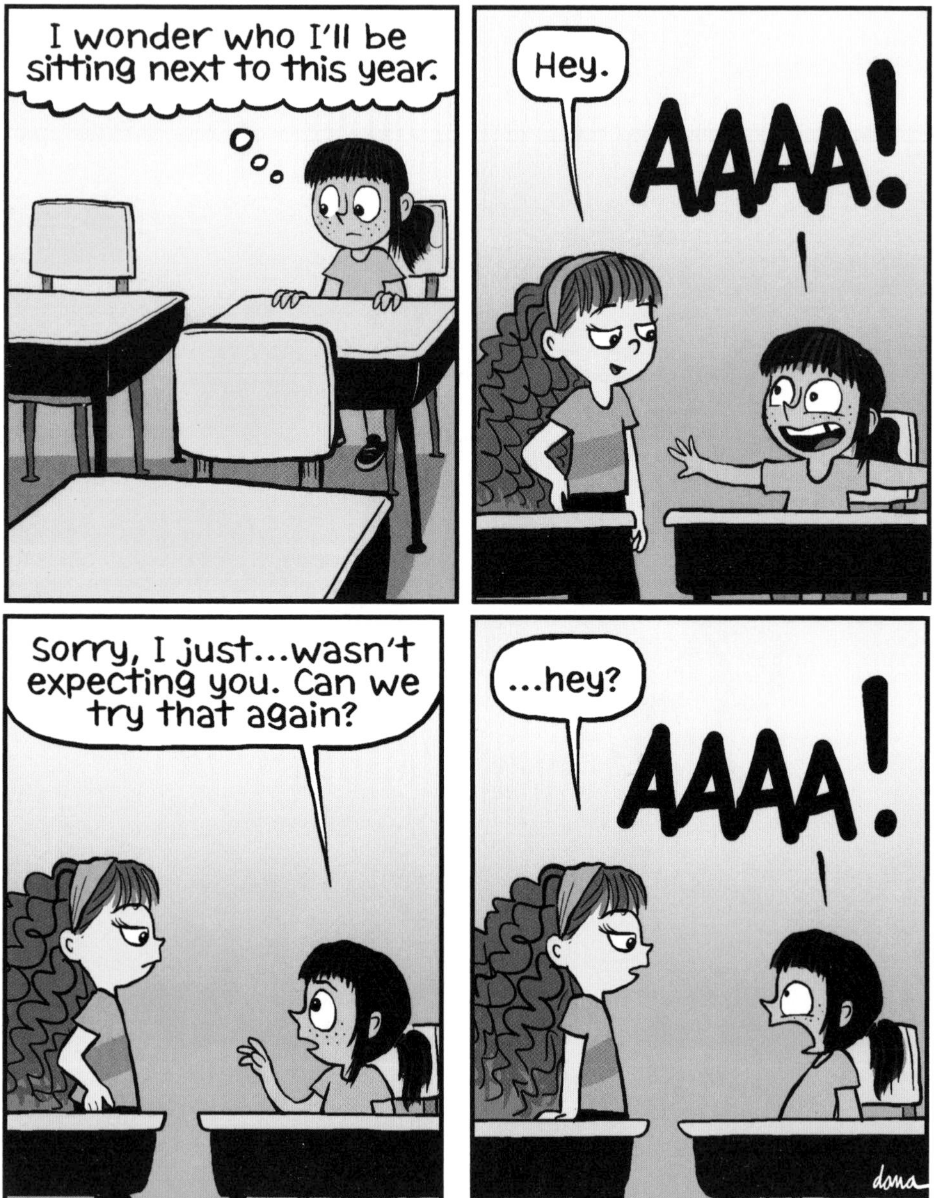
I wonder who I'll be sitting next to this year.
Hey.
AAAA!
Sorry, I just...wasn't expecting you. Can we try that again?
...hey?
AAAA!
dona

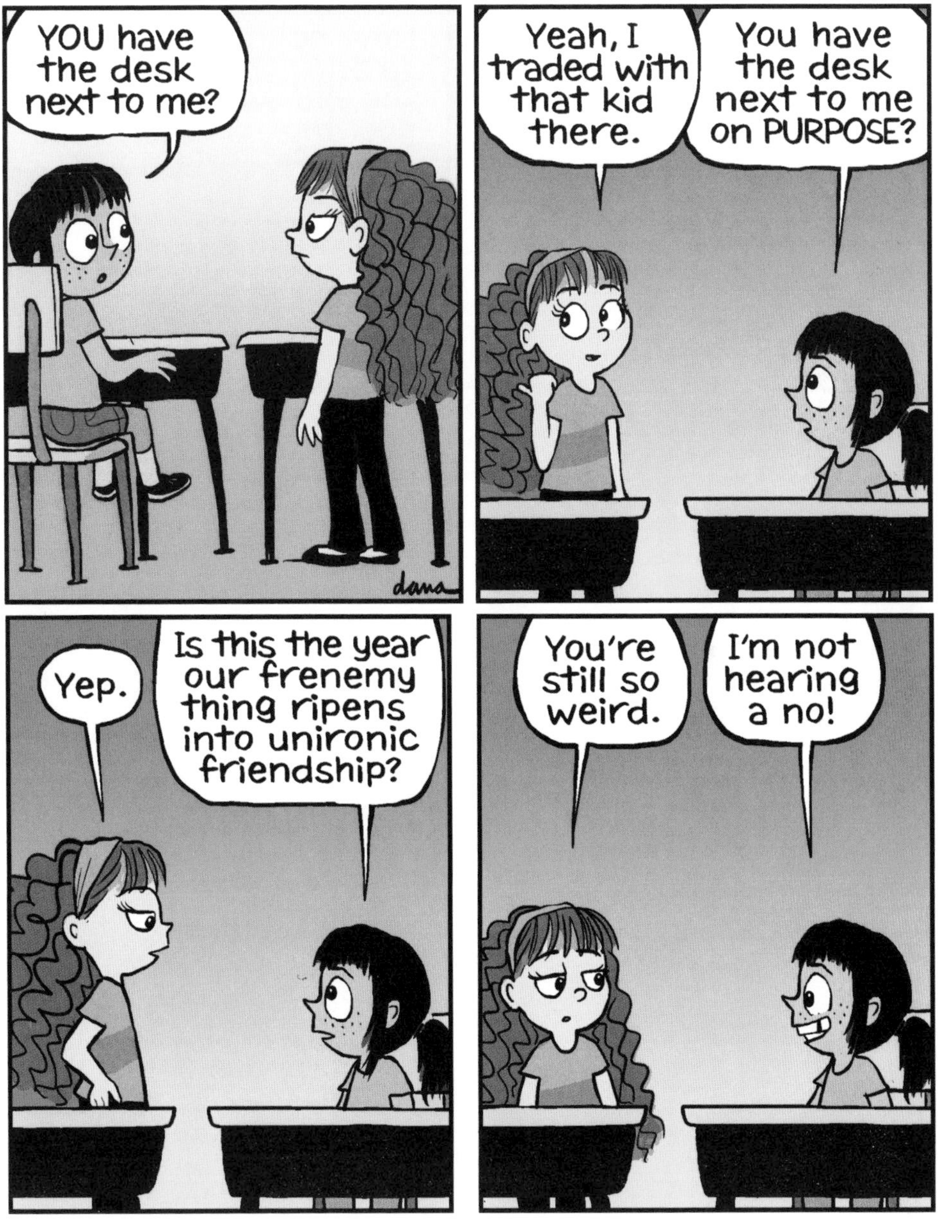
YOU have the desk next to me?
Yeah, I traded with that kid there.
You have the desk next to me on PURPOSE?
Yep.
Is this the year our frenemy thing ripens into unironic friendship?
You're still so weird.
I'm not hearing a no!
dana

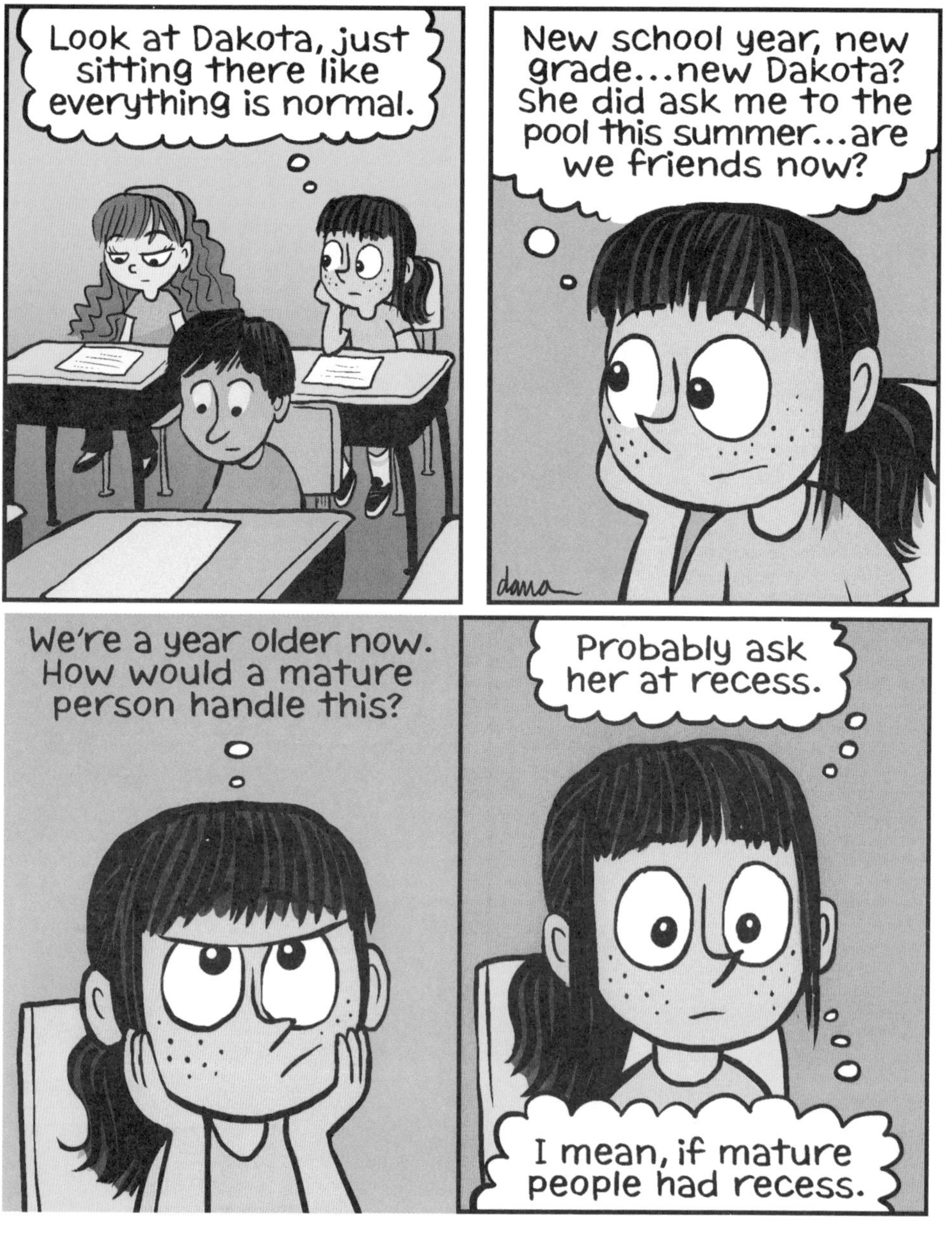

Look at Dakota, just sitting there like everything is normal.
New school year, new grade...new Dakota? She did ask me to the pool this summer...are we friends now?
dana
We're a year older now. How would a mature person handle this?
Probably ask her at recess.
I mean, if mature people had recess.

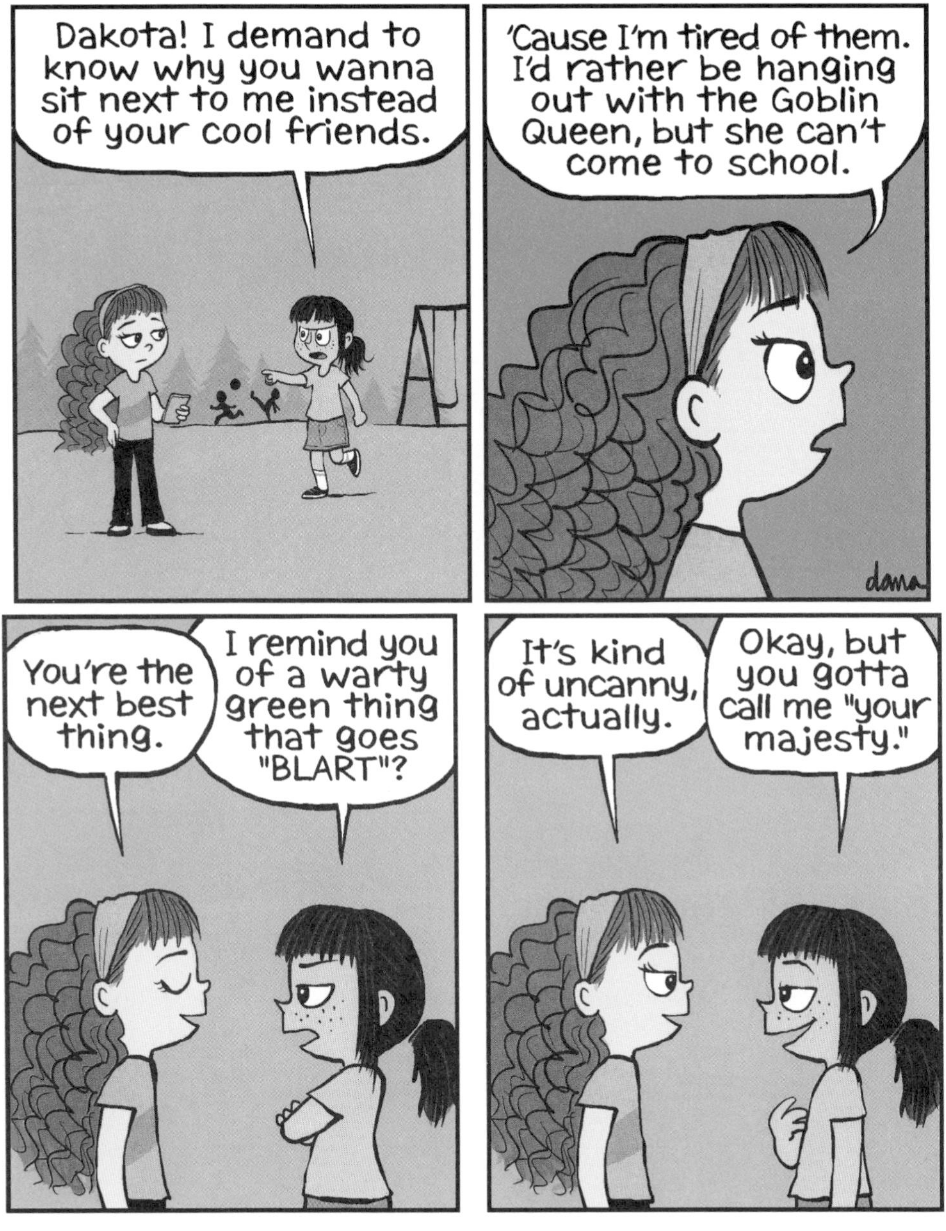
Dakota! I demand to know why you wanna sit next to me instead of your cool friends.
'Cause I'm tired of them. I'd rather be hanging out with the Goblin Queen, but she can't come to school.
dana
You're the next best thing.
I remind you of a warty green thing that goes "BLART"?
It's kind of uncanny, actually.
Okay, but you gotta call me "your majesty."

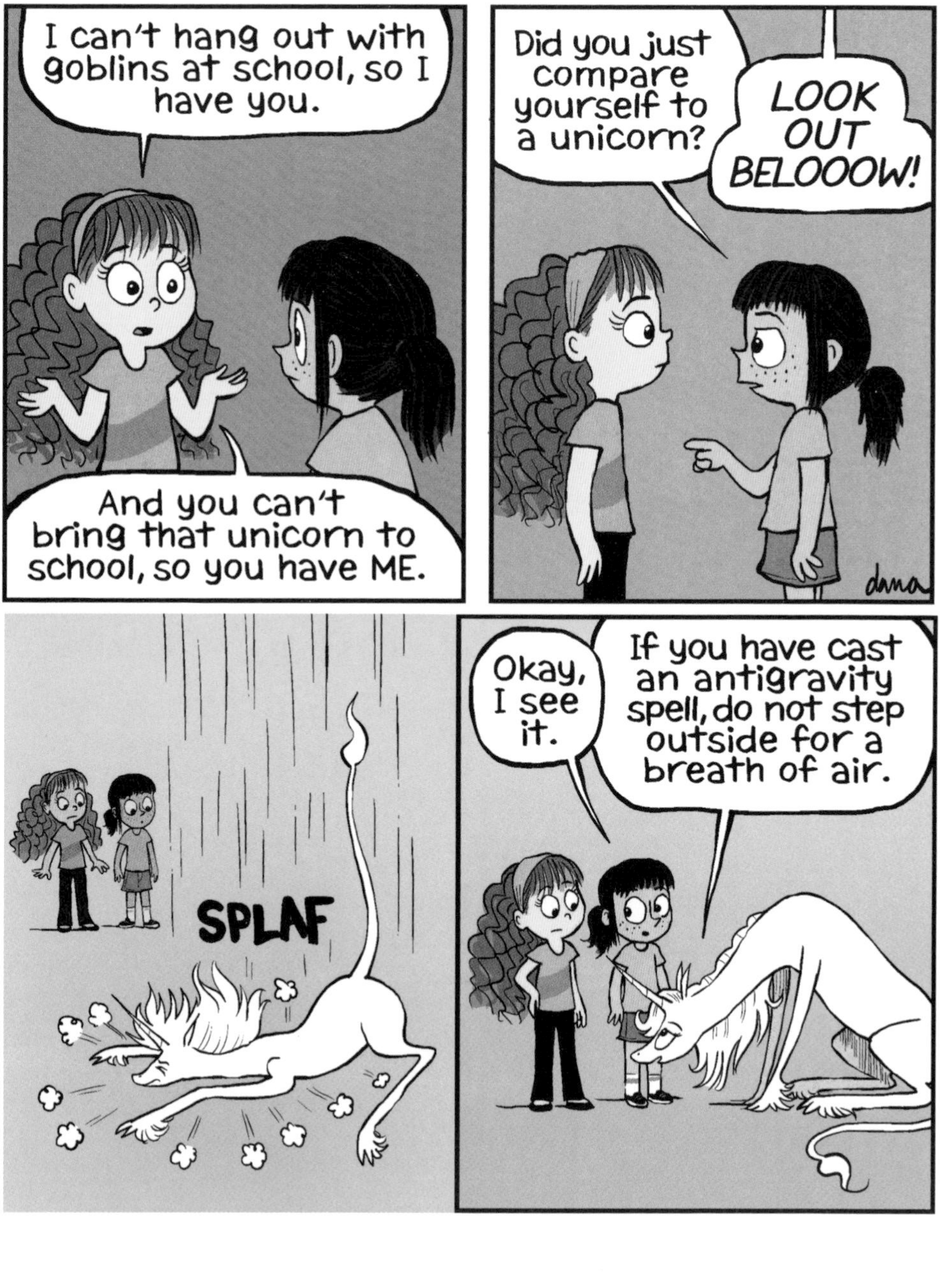
I can't hang out with goblins at school, so I have you.
And you can't bring that unicorn to school, so you have ME.
Did you just compare yourself to a unicorn?
LOOK OUT BELOOOW!
dana
SPLAF
Okay, I see it.
If you have cast an antigravity spell, do not step outside for a breath of air.

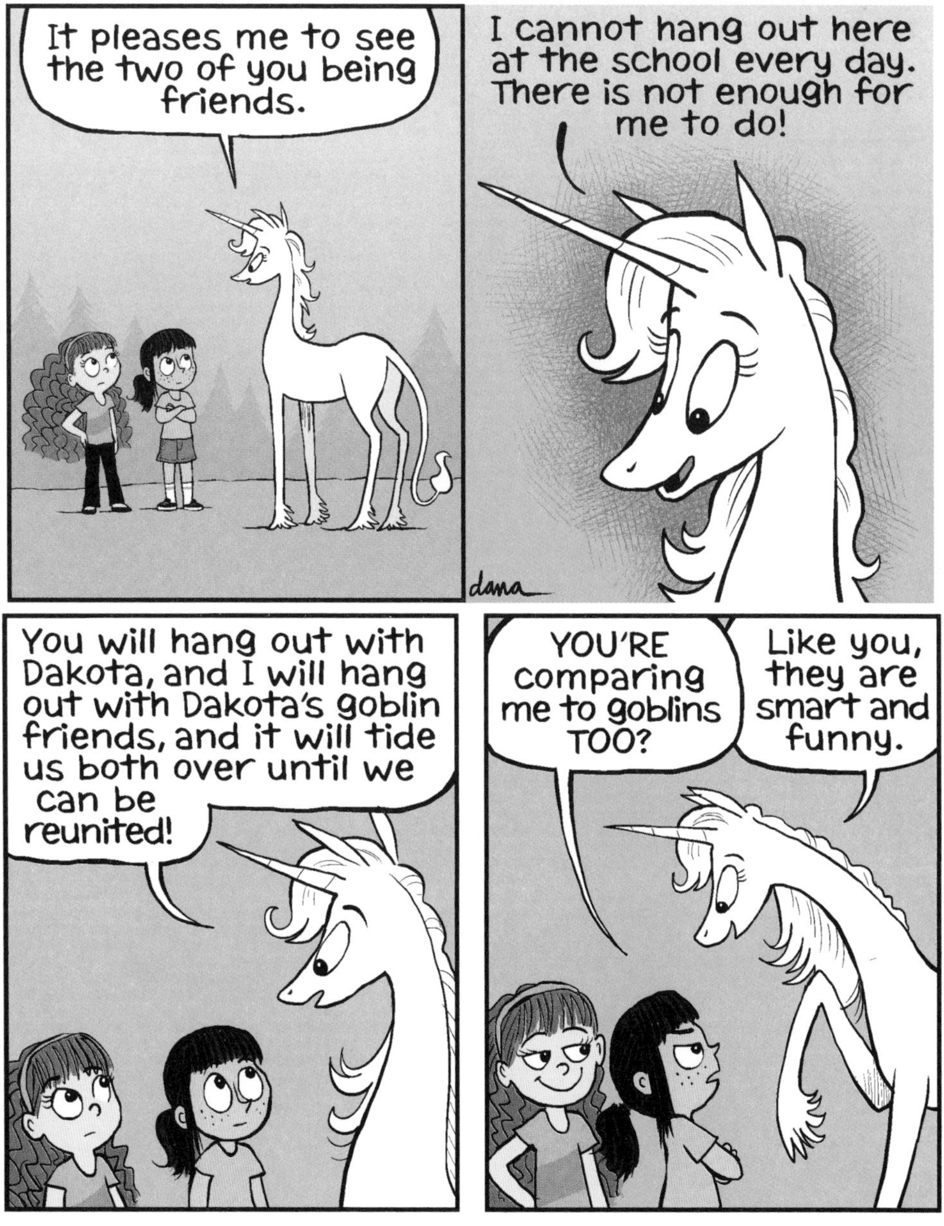
It pleases me to see the two of you being friends.
I cannot hang out here at the school every day. There is not enough for me to do!
dana
You will hang out with Dakota, and I will hang out with Dakota's goblin friends, and it will tide us both over until we can be reunited!
YOU'RE comparing me to goblins TOO?
Like you, they are smart and funny.

See you, Marigold!
Have a good day at school!
MAGIC CREATURE KARAOKE
dana

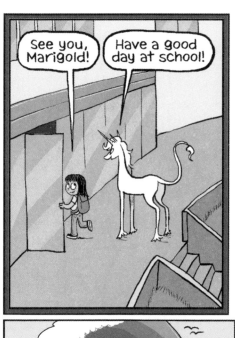

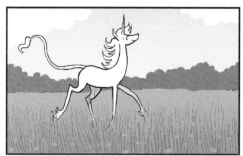

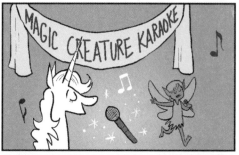

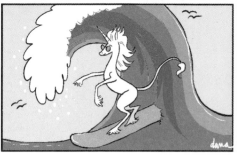

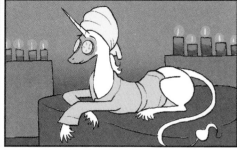

Woo! What a day. How was yours?
Average.

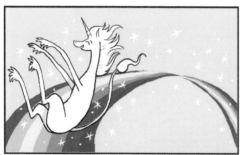

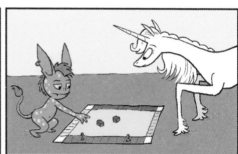

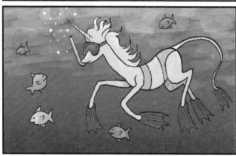

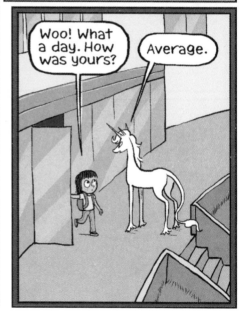

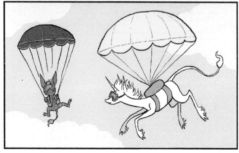

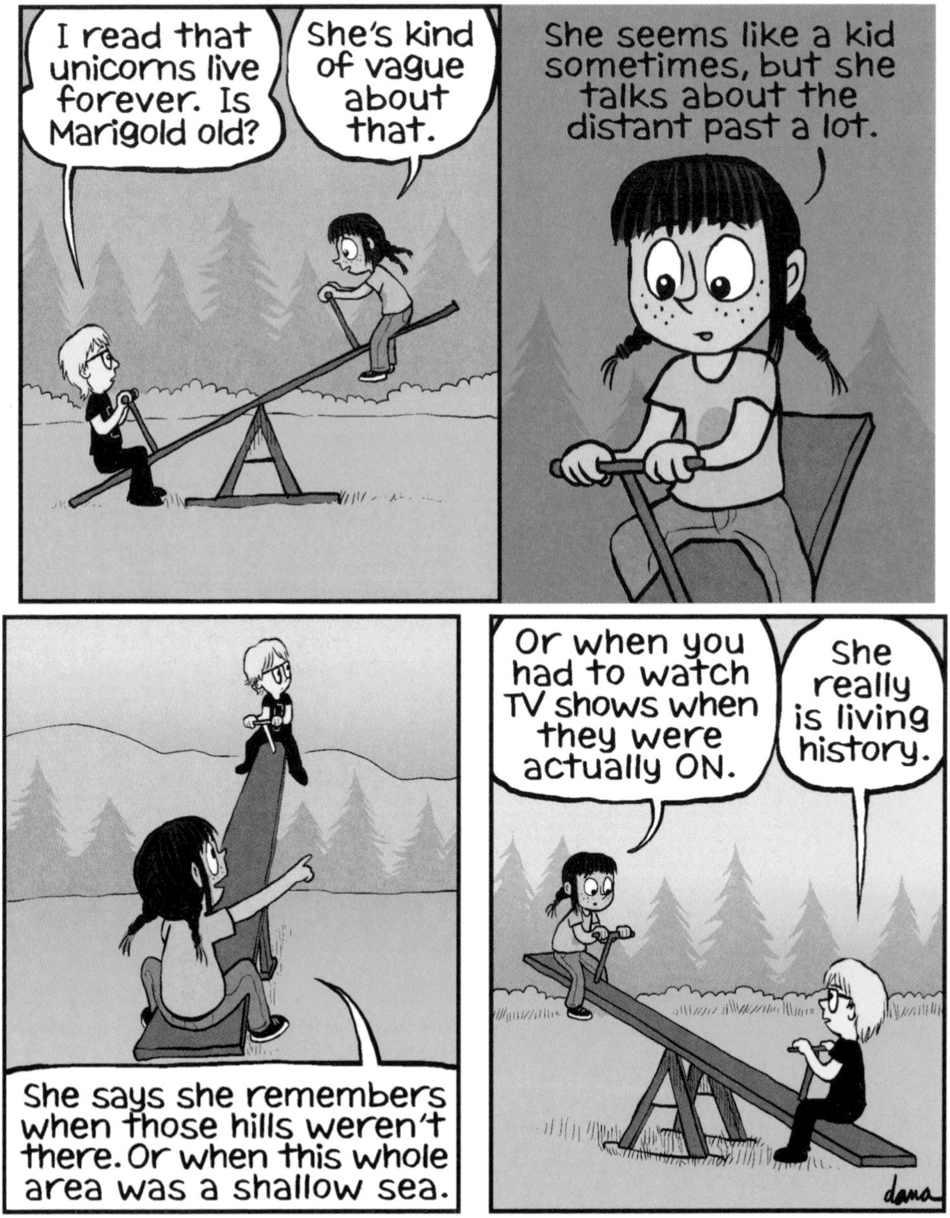
I read that unicorns live forever. Is Marigold old?
She's kind of vague about that.
She seems like a kid sometimes, but she talks about the distant past a lot.
She says she remembers when those hills weren't there. Or when this whole area was a shallow sea.
Or when you had to watch TV shows when they were actually ON.
She really is living history.
dana

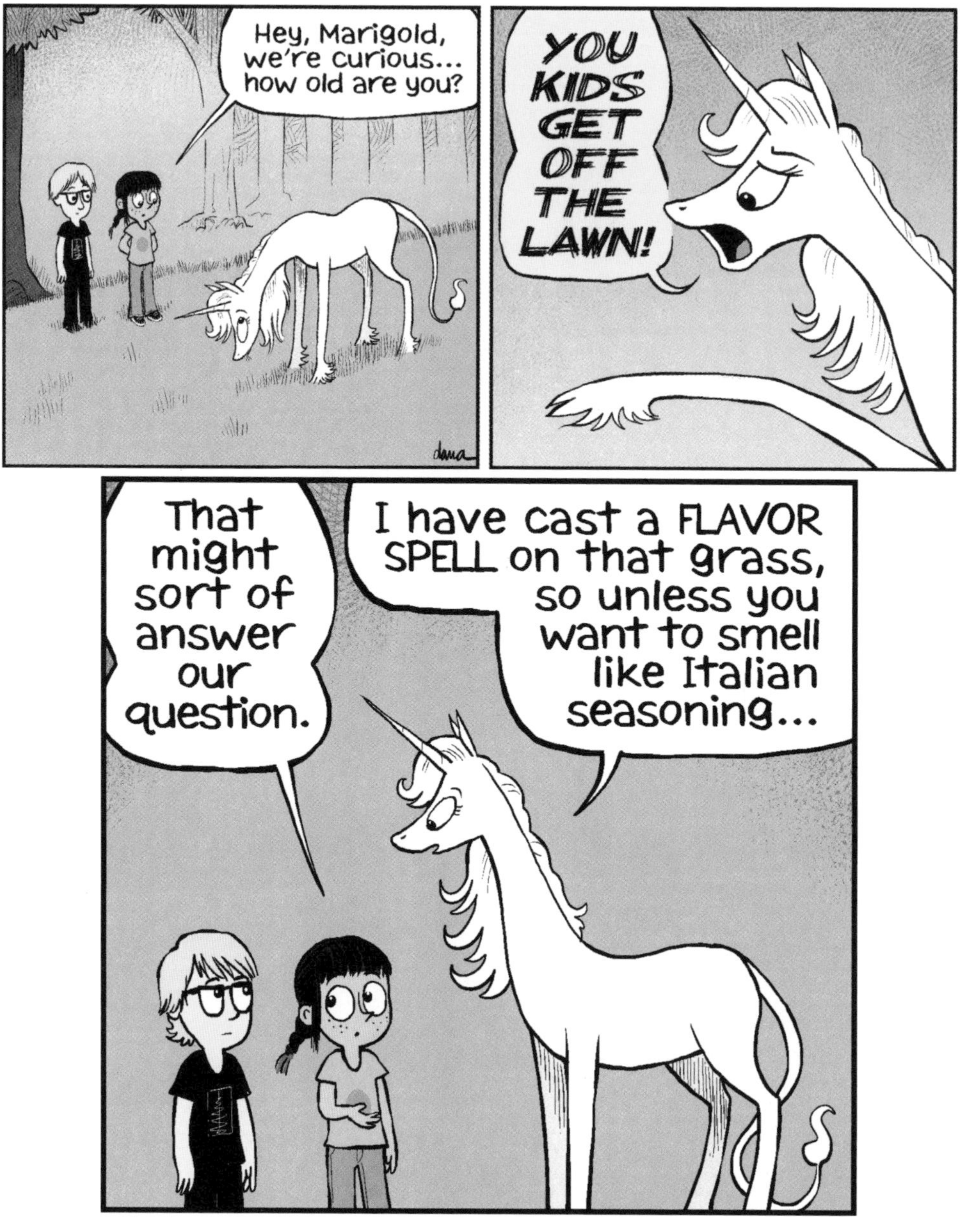
Hey, Marigold, we're curious... how old are you?
dana
YOU KIDS GET OFF THE LAWN!
That might sort of answer our question.
I have cast a FLAVOR SPELL on that grass, so unless you want to smell like Italian seasoning...

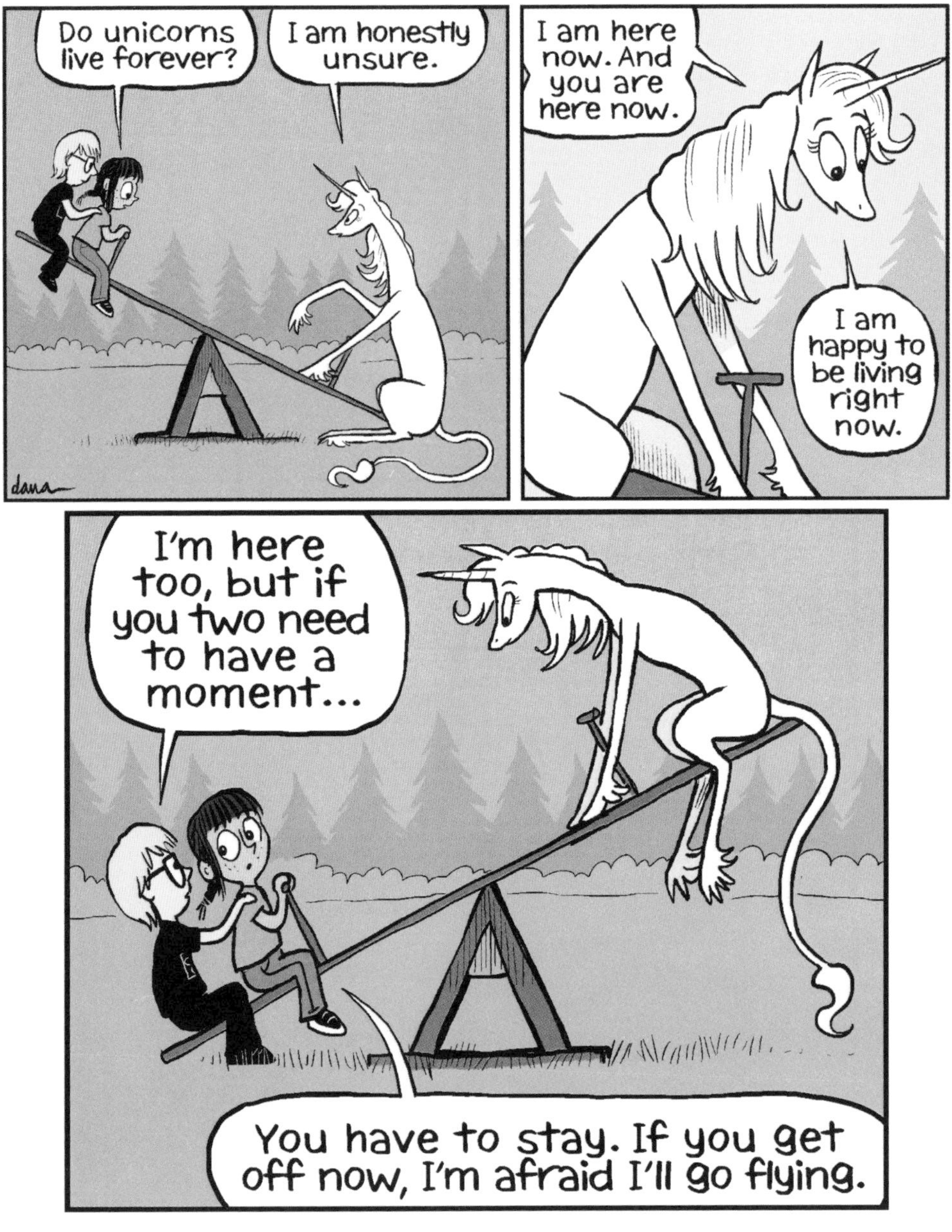
Do unicorns live forever?
I am honestly unsure.
dana
I am here now. And you are here now.
I am happy to be living right now.
I'm here too, but if you two need to have a moment...
You have to stay. If you get off now, I'm afraid I'll go flying.

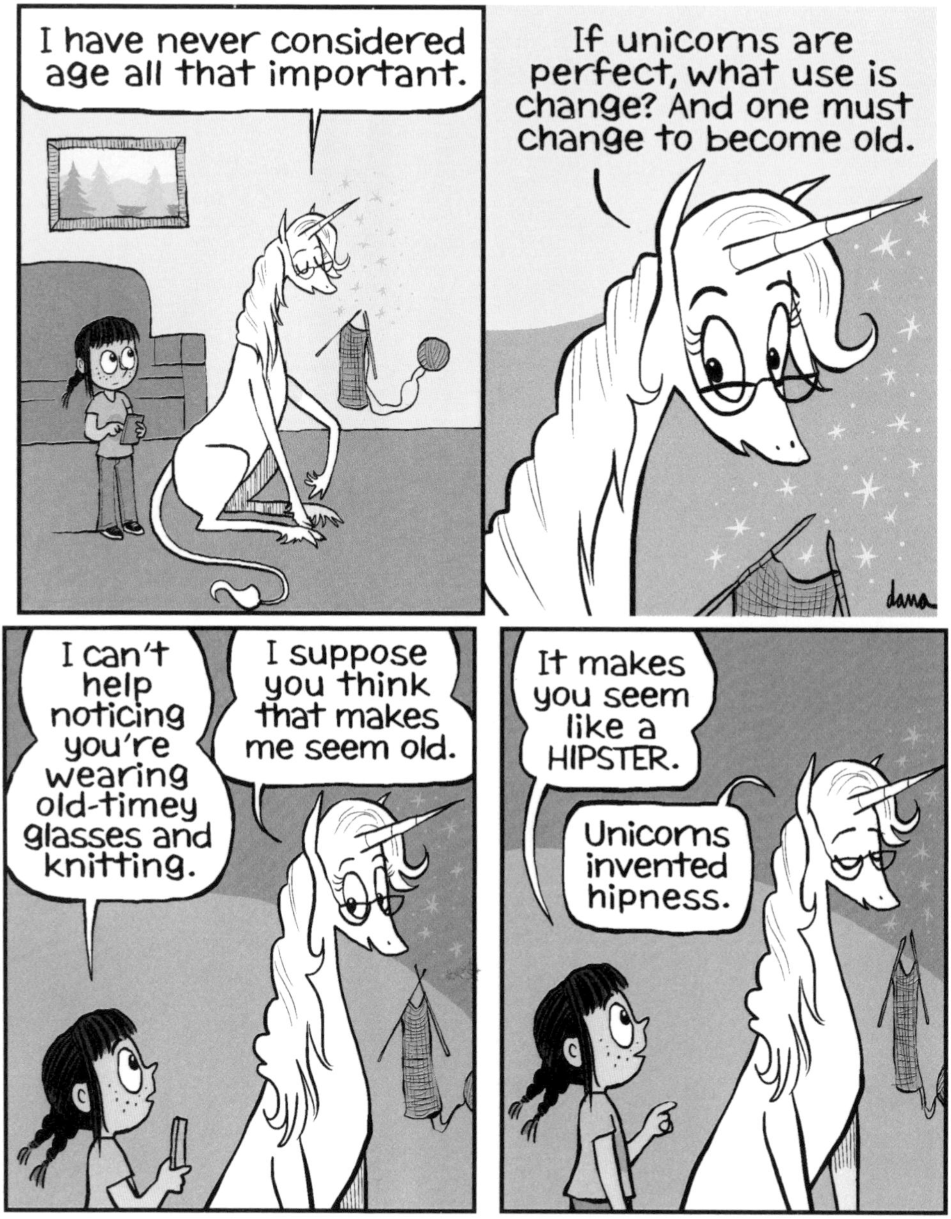
I have never considered age all that important.
If unicorns are perfect, what use is change? And one must change to become old.
dana
I can't help noticing you're wearing old-timey glasses and knitting.
I suppose you think that makes me seem old.
It makes you seem like a HIPSTER.
Unicorns invented hipness.

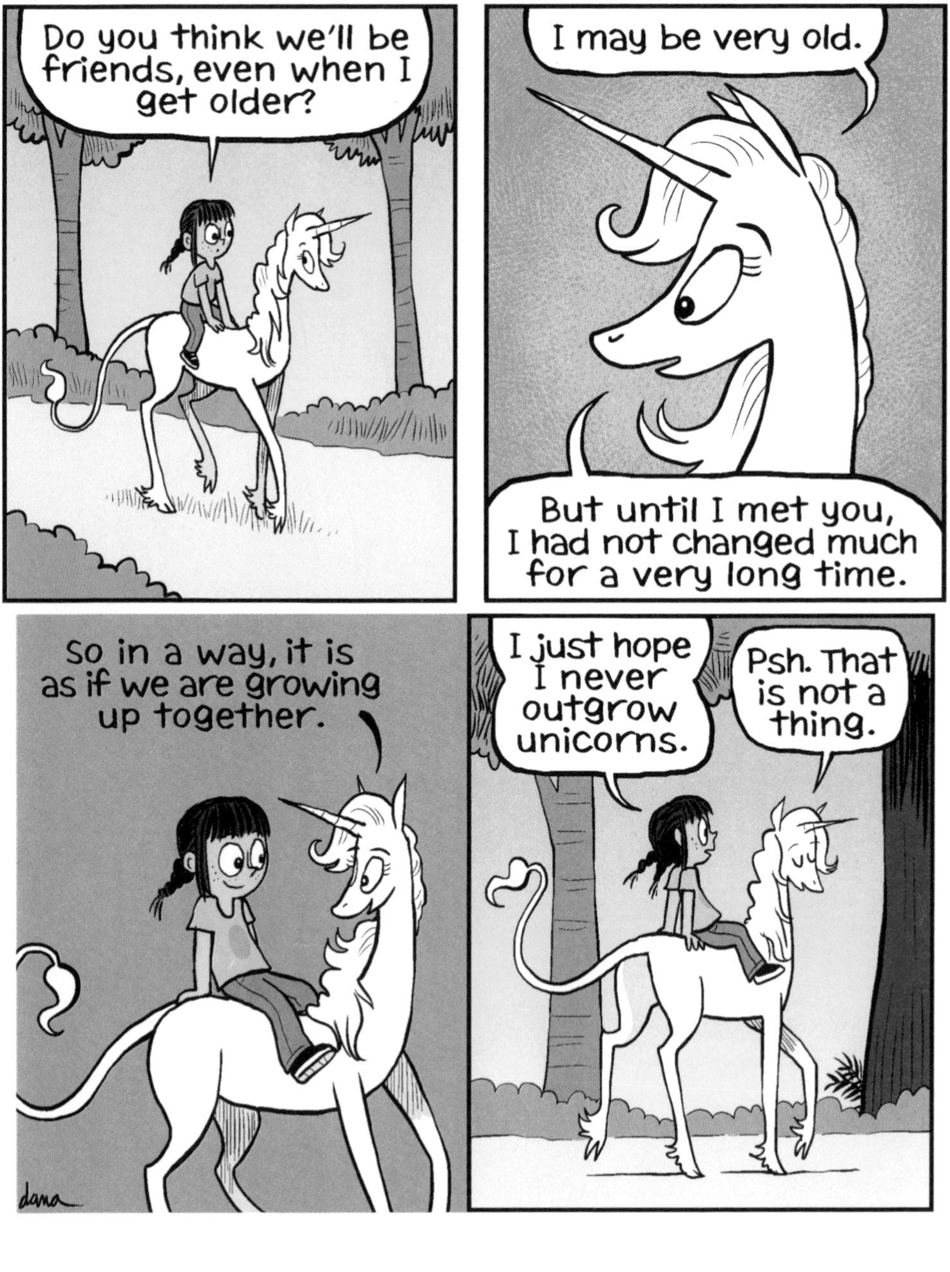
Do you think we'll be friends, even when I get older?
I may be very old.
But until I met you, I had not changed much for a very long time.
So in a way, it is as if we are growing up together.
I just hope I never outgrow unicorns.
Psh. That is not a thing.
dana

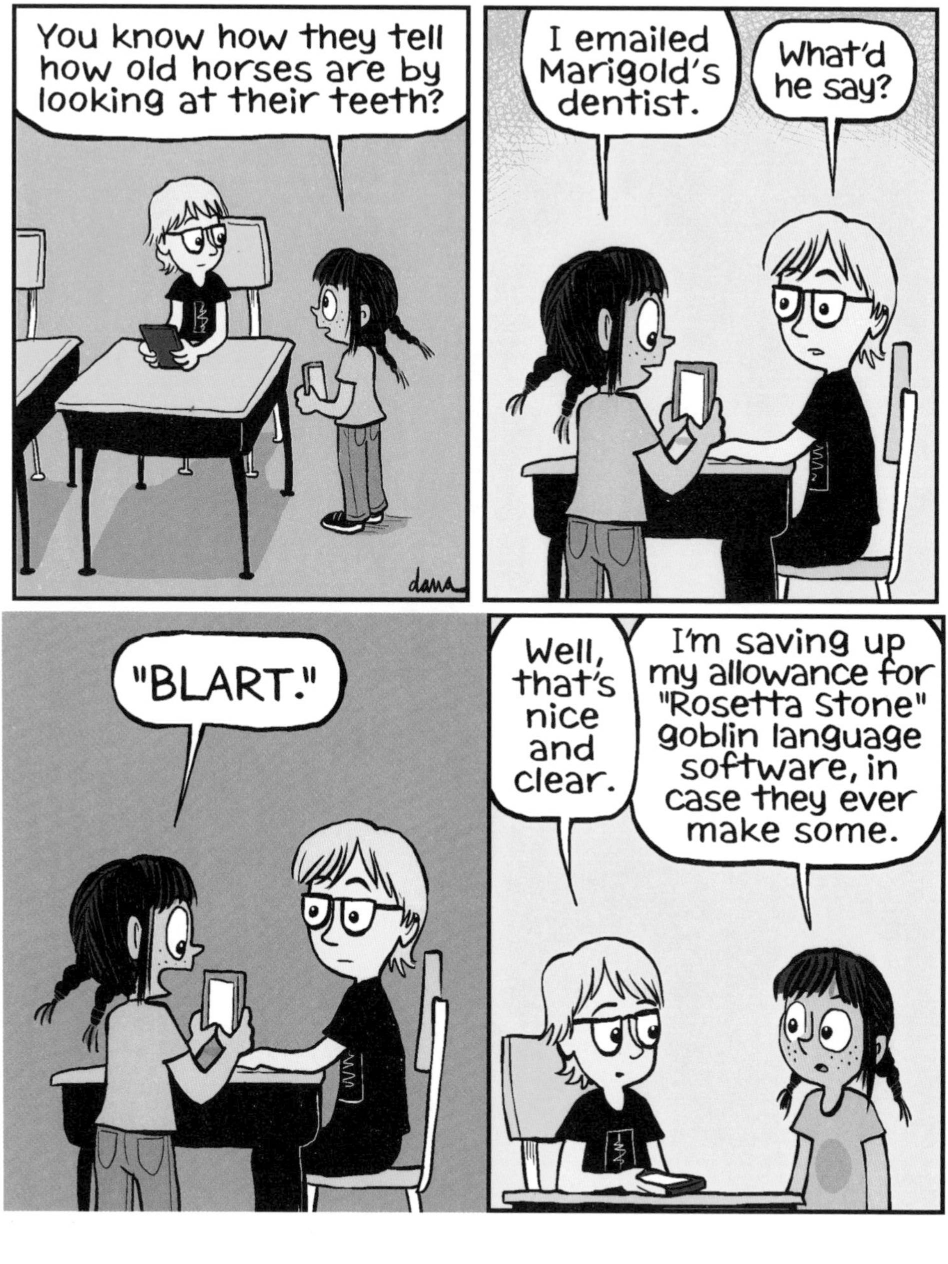

You know how they tell how old horses are by looking at their teeth?
I emailed Marigold's dentist.
What'd he say?
"BLART."
Well, that's nice and clear.
I'm saving up my allowance for "Rosetta Stone" goblin language software, in case they ever make some.
dana

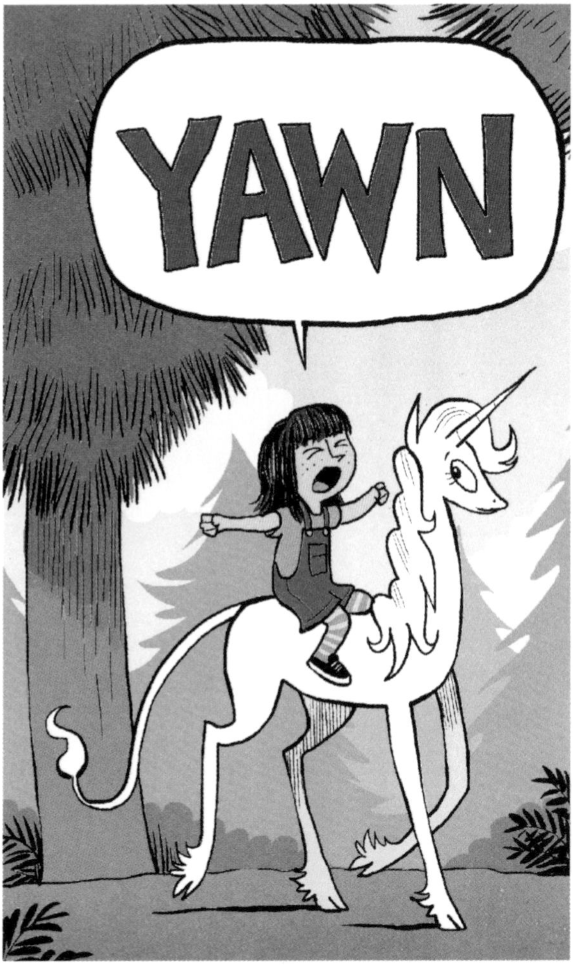
YAWN

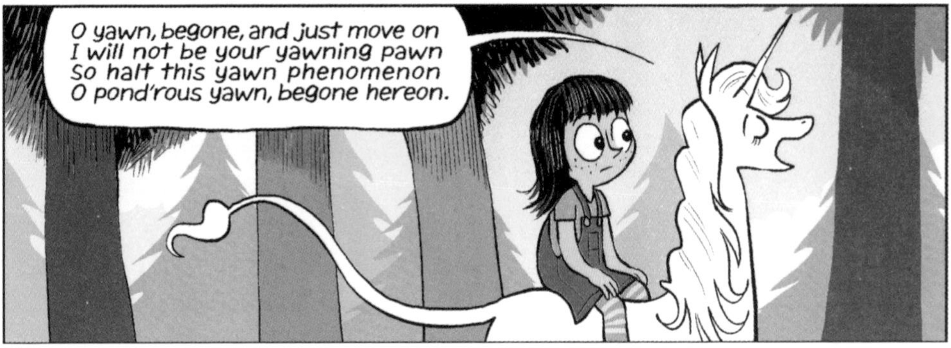
O yawn, begone, and just move on
I will not be your yawning pawn
So halt this yawn phenomenon
O pond'rous yawn, begone hereon.

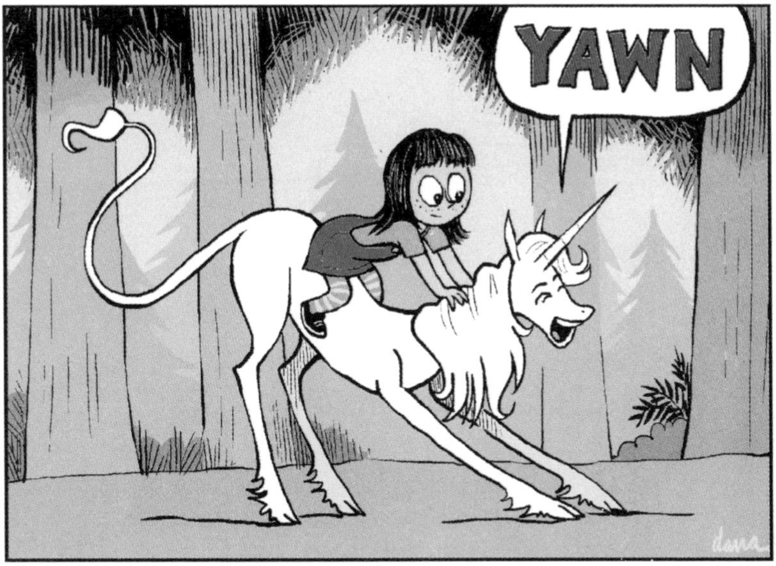
YAWN

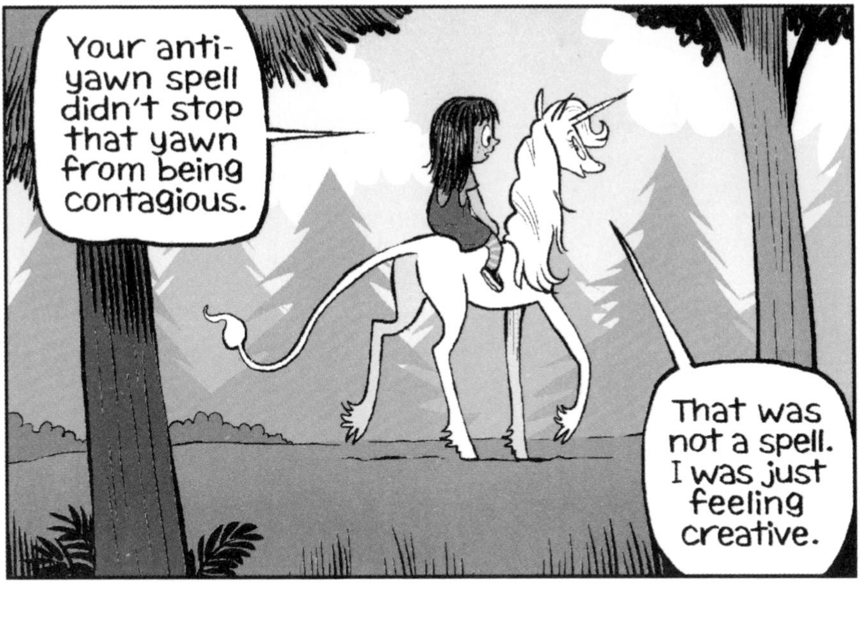
Your anti-yawn spell didn't stop that yawn from being contagious.
That was not a spell. I was just feeling creative.

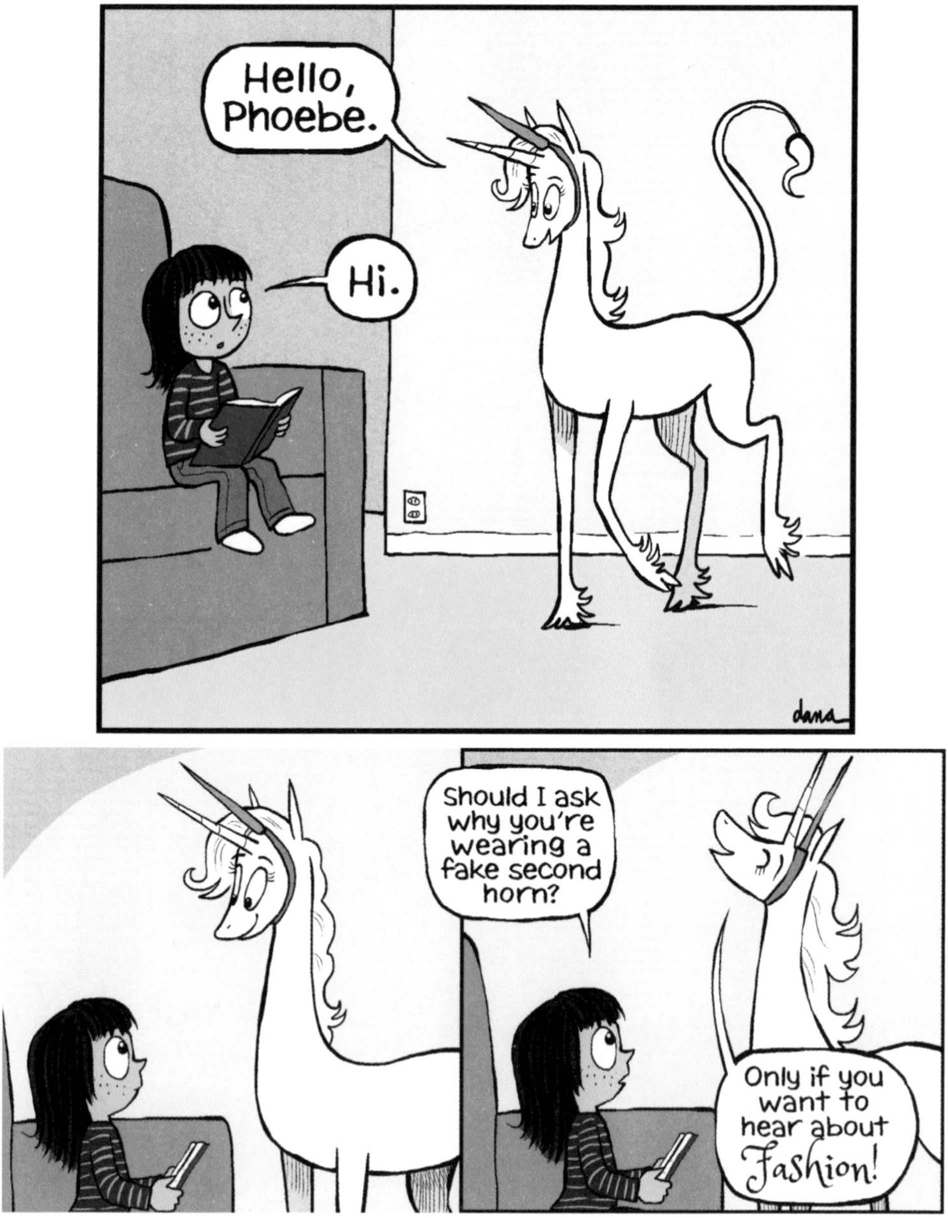
Hello, Phoebe.
Hi.
dana
Should I ask why you're wearing a fake second horn?
Only if you want to hear about Fashion!

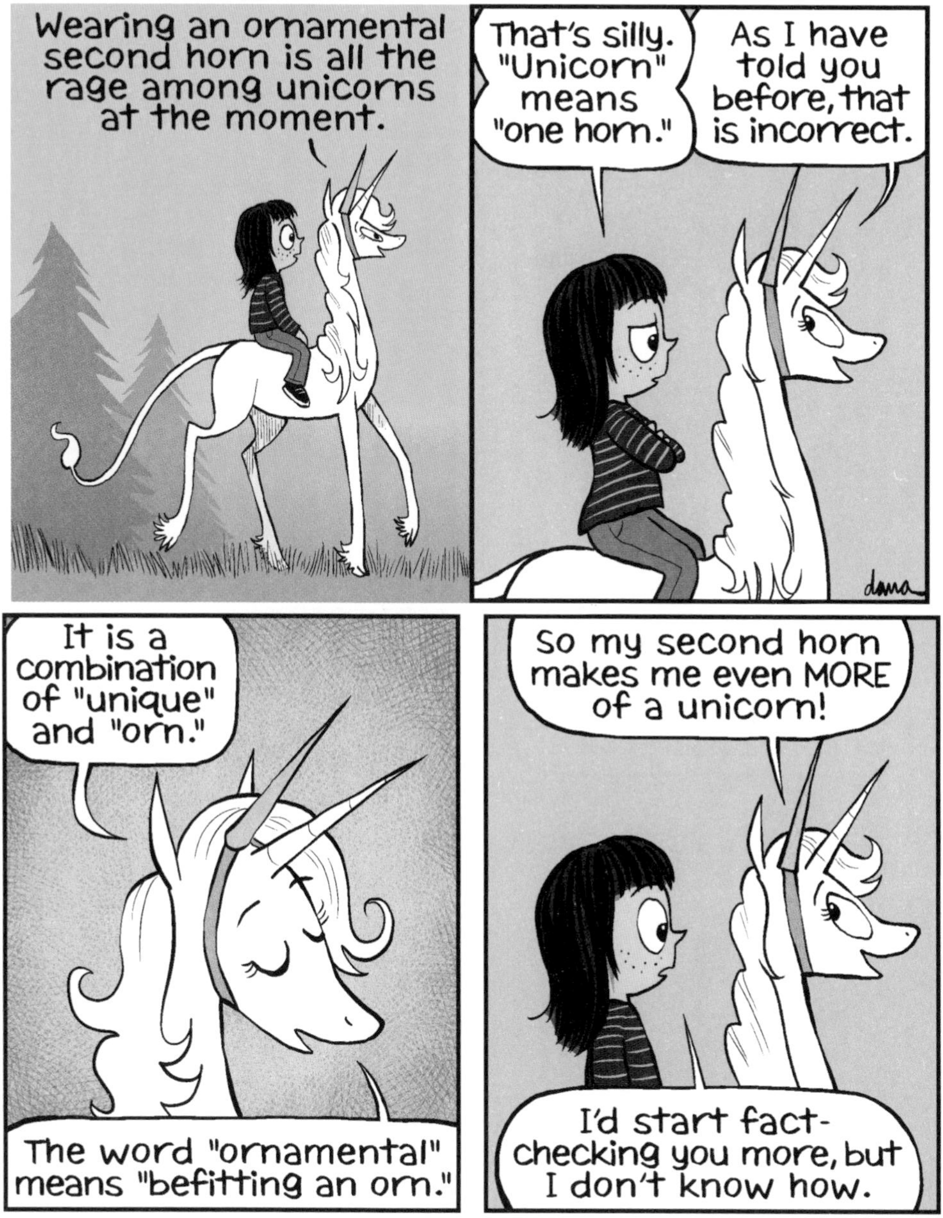
Wearing an ornamental second horn is all the rage among unicorns at the moment.
That's silly. "Unicorn" means "one horn."
As I have told you before, that is incorrect.
dana
It is a combination of "unique" and "orn."
The word "ornamental" means "befitting an orn."
So my second horn makes me even MORE of a unicorn!
I'd start fact-checking you more, but I don't know how.

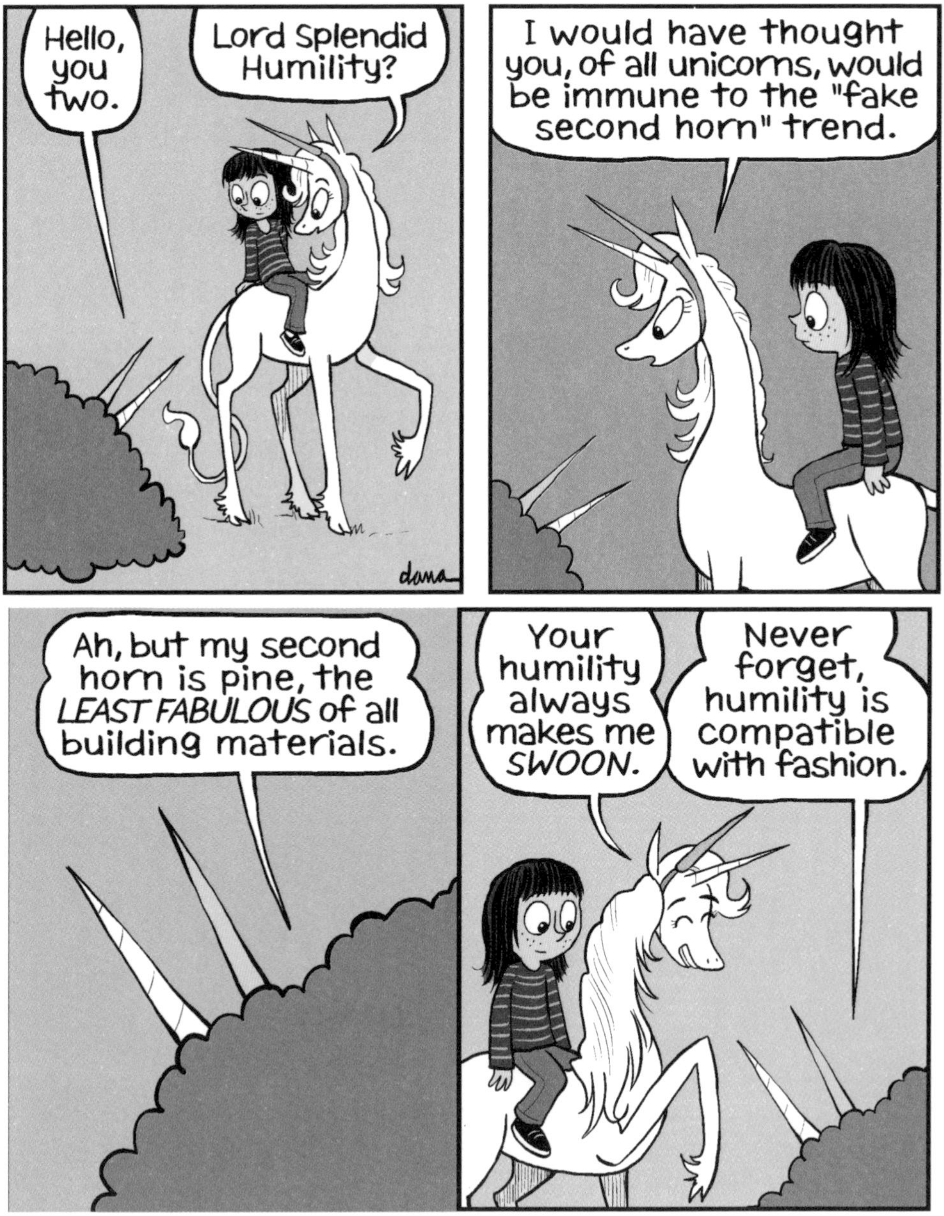
Hello, you two.
Lord Splendid Humility?
I would have thought you, of all unicorns, would be immune to the "fake second horn" trend.
Ah, but my second horn is pine, the *LEAST FABULOUS* of all building materials.
Your humility always makes me *SWOON.*
Never forget, humility is compatible with fashion.
dana

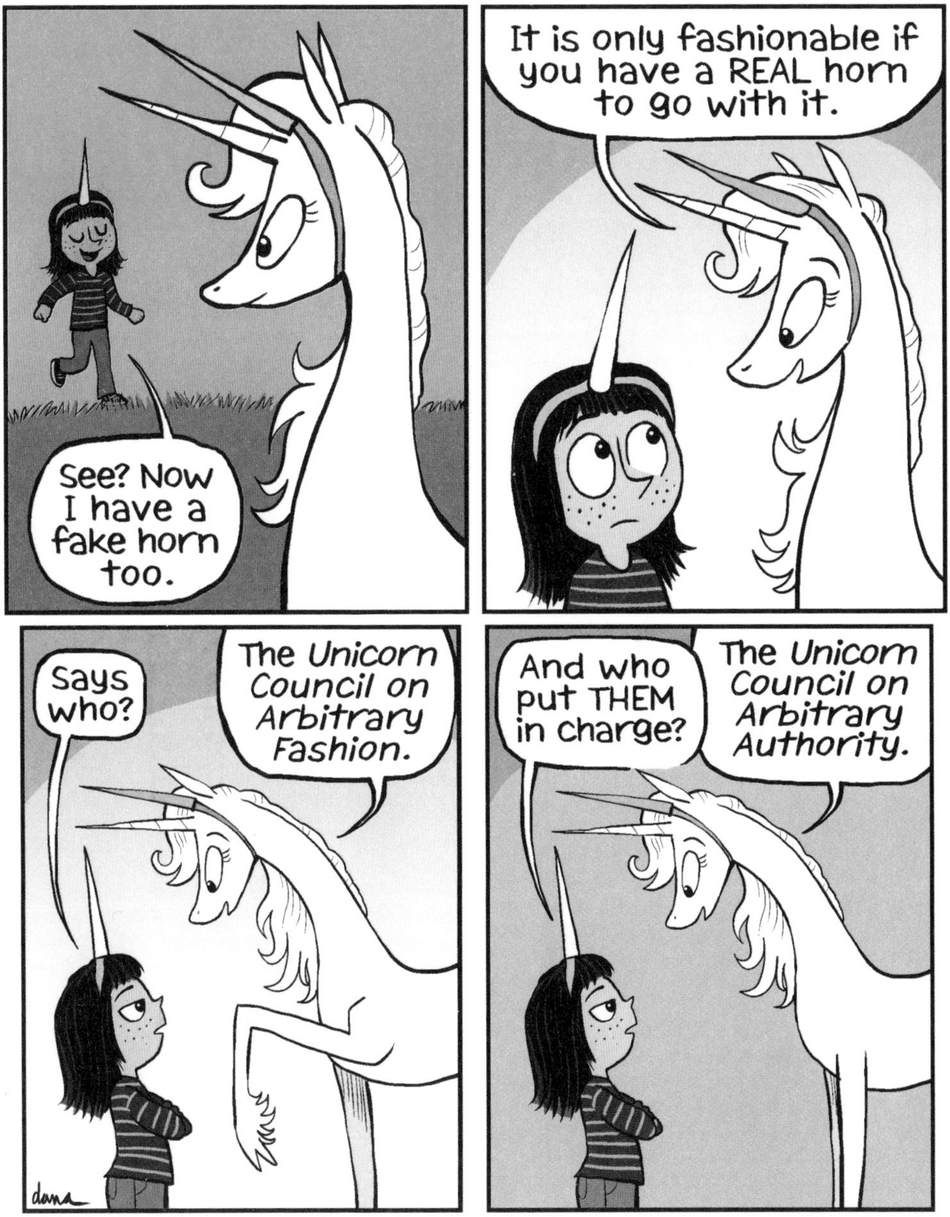
See? Now I have a fake horn too.
It is only fashionable if you have a REAL horn to go with it.
Says who?
The *Unicorn Council on Arbitrary Fashion*.
And who put THEM in charge?
The *Unicorn Council on Arbitrary Authority*.
dana

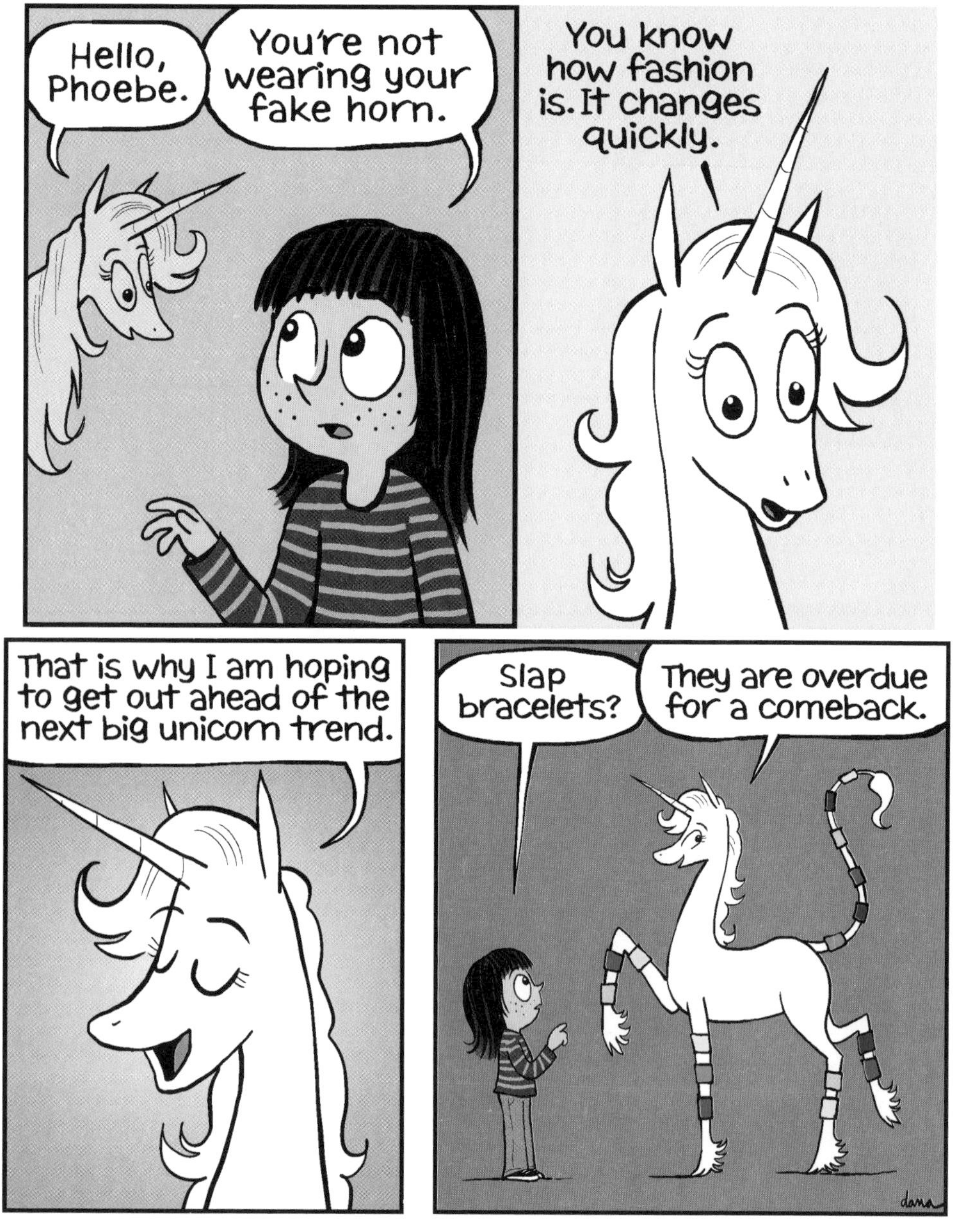

Hello, Phoebe.
You're not wearing your fake horn.
You know how fashion is. It changes quickly.
That is why I am hoping to get out ahead of the next big unicorn trend.
Slap bracelets?
They are overdue for a comeback.
dana

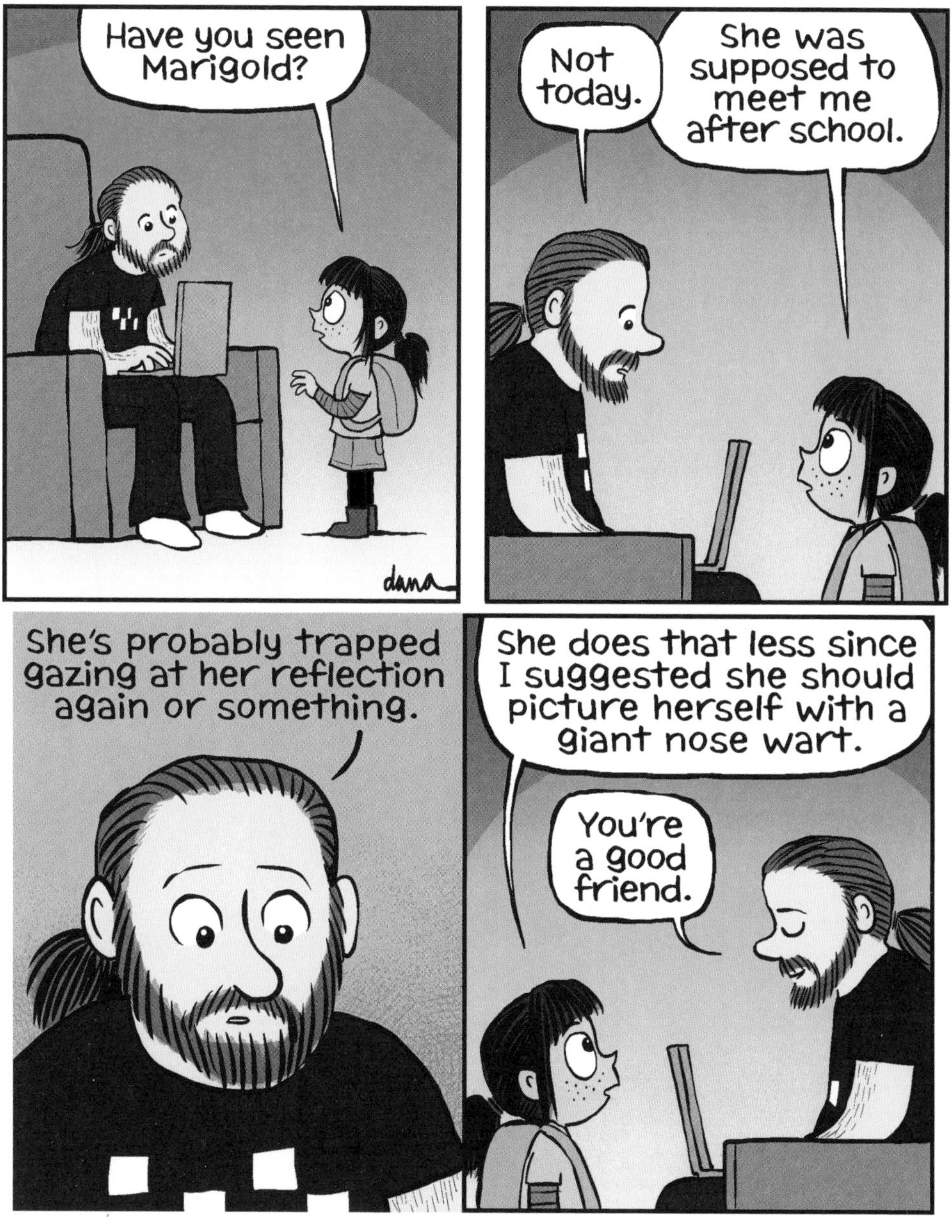
Have you seen Marigold?
Not today.
She was supposed to meet me after school.
She's probably trapped gazing at her reflection again or something.
She does that less since I suggested she should picture herself with a giant nose wart.
You're a good friend.
dana

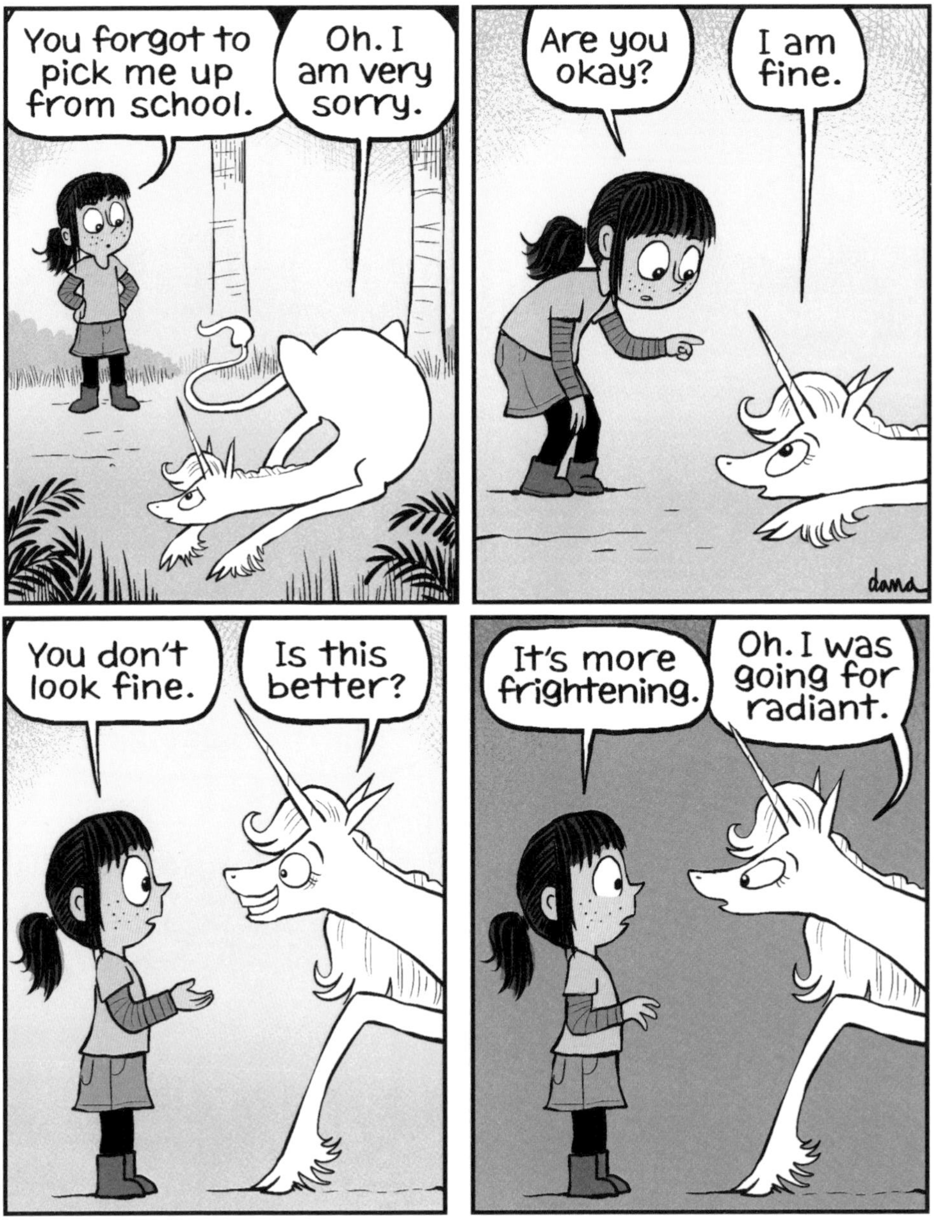
You forgot to pick me up from school.
Oh. I am very sorry.
Are you okay?
I am fine.
dana
You don't look fine.
Is this better?
It's more frightening.
Oh. I was going for radiant.

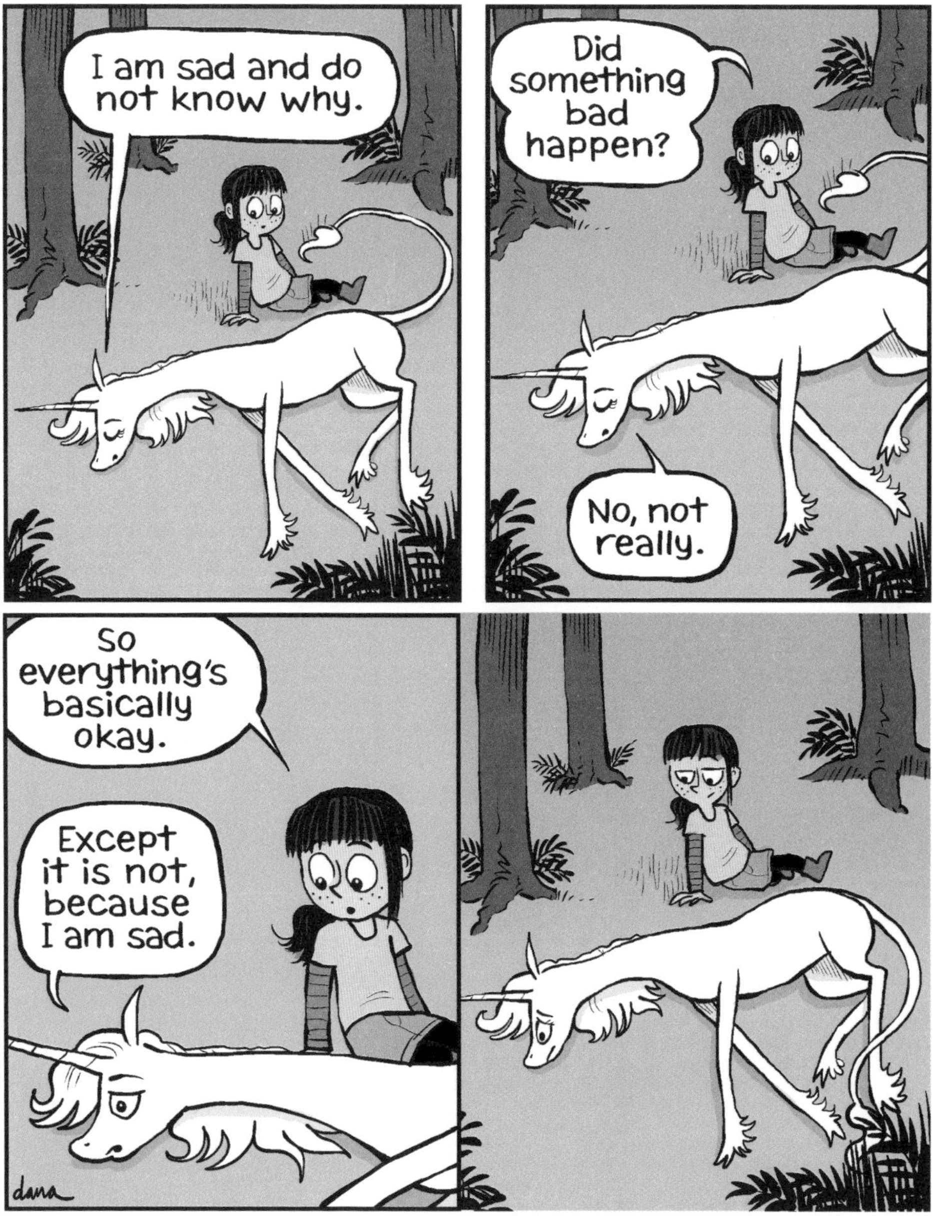
I am sad and do not know why.
Did something bad happen?
No, not really.
So everything's basically okay.
Except it is not, because I am sad.
dana

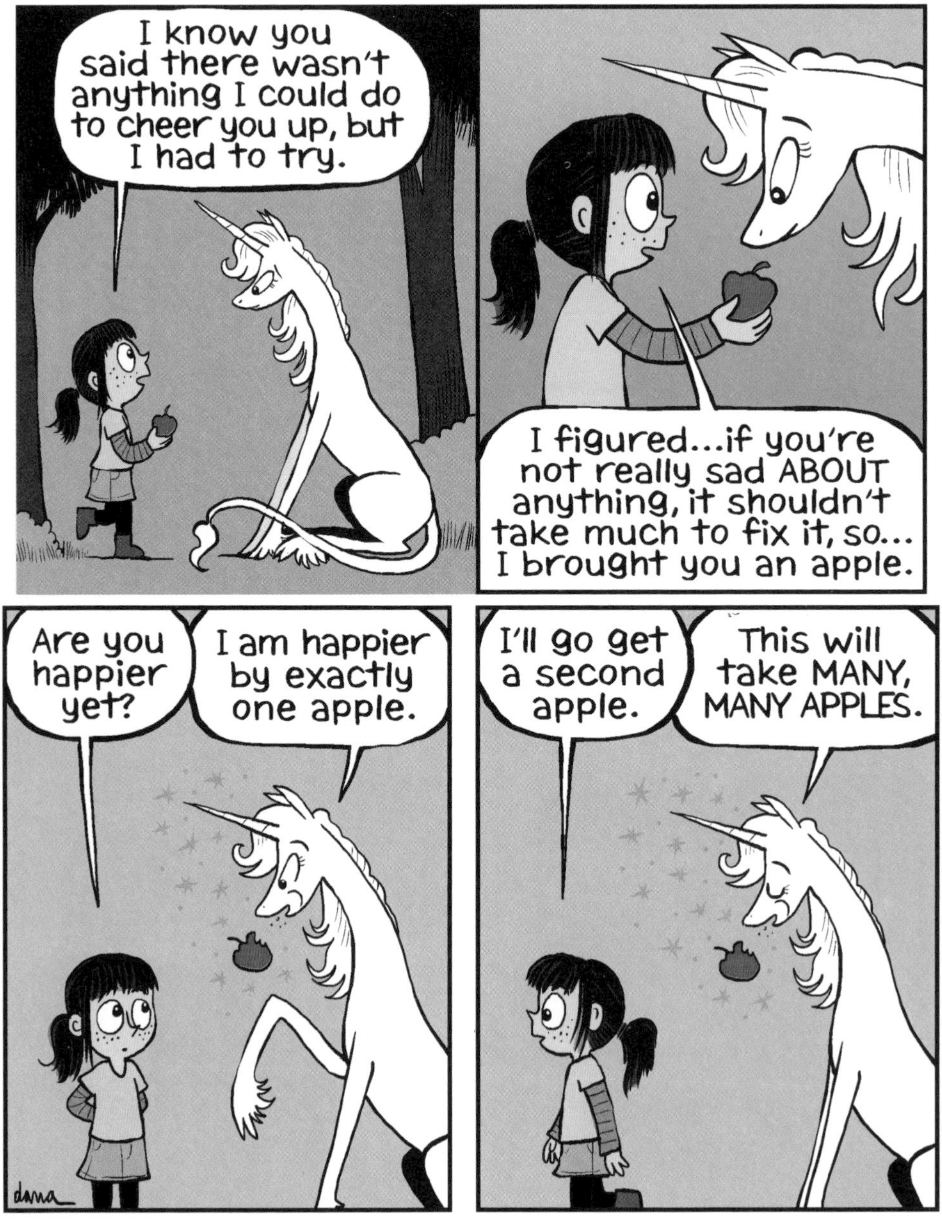
I know you said there wasn't anything I could do to cheer you up, but I had to try.
I figured...if you're not really sad ABOUT anything, it shouldn't take much to fix it, so... I brought you an apple.
Are you happier yet?
I am happier by exactly one apple.
I'll go get a second apple.
This will take MANY, MANY APPLES.
dana

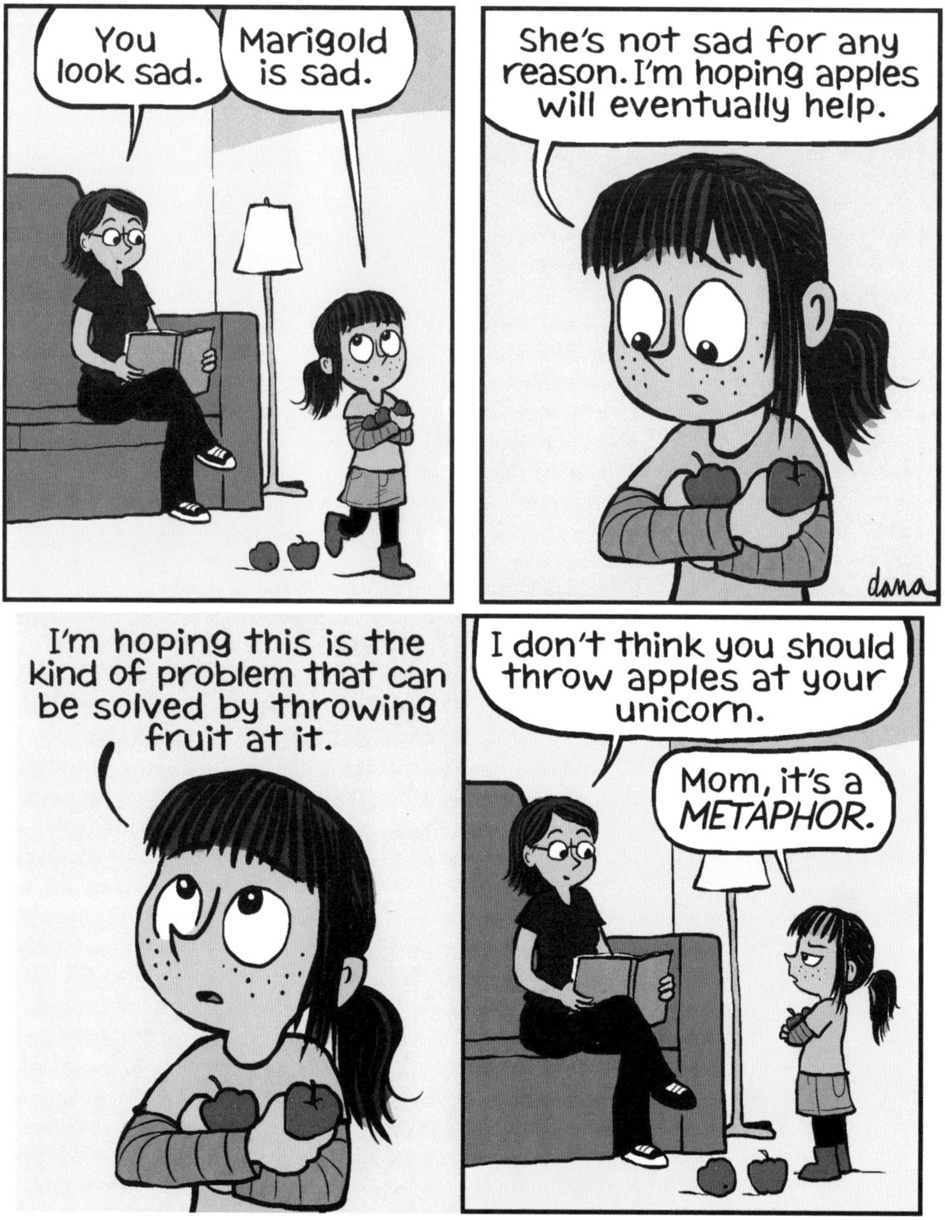
You look sad.
Marigold is sad.
She's not sad for any reason. I'm hoping apples will eventually help.
dana
I'm hoping this is the kind of problem that can be solved by throwing fruit at it.
I don't think you should throw apples at your unicorn.
Mom, it's a *METAPHOR*.

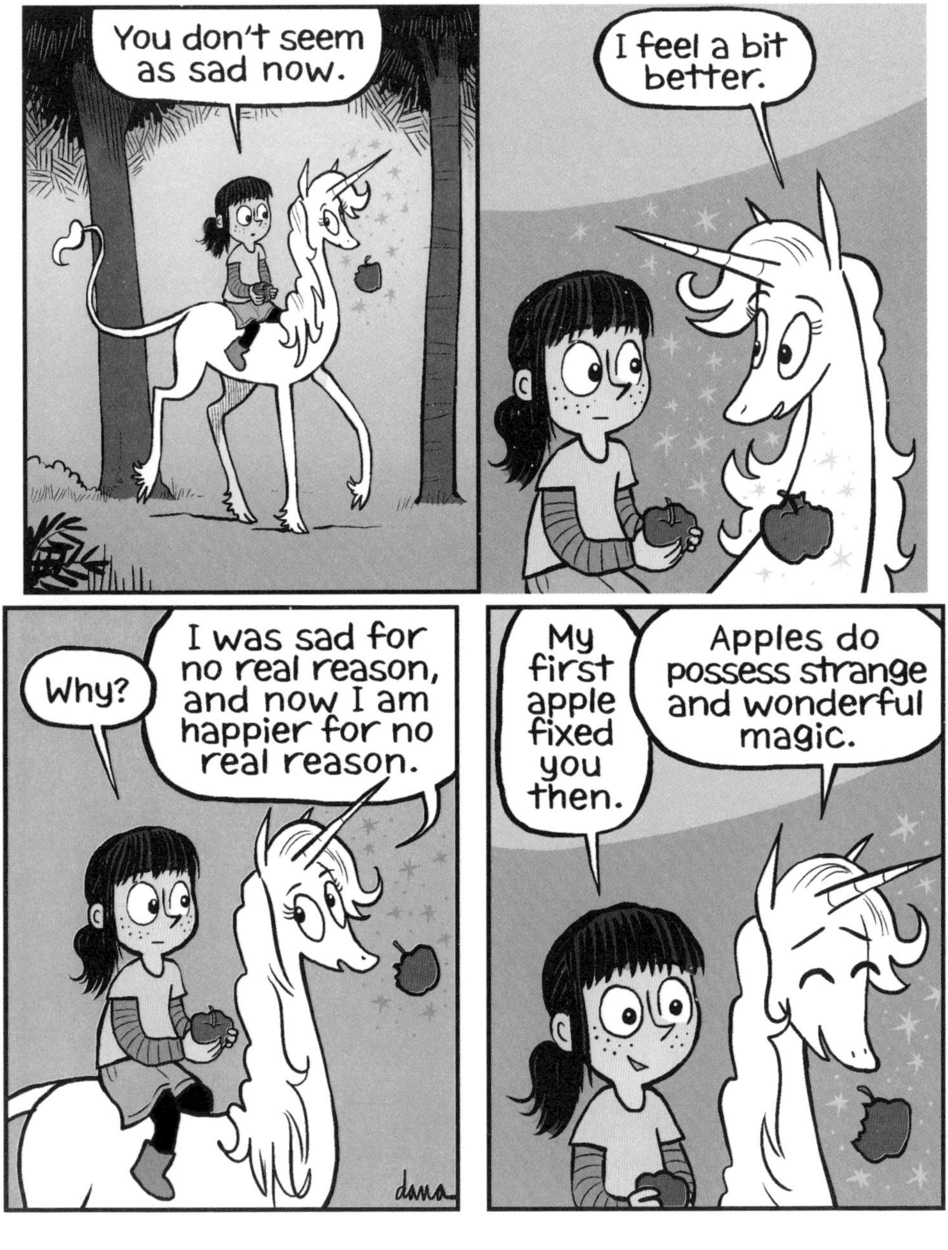
You don't seem as sad now.
I feel a bit better.
Why?
I was sad for no real reason, and now I am happier for no real reason.
My first apple fixed you then.
Apples do possess strange and wonderful magic.
dana

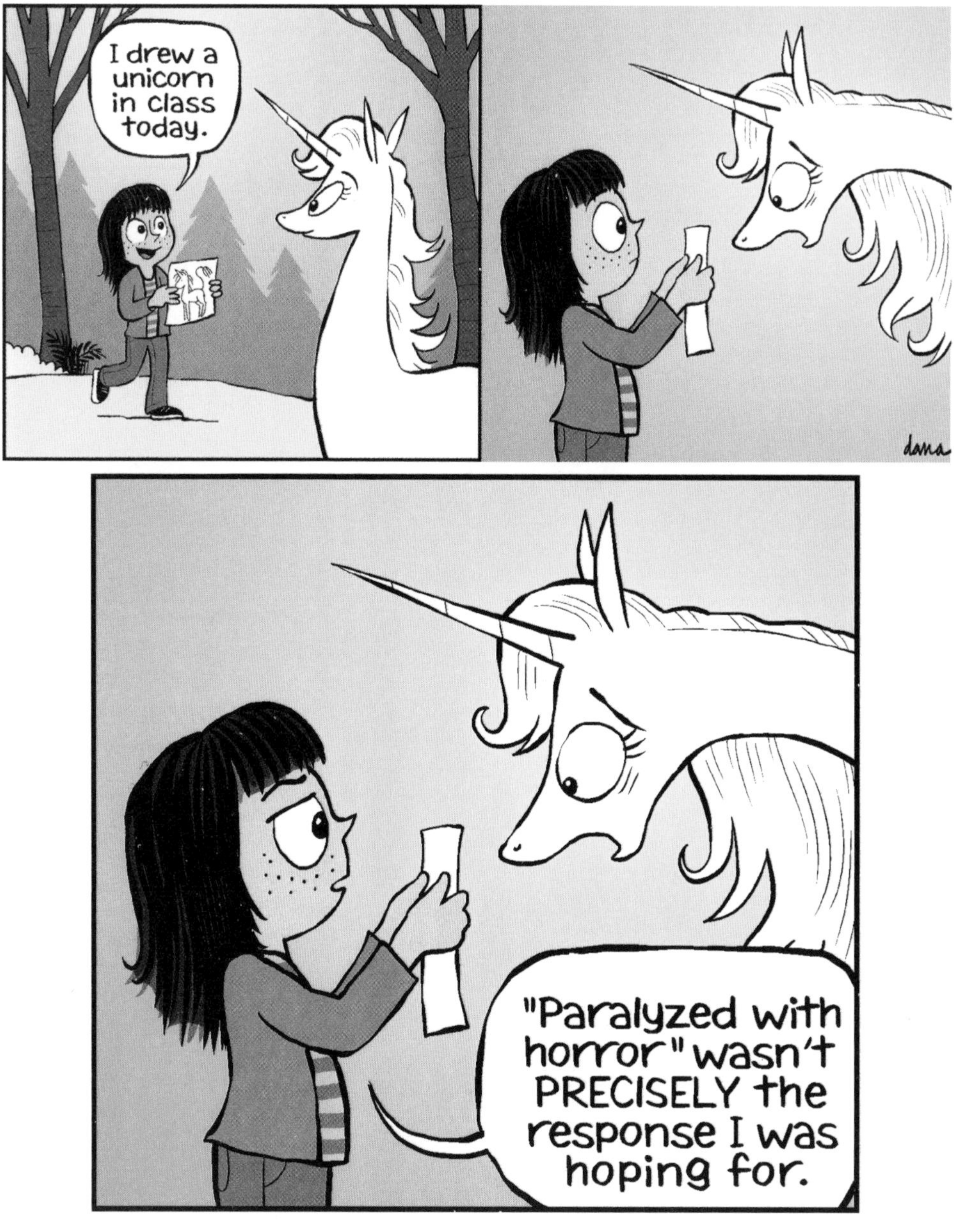
I drew a unicorn in class today.
"Paralyzed with horror" wasn't PRECISELY the response I was hoping for.
dana

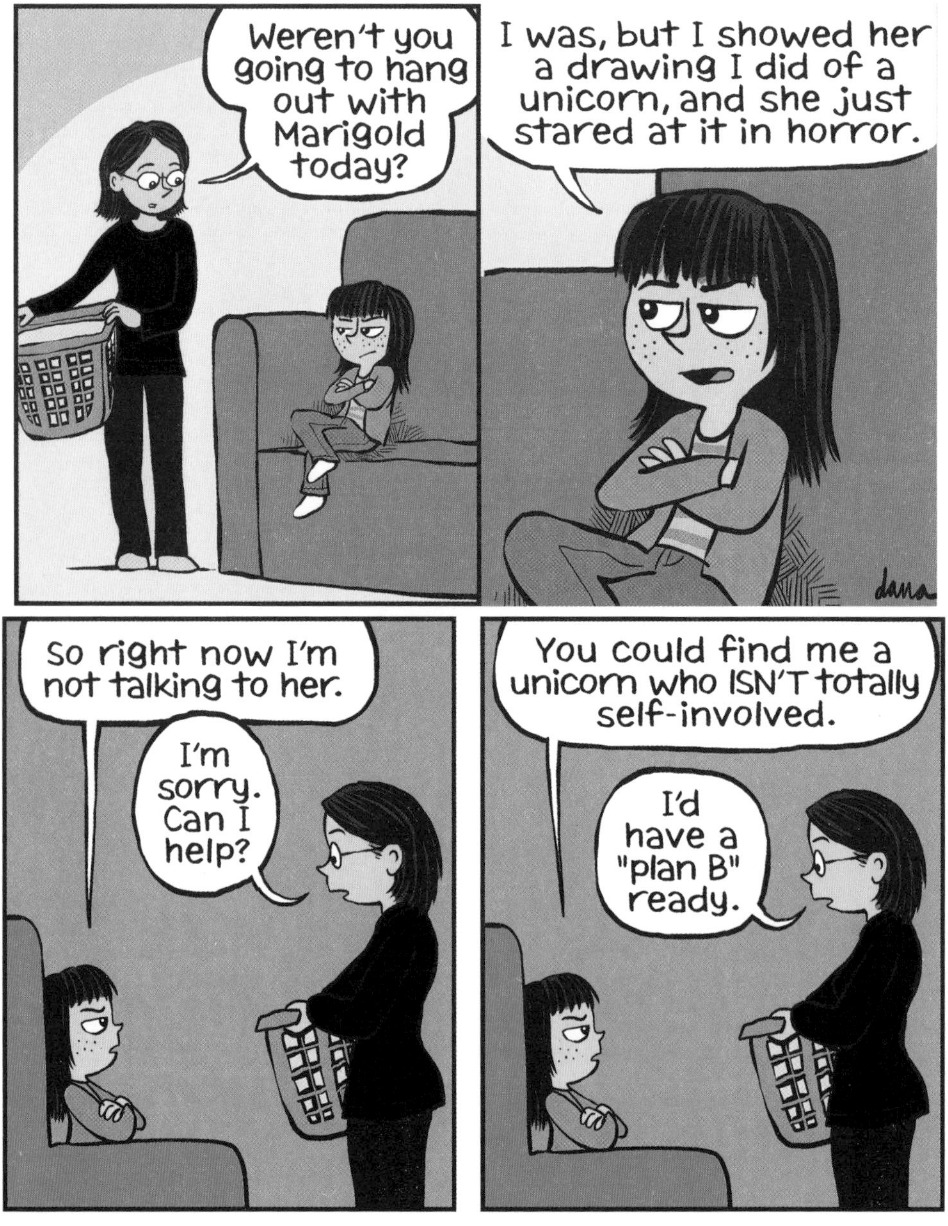
Weren't you going to hang out with Marigold today?
I was, but I showed her a drawing I did of a unicorn, and she just stared at it in horror.
dana
So right now I'm not talking to her.
I'm sorry. Can I help?
You could find me a unicorn who ISN'T totally self-involved.
I'd have a "plan B" ready.

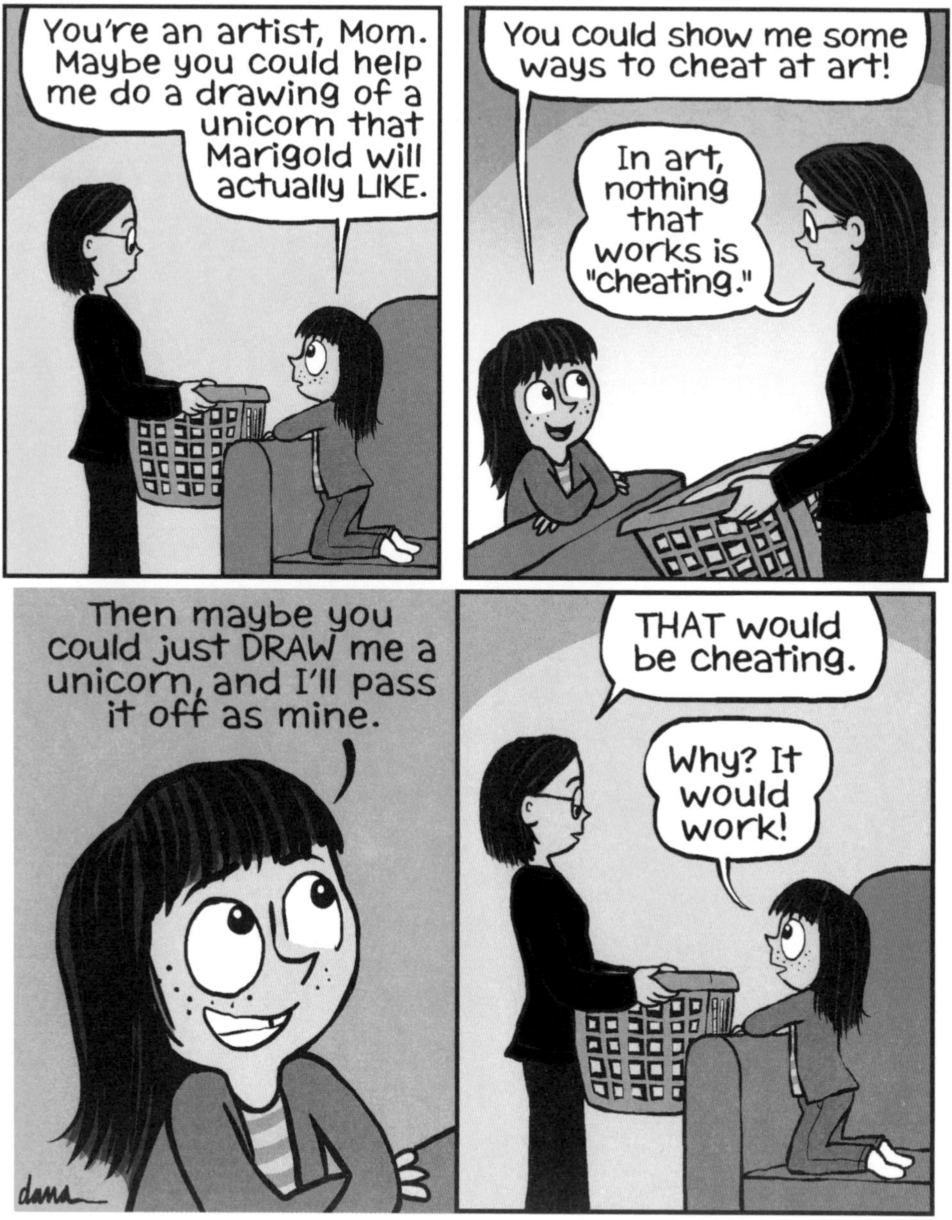
You're an artist, Mom. Maybe you could help me do a drawing of a unicorn that Marigold will actually LIKE.
You could show me some ways to cheat at art!
In art, nothing that works is "cheating."
Then maybe you could just DRAW me a unicorn, and I'll pass it off as mine.
dana
THAT would be cheating.
Why? It would work!

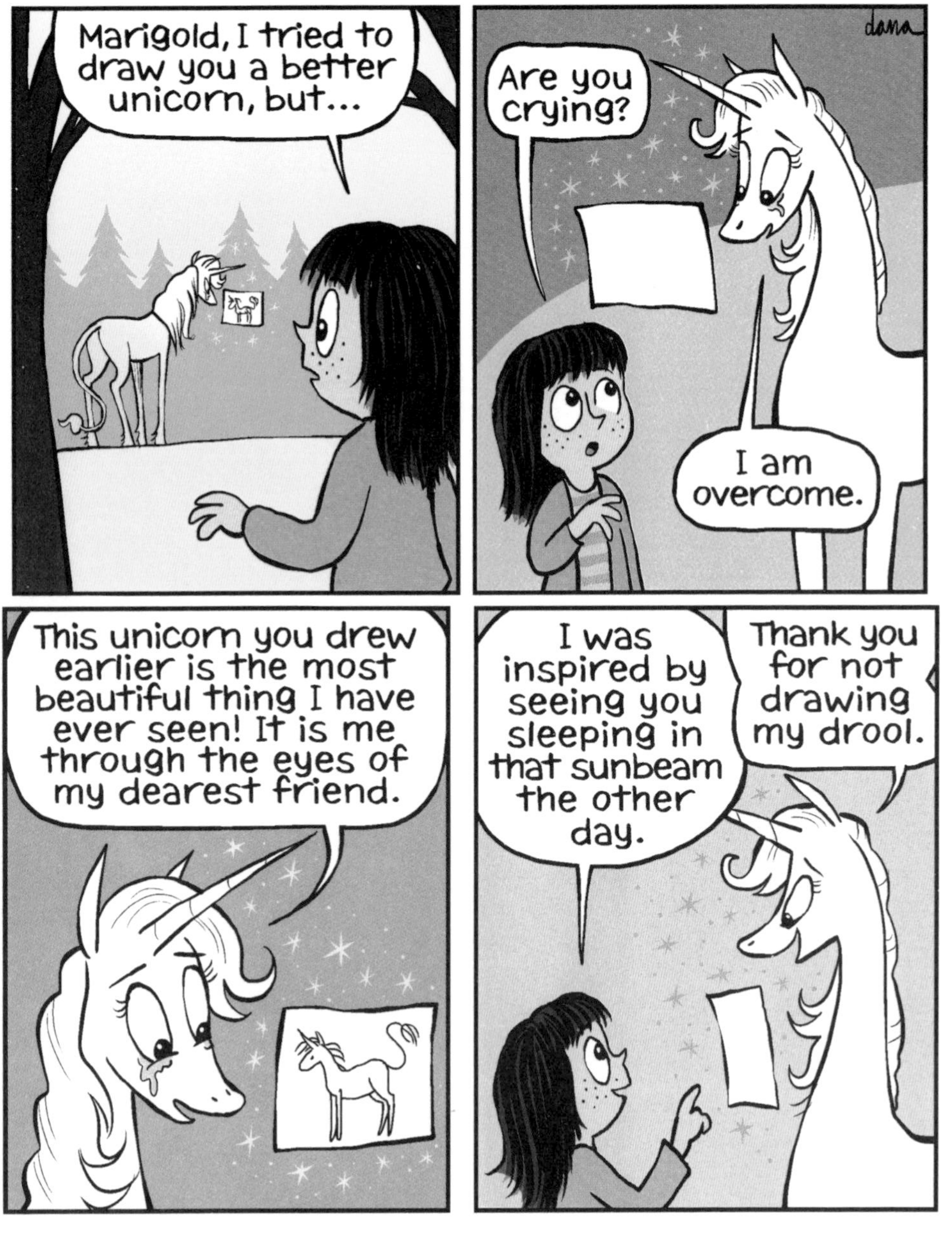
Marigold, I tried to draw you a better unicorn, but...
dana
Are you crying?
I am overcome.
This unicorn you drew earlier is the most beautiful thing I have ever seen! It is me through the eyes of my dearest friend.
I was inspired by seeing you sleeping in that sunbeam the other day.
Thank you for not drawing my drool.

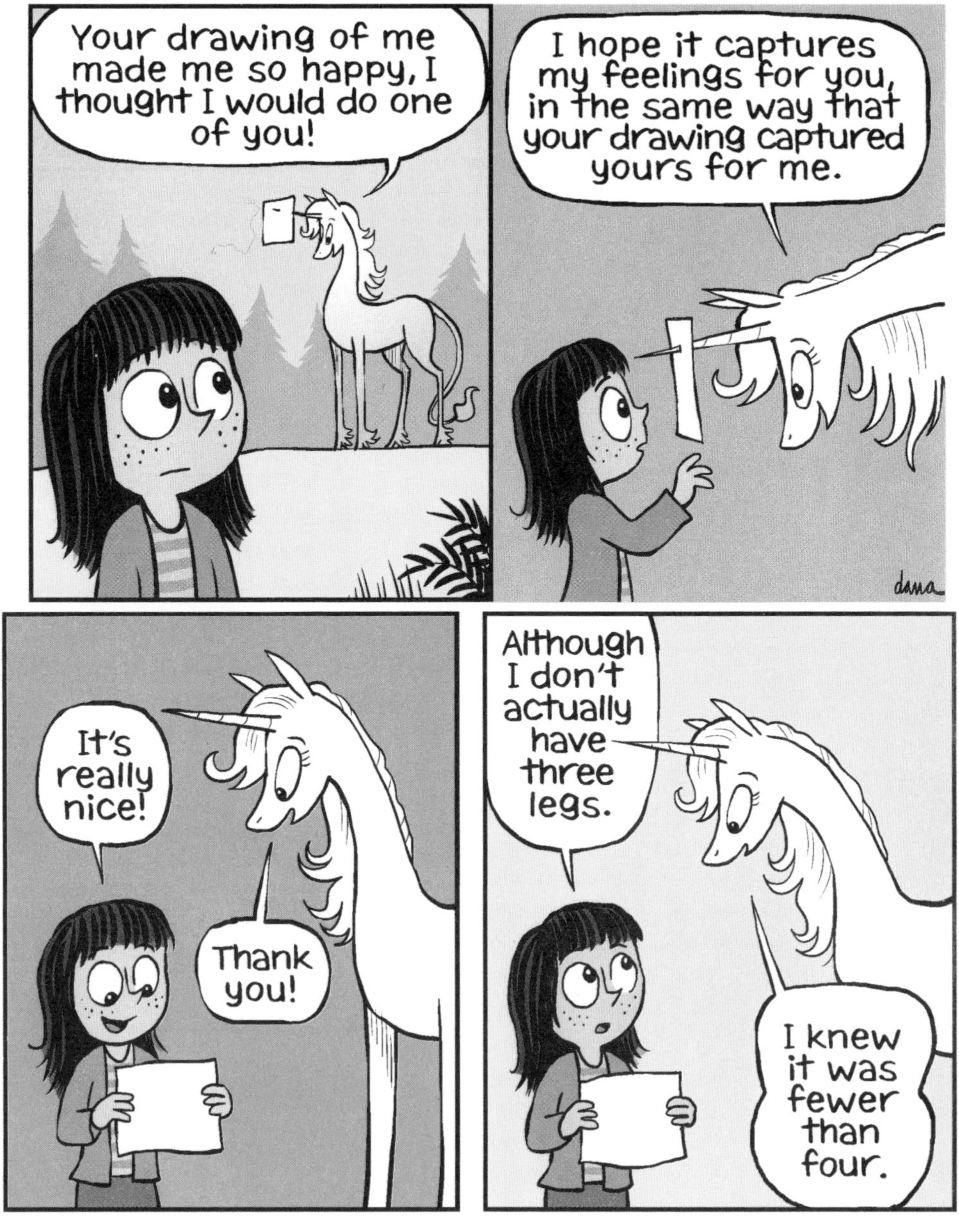
Your drawing of me made me so happy, I thought I would do one of you!
I hope it captures my feelings for you, in the same way that your drawing captured yours for me.
dana
It's really nice!
Thank you!
Although I don't actually have three legs.
I knew it was fewer than four.

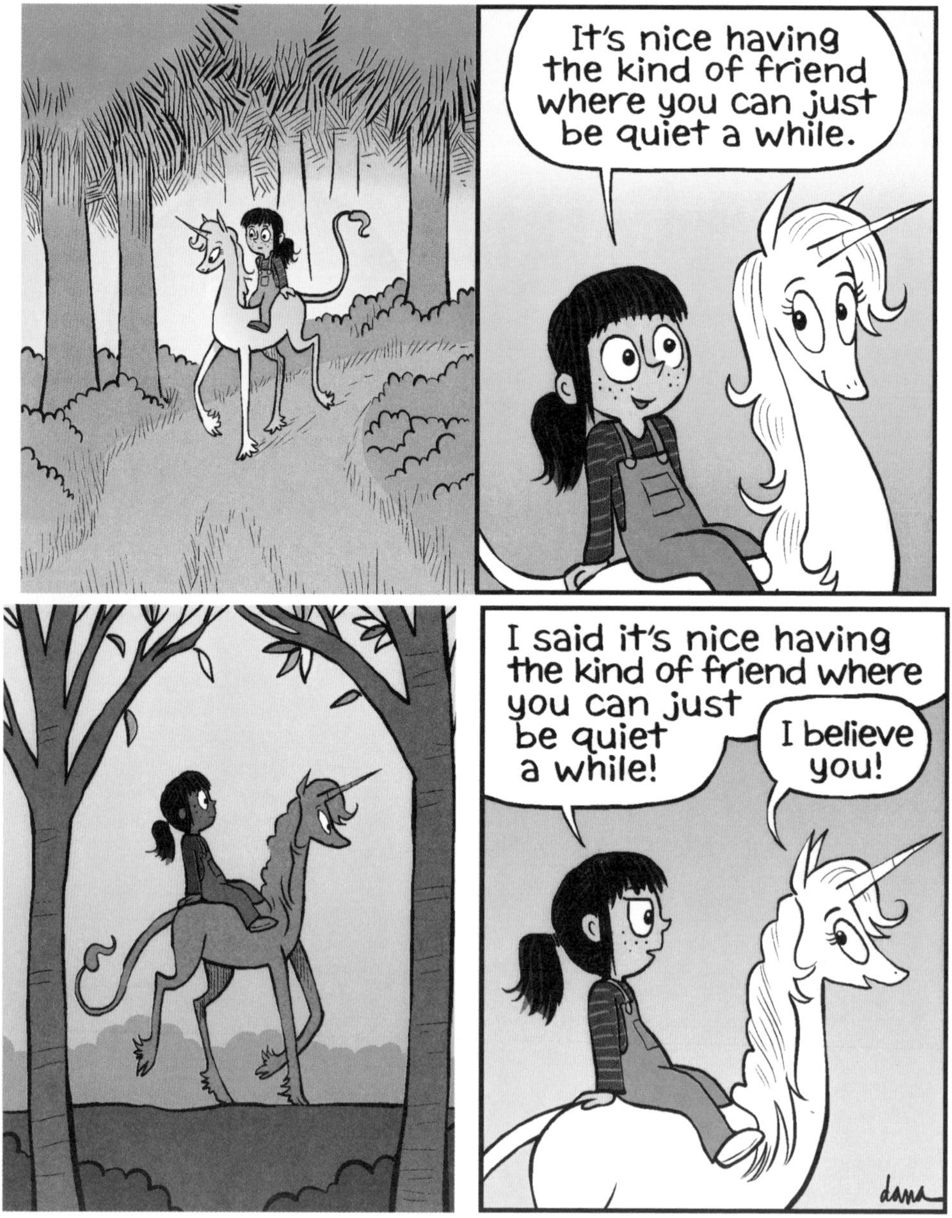
It's nice having the kind of friend where you can just be quiet a while.
I said it's nice having the kind of friend where you can just be quiet a while!
I believe you!
dana

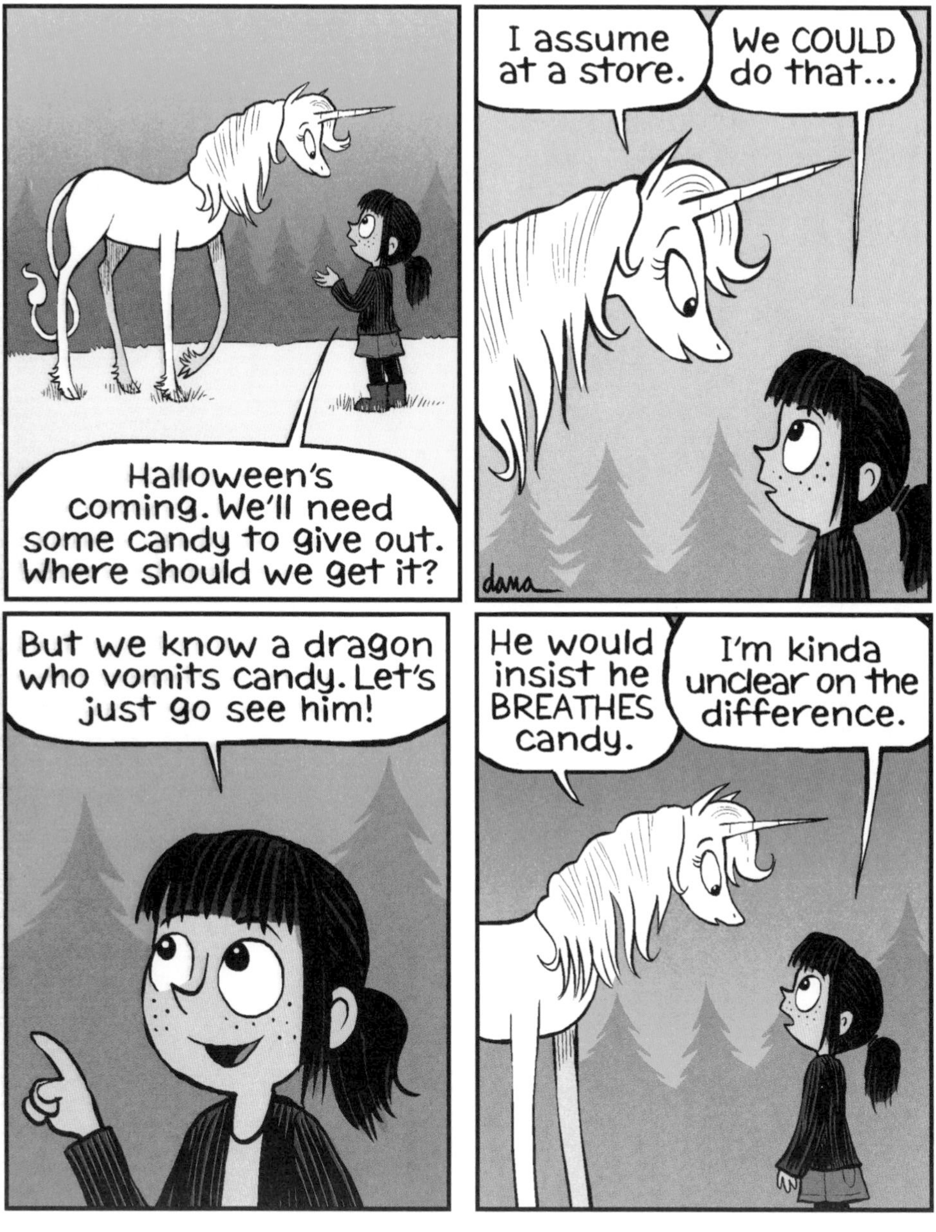
Halloween's coming. We'll need some candy to give out. Where should we get it?
I assume at a store.
We COULD do that...
dana
But we know a dragon who vomits candy. Let's just go see him!
He would insist he BREATHES candy.
I'm kinda unclear on the difference.

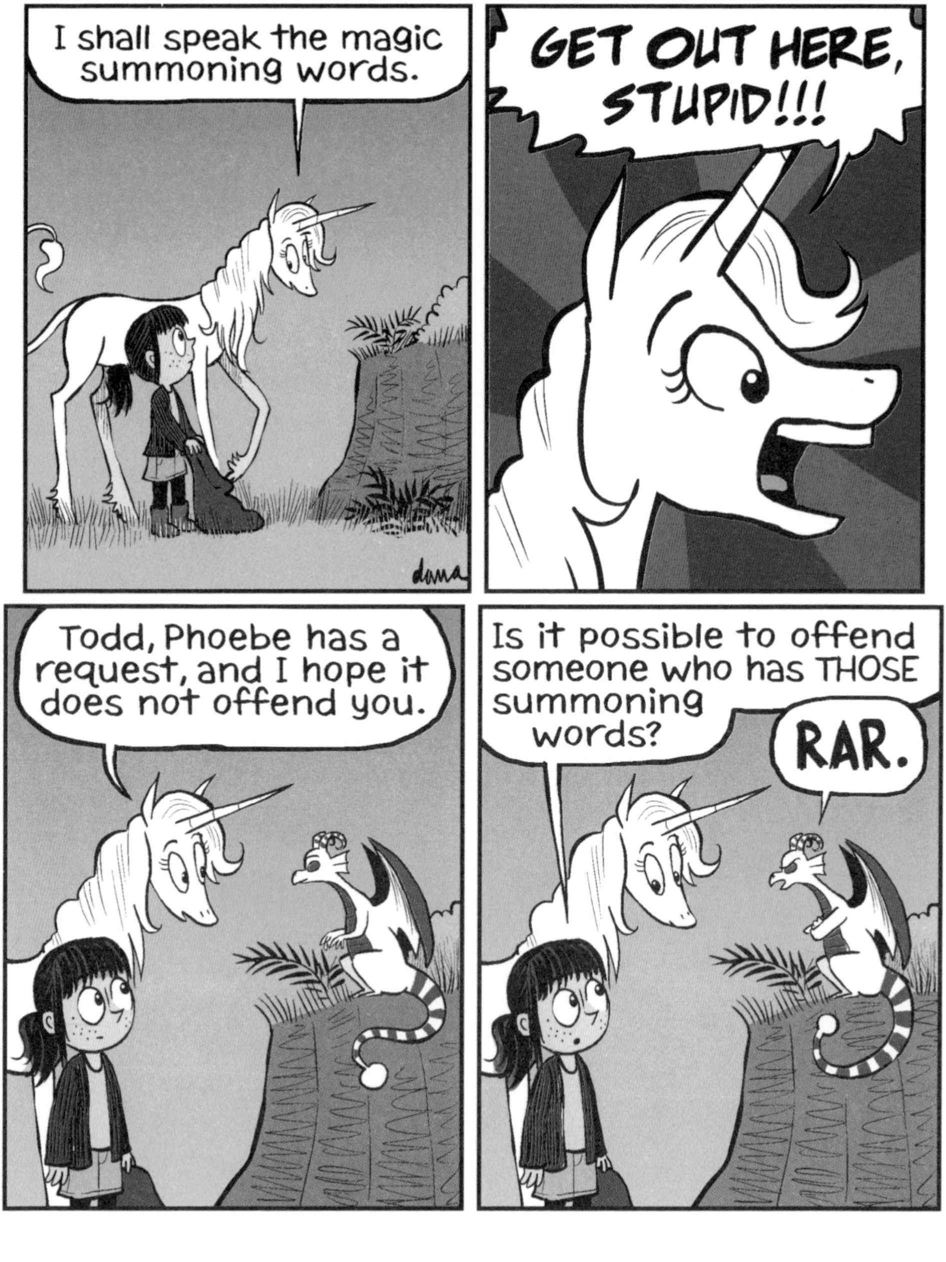
I shall speak the magic summoning words.
GET OUT HERE, STUPID!!!
Todd, Phoebe has a request, and I hope it does not offend you.
Is it possible to offend someone who has THOSE summoning words?
RAR.

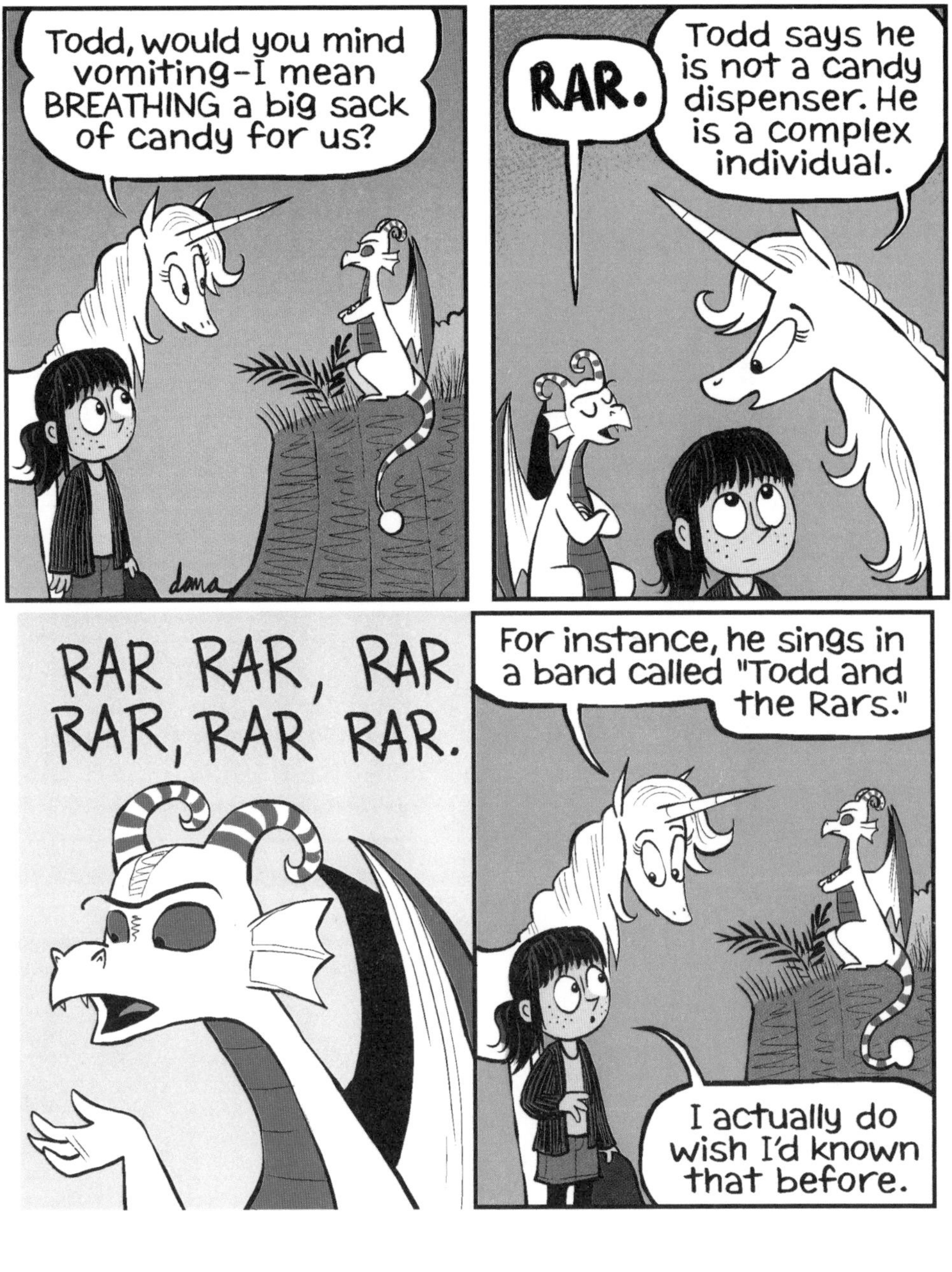
Todd, would you mind vomiting—I mean BREATHING a big sack of candy for us?
RAR.
Todd says he is not a candy dispenser. He is a complex individual.
RAR RAR, RAR RAR, RAR RAR.
For instance, he sings in a band called "Todd and the Rars."
I actually do wish I'd known that before.

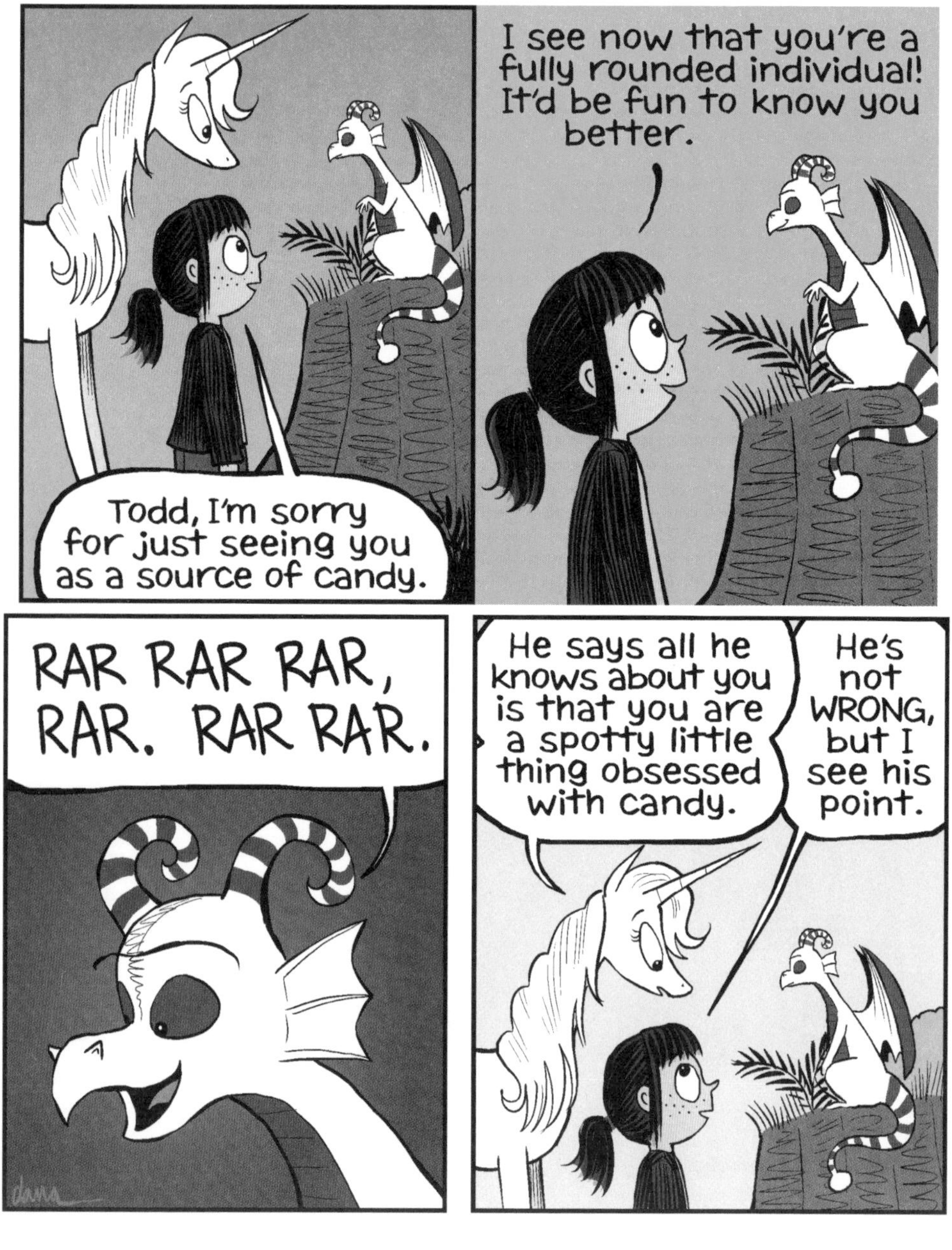
Todd, I'm sorry for just seeing you as a source of candy.
I see now that you're a fully rounded individual! It'd be fun to know you better.
RAR RAR RAR, RAR. RAR RAR.
He says all he knows about you is that you are a spotty little thing obsessed with candy.
He's not WRONG, but I see his point.

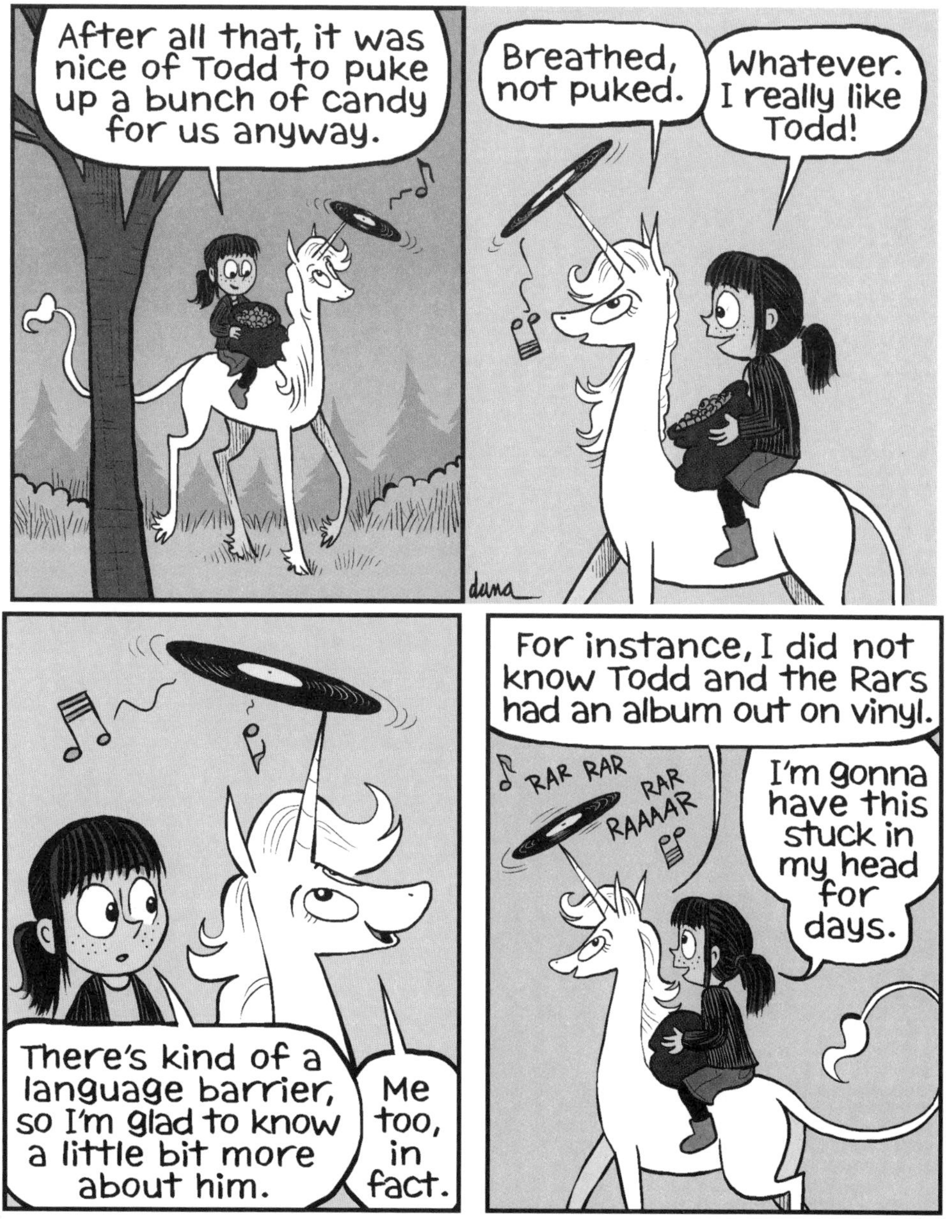
After all that, it was nice of Todd to puke up a bunch of candy for us anyway.
Breathed, not puked.
Whatever. I really like Todd!
dana
There's kind of a language barrier, so I'm glad to know a little bit more about him.
Me too, in fact.
For instance, I did not know Todd and the Rars had an album out on vinyl.
RAR RAR
RAR
RAAAAR
I'm gonna have this stuck in my head for days.

Once upon a time, there was a princess who lived in a pink castle.

Her best friend was a pink unicorn.

Then she gave a speech in the pink room at the U.N.

And then she and her unicorn ate a pink pizza.

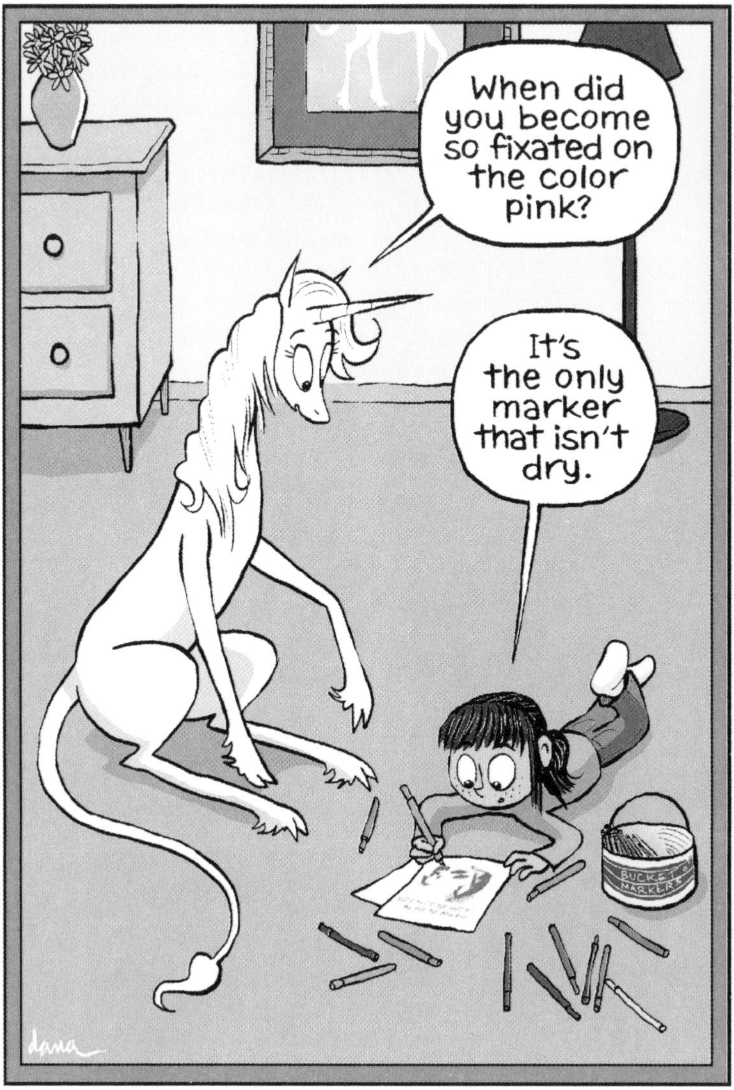
When did you become so fixated on the color pink?
It's the only marker that isn't dry.
BUCKET O' MARKERS
dana

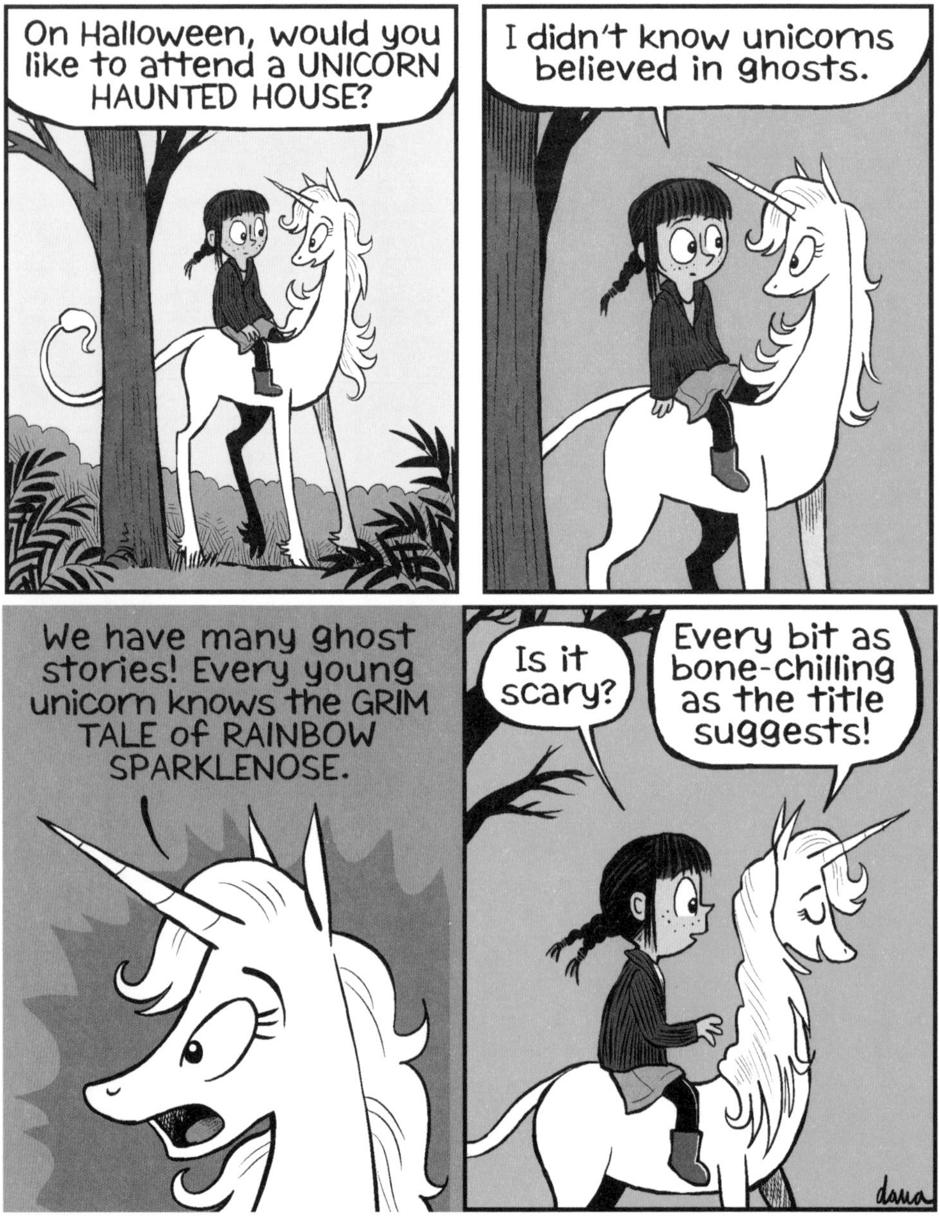
On Halloween, would you like to attend a UNICORN HAUNTED HOUSE?
I didn't know unicorns believed in ghosts.
We have many ghost stories! Every young unicorn knows the GRIM TALE of RAINBOW SPARKLENOSE.
Is it scary?
Every bit as bone-chilling as the title suggests!
dana

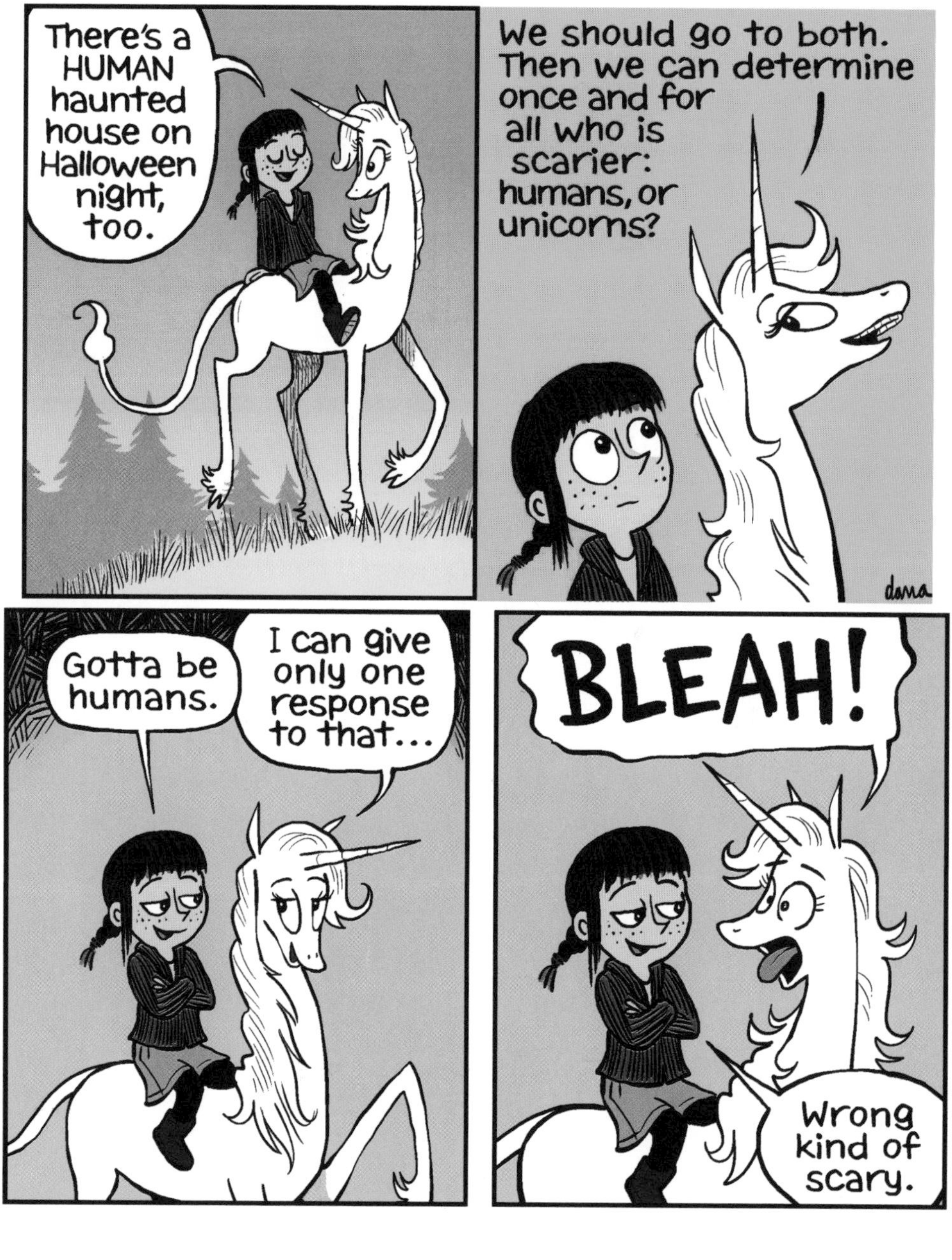
There's a HUMAN haunted house on Halloween night, too.
We should go to both. Then we can determine once and for all who is scarier: humans, or unicorns?
dana
Gotta be humans.
I can give only one response to that...
BLEAH!
Wrong kind of scary.

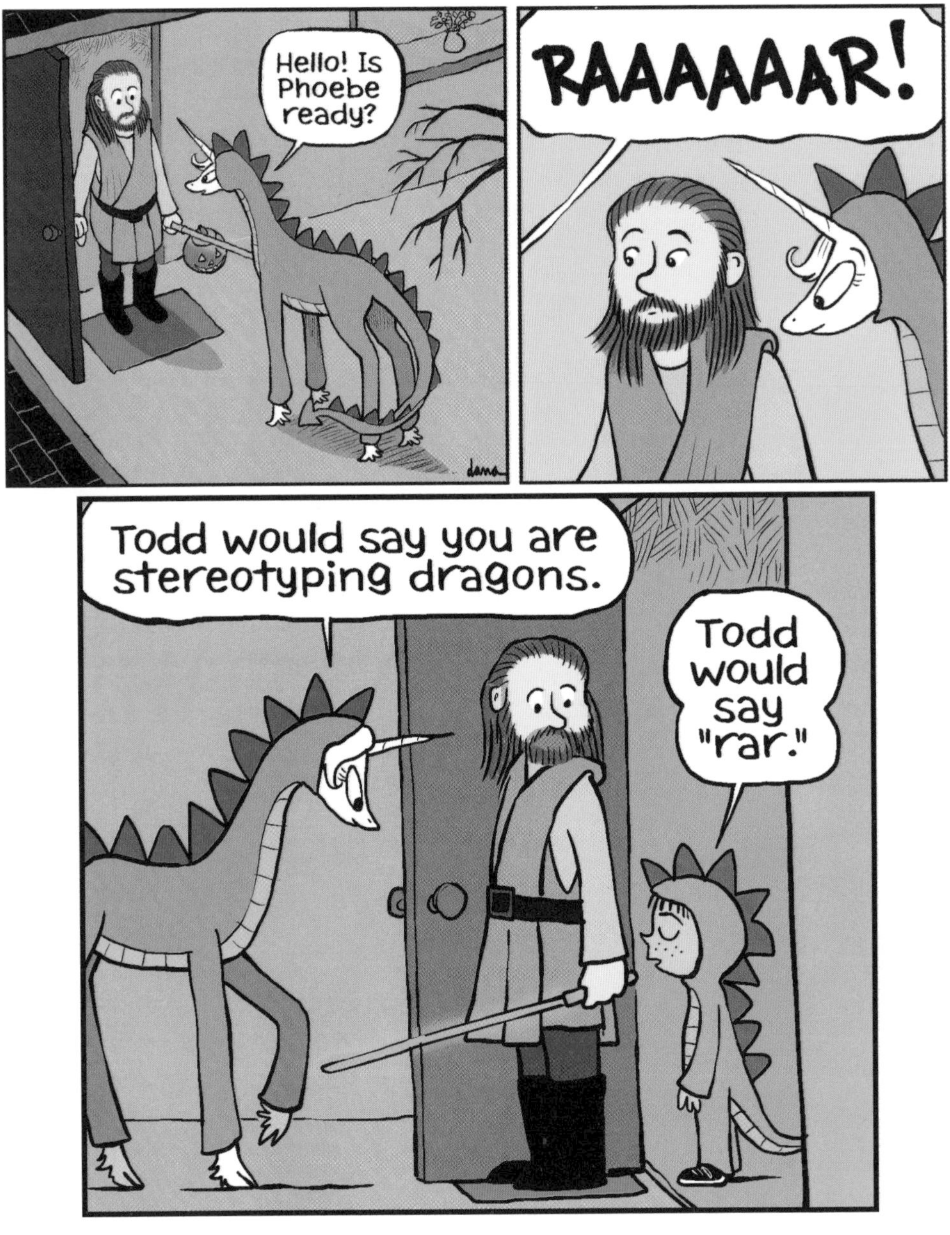
Hello! Is Phoebe ready?
RAAAAAAR!
Todd would say you are stereotyping dragons.
Todd would say "rar."

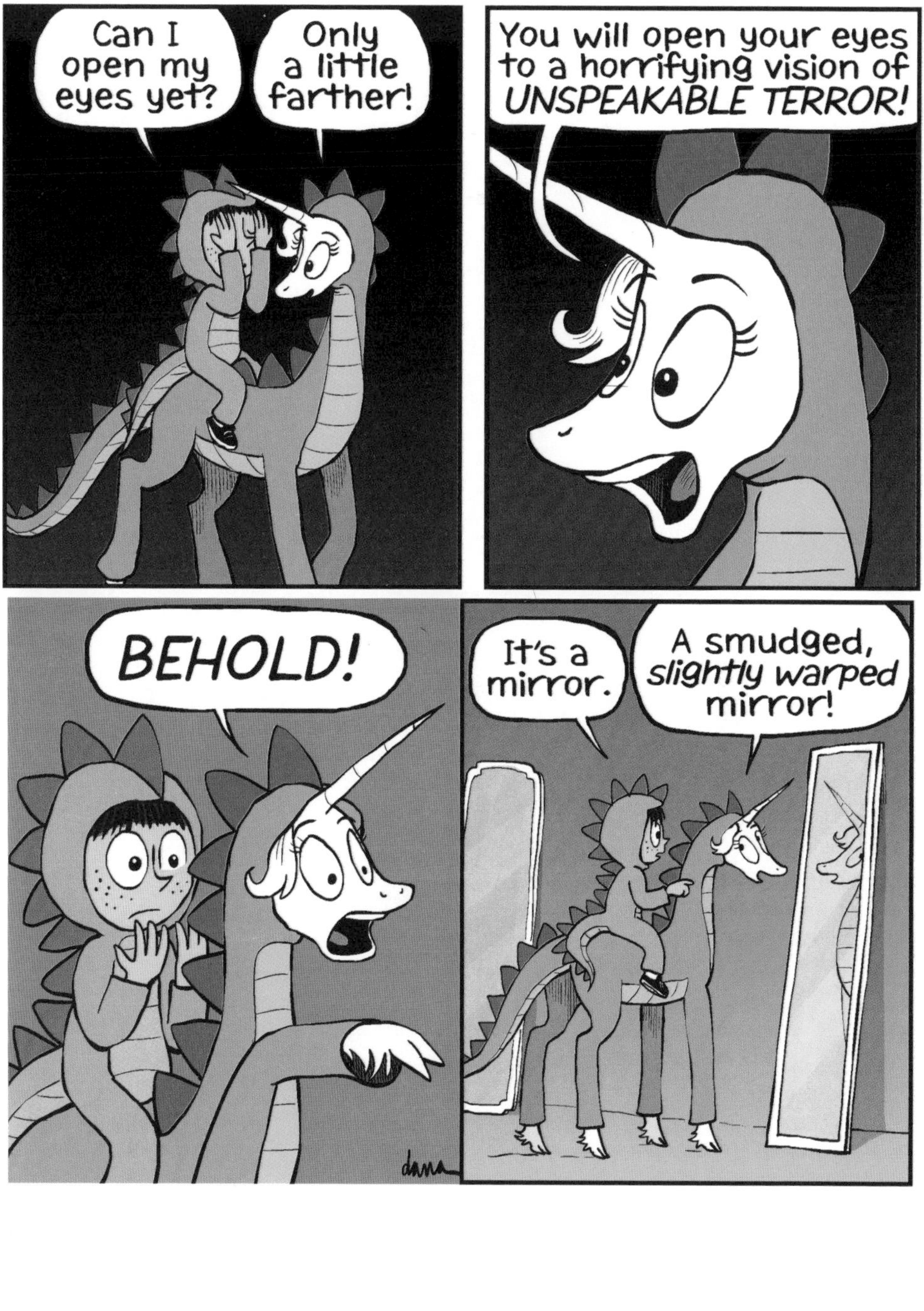
Can I open my eyes yet?
Only a little farther!
You will open your eyes to a horrifying vision of *UNSPEAKABLE TERROR!*
BEHOLD!
dana
It's a mirror.
A smudged, *slightly warped* mirror!

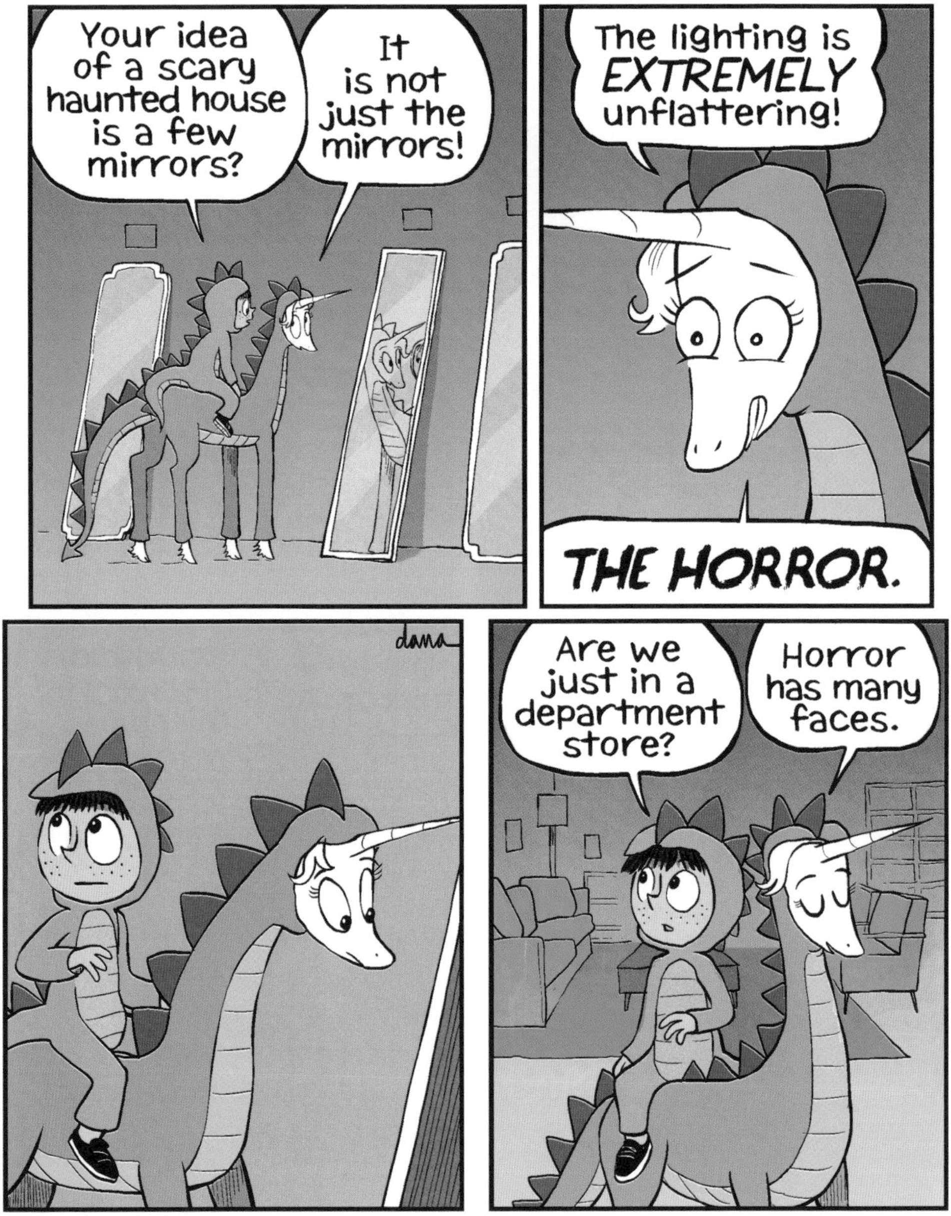
Your idea of a scary haunted house is a few mirrors?
It is not just the mirrors!
The lighting is EXTREMELY unflattering!
THE HORROR.
dana
Are we just in a department store?
Horror has many faces.

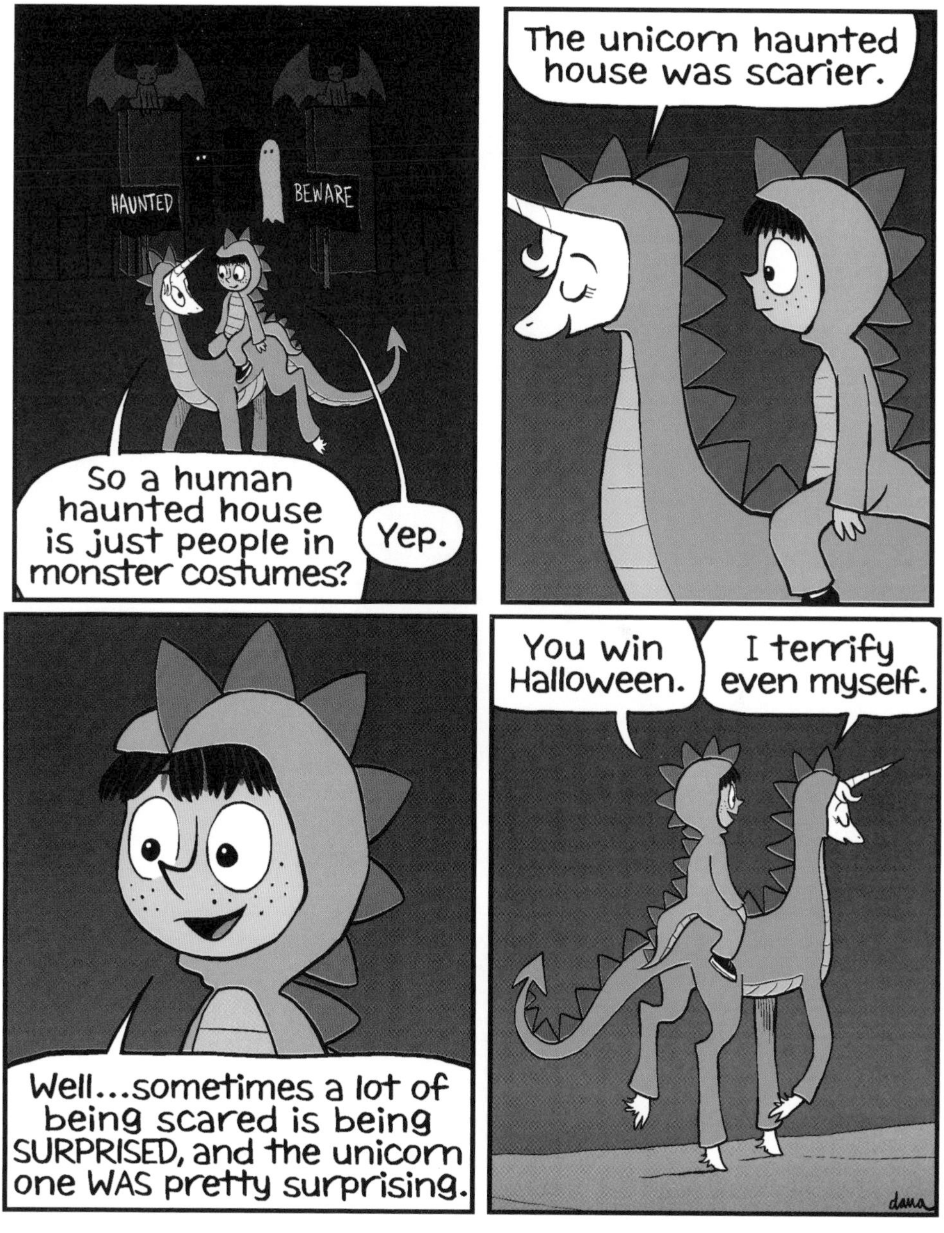
HAUNTED
BEWARE
So a human haunted house is just people in monster costumes?
Yep.
The unicorn haunted house was scarier.
Well...sometimes a lot of being scared is being SURPRISED, and the unicorn one WAS pretty surprising.
You win Halloween.
I terrify even myself.
dana

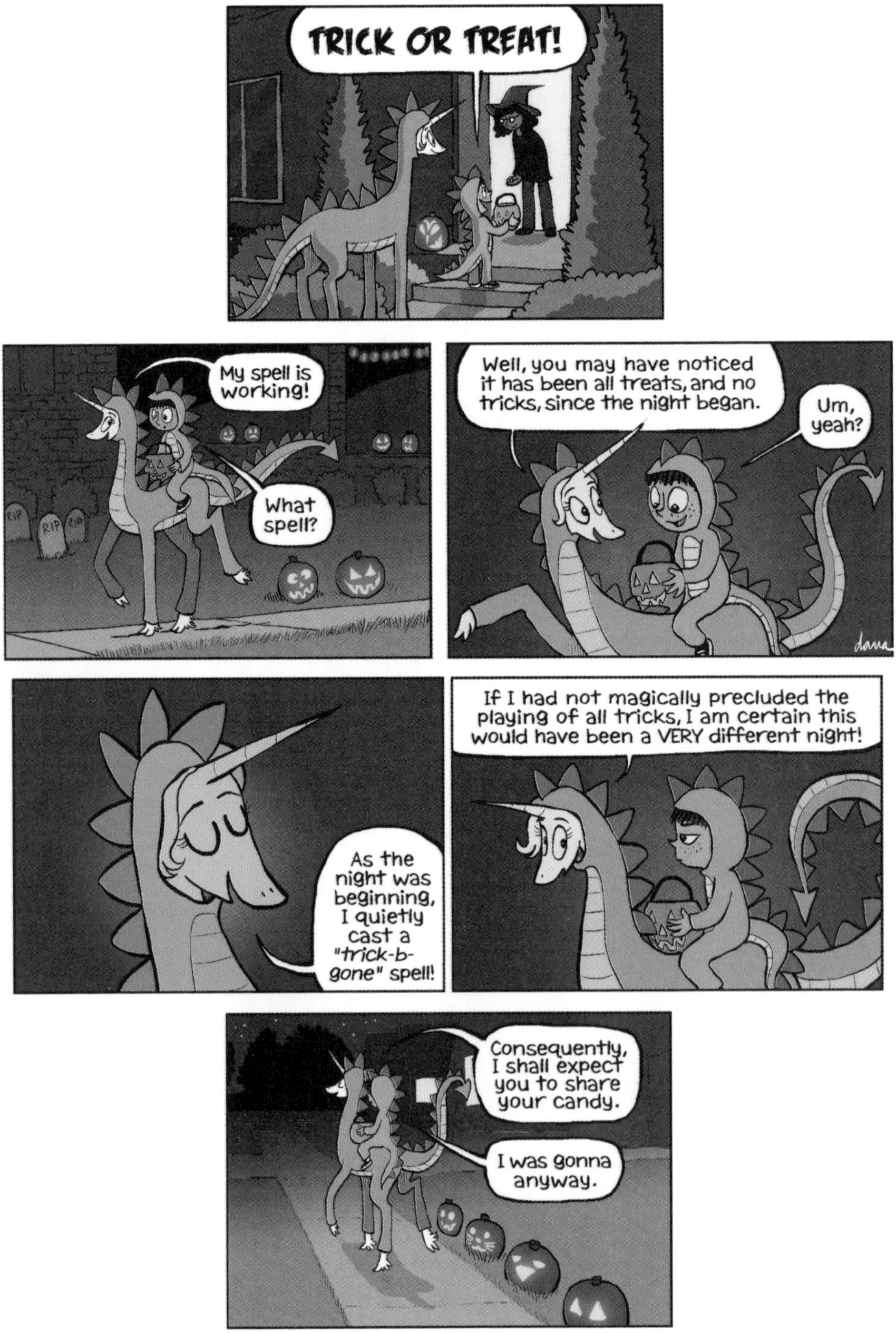
TRICK OR TREAT!
My spell is working!
What spell?
Well, you may have noticed it has been all treats, and no tricks, since the night began.
Um, yeah?
As the night was beginning, I quietly cast a "*trick-b-gone*" spell!
If I had not magically precluded the playing of all tricks, I am certain this would have been a VERY different night!
Consequently, I shall expect you to share your candy.
I was gonna anyway.

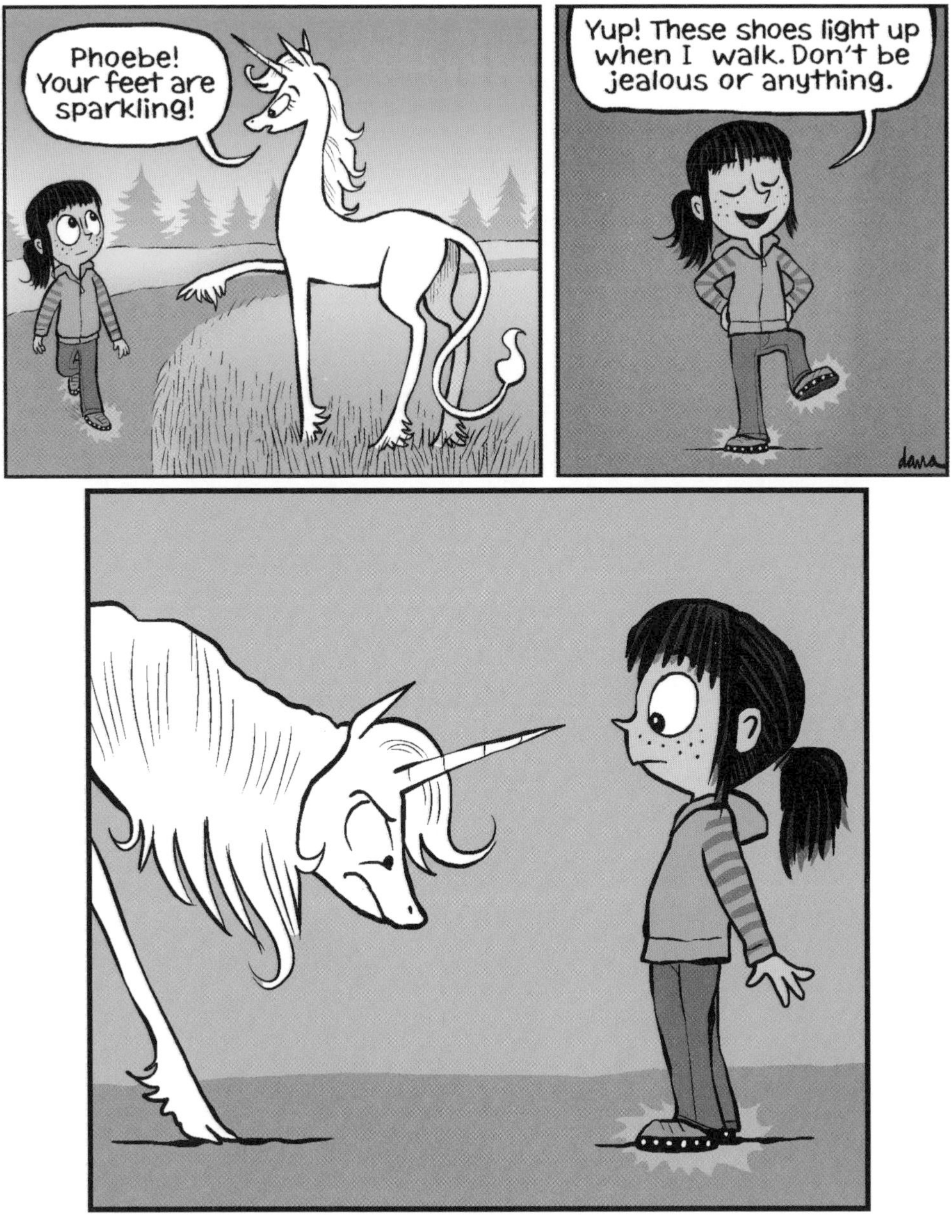
Phoebe! Your feet are sparkling!
Yup! These shoes light up when I walk. Don't be jealous or anything.
dana

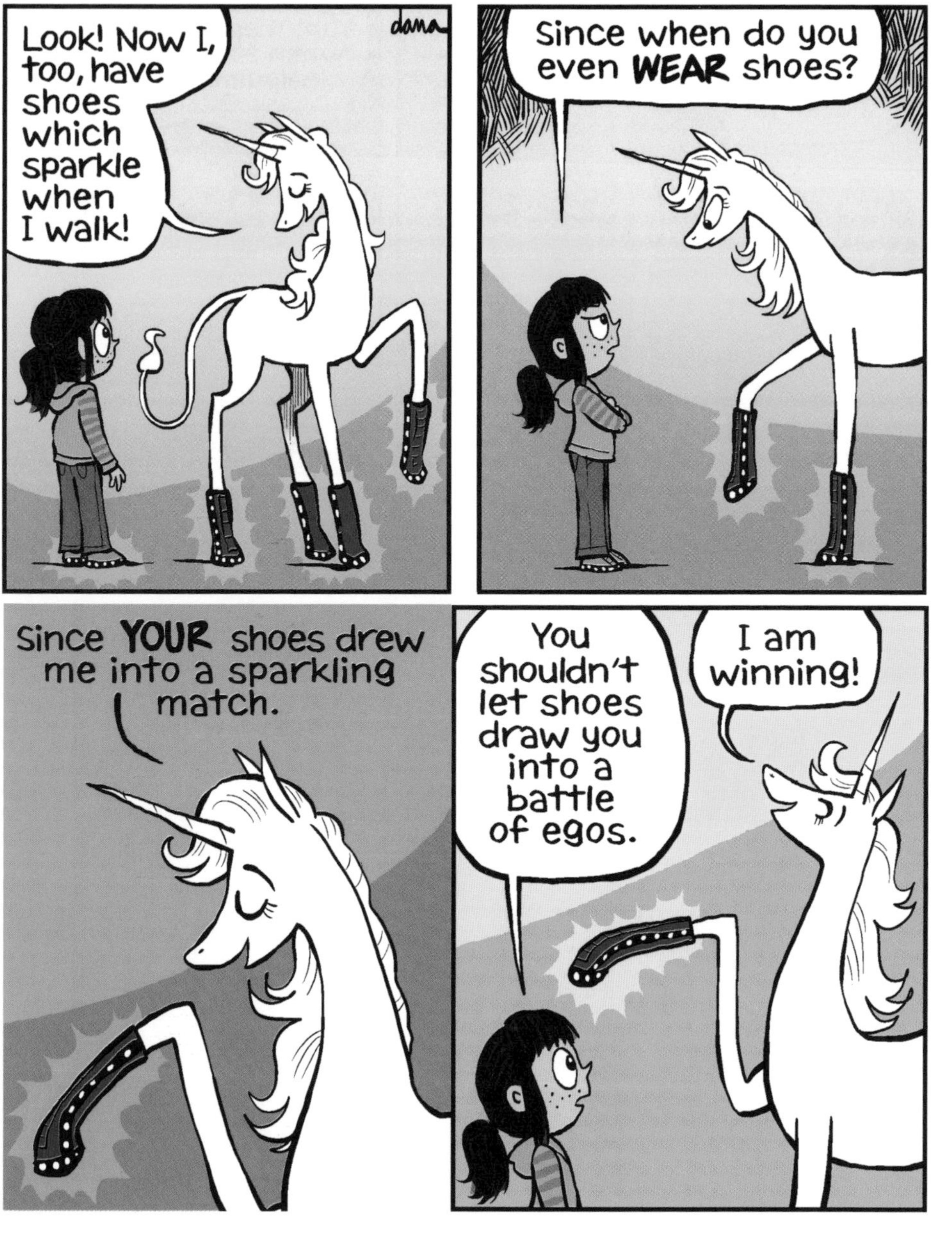
dana
Look! Now I, too, have shoes which sparkle when I walk!
Since when do you even WEAR shoes?
Since YOUR shoes drew me into a sparkling match.
You shouldn't let shoes draw you into a battle of egos.
I am winning!

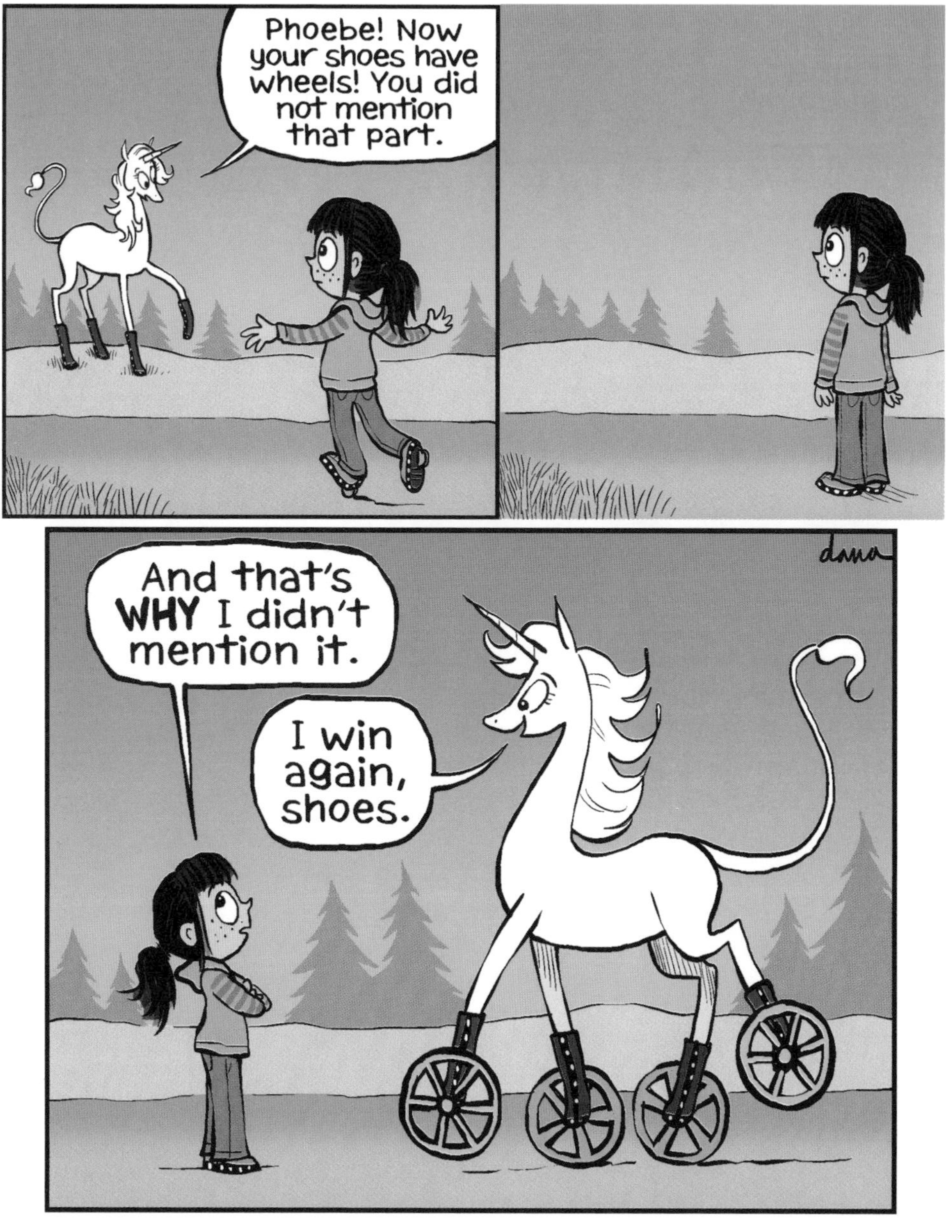
Phoebe! Now your shoes have wheels! You did not mention that part.
And that's **WHY** I didn't mention it.
I win again, shoes.
dana

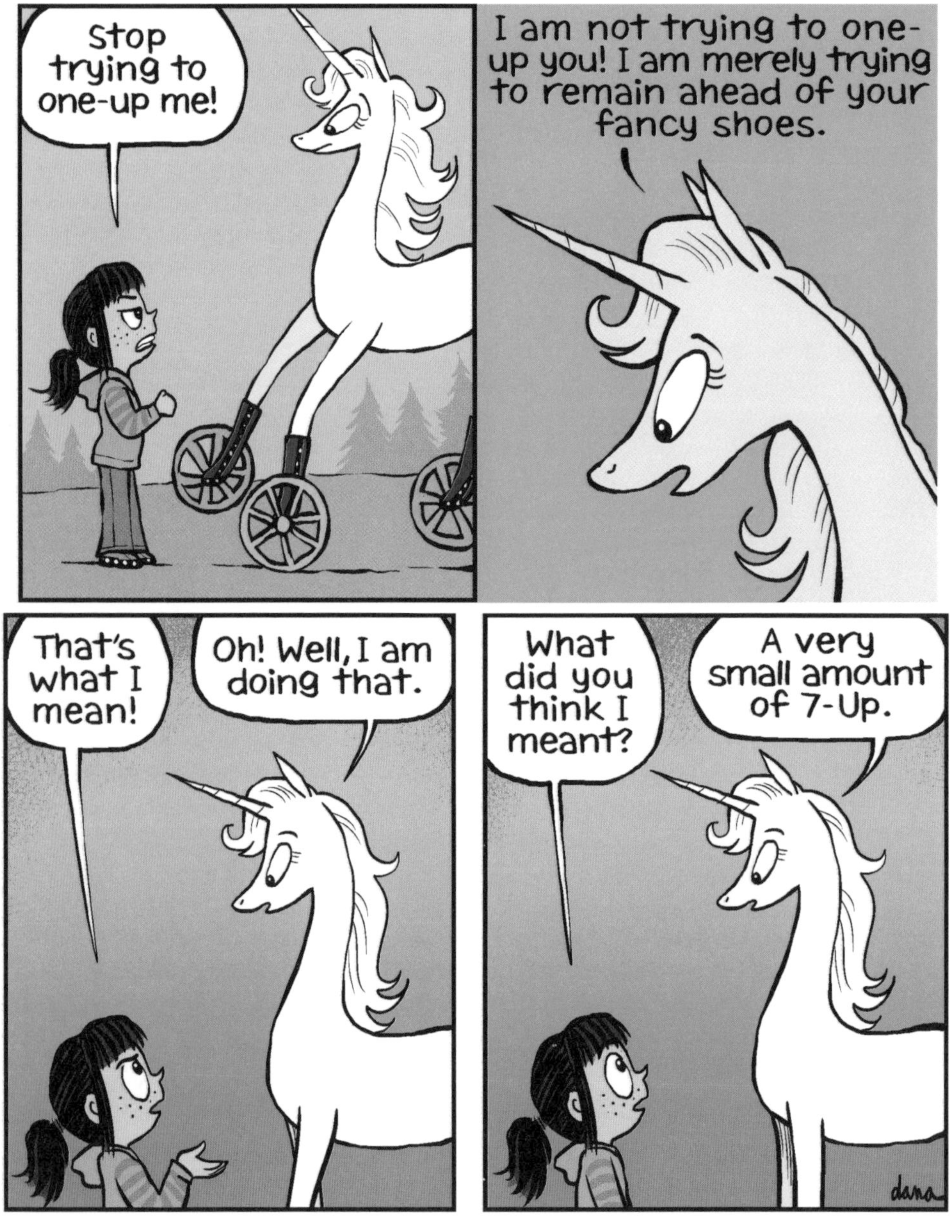
Stop trying to one-up me!
I am not trying to one-up you! I am merely trying to remain ahead of your fancy shoes.
That's what I mean!
Oh! Well, I am doing that.
What did you think I meant?
A very small amount of 7-Up.
dana

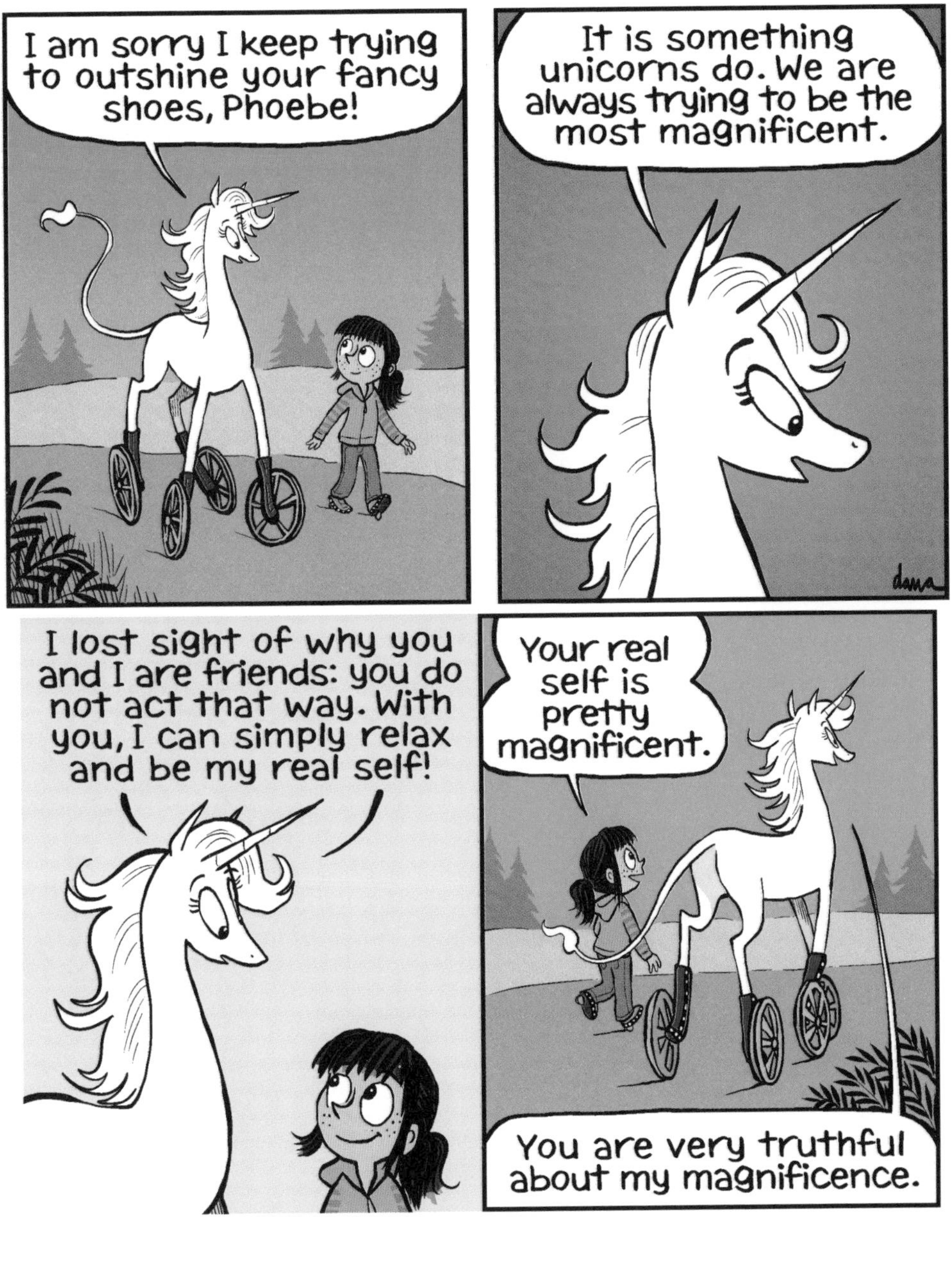
I am sorry I keep trying to outshine your fancy shoes, Phoebe!
It is something unicorns do. We are always trying to be the most magnificent.
dana
I lost sight of why you and I are friends: you do not act that way. With you, I can simply relax and be my real self!
Your real self is pretty magnificent.
You are very truthful about my magnificence.

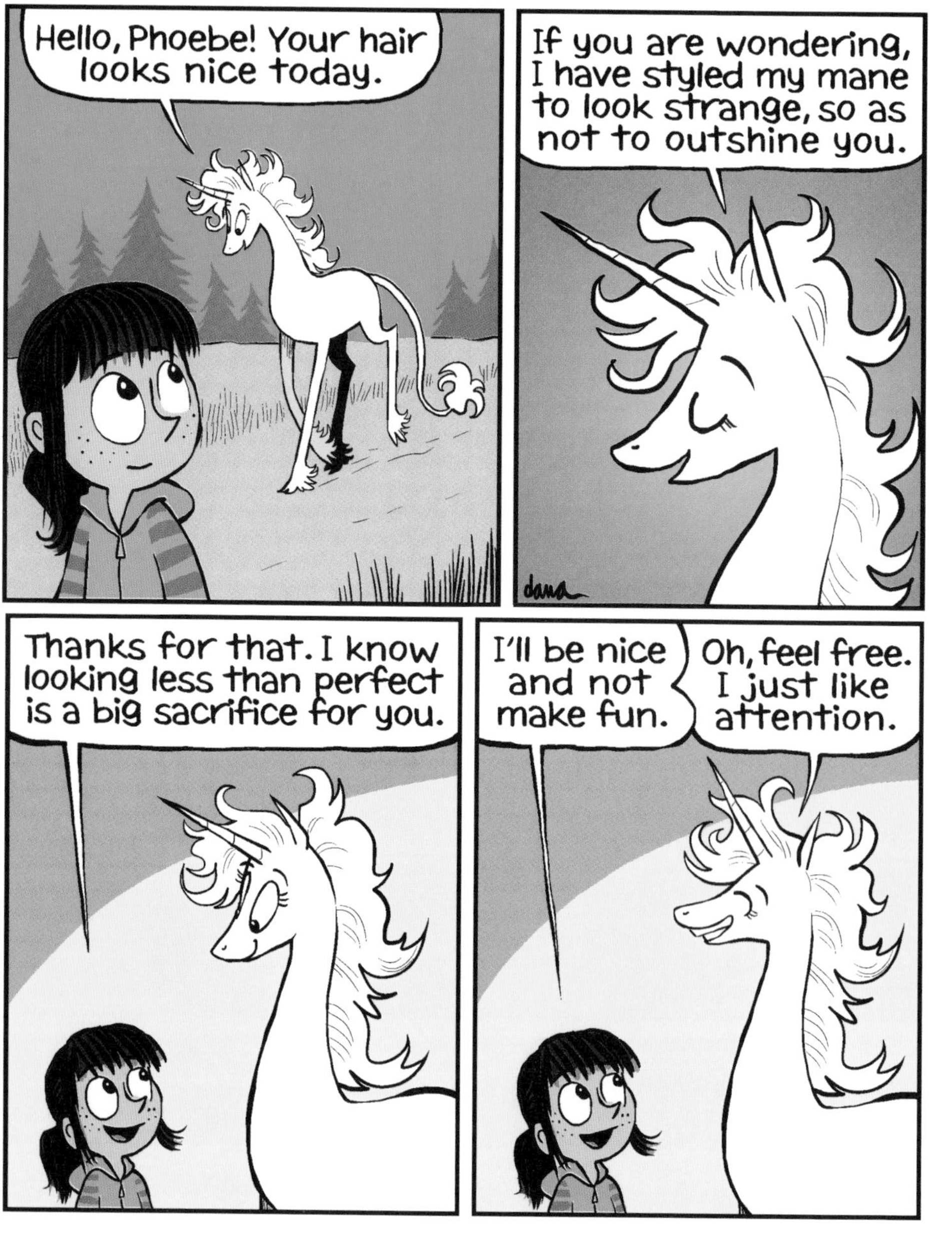
Hello, Phoebe! Your hair looks nice today.
If you are wondering, I have styled my mane to look strange, so as not to outshine you.
dana
Thanks for that. I know looking less than perfect is a big sacrifice for you.
I'll be nice and not make fun.
Oh, feel free. I just like attention.

MORE TO EXPLORE! A special section featuring words to learn!

GLOSSARY

ambivalence (am-bi-va-lents): pg. 108 – noun / mixed feelings or ideas about someone or something

arbitrary (are-bi-trair-ee): pg. 139 – adjective / based on a single preference or convenience rather than by logic or need

atrophied (a-tro-feed): pg. 30 – verb (past participle) / having weakened or shrunk from disease or lack of use

beset (bi-set): pg. 71 – verb / to trouble or surround

continuity (kon-ti-noo-i-tee): pg. 28 – noun / consistency over a period of time

devastatingly (dev-uh-stay-ting-lee): pg. 17 – adverb / in a very damaging or destructive way

figurehead (fig-yer-hed): pg. 15 – noun / a person who is the head of an organization or group but doesn't have any real power or authority

garish (gare-ish): pg. 62 – adjective / extremely bright or vivid; flashy

humility (hu-mil-i-tee): pg. 138 – noun / feeling humble; the state of being or acting modest

inedible (in-ed-i-buhl): pg. 89 – adjective / not able to be eaten

metaphor (met-a-for): pg. 145 – noun / a figure of speech in which a word or phrase is used to make a comparison between two things that are different but have something in common

misconception (mis-con-sep-shun): pg. 63 – noun / a wrong or untrue idea

ominous (ah-mi-nus): pg. 108 – adjective / forecasting or implying evil or danger is coming

ornamental (or-na-men-tal): pg. 137 – adjective / serving as a decorative object, usually without any use or purpose

pathos (pay-thos): pg. 93 – noun / a quality that causes the emotion of pity or sympathy

pretentious (pre-ten-shis): pg. 79 – adjective / excessive confidence; exaggerated importance or worth

prodigy (pra-di-jee): pg. 23 – noun / a person, especially a young one, who has extraordinary talent or ability

static electricity (sta-tick i-lek-tri-suh-tee): pg. 41 – noun / electricity that is made up of single charges (such as friction)

uncanny (un-ca-nee): pg. 123 – adjective / beyond what is normal or considered natural; supernatural or magical

vicinity (vi-sin-i-tee): pg. 89 – noun / the surrounding area

vinyl (vie-nuhl): pg. 157 – noun / a format for musical recordings (usually called a "record"), much like a CD except larger and made with a plastic coating